EVERY
SINGLE
SECRET

ALSO BY EMILY CARPENTER

Burying the Honeysuckle Girls
The Weight of Lies

EVERY
SINGLE
SECRET

A NOVEL

EMILY CARPENTER

AUTHOR OF **THE WEIGHT OF LIES**

LAKE UNION
PUBLISHING

Text copyright © 2018 by Emily Carpenter
All rights reserved.

Published by Lake Union Publishing, Seattle
www.apub.com

Amazon, the Amazon logo, and Lake Union Publishing are trademarks of Amazon.com, Inc., or its affiliates.

ISBN-13: 9781503951907
ISBN-10: 1503951901

Cover design by Rex Bonomelli

Printed in the United States of America

For Rick,
who is better than anything a Brontë
could've dreamed up

*The curate might set as many chapters as he pleased
for Catherine to get by heart, and Joseph might thrash
Heathcliff till his arm ached; they forgot everything the
minute they were together again . . .*

Emily Brontë, Wuthering Heights

Friday, October 19
Afternoon

There are monsters all around us—people who have to hide because the world can't bear to see them for who they truly are. They're good at keeping secrets, the monsters. Sometimes, too good.

Which is why I've always suspected that I am one of them.

A girl I once knew used to call me names: *Egg Salad*, *Pizza Face*, *Fat Fuck*. She claimed a family of cannibals wanted to adopt me and put me in their cellar, and that when they did, I would forget my name and who my mother was and become one of them. It was a cruel thing to say, but I saw the blackness of my own soul pretty clearly for a kid, so part of me believed her.

The strange thing was, when it came to predicting the future, she wasn't that far off. Now I wonder if she hadn't been, in fact, warning me.

᷄

Perched high on a lichen-crusted rock ledge, I look past the scuffed tips of my hiking boots at the waving branches of red and orange and russet below. I clutch an iPad to my chest, and the cold wind whips my hair, making my eyes water behind my glasses. The dampness is so thick it has a weight to it, even though it isn't actually raining. It pierces through the too-big canvas coat I'm wearing, right through to my bones.

This day is nothing like the crisp blue night the name-calling girl—Chantal—died. That night was brilliant. The perfect night to lie under a canopy of stars.

I brush the thought away. It's true I'm a bit of an oddball, and not just because of Chantal. I am what people call *guarded*. I don't blog. I don't post. I don't share. I don't love people in that beaming, open-armed way you're supposed to, but there is a good reason for it. Dark things vein through me, the way precious metal shoots through the heart of a mountain. Dark things that should stay hidden, embedded deep within the rock. It is for the greater good that I stand guard over my mountain, over my past.

This particular mountain is only the dog tail of the Blue Ridge range, but standing here with the gorge dropping away beneath me makes it feel like the highest, loneliest point on earth. I've been staying in the crook of this mountain nearly a week, and I don't even know the name of it. I do know, from my stellar Georgia education, circa fourth grade, that white men discovered gold in this area a century ago and took this mountain and all the rest of the northeastern part of the state from the Cherokee.

They ripped the gold out of the mountain, and after that came death and disaster.

I know another thing about this mountain, having seen it from the trail below. The cliff I'm standing on curves back under itself, creating a jutting shelf. I wouldn't even have to jump out to fall. I could just take one small step, and it would all be over. I might crash straight down through branches and needles before I hit something solid, but eventually I would hit.

And it would hurt. Just like it must've hurt Chantal.

The cliff, the whipping wind, the thoughts of death—the whole scenario is so over-the-top gothic, it almost makes me laugh. But it is poetic justice. Full-circle closure. I am a runner, always have been, in different ways. And now, after all the years of running—in my head and heart and even physically, every dawn at the track down the street from my house—I'm finally being forced to stop. To decide what I really want.

Do I stay? Or do I throw myself off the cliff and end it, once and for all?

To my left, down the trail but still out of sight, I hear the rustle of leaves and breaking twigs. Someone is struggling up the path. Someone I know. My time is up. I have to decide. Quickly, before I go back down the trail to that house and everything gets confused again. Before I lose my way.

Suddenly, another sound. The cry of a bird, in the blue above me. A hawk is tracing figure eights. He's relaxed, scanning the trees for dinner. Not a care in the world. No idea of the drama unfolding below him. And then, beside him, a darker form. A vulture? Can he have already smelled what's happened here?

If I go over the cliff, he will find me too, eventually. That's the way it works.

Suddenly, the reptilian section of my brain kicks into gear, and I realize with a jolt that I can feel my blood pulsing through my veins, infusing every inch of my body with life. My body is still working, still doing its job, even as my thoughts turn to death. I guess no matter what kind of person I might be, no matter what I've done up to this point, I am a person who wants to live.

I want to live.

And then I go—scrambling down the side of the mountain, stumbling over roots and rocks, barely managing to keep myself upright. I press the iPad against my chest, gasping in the thin, cold air, but I keep going. There's no trail here, but right now getting lost is better than being found.

I will not die for anyone—not for Chantal, not even for the girl I was.

I am running. Again.

If that makes me a monster, so be it.

Chapter One

My fiancé, Heath Beck, sat all the way at the back of the crowded bar. I could see his reflection in the mirror behind the liquor bottles. Dark hair hiding his eyes. Shoulders hunched over the glossy oak slab, tipping a glass of brown liquid into his mouth. Seeing him like this felt artificial, like a scene out of a movie. This was the last place Heath would come—this bar on East Howard—hence the last place I thought to try. And yet here he was.

My know-it-all brain helpfully told me why.

He's hiding from you.

I stood just inside the door, my legs gone wobbly beneath me. From dinnertime to just past midnight, I'd been driving around the city, checking out his favorite haunts, fueled by surging adrenaline. Now that I'd found him, the chemical was receding, leaving my limbs trembling and weak.

The bar was called Divine. Major branding irony, as the place was a discordant hell of shouted conversation, clinking glasses, and migraine-inducing techno-pop. The clientele—youngish, hollow-eyed metro-Atlanta professionals—milled around, sizing each other up for future business deals or a late-Saturday-night hit-and-run.

Heath hated this place. At least, that's what he'd always said.

I pressed back against the wall and eyed him. Like always, twin bolts of disbelief and desire shot through me. Desire for his jaw-dropping handsomeness. Disbelief that he was truly mine. It always hurt, just a little bit, to look at Heath. There was a woman on the stool next to him. Young, with dreadlocked hair gathered into a tangled bun. She was wearing a transparent peasant blouse with no bra, but Heath didn't seem to be the least bit aware of her. No surprise there. He wasn't a cheater, not even a flirt. He'd never given me a reason to worry, not in that respect.

Dreadlocks grabbed her purse, slid off the stool, and walked toward the bathroom at the back of the bar, giving me my opening. I wanted to rush up to him, hug him, and smother him with kisses, but resisted the urge. This wasn't a happy reunion; it was a confrontation. I needed to know what the hell was going on.

The nightmares had started a couple of months ago. They'd wrecked the bliss of our engagement, exhausted us and made us tiptoe around each other. And then came that first night when Heath didn't return home from work. It hurt, of course. But more than that, it scared me. What did he need that I couldn't give him? What was he doing that he couldn't share? As it turned out, it was the first night of many. A new normal for us.

I could hear Lenny now, drawling in her posh, old-money Buckhead accent. *This is why you give a man at least five years before you let him put a ring on it.* She was my best friend, my partner in our corporate design business, and she was always looking out for my interests, but when it came to Heath, I took her advice with a whole saltshaker. She didn't have the full story. She assumed I'd fallen fast and hard for Heath because he looked like he'd taken a wrong turn out of a Greek myth. She had no clue, but it wasn't her fault. It was because I'd never told her. I'd never uttered the two words that would've explained everything: *soul mate.*

I couldn't have said those words and expected her to keep a straight face. Nobody said old-fashioned stuff like that anymore. It made people gag and roll their eyes and pity your naïveté. The idea of a soul mate was a cliché. An invitation for mockery—even if it happened to be true. Even if it was the only term that came close to describing the connection you felt.

Somehow Heath and I had short-circuited the customary "Show me yours, I'll show you mine" dating process and arrived at a perfect understanding of each other. "I have a story," he'd said on our second date at a cramped Italian restaurant in an out-of-the-way corner of the Westside. "A long, sad story that I don't particularly enjoy talking about."

I nodded. *You and me both.*

He sighed. Took my hand. "It stars a single mom, some of her particularly unfriendly boyfriends. She passes away. There are a lot of nights sleeping on friends' couches." He looked down at our interwoven fingers. "The thing is, I don't believe therapy is the answer. I don't believe you find strength in talking about your past. I think you find it in a person. The right person."

I was mesmerized by the elusive logic of it all. Crazy how, in one instant, everything you could never express can suddenly make perfect sense. I wondered if I was the right person, if he was mine. And then he jutted his chin at the speaker above us, which had been playing a steady stream of Sinatra all evening. Now "Why Can't You Behave?" slithered through the patio.

"This guy," he said. "He's always made my skin crawl."

I laughed. I hated Sinatra too.

With that, loving another person became the most effortless, beautiful thing I'd ever experienced. Our silences were more precious to me than all the conversations I'd ever had with other men. Even after nine months together and getting engaged, Heath knew very little about me. But he knew the things that mattered. He knew I loved him. That I would never leave him. Not even with the nightmares, or the distance, or this ghosting routine he was putting me through. Not ever. Maybe it sounded desperate, but I had been searching my whole life for something I didn't know existed. Now that I had it, now that I had him, there was no way in hell I was going to let it go.

Dread, like warm bile, pushed up my throat as I threaded through the crushing tide of people in Divine. I slid onto the vinyl stool the dreadlocked woman had deserted, and Heath straightened, a look of surprise on his face.

"Daphne." He'd been playing with a white business card, rotating it between his fingers, but now he held it still, poised like a flag.

I fought the urge to put my hand against his cheek. "Hi."

On the other side of Heath, a knot of girls in tight club dresses and impossible shoes not-so-subtly checked him out. I wondered how long they'd been standing there. Posing. Baiting him.

One, in particular, was really locked in. She had long honey-colored, flat-ironed hair, beige lipstick, and bright-blue eyelash extensions. College student, probably. A baby. I almost wished I could pull her aside:

Stay one night with him, I dare you. See how it feels to wake up to him screaming and ripping the sheets off the bed. Trying to climb through the window. Breaking the wedding dishes you picked out together at Crate and Barrel. See how sexy that shit is.

I hung my purse on the hook by my knees, caught her eye, then pushed up my glasses with my middle finger. Not super classy, but you know what they say—you can take the girl out of the Division of Family and Child Services . . .

Blue Eyelashes tossed her stick-straight tresses and turned back to her posse. She said something that made them all titter, then they aimed a collective sneer at me. Out of the corner of my eye I saw the bartender chuckling to himself.

"I'm sorry I made you come looking for me," Heath said.

I met his eyes. "Please don't apologize. Not if you don't mean it. Not if you're just going to keep doing this every night."

He started to say something but stopped, and in the sudden flash of light from the TV screens above the bar, I realized his eyes were red and damp.

"Not here," I said quickly. "We can talk at home."

"No. I can't go home, not yet. I'm just . . ." He shook his head. "I need to tell you what's going on. You've been really patient, and you deserve an explanation."

I exhaled evenly. This was going to get tricky, I could feel it. Yes, I wanted Heath home, and yes, I wanted the nightmares to stop, and yes, maybe even an explanation from him would be just the thing to get us over this rough patch. But talking led to other, unwelcome things. Talking led to openness. To heartfelt statements, honesty, and confessions. Dangerous and unknown places. Places that terrified me.

Talking, for me, wasn't an option.

Heath rubbed his eyes, and in the seconds he wasn't looking, I picked four cashews out of a nearby bowl. I clenched them in my hand under the bar, feeling their reassuring kidney shape against my skin. Immediately the electrical storm in my head cleared, and I felt calmer.

I drew in a breath and let it out slowly. The counting was residue from my ranch years. A weird habit—or tic, whatever—that so far I'd been able to keep from Heath. Back then, it was always about food— how much was available and would I have access to it when I needed it. Now the counting alone seemed to settle my nerves. It always had to be an even number, preferably four. Four cashews, four stones, four pens. I knew it wasn't normal—and sometimes I could curtail it with a quick snap of the elastic hair band I kept around my wrist, hidden among a stack of bracelets—but it did make me feel better. Particularly in moments of high stress. Like this one.

"Do you remember what you told me when we first met?" he asked. "About closure?"

I swallowed. Of course I remembered. It was the same thing I had said to every new friend I made, every guy who'd ever pressed me to talk about my past.

"You said closure was an illusion," he went on. "You said we can't go back. We can't fix things. And trying only brings more pain."

I waited. There was a *but* coming.

"I so admired you for believing that. For living it out every day. I wanted to be like you. I tried and tried, Daphne, but I'm not as strong as you. I want closure. I need it . . . and I need help finding it."

He pushed the business card he'd been holding at me. I stared at it numbly.

Dr. Matthew Cerny, PhD, the elegant font read. *Baskens Institute. Dunfree, Georgia.*

"He's a therapist. A psychologist," Heath said.

A therapist. Someone whose sole job it was to make you tell your secrets. To poke and prod at you until you voluntarily gave up information that ruined your life—or someone else's. I had opened up to a psychologist once, and it had torn a good man's world apart. Torn mine apart too. The dread I'd been swallowing since I set foot in this place snaked up into my chest and lodged there.

"Are you okay?" he asked.

"You said you didn't believe in therapy." My voice was faint.

"I didn't, but maybe I've been wrong. Too stubborn to admit it's the one thing I need."

"Okay." I hesitated. "It seems like a big shift, all of a sudden. But even if you've changed your mind, there's no reason to go all the way to Dunfree. That's at least three hours away, right? Up in the mountains? I'm sure you can find a doctor down here in Atlanta. Somebody who can help you get closure."

The bartender pointed at me, his eyebrows raised, but I shook my head, and he turned back to the bar. I squeezed the cashews.

"I'm sure there are plenty of good doctors around here," I barreled on. "Hell, Lenny could probably recommend a battalion of them, knowing her crazy family." I touched his arm. "Growing up the way you did. Your mom and her boyfriends. Maybe that's why you're having the nightmares—"

"Heath. Dude."

A young man in a badly tailored blue suit had materialized behind us. A basketball buddy or an old college friend. I didn't recognize him. He clapped Heath's shoulder and thrust out a hand. "Where've you been?"

Heath swiveled to face the guy. "Busy, man. Working. I've got a new thing."

I kept my back to them and let out a whoosh of breath, half listening to Heath describe the warehouses on the outskirts of Cabbagetown that he was developing into condos. Heath didn't bother to introduce us, rightly sensing I was in no mood to chat up strangers, and for that, I was grateful. I signaled the bartender. He braced his arms against the bar's edge, and in a low voice I made my request. He raised his eyebrows at my credit card but took it. When he moved back down the bar, Heath was sending the guy in the suit on his way.

"So the therapist," he said.

Out of the corner of my eye, I could see the bartender was talking to the girl with beige lipstick. Her gaze slid over to me once, then back to him.

11

"He's based near Dunfree, up on the mountain. It's an old mansion that he uses as a relationship-research lab and retreat center," Heath said. "He's one of the best in his field, been leading these retreats for over a decade. He observes how couples interact—he studies their body language, their conversation, all with hidden cameras in their suites."

"Seriously?"

"He gets amazing results, apparently. And he'll be able to observe me while I sleep. It's like a total break from reality up there. Very intense—they don't let you have cell phones or computers."

I just shook my head.

"People from all over the world want to see Dr. Cerny. Baskens is really hard to get into."

"But you did."

"A guy in the office told me about him, and he must've put in a good word, because I called today and got the green light."

I cleared my throat. "You know, you could just talk to me."

He smiled gently. "Interesting you should say that."

"What do you mean?"

"If I told you all about my past, but you keep yours hidden, it would throw off our balance. The perfect, precarious balance that's made this thing work so well. Don't you agree?"

I didn't answer. It was the first time Heath had ever referred to my past—and with such confidence that I wouldn't want to talk about it, even if he opened up about his. It was a new feeling—like he was indulging my insecurities, like he was a parent whose child was convinced there was a monster hiding under the bed.

"I wouldn't put this on you anyway, Daphne. Dr. Cerny's a professional. He's done everything—couples' therapy, relationship research, dream therapy too. He does this thing called EMDR. Eye Movement . . . um, something something? It's a technique they use to help people remember past events. Childhood trauma."

A trickle of sweat ran down the back of my neck; I rolled the cashews inside my palm.

"I'd like to go there," he said. "To the Baskens Institute, to meet with him. But"—he hesitated—"it's seven days."

My skin goosepimpled. "What's seven days?"

The whole bar broke into a round of barking in response to the game playing over our heads, and I leaned closer to Heath.

"The retreat," he said louder. "Dr. Cerny's retreat for couples. It starts Monday morning and ends Sunday. When I called, he suggested we should register for it. That it might be a really good idea, for the both of us."

"But if it's you that wants therapy, why do we need a couples' retreat?"

"He suggested since we're going to be married, whatever I had to deal with involved you too—"

"But it doesn't," I blurted. "And, frankly, I don't buy that the only solution to what we're dealing with is a weeklong couples' getaway. How much is this thing, anyway? I'm sure it's not cheap. I mean, think about it. This guy's a salesman. He's selling a product."

"That's a cynical way to look at it."

"Heath. You don't need to sit in some airless office and talk for seven days straight so some arrogant, money-hungry PhD can tell you why you're having nightmares. I mean, there's a billion-dollar self-help-book industry out there, probably scores of books on why we dream what we dream. And not that you want to hear this, but you could just take a knockout pill to help you sleep better. I mean, they're not going to make you turn in your man card for taking a fucking Ambien."

I was babbling now, but he only watched me, his eyes patient. The look filled me with more fear than everything he'd just said.

"Look—" I started again.

He put out a hand. "Listen to me for a second. Dr. Cerny said if you weren't comfortable meeting with him, that it would be fine. You could still come up, be with me when I'm not in sessions, spend time around the institute. The house is really old, and I hear the grounds are beautiful. You could just rest. Relax. Would a week off kill you?"

"No." I sounded petulant even to myself.

"He said there was a possibility you could offer some insight into the nightmares, too, if you were open." He looked down at his drink. "If you don't want to, that's your choice, of course. But, Daphne, here's what I'm saying. Whether you go with me or not, I'm leaving tomorrow."

This was the point where he was supposed to say he was kidding— that all this therapy talk was just a huge joke, and really what he wanted to do was go home with me so we could make love and then fall asleep in each other's arms. But he wasn't saying that. He was just staring down at that stupid business card lying between us like it was some kind of magic key, given to him by a fairy godmother. The promise of a better life. I already felt like I was being left behind.

He was very still. "I don't want to do anything without you. But if we don't figure this out, Daphne, I don't . . . I don't know what's going to happen to us."

"So you're saying . . ." My voice was shaking. "You're saying it's the therapy or we're finished?"

He cleared his throat carefully. "What I'm saying—"

"Heath—"

"—is I don't know if the way we're living—the way we've chosen to relate to each other—is sustainable for the long term."

These weren't his words. They were something a therapist had said to him and now he was repeating back to me. But it didn't matter where the words had come from. It was clear—Heath wanted to deal with his past. Bring it out into the open. And then—as surely as thunder followed lightning—mine would be next.

The dark, crowded bar felt airless. Like it was gradually shrinking and I would be crushed if I stayed. I lifted a finger to the bartender.

"He'll have another one." I dropped my credit card back in my purse, then faced Heath. "Drink it slow. When you're done, come home, and we'll talk. And whatever you do"—I slipped off the stool—"never, ever make me come looking for you again."

As I pushed my way back through the crowd, a cross between Joan of Arc and Beyoncé, I burned with humiliation and defiance. I could feel Heath's eyes on me. And the eyes of the blue-lashed girl. I hadn't been able to resist striking first. Paying her tab for the night, and thus sending her an unmistakable message: *Don't mess with me; don't mess with my man.*

If the system had taught me one thing, it was that acting tough was a perfectly good substitute for actually being tough. Just like this bar and the people drinking away their Saturday night in it. Heath's basketball buddy, the girl with the blue eyelashes, the laughing bartender. We all acted like a bunch of badasses with nothing to lose. But I knew it was a lie.

I was a lie. I was weak and I was scared. Losing Heath, losing my soul mate, would be like watching a sand castle that had taken twenty-eight painstaking years to construct be swept away by a single wave. It would end me, if not in body, then in spirit.

I couldn't let that happen.

Outside the bar, I found a trash can and watched the cashews fall from my hand. I wiped the salt off my palms and stood there for a minute, thinking over my plan.

I would go with Heath to the retreat. Play the supportive fiancée while he met with the doctor and searched for his elusive closure. And in the meantime, I would do some digging of my own, try to get out in front of the situation. If I could somehow figure out what was causing Heath's nightmares before this Dr. Cerny did, maybe I could cut this process short and get us home where we belonged. Get everything back to normal.

I did have something to start with, something I hadn't given much attention to when it first happened because I'd been so rattled. Now I realized it was a clue, if only just a seed of one. Words Heath had said during one of his bad dreams, his voice raw and ragged with terror.

Break the mirror, he had chanted over and over until it reverberated in my brain. *Break the mirror.*

Chapter Two

Sunday, October 14
Five Days Before

The house lay at the end of a rutted gravel road that seemed to stretch on endlessly, rising, switching back, then rising again until I felt nauseated. It stood in a cove of dark pines, its steep crimson gables and stained-glass windows regarding our arrival with a stern expression.

A house with eyes.

I wasn't being paranoid or dramatic. Like Heath had said, the cameras were actually part of the deal at Baskens Institute. Couples attending the famous Baskens retreats were not only paying for therapy sessions but also for the privilege of being observed while they twiddled their thumbs or engaged in their everyday spats. A bunch of lab animals, paying for their own exploitation.

I unfolded myself from Heath's battered Nissan. The air smelled of moss and rotted wood and was at least ten degrees cooler than down in Atlanta. A cloud blotted out the sun, dousing blue sky and green forest in an inky gray, then moved on again. I shivered in the sunlight and thought of my iPad, which I'd tucked safely under the mat in the back seat. Heath hadn't seen me hide it. I hoped it would be safe until I could retrieve it later.

"Where do you think the cameras are hidden?" I polished my cloudy glasses on the scrunched-up sleeve of my sweater. Ours was the only car in the circular drive. I wondered if the other two couples attending the retreat had flown in and been shuttled up the mountain. I hadn't heard anything about them.

"They're inside the rooms. Not out here."

Heath climbed out, popping his neck and stretching. The drive from Atlanta had only been three hours, but in his tiny car it felt like twelve. The Nissan, an unfortunate iridescent royal blue, was a holdover from his college days that he swore he'd never give up, no matter how important the job he happened to have. His holding on to the old car was just one of the things I loved about him. He didn't judge things by their outward appearance; he saw below the surface.

In the bright mountain sunshine, Heath sneezed twice in quick succession.

"Bless you," I said.

"Something's blooming." He went around to the trunk.

Everything was dying as far as I could see, fall's brown and red and gold emerging on the hillsides. A series of terraced lawns bordered the western side of the house, dropping out of sight down the slope of the mountain. Dense forest flanked the rear and eastern sides. Farther off, higher up on the shoulder of the mountain, I caught a glimpse of a thin waterfall tumbling between granite rocks.

The house was painted a deep crimson—the wood siding, the shutters, even the intricate gingerbread trim. Except for the door, which was a vibrant mustard yellow. The facade was dominated by a large overhanging gable, but the rest of the thing was a collection of off-center wings, jutting eaves, and precarious spindled balconies. There was an L-shaped wraparound porch and a hexagonal tower that rose from the top floor. An orgy of Victoriana.

The place was grand, but this close, it was impossible not to notice the faded, peeling paint and mildew-rotted eaves. The way the tops of the window frames sagged. How the roofline and walls joined at odd angles. And the house was wedged into the side of the mountain, too, good and tight. No place for me to go jogging, not unless I wanted to risk falling off a cliff.

I did an automatic count—two doors, four chimneys, eighteen panes of glass on that large, front-facing gable that appeared to be an enclosed balcony. I felt a little better, then. It was important to stay calm. I couldn't let myself slide into panic.

"How in the world do people find this place?" I said.

Heath hoisted our bags from the trunk. "Dr. Cerny's retreats are all based on word of mouth and referrals. Under the radar, super exclusive. Word is, he's the guy who handles Bill and Hillary's tune-ups."

"I wonder if we'll get their room. Sleep in their bed."

He dropped our bags. "Would you like that?" He raised his eyebrows and we shared a smirk. For a moment, just a moment, things seemed perfect between us, like the conversation at Divine had never happened. Like we were just a normal couple who'd gotten out of the city for a last-minute mountain getaway. But I couldn't pretend.

The night before, when I'd gotten home from Divine, I'd spent an hour on the computer, first Googling *Baskens Institute*, then rescheduling the rest of my appointments for the upcoming week so I could leave the next day.

The search results were sparse: there was no official website for the retreat center and only a smattering of pieces written about it, most of them years old. One, an article in the *Wall Street Journal* about Baskens's reputation as a center for platinum-level relationship rescues, emphasized the exclusivity of the place. Nondisclosure agreements prevented clients from leaking any details about Cerny's unconventional methods, but rumors of juicy scandals abounded—celebrity dirt or perverse deeds the Baskens surveillance cameras may have captured.

I moved on to shuffling the upcoming week's tasks onto Kevin and Lenny. I dashed off a succinct, overly cheery email to each of them, glad that it was late enough not to have to deal with a million questions I didn't want to answer.

Yes, Daphne Amos, who scoffed at psychotherapy, was accompanying her fiancé up to the mountains for a full week of it. No, I wasn't taking part; I was tagging along to cheer him on and, in the process, dumping a crap-ton of extra work onto my partner and our employee. I could practically hear Lenny screeching in disbelief when she read the email.

Moving on to my final task, I opened Instagram, and, holding my breath, typed in a name. I'd heard it only once, from Lenny, that very first day I'd met Heath. *Annalise Beard.*

On Instagram, she was @fairlyweirdbeard, and she was a prolific poster. Of frosty, fruity drinks, beach sunsets, and a wan-faced cocker spaniel, mostly. The scattered selfies showed a long-limbed woman with tangled blonde beach hair, a knowing twist to her lips, and an impressive collection of fedoras and ankle boots. Actually, she looked a bit like me. Or maybe my prettier, more socially confident sister. I followed her, then clicked over to type in a message.

After I was done, I powered down the computer, tucked it in the bottom drawer of my desk, and went to bed. Later—much later— Heath slipped between the covers and curled against me. He was cold and smelled like the autumn night air and fallen leaves. He must've been out walking, not hanging out in the bar, drinking, like I'd been imagining and worrying about.

In relief, I rested my hand on his bare chest and draped a leg over one of his. I told him that yes, I would go with him to the retreat, but I still refused to meet with Dr. Cerny. We made love for the first time in weeks. As I drifted off to sleep, I tried not to think about pretty Annalise Beard, whose help I now so desperately needed.

Heath slept peacefully the rest of the night and woke in a good mood. Which was something, I guessed. And on the way up to the mountains, he'd seemed unusually lighthearted, chatting and singing along with the radio. Now, standing in front of the rambling crimson Baskens, I resolved to act supportive, even if I didn't feel that way. Even if I was low-level panicking at the very idea of being an overnight guest at a relationship-research facility.

I inhaled and sent Heath a sly grin. "If sleeping in the same bed where Bill and Hillary slept is what it takes to save us, I will do it," I said. "I will find it ironic, but I will do it."

He caught my wrist and pulled me closer. I buried my face in his shoulder and inhaled his scent—soap and deodorant and the stuff he put in his hair. Who needed therapy when you had your own personal, six-foot-two mood stabilizer?

The whiskers on his jaw scratched my temple. "Always us," he said in a low voice.

"Always us," I replied. "And Bill and Hillary, if need be."

A young man with a shiny face, tortoiseshell glasses, and a swoop of muddy brown hair shouted a greeting at us from the porch. He hadn't been there when we'd first driven up. Maybe he'd seen us approach on the hidden cameras. He bounced down the porch steps and across the expanse of grass.

"Ms. Amos? Mr. Beck?" The man extended a plump hand toward me. Crescents of sweat stained the underarms of his starched oxford button-down, and his khaki chinos were just a hair too short. "Dr. Reginald Teague. Reggie, though, please. Welcome to Baskens. I'll have your car parked around back, if you don't mind."

Heath handed him the keys, and Reggie nodded at our bags.

"Give you a hand with those?"

Heath slung the strap of my bag across his shoulders. "I got it, thanks. Just point me in the right direction."

"Of course. Right this way." He led us up the front walk and then the porch steps, talking over his shoulder. "The other two couples, the Siefferts and the McAdams, have already arrived and are getting settled. You'll have your private tour, meet the doctor, and then dinner in your room. Tomorrow after breakfast, Mr. Beck, you'll have your initial session with Dr. Cerny."

I expected some side-eye from Reggie because of my refusal to take part in any sessions, but without so much as a hiccup, he ushered us through the mustard door, and we stepped into the front hall. I stopped in my tracks.

"Wow."

I was used to the vast, open floors of modern office buildings—prefab cubicles, collaborative meeting rooms, and dog-friendly court-yards. Everything was bright and visible in those places. All things movable, adjustable, temporary.

This house looked like it had been here a thousand years, like it breathed the moldered air of a long-ago past. The lower halves of the walls were paneled in coffered oak, the upper halves in cracked leather embossed with a trailing-vine design. The floors were a dingy brown veined marble, and an oak staircase with multiple landings rose from the middle of the room to the floors above. The stairs seemed to have as many switchbacks as the road we'd just driven up.

Chairs upholstered in frayed silk were scattered among monstrously oversized sideboards. Ornate brass gas lamps converted to electric did their utmost to light the room, but the place was still oppressively dark. The air felt stale, like the windows had never been opened. I tried to ignore a creeping sense of claustrophobia, looking into the rooms just off the front hall. There were several—a dining room, a salon, maybe, or music room. A library. But their doors were closed or they were dark and I couldn't see inside. Old houses with cloistered rooms and layers of bric-a-brac always did this to me. I snuck a look at Heath but couldn't gauge his reaction to the place. His face was a blank.

Reggie brightened. "Ah, surprise, surprise. Looks like the McAdams are back downstairs. We can meet them before the tour."

Heath dropped our bags, and Reggie ushered us into a library, done up in more dusty silks and somber velvets, with one wall a massive, carved bookcase. Twelve shelves, all filled with old books. I turned away, fiddling with the hair band around my wrist, and focused on the couple standing beside the bay window. They were in their midthirties, the man sporting a pair of Oakleys looped around his neck by a camouflage neoprene strap, the woman dressed in a swingy paisley dress and cowboy boots. Both of them held crystal goblets of red wine.

"Heath Beck and Daphne Amos, I'd like you to meet the McAdams, Jerry and Donna. They're one of our three lucky couples at this month's session."

Three. Why does it have to be three?

I took a deep breath and forced a smile. After the flurry of handshakes and greetings, I turned to the woman. "Are you from around here?"

She glanced at Reggie.

"Actually, Ms. Amos," he said, "we ask that all Baskens participants not share personal details with each other. You'll be seeing very little of the other couples this week. All meals are delivered to you in your private suites by Luca, our cook—who speaks very little English. Sessions are scheduled with everyone's utmost privacy in mind. You may see the other couples on the grounds during free time, but Dr. Cerny asks that you respect the intensity of everyone's experience and refrain from socializing. The doctor believes the fewer the distractions, the more you can adequately focus on your partner and open yourself up to the therapy. It's one of the hallmarks of Baskens's unique approach. Speaking of which, you read the agreement regarding your cell phones, correct?"

"Yes," Heath said.

"The gift of silence, that's what we like to call it." Reggie produced a small basket and held it out. Heath dropped his cell phone in. "Dr.

Cerny and I both have telephones in case of emergency. The nearest village down the mountain, Dunfree, has a fire department and hospital, if needed. Though it never has been," he rushed to add.

I tried not to imagine the awfulness of driving back down that rutted gravel road with some sort of medical emergency. I couldn't believe people actually chose to live up here, almost completely cut off from society. And SuperTargets.

"Babe," Heath said.

I dug my phone out of my purse. "Oh, right. One sec. Just something from work I should check real quick." I turned and tapped open Instagram. A couple of notifications—@fairlyweirdbeard had followed me. And left me a message. I opened it.

I was wondering when I'd hear from you. Emailing you now.

"Daphne," Heath said.

I switched off my phone and let it clack into the basket. Annalise Beard was emailing me. This was a good sign. Better than good.

Reggie checked his watch. "All right, then. I'll take you to your suite. You can unpack, rest a bit from the trip. Luca will deliver your dinner at seven o'clock—fish, I believe—along with a complimentary bottle of wine."

"Fish," Heath said under his breath.

I furrowed my brow at him, but he looked away.

"It's actually scallops in some kind of cream sauce, if I'm not mistaken. You're not allergic, are you?"

"He's not allergic," I interjected. I glanced at Donna McAdam, smiled, and rolled my eyes. A prim look was all I got in return.

Reggie cleared his throat. "After dinner, the doctor will meet with each couple in his study, so we'd like to get your private tours of the house and grounds in before that. There are a few quirks to the property, and we want everyone to feel comfortable during your stay. The Siefferts have already had theirs. The McAdams are next, and then I'll take you."

I looked over at the McAdams. They'd migrated back to the windows, still holding their wine.

In the main hall, Reggie led the way upstairs. "You can drop your things in your room, freshen up if you like, and then we'll meet back downstairs for your tour. Do either of you know why the house is called Baskens?"

Heath spoke up. "The property and house originally belonged to the Baskens family, from Dr. Cerny's maternal side—built back during the gold rush. Dr. Cerny inherited the place, lived here a while, and eventually turned it into a counseling retreat."

"Wow," I said. It was certainly more than I'd been able to dig up online.

"Very good," Reggie said.

"Mason, the guy from work, told me that," Heath said.

"Here we go," Reggie puffed, and Heath hooked a finger through one of mine.

As I stepped onto the first landing, I happened to look back. I could just see—through one arched opening—a woman standing in the dark dining room. She had silver or blonde hair that shone, even in the shadows, and a long, elegant neck. I thought, at first, that was all I could see, but it wasn't exactly true. There was something more, something strange. She was staring at us—at me, specifically—with an expression of naked, undisguised curiosity.

Chapter Three

In January, the *Atlanta Business Chronicle* picked Lenny and me to participate in their annual "Thirty Under Thirty" issue, which was an incredible coup for us—a PR rocket booster that meant our little company, the Silver Sisters, could leapfrog to the front of the line and bid more prestigious jobs.

It also meant we were morally obligated to go out (along with Kevin, our one employee, an assistant-slash-bookkeeper) and blow our expense budget on a three-course dinner and a bottle of real French champagne. The next day, still gloriously hungover, Lenny and I met the reporter for lunch at Farm Burger, where the two of us put on our dog-and-pony show about how we'd started the Silver Sisters.

Well, Lenny put on the show. I sat quietly and snapped the hair band on my wrist so many times the skin on the inside of my wrist burned in the shower later that night.

Lenny explained to the reporter that both of us were only children, each having always longed for a sister. Friends who'd met at Savannah College of Art and Design, a pair of starry-eyed, scrappy girls; we'd dreamed of starting a business together since the day we met in Space Planning our freshmen year. After graduation, we finally did it, me with the design talent and Lenny with the kick-ass business savvy. Through sheer force of will (and a nice pile of startup cash from her father), we created our own business as well as the sisterhood we'd always longed for.

Of course, the story made me sound as if I'd shown up at art school like Athena springing from the head of Zeus, but the real story was different. The truth was I'd gotten there the hard way—seven years at a group foster home southwest of Macon, during which time my absentee mother died of a drug overdose. I made it through those early years mostly unscathed, my only visible scar a secret but mostly controlled obsession with food.

Thanks to a state scholarship program, I attended SCAD, where I met Lenny Silver. Lenny took an instant liking to me and swept me under her motherly wing. My reluctance to talk about the ranch or my mother's death must've frustrated her, but she never let it stop her from deluging me with her friendship. After we graduated and moved to Decatur, just outside Atlanta, her parents absorbed me into their warm, chaotic family like I was a stray pup. At Hap Silver's insistence, I moved into one of his properties, an adorable updated bungalow on Ansley Street. I paid him a laughably low monthly rent and furnished it with Barbara Silver's exquisite nineteenth-century castoffs. I walked to Agnes Scott College every morning in the soft dawn and sprinted around the track until any jagged memory from Piney Woods Girls' Ranch that may have poked through my formidable psychic walls and into my consciousness was safely stuffed away again.

And the food-hoarding thing eased, thanks to the stability provided by the Silver family. I no longer stashed cookies and granola bars under my mattress. Now when I felt anxious, I just silently counted whatever happened to be nearby. My slimmer physique reflected my new calm (and the running I'd taken up), and although I didn't date much—I hadn't met anyone I felt a strong connection to—I was content with my life. Work kept me busy enough. It was all the therapy I needed.

The photo shoot for the *Chronicle* feature was held in midtown, at a drab warehouse on a side street off Ponce de Leon. The thirty anointed ones (Lenny and I counted as one) gathered in the frigid space for a group shot. The wardrobe guy wheeled around us, slapping shirts and blazers and scarves on those deemed underdressed, while two makeup artists scuttled frantically between the women, spackling and dabbing and hair fluffing.

They spent an inordinate amount of time on me, I thought, sniffing over my pale skin, which they predicted would blow out the shots, and my long, lank blonde hair that "just lies there." One of them kept pulling off my glasses and saying my eyes were pretty. But I couldn't see a damn thing, so I put them back on.

After the group shot, the woman in charge told us they'd take the individual pictures in rapid-fire, fifteen-minute windows. Everybody scattered to check their phones. Lenny and I were last on the list, so I settled in to wait at the craft-services table and try not to count every last Cool Ranch Dorito.

The photographer, an elfin woman with a fuzz of snow-white hair and tight black leather pants, went to work, positioning the first subject, a stunning female lawyer from the state's attorney general's office. The attorney struck poses like a *Vogue* model, and I felt fear begin to gnaw in my gut. There was no way I was going to be able to pull off that level of confidence. No way I could even fake it.

To distract myself, I assessed the offerings at the craft table. Heaps of fresh fruit, chips, crackers, popcorn, and cookies, all gourmet, tumbled over the table in reassuring mounds. Grateful for the low lights, I busied myself assembling a plate. Feeling calmer, I nibbled on the food while Lenny worked her way around the room.

I had started in on an oatmeal-raisin cookie when I realized the cavernous studio, which had previously been buzzing with conversation, had suddenly hushed around me. In unison, everyone seemed to have angled themselves toward the black-paper backdrop, where a guy I hadn't seen until now, tall and broad-shouldered, stood in the pool of light created by hot tungsten bulbs and silver umbrellas. He was gorgeous, but that wasn't all. There was something more interesting about him. He was . . .

Like me, I thought—surprised, yet somehow not. *He is like me.*

It was a bizarre, out-of-the-blue thought, as the guy in the lights was an arresting sight, beautiful and brooding—clearly nothing like me. At best, I was average, maybe a little above, and that was on a cute-hair day. He was also at ease in front of the camera, self-contained and mysterious, which was surely not going to be the case with me.

Regardless, there was something about him, something that struck me in a very particular but indefinable way. I couldn't look away from him. A tiny burst of electricity zipped through me—a charge that sizzled under my skin all the way down to my toes. How had I not noticed him earlier? Where had I been? This guy was not the sort of person you missed. Pale skin, sharply angled cheekbones and jaw, with shaggy, slightly-too-long coal hair and wide-set deep-brown eyes.

"Heath Beck." It was Lenny, at my five o'clock, whispering in my ear. "Real-estate wunderkind. Works with the Holland Company. He negotiated the sale of that entire area between Foster and Spring."

She went on. About how the Holland Company was at the forefront of the revitalization of some of these neglected pockets of Midtown and the Westside, about how she'd heard that he personally had bought a derelict warehouse in Cabbagetown that he was going to develop into high-end loft apartments. I could barely process what she was saying. Heath Beck's silhouette, lit like an angel, turned her voice to a mosquito's buzz.

"It's ridiculous, really," she concluded, reaching for a can of Diet Coke.

"What is?"

"He's supposedly dating someone, but I don't think I've ever seen them together."

I whipped around to face her. "Who is he dating?"

"That publicist, Annalise Beard, the one who works for the Hawks. She's gorgeous. But, like I said, never around. Let me tell you, if I was dating that? One hundred percent never let it out of my sight." She laughed at her own joke, then looked at me and narrowed her eyes. "Oh, no. Really? Seriously? Are you kidding me?"

I turned back to look at him again.

"So the woman who won't give any man the time of day finally succumbs," she marveled. And my friend was right. I had officially succumbed.

Later, when Lenny had gone off to work the room some more, Heath Beck appeared on the other side of the craft table. He was wearing a fitted blue dress shirt, a black tie, and a pair of criminally well-tailored black pants. I lowered my plate of snacks and tried to swallow the remnant of a cheese straw.

Up close he was even taller than I'd realized. Nice smelling and muscular. I tried not to stare directly at him. Or into his eyes, which were warm and brown and so intense that it felt like they were literally piercing my skin. I coughed. The cheese straw wouldn't go down.

He took a swig of water. "Fair warning? That is one hell of a hellish experience."

I laughed, clearing my throat as unobtrusively as I could. It sounded like a donkey bray. "You looked great. Totally aced it all the way." I flushed furiously. I sounded like a teenage girl. I sounded like I liked him.

"I'm Heath." He looked at me for what seemed like a long time. So long that I felt my entire body grow warm. "What was your name again?" He asked it quietly, purposefully, like he'd been practicing the question in his head before he walked over.

"Daphne," I said. "Daphne Amos."

"Your company is the Silver Sisters, right?"

"Daphne!"

It was Lenny, calling me from across the studio. We were up. I scuttled toward the nimbus of lights, aware that Heath was still standing back at the craft table and was probably—no, definitely—noticing the weird plate of snacks (four cheese straws, four grapes, four sea-salt-and-dark-chocolate-covered almonds) that I'd just set down on a stack of four cocktail napkins.

Like I'd anticipated, the photo shoot was excruciatingly awkward. Lenny vamped and puckered and pouted at the camera while I stood beside her, trying to obey the photographer's encouragement to give her some attitude. I wanted to give it to her, I really did, but instead my face went immobile, I stiffened up, and I had the overwhelming urge to pee.

Somewhere in the middle of the horrific process, Heath ambled up behind the photographer and whispered in her ear.

"Take five, ladies." She stepped away, her assistant scurrying after her. Heath joined Lenny and me under the lights.

"Lenny Silver-Hirsch," Lenny chirped, offering her hand.

"Heath Beck," he said. "Would you mind if I stole your partner for a second, Lenny?"

Lenny's eyes went wide. She smiled. "Be my guest."

Heath put his hand on my arm—actually, just inside the upper part of my arm, the spot a little above the elbow—and led me outside the pool of light. In the darkness, he leaned toward me, and I inhaled. He smelled amazing—of some kind of intoxicating scent that I couldn't place. My arm was tingling where he'd touched me.

"You don't like this," he said.

"This?" I asked, waving my finger in the space between us. He couldn't have been more wrong. I liked it very much.

He smiled. "I mean having your picture taken."

"Oh, right. No. I mean, yes. I hate it."

"Me too."

I blinked at him. "But. You were great up there. Like, completely . . . great." My face was burning. I was glad we were outside the light.

"I have a trick. A secret that helps me get through things like this." I stared at him.

"Do you want to know what it is?" he asked gently.

I cleared my throat. "Absolutely. Yes."

"I pick out the sexiest woman in the room, and I pretend I'm approaching her. Imagine I'm standing in front of her, about to ask her out for the very first time. I muster all my resources—all my charm and wit and confidence—and then I just slay her with all the amazingness that is me."

He was still smiling, but when I looked into his dark eyes, they were locked onto mine.

He is like me . . . We are the same . . .

"You understand?" he asked.

Somehow I managed to speak. "I think so. Slay with my amazingness."

"So go ahead. Do it. Look around and pick out the sexiest guy in the room."

"Oh." It was all I could do to tear my eyes away from his and scan the room. My gaze fell upon the guy who'd stood next to me in the group picture, a plastic surgeon. A red-faced, somewhat sweaty guy with caterpillar eyebrows and a scraggly goatee. He wore a giant gold pinky ring.

"Really? That guy?" Heath sounded incredulous. A little crestfallen.

I smiled, then covered my mouth. "I, uh—"

"No, no. It's fine. I didn't mean to criticize. I just . . . I guess I expected somebody . . . else. But, different strokes." He grinned broadly and touched my arm again. My skin goosepimpled.

"When she takes the picture, all you have to do is pretend you're standing in front of that guy—that strapping fellow you just selected. You stand in front of that guy like the strong, beautiful, intelligent woman that you are. And you give him a look that says, *Hey, sweaty guy with that sad beard and pinky ring. We should go out for burritos later.*"

I raised an eyebrow. "Burritos?"

"That's right, burritos."

He gave me a gentle push back into the lights. The next thing I knew, Lenny and I were draped all over each other, laughing and posing. The camera clicked nonstop, and all the while, I couldn't tear my eyes away from Heath Beck, who, incidentally, wasn't standing anywhere near the guy with the sad beard and pinky ring.

Later, as Lenny and I made our way through the parking lot to her car, my phone vibrated with a text. Only one word, from a number I didn't recognize.

Daphne.

I stopped, my heart thudding while Lenny danced around me, oblivious, chattering about the shoot and her husband, Drew, and how much he was going to love the photos.

"Did you give him my number?" I asked her.

She just grinned, and then another text appeared, directly under the first.

We should go out for burritos.

Friday, October 19
Evening

I am sliding sideways down the face of the mountain, skiing over the blanket of wet leaves, using the slender beech trees for balance. The big coat flaps around me, and I've wedged the iPad against my back in the waistband of my jeans. My glasses keep slipping down. They're fogged too, but I don't bother to stop and wipe them. I don't have time. I need to find the road, wherever the hell that may be, before it gets dark.

I'm not a woods person, even during the day. Past sundown, they'll feel like they've grown deeper, darker, more labyrinthine, the setting of a monstrous fairy tale. There are bears and coyotes and God knows what else out here prowling, stalking. But there is also a man. And I am more afraid of him than I am of any wild animal.

I'm soaked through now, from my own sweat and maybe even blood, but I keep going. All those dawns on the track come back to me. Funny how I was always trying to push myself harder for some reason. It must've been all for this moment.

Chapter Four

Sunday, October 14
Five Days Before

The stairs to the second floor led up to a long hallway filled with more sideboards, wardrobes, and chiffoniers—scrolled mahogany behemoths from a bygone era. Along the hall, I counted three doors and one at the very end. All closed.

Reggie executed a perfect flight-attendant gesture. "That first room is vacant and the door is locked. The McAdams and Siefferts are in the next two rooms. You"—he pointed at the far end of the hall—"will have that room, the largest suite, which overlooks the front of the house."

"What's back that way?" I pointed at a closed pocket door, only a few feet from the stairs, which blocked the other end of the hall.

"That's Dr. Cerny's suite. The entire wing is strictly off limits, but he has his own set of stairs that lead down to the kitchen and back door. Another set lead up to the attic. The attic is off limits as well, of course."

"Say it one more time, and I guarantee you somebody sneaks in there." I grinned, but he didn't return it, just led the way to our room, swung the door open, and stepped back. He puffed his chest, and as I entered, I turned a slow, appreciative three-sixty and saw why.

Our bedroom was the one I'd seen when we'd first driven up. Nearly all glass, the walls retrofitted over the spindles of what had formerly been a porch. Heavy cream silk curtains lined the wall of windows, and every piece of furniture—bed, nightstands, dresser, and desk—was a meticulously restored Danish-modern original. At the far end of the sitting room, a leather-and-walnut recliner was artfully arranged beside a Delft-tiled fireplace. Which was, of course, invitingly laid with wood, ready to light. The room was bright and spotless and smelled of lemon verbena.

Heath shed the bags in a heap at the foot of the bed and moved toward a small oval mirror hanging over a blond-wood dresser. He glanced at his reflection, then moved to the wall of windows. The sun must've broken through the clouds and pierced the heavy canopy of trees, because all at once the room was filled with light.

I bent over to examine the fireplace and yelped in surprise.

"Oh, yes," Reggie said. "I should've warned you."

Heath turned.

"It's a face, in the back," I said.

"We call him the fiery fiend," Reggie said. "He's in every fireplace in the house. Part of the original design, I'm told."

I glanced around the room. "And what about the cameras? Where are they? There's not one in the bathroom, I hope."

Teague tilted his head. "Camera, singular. It's in the main room. And my advice is to forget all about it. Pretend it's not there. The more naturally you behave, the more you are yourselves, the more Dr. Cerny will have to work with."

Heath had unlocked several of the windows and thrown them open. Cool air blew in, the scent of river and rock and pine overpowering the lemon smell.

"The cameras are activated every morning at eight a.m. and shut down from ten p.m. until midnight, at which point they run again until five a.m. They're also down briefly from one thirty to two thirty every afternoon. A free block." He raised his eyebrows, giving us a moment, I supposed, to get his meaning. "I know it feels somewhat uncomfortable, but keep in mind, filming patients is a legitimate technique for research and diagnosis. There are several well-regarded labs all over the world that employ it to great success. Learman's Intimacy Institute at BYU and James Deshpande's facility that explores work-related violence."

I snuck a look at Heath. He was leaning out one of the windows, gazing off into the distance. Unfazed by the fact that we were being watched like zoo animals. Or criminals.

Reggie clasped his hands. "Well, then. I'll let you two get settled, freshen up, then in exactly fifty minutes, we'll meet downstairs for the tour and your meeting with Dr. Cerny. We'll have you around the place and back to your rooms by seven for dinner."

He left, and as I unpacked, Heath disappeared into the bathroom. "So the schedule around here seems really precise," I called out. There was no answer. When he came back, he returned to the opened windows and leaned out into the darkening night air.

"You okay?" I said. "It seems a little chilly to have the windows open."

"I like the way the mountains smell." He turned to me, a playful look in his eye. "You know, Reggie said we have fifty minutes."

"Well, more like forty-five now." I pointed around the room. "But more importantly, it's showtime, remember? We're being watched. Even though, I should point out, we haven't signed the releases yet."

"I bet the Siefferts are in their suite, banging it out hard-core." He kicked back on the bed and aimed his blindingly sexy grin at me.

I turned away. Mrs. Sieffert, or whoever it was who'd been lurking in the dining room watching us, was certainly, one hundred percent, not upstairs banging it out with her husband.

"Come on, Daph. Real quick."

I raised an eyebrow. "Are you kidding me?"

"Come. Here." He said it in that voice—the one with the deep, slow cadence that made the area below my stomach twinge. He crooked one finger, and I moved to the bed, only a hair out of his reach.

"You want me to come closer?" I asked. "Never say *real quick*."

I bent to him, just so my hair fell over his face and my breasts brushed his chest. He moaned. He reached for me and I crawled up beside him. Cradling me with one arm, he pulled the white comforter over us, and I closed my eyes as he fitted the length of his body against my back and legs. He was already hard.

I spoke. "There was a woman when we came in. Kind of spying on us from downstairs. Did you see her?"

"No." He nuzzled my neck.

"She was staring at us, like . . ."

He kissed my neck gently, reached around and removed my glasses. "Like . . ."

He whispered in my ear. "Whatever happens—no matter what I do—don't move."

I didn't, not when he unzipped my pants under the covers, then eased them down past my knees, ankles. Not when he did the same with my underwear. Not even when he ran his hand along the inside of my thigh.

I let him touch me for as long as I could stand it, then guided him into me, turning my face into the pillow. After it was over, he buried his head in the crook of my neck and whispered one last time, "Always us."

Maybe it was the sex or just that I hadn't had a good night's sleep in months, but right after, I fell fast and hard into a dreamless sleep.

When I woke, the room was lit with the soft glow of the bathroom night-light, and Heath was sleeping beside me. The window was still open and I inhaled a lungful of cool, pungent air. I guessed the months of nightmares really had depleted both of us, more than I'd realized. If nothing else, the two of us might actually be able to catch up on all our lost sleep in this creepy house. I groped around on the nightstand for my phone. *Right.* I'd turned it over to Dr. Teague. Reggie. *Crap.*

I found my glasses under my pillow, then dug under the comforter for my pants. Easing out of bed, I crept to the fireplace, trying not to think about the fiery fiend's grotesque, leering face. I ran my hands along the mantel. A small brass clock on it ticked softly: 9:40 p.m. I bit my lip. I couldn't remember the last time I'd slept like that.

We'd missed our first meeting with Dr. Cerny. As well as the tour and the signing of the releases, which was not at all the way I'd planned to start things off. I was not usually one to oversleep, arrive late to an appointment, or forget details of clients' orders. But then again, I usually had a phone glued to some part of me, pinging alerts right and left.

We'd also missed dinner. Damn. Scallops, I remembered with longing. Reggie had said it was scallops and wine. It was possible somebody had saved our meals in the fridge or something. Possible, but not for sure, and that was the thing that really got me, the not knowing. And right now, with the house spreading out like a maze around me, the worry that I wouldn't be able to find anything to eat—I could feel the old food obsession dancing around the edges. Could feel myself close to panicking.

Daphne. Stop.

I went into the bathroom and dug in my makeup bag, pulling out a hair band and slipping it over my hand. I snapped it against my wrist—once, twice, three and four times. Then inhaled and exhaled, letting the pain pull me back to the physical room. I couldn't panic. Not now. I needed to get organized, be thinking about my plan. How I was going to find the car and check my email. How I was going to deal with the information, if any, that Annalise Beard decided to share.

I peeked through the door at Heath and watched him breathe for a moment. It was a relief to see him like that—practically comatose, arms flung out and mouth open. How odd that he couldn't sleep in our cozy little house, but here he conked out like an innocent babe. I had the feeling sleep wasn't going to return so easily for me, not with my gnawing stomach and my nerves. But being up wasn't such a bad thing. I might as well try to find where Reggie had put our car keys.

Out in the dark hallway, all the doors were shut. The McAdams and Siefferts must have turned in early too. The pocket door with tarnished brass fittings at the opposite end of the hall—the one leading to Dr. Cerny's quarters—was open just a couple of inches.

I tiptoed to it and peered through the crack. Beyond it was a spacious landing area, as big itself as our bedroom. At the far end, I saw another closed door—Cerny's suite, no doubt. On the left side of the landing, there was a set of stairs that probably led down to the kitchen. From the right, another set of stairs, narrower than the others, wound up to the next floor.

The attic.

I heard a noise, coming from the attic stairs. A clicking sound, then a low drone. I glanced at Cerny's door at the opposite end of the landing. It was far enough away that I could probably slip in unheard, if I was careful. I pushed the pocket door open and eased through.

I crept to the attic stairs, put my foot on the first step. Waited. When nothing happened, I mounted the next step, then another and another, keeping to the edge so the boards wouldn't creak. At the top of the stairs, I found a black fireproof door, cracked open just the slightest bit. The drone was louder; I had definitely found the source. I listened for any indication that I'd disturbed Cerny. When I heard nothing, I pushed open the door and walked in.

The tiny, hexagonal garret was crammed to bursting with all sorts of oversize metal hardware. Machinery and shelving ringing the room like a cabal of mechanical giants. Dozens of thick black cords snaked across the bare wood floor. To my right, a row of three boxy video monitors sat on a sagging plywood shelf. On the left were two enormous machines as big as refrigerators, covered with rows of multicolored buttons, dials, and gauges. And more unidentifiable machines next to those.

"Hello, Dr. Strangelove," I whispered.

In the center of the room, a battered metal desk and folding chair faced the monitors. Only a yellow legal pad and pen were on the desk. I opened the drawers—all six of them—but they were empty. No car keys. I crept around the desk, taking in the strange setup. The computers, if that was what they were, must have been the main servers, linked to the cameras downstairs and to the monitors up here. To timers, as well, most likely. And there was probably, somewhere, a mechanism for recording the captured footage so Dr. Cerny could review it later. I could see slots that looked like they might fit VHS tapes, but I was hopeless at technology, and the rest of the knobs and buttons and dials were meaningless to me. Frankly, the whole tableau looked very KGB circa 1980.

I examined the monitors. Feeds from our in-room cameras, maybe? They were dark, at least they appeared to be at first glance—but then a curtain fluttered in the corner of one, and I jumped in fright. The cameras were running, even though it was after ten. Either somebody had screwed up or the timers were off.

I moved closer.

Each camera must have been mounted near a fireplace mantel, allowing for a wide shot of the suite, even a bit of the windows. On our monitor, the one on the far right, I could see the bed, the door to the bathroom, and the small sitting area. The monitors were illuminated the slightest bit, by some light source outside the house, maybe. The moon or a floodlight on one of the eaves.

Heath was still sprawled out, his leg kicked out from under the comforter now. On my side of the bed, the comforter was thrown back, and I noticed, with a guilty flush, the twist of underwear lying on the floor. I turned my attention back to my fiancé—that beautiful, strong, tormented man—and, as I watched him sleep, thought back six months ago, to the night of his first nightmare.

Heath asked me to marry him on a perfect April night.

We were at our house—the bungalow Lenny's father had agreed to sell to us to bolster Heath's fledgling private foray into Atlanta real estate. We'd eaten pizzas loaded with every leftover vegetable I could scrounge from the fridge and now were relaxing on the back deck. The sky was perfect and clear, promising a star-sprayed canopy after the crisp spring dusk had passed.

We were stacked together on one of Barbara Silver's hand-me-down Adirondack chairs, my head resting back against Heath's shoulder. As we'd watched the night settle around us, he'd been gathering my hair over my shoulder and gently twisting it. It felt so good, I'd nearly fallen asleep.

After a while, he ran one finger down the length of my arm. His skin, pale like mine but with an olive tint, was warm. He turned up my hand and laid a ring in the center of my palm. It looked like an antique, a simple silver band, but heavy, engraved, and set with diamonds. The lines of my palm converged in the ring's center.

"It was my grandmother's." Heath's voice was soft in my ear. I tore my eyes from the ring, twisted in the chair to look at him. The kitchen window was a bright block of light behind him, so I could barely make out the expression on his face, but I knew he was smiling.

The Silvers were wonderful, but I'd never had a family, not a real one of my own. All my junkie mother had left me with was an enormous need for privacy and an annoying eating disorder, not family heirlooms. But now, starting that night, everything would change. I was about to become a part of a new family. The family Heath and I created together.

"Daphne," he said, and this time his voice had a ragged edge to it. A vulnerable, open need that made me feel scared and exhilarated, all at the same time.

"Yes," I said. "Yes." Then I reached up and laced my fingers through his thick black hair and drew his face to mine. He took off my glasses and kissed me, and I thought, for the thousandth time since meeting him, I'd never been kissed so well in my life.

In the bedroom, I was impatient, peeling off my shirt and then Heath's, but he gripped my wrists to make me slow down. I pulled him to the bed, but the more urgently I moved, the more he resisted. Every time I pressed against him, he would pause whatever incredibly delicious thing he was doing, fix his eyes on mine, and gently push me away. He grazed his fingers over every plane of my face.

In the light from the hallway, I could see that his brown eyes had lightened to a pure, reflective amber—the way they did anytime he was tired. His lips parted, then pressed together. It seemed like there was something he wanted to say.

"What is it?" I gave him a playful shake even as alarm shuddered through me. This was always tricky territory for me—opening up, talking about my feelings. And Heath and I didn't usually go there, but this night felt different. He shook his head and kept staring at me with those amber eyes. There was something more than tiredness in them—something I'd never witnessed before. He was afraid, afraid to tell me something.

Suddenly I was afraid too. I had a crazy urge to cover his mouth with my hands or to run out of the room. But I didn't do either. Instead I calmly pulled aside the sheet, tugged down his underwear, and went to work on his body until all thought of conversation had been forgotten.

Later, he pulled the sheet over my shoulders and murmured in my ear. A simple wedding, he said—maybe in our backyard, or even at the courthouse. A honeymoon in the Caribbean. I nodded to all of it. The details of a wedding were irrelevant to me. Neither of us had enough family to count and only a handful of friends. What mattered was we were back to normal. Whatever he might have wanted to say, he'd changed his mind. The delicate balance between us was restored. I was safe.

Heath pressed a kiss against my hair, and I burrowed into the blankets, my eyes fixed on the diamond band on my left hand. It winked in the bar of light from the bathroom. Heath had gotten it sized to fit me perfectly.

It was perfect.

Everything was perfect.

Sometime in the night, I felt the blankets jerk and I woke, disoriented. The streetlights had shut off and the room was ink black. Heath, on his hands and knees, was mumbling and pawing at the covers, like he was searching for something.

"Break the mirror," he said. "Break it. Smash it."

He leapt up and darted across the room, yanking up the blinds on the bay of windows in our bedroom. He laid his hands on the wavy old pane of the center window, gently at first, his fingers spreading outward. Between them, I could see the cloud of his breath on the glass.

"Heath?" I said, but there was no answer. Only the sound of his breathing. It was heavy, like he'd just burst over some invisible finish line.

"We can open the window, if you want." I could hear a tremor in my voice. Maybe he was having a panic attack and needed fresh air. I told myself to stay calm.

"Do you—" I started.

With no warning, he balled his hands into fists and smashed them into the window. The glass cracked but didn't shatter. I gasped, then he drew back again, ramming his fists clear through to the other side. The window splintered, breaking into a million triangles.

A moth fluttered around his head, and the sheer voile curtains billowed behind him. He held his hands out, palms up, and a beaded line of blood trickled down his forearms. His eyes were wide open but hollow, and the look on his face stopped my breath. It was a triumph I'd never witnessed on anyone's face before.

"I did it, Mom," he said.

I shrank back against the wooden headboard and waited—for what, I didn't know. After a few seconds, Heath moved to the bed and lay down again, curling his body away from me. I heard him sigh once, deeply, then begin to snore.

I eased off the bed and crept around to the other side. It was hard to see in the dim light, but the worst cut seemed to run along the edge of his hand, all the way down past his wrist—a good three inches and a series of angry, oozing crosshatches across his knuckles. But the bleeding had already slowed, even though some of it had soaked into the blue sheet beneath him.

In the kitchen, I made myself a cup of tea and drank it standing up, staring out the back door, willing my hammering heart to slow. I flung open the door of the pantry. Rows of cans and boxes and packages lining every shelf. Plenty of food for now. Plenty for always. I counted until my breath evened out.

The next morning, when I got out of the shower, Heath was sweeping the floor. He shook his head when I asked him what the dream had been about.

"I don't remember." He squatted and swept the glass into the dustpan.

"You don't remember anything?"

"No." He dumped the pan into a garbage bag.

"Was it something about your mother?" I asked, my throat closing with dread.

The question hung in the air between us. Here was his chance to tell me anything he'd held back. Here was my chance to do the same.

"You said something about a—"

"Daphne," he interrupted. "It was just a bad dream. No point in talking about it. But I'm sorry about the window."

He slung the bag over his shoulder. Something in the clipped tone of his words, the closed look on his face that I'd never seen before, kept me from pushing any further. I had the distinct impression that we'd ventured into a tenuous place. That if I wasn't careful, I could lose him. I nodded my assent, and he left the room.

The nightmares continued, at least two or three times a week. Occasionally Heath got physical, delivering a particularly fierce kick or jab to my ribs. Once I caught an elbow on my jaw, leaving me tender and bruised. When Lenny saw me at the office the next day, her eyes got big, and she sent Kevin on a coffee run.

Her silence made me nervous. "It was an accident," I said. "He was asleep—dreaming—and got agitated. I just happened to be in the way, that's all."

"Did he mention what he was dreaming about? Zombie Nazis? Killer T. rexes? The IRS?"

I avoided her gimlet eye. "He said he didn't remember."

"Maybe it was about his mysterious, murky past, that he doesn't like discussing with you or anyone. Which you let him get away with because y'all seem to have this weird pact where you don't talk either."

I sighed. "Everybody has a right to privacy. Some of us just need more than others."

"I know," she said. "And I'm not trying to pry, I swear. I'm just . . . I love you, Daph. And I think it might be a relief to let it all go."

"Mm-hm," I said.

"Something to think about," she said. "That's all."

"We need to put the Mathison drawings into CAD," I threw over my shoulder as I stalked off in the direction of our minikitchen.

"I love you," she yelled after me.

"I love you too," I yelled back, and that was the end of that.

She might've been off base thinking Heath was an abuser, but she was right that the nightmares were a sign of something more going on with him. The truth was, I had known for a while now that below Heath's perfect exterior, inside him, lay a wilderness—I had recognized it that first night because I had the same thing. Before, it had made me feel connected to him in a way I couldn't put into words. But now I knew there was something seriously wrong—something my fiancé didn't think he could tell me.

And it occurred to me, for the first time, that both of us could end up lost—so easily and without any hope of rescue—in that vast, hostile wilderness.

Chapter Five

The monitor at the left end of the shelf showed a room furnished with Victorian pieces like they had downstairs, rather than the modern style of ours. A couple slept peacefully in the bed. The room on the middle monitor looked almost identical, except it was papered in an old-fashioned rose pattern.

A movement caught my eye, and I inched closer to the screen. The couple—presumably the Siefferts, the ones who'd arrived before us—were awake. I hadn't noticed this before, but they weren't in bed. They were sitting on a matching pair of ottomans positioned close to the camera. And it appeared that they were fighting. Mr. Sieffert slumped back, arms folded across his chest, and his wife leaned forward, her chin jutted, lips moving fast. She was mad about something, that was for sure.

It was hard to tell with the low lighting and the grainy picture, but she looked like she might be the same woman I'd seen earlier, watching us from the dining room. She was slim, and her hair was the same lightish tint, blonde or gray, pulled back in a clip.

"How do you turn up the volume on this thing?" I murmured.

I twisted a couple of knobs along the bottom of the monitor, but nothing happened. Maybe there was another volume control. Or maybe Cerny disabled the sound at night. I drew back, chewing at my thumbnail, momentarily ashamed for prying into their private moment. The feeling didn't last long, because another blip from the left monitor caught my attention.

Jerry McAdam—no more than a fuzzy gray blob on the screen—was climbing out of bed, easing out slowly from between the sheets. He disappeared into the bathroom, then a few seconds later returned and crept toward the sitting area. He eased himself down, threw a glance over his shoulder at the bed, and began thumbing at an old-school flip phone.

"Jer, you sneaky bastard," I breathed, moving closer to the monitor. "You smuggled a phone into Baskens? I call a flag on the play."

He set it on the arm of the chair. A few seconds later it flashed; he snatched it up and started typing again.

"Texting somebody, are we? And not your wife, obviously, as she's just a couple of feet away."

Suddenly, behind me, I heard a loud click and a whir. I leapt backward, bumping into the desk, bashing my hip bone. I yelped, then clapped a hand over my mouth. As I limped to the other side, the yellow pad caught my eye, and I smoothed the page. There were four names written on it, in all caps.

SIEFFERT.
MCADAM.
AMOS/BECK.

I looked back up at the monitors. The woman, Mrs. Sieffert, was alone now, her husband out of the frame. He must have gone to the bathroom. She had her head in her hands, and her shoulders were shaking. She was crying.

The apparatus behind me beeped again, one long, tinny whistle, and the monitors went black, dousing the room in darkness. I froze, my heart pattering. *Holy shit.* This room was a minefield of cables and metal corners. How was I going to get out of here without impaling myself? Arms extended, I picked my way out of the room, managing somehow not to trip or bang any more body parts. After gently pulling the door closed behind me, I hurried down the stairs. At Dr. Cerny's room, I paused for a quick beat, then continued down the stairs that I hoped would lead me to the kitchen.

I was right, thank God, finding myself in Baskens's thoroughly modern and spotlessly clean kitchen. Commercial appliances gleamed; above them, shelves stacked with pots and pans and every conceivable cooking implement. Just beyond the massive double refrigerator, I spotted a door and was immediately rewarded with a pleasurable little spike of dopamine.

Ah, yes. The pantry.

I opened the door. Inside, wooden shelves lined the wall, one stacked with cans of soup and pickles and sun-dried tomatoes, another with dry goods. The rest were bare. I looked around, not quite able to stop myself from counting as I took it all in. There was a hanging basket with a few potatoes, onions, and apples. A glass jar of candy bars. Two boxes of cereal. Not exactly the bounty I'd expected to see. But maybe the cook brought in fresh food every day.

I snagged a couple of packages of peanut-butter crackers, an apple, and a bag of M&M's, and, kicking the door shut behind me, carried my windfall back into the kitchen. As I did, one package of crackers slipped from my grasp and went spinning across the floor. I scuttled forward, anchoring everything with my chin, and reached for them, only to be met by the sight of a pair of expensive-looking black leather loafers.

I straightened, my face already hot.

The man, dressed in a dark sweater, tailored trousers, and the loafers, was in his late sixties. He had an impressive head of thick hair, mostly gray with streaks of honey, and a neatly trimmed beard. A smile played around his lips, deep dimples cleaving his cheeks, and I felt something twist hard and fast inside me, and the pain was so unexpected it took my breath away. He looked so familiar, like someone I'd known. Someone I'd loved . . .

It was Mr. Al, I realized. From Piney Woods.

He held out the package of crackers. "My apologies, I didn't realize you were awake."

I accepted them. "I'm sorry. Heath and I—we slept through dinner."

"No apologies necessary. I'm Matthew Cerny. It is my great pleasure to meet you."

"Daphne Amos."

We managed an awkward handshake. His grip was firm, warm.

"I was hoping you didn't stand me up because you were unhappy with something. Your accommodations, possibly. Something Dr. Teague said." He grinned again. And there was that twisting sensation once more, deep in my gut. I felt breathless.

"Daphne?"

"Excuse me. No, everything is lovely. We just . . . we were so tired from the trip."

"Feeling better now? More rested?"

"Yes. Thank you."

"Would you like your dinner?"

"Oh, this will be fine."

"Don't be silly," he said. "Sit." He gestured to a small table by the window. I sat and deposited my haul as he swung open the refrigerator and began pulling out an array of plastic containers. "We have a wonderful cook, Luca, but he goes home, back down to Dunfree, every night and doesn't return until morning. So I'm afraid you're left with me. No fear, however. I am well versed in the ways of the microwave." He spooned leftovers onto a plate.

"You really don't have to," I protested.

"No, please, allow me. It's a first, someone paying for one of my retreats but declining to meet with me. I have to admit, on one hand, it's been making me feel like the last one chosen for the kickball team."

I gulped.

"On the other . . ." He turned now and regarded me with a thoughtful expression. "It means we can be friends. I think I'll rather enjoy running into someone this week who isn't a client." He put the plate in the microwave and punched a few buttons. He drew two wineglasses hanging from a rack above the counter toward him. "How about something to drink? How about a red?"

"Water's fine," I said.

"Problems with alcohol?"

I hesitated. "No. I just don't want you to go to any trouble."

"It's no trouble. And I'd like a glass myself." He inspected a bottle on the counter. "They left us half." He filled both glasses, then held his aloft. "*I wish I were a girl again, half-savage and hardy, and free.* Do you know the quote?" He looked hopeful. And even more like Mr. Al than I'd thought at first. It was the cowlick, just above his left eye. On Mr. Al, it had been endearing—made him look like a wide-eyed boy. It lent a certain charm to the doctor as well.

"No, sorry," I said.

"It's from *Wuthering Heights*. A classic."

"It's a good one. Evocative." *If a little bizarre for a toast.* He clinked his glass on mine, and we drank the strong, mellow red. "When I looked at you, that's immediately what came to mind. Heathcliff's girl, making her way back to the old house, searching for her lost innocence. Her childhood love."

The microwave beeped, and he pulled out the steaming plate.

"It's just Heath, by the way. My fiancé's name. Not Heathcliff."

"Noted." He set the food in front of me, along with utensils and a cloth napkin, then settled in the other chair. "So, shall we discuss the elephant in this shadowy kitchen?"

I blushed.

"Your distaste of psychotherapy."

I concentrated on the scallops. "Trust me. You're not missing much by not meeting with me. I'm kind of boring."

"Oh, I doubt that." He poured more wine. "In particular, I'm interested in why you don't want to talk."

"Therapy's not my thing."

"Ah." He laced his fingers. "You've had a negative experience."

"Not necessarily. It's . . ." My eye fell on a toaster on the counter. The doctor and I looked like a Picasso painting on its gleaming surface.

And that was exactly what I wanted to say to the doctor. That the past was like the surface of a crazy mirror. When you spoke certain things aloud, when they left your mouth, they changed. The words became either oddly magnified—blown out of proportion—or squeezed down to nothing. Right could appear wrong, good could look like evil, depending on the spin. No one talked about their past without things getting distorted—and without consequences. There were always consequences.

"It's complicated," I finally said.

Cerny's lips curled. "Ah, complicated. That magical word that has the power to end a conversation."

"Sorry."

"No apology necessary. It's none of my business. But I couldn't help but notice the . . ." He nodded at the hair band around my wrist. I realized it must stand out, especially to someone in his field. A tip-off to who I was.

I cleared my throat. "I read about it somewhere, a few years ago. I use it to bring me back to reality when I get . . . off track." Maybe a smidge of self-revelation would satisfy his curiosity, prevent him from prodding any deeper. "I was a foster kid. Raised on a girls' ranch in south Georgia from age eleven to eighteen. Not a great place, but not as bad as it could've been. There was a man—one of the housefathers—that I was close to. Long story short, he was a good guy, but he ended up going to jail. Felony drug possession and child endangerment."

I felt short of breath, disoriented. Like some foreign entity had just taken over my body and unleashed a torrent of words in an unknown language.

"I'm so sorry to hear that," he said quietly. "It must've been very difficult for you."

"It was." I pushed the four scallops remaining on my plate into an orderly row. Counted them absently with the tines of my fork.

He leaned back. "Thank you for sharing with me, Daphne. I appreciate your trust and don't take it lightly. Go ahead, finish your dinner, and I'll let you get back to your room."

But I couldn't eat any more. Cerny refused to let me help with the dishes and, instead, escorted me up the rear stairs—his private stairs—past his room and the steps to the attic. We stopped at the far end of the hallway, where I could see the door to our room cracked open just the slightest bit.

"Goodnight, my circumspect friend." Cerny bowed slightly, his eyes twinkling in the dark.

"One thing," I said.

"Yes?"

"I wondered if I could get our keys. I left something in the car."

"I'm sorry. We collect and keep everyone's keys for the duration of the retreat. I hope you'll understand." Then he took my hand and turned it up, depositing the two packages of peanut-butter crackers, an apple, and the bag of M&M's. Four, just how I liked it. "Sleep well."

He left me there, standing alone in the dark hall, my hands cupped protectively around the snacks.

Friday, October 19
Evening

The open forest gives way to a tangled mass of branches that seems to exist solely to slow my progress. I do slow, then stop altogether. The woven tunnel is made of mountain laurels, their curvy, leggy jumble blocking my view. Layers of long dark-green leaves form an impenetrable canopy over my head.

I've been going in the right direction, I think. But now it's impossible to know for sure. The fretwork of boughs blocks my view of anything more than a few feet in front of me. The only thing I can see is bits of the darkening sky above.

I can feel myself dipping into panic, counting the number of leaves on a branch near me. Counting roots at my feet, then the metal eyes on my boots. My brain is bubbling with half-formed thoughts, ill-conceived solutions. The reality is, I may be more afraid of the panic than I am of the man. I can't lose control. He'll catch me if I do.

So I won't. It's just that simple. I'll claw through the branches, keep heading down, and hit a creek or a road, either of which I could follow to town.

I have to get to town.

Chapter Six

Monday, October 15
Four Days Before

Rain lashed at the windows, rattling the panes so hard I woke. I slung an arm around Heath's body, and he twisted around, sleepy-eyed and warm. He rolled on top of me, then lowered his lips to mine.

"Wait, what time is it?" I mumbled into his mouth.

"Do we care?" His lips traveled down to my shoulder.

I thought of the monitors in the cramped attic room. The yellow legal pad.

"Yes, we care. I don't remember. What did Reggie say? The cameras go off at five until . . ."

"Eight." He propped on his elbows, and looked at the clock on the mantel. "And it's five after eight. Dammit." He flopped off me. "I hate this place."

I smiled. "Ironic, since it was you who insisted we come here. But it's going to help us figure everything out, so buck up, soldier. Also"—I bit his earlobe and whispered—"if you meet me back here at one thirty, the cameras'll be off."

He rolled over and looked into my eyes. "I can't wait."

"Anticipation's half the fun."

"If you think that, I'm not doing it right."

I traced the line of his jaw. "Oh, trust me. You do it right."

He sat up with a groan. "You're killing me, woman."

I stroked his bare back. His skin goosepimpled under my fingertips. "Any nightmares?"

"Nope. Not a one."

I fluttered my fingers up his spine, smiling at how I raised a whole new crop of goose bumps with each move. I leaned close, my lips at his ear. "I found something interesting last night. In the attic. A room with a bunch of old-school surveillance equipment. I'm pretty sure it's where they watch us."

He whipped around to look at me. "You left the room last night?"

"Shh." I grinned. "I woke up and we'd missed dinner. I was starving."

"You shouldn't have gone snooping around," he whispered sternly.

"Why not?"

He turned back and made a little shrugging move so I'd keep on scratching. "It's just that we don't know the other people here. We don't know Dr. Teague or Dr. Cerny."

"Are you mad?"

"No. I just think you should be careful. And you heard the rules about places being off limits."

"I was careful. You know, Jerry McAdam has a cell phone."

He glanced around the room, like he was worried the camera could pick up on our body language. "You watched the other couples?"

"For just a minute or two, yeah."

"Daphne, Jesus," he said. "You're not supposed to be spying on people. They're here because they have problems, which makes them vulnerable. Besides that, maybe you're somehow compromising the doctor's methods." He turned away.

I sighed. "I know. Okay? I know that." I laid my head against his back. Let my hand travel around to his chest, then abdomen. "The door was open, and I was curious."

He made a reproving sound. "What if they stumbled upon that room and decided to watch us? Watch you?"

"You mean to tell me, if you saw an open door with a wall of surveillance monitors, you wouldn't feel the slightest bit intrigued? You're telling me you would walk on past without even a peek?"

"I wouldn't watch," he said, so fiercely I pressed my lips together.

I wasn't about to tell him about running into Dr. Cerny. I was pretty sure he wouldn't be thrilled about me sharing a bottle of wine with the guy he was about to spend a week of intensive therapy with. Anyway, I was tired of whispering. So there was another secret. I guessed I could add it to the one I was keeping about reaching out to his ex-girlfriend.

A sharp knock startled me. When I opened our door, there was no one there, just an intricately scrolled silver tray at my feet, laid with an elaborate collection of china, crystal, and silver. The sharp scent of coffee and fresh-baked *somethings* that rose from it made my mouth water. I must've just missed Luca, the phantom, non-English-speaking cook.

A note sat to one corner, heavy cream stationery. I popped on my glasses and read it aloud to Heath while he laid out the meal.

> *8 a.m. Breakfast (room)*
> *9 a.m.–9:50 a.m. Heath Beck session (sunroom)*
> *10 a.m.–10:50 a.m. Heath Beck reading assignment*
> *(Dr. Cerny In Session)*
> *11 a.m.–11:50 a.m. Heath Beck assessments*
> *(Dr. Cerny In Session)*
> *12:30 p.m. Lunch (room)*
> *1:30 p.m.–2:30 p.m. Free block (cameras off)*
> *3 p.m.–3:50 p.m. Heath Beck session with*
> *Dr. Cerny (sunroom)*

> *4 p.m.–4:50 p.m. Heath Beck writing assignment*
> *(Dr. Cerny In Session)*
> *5 p.m.–5:50 p.m. Heath Beck meditation*
> *(Dr. Cerny In Session)*
> *6 p.m.–7 p.m. Free block (cameras on)*
> *7 p.m. Dinner (room)*
> *8 p.m.–10 p.m. Free block (cameras on)*
> *10 p.m.–12 a.m. Free block (cameras off)*

I tossed the note on the bed. "According to this, you've essentially signed up for six hours of daily therapy."

"It's not all therapy." He tucked into the scrambled eggs. "There are personality tests. Reading and journaling. Meditating."

"Free blocks," I couldn't resist adding.

"Don't knock it till you try it," he said mildly, cutting a sausage in half.

"You've never meditated a second in your life."

"That you know of."

I sat opposite him and poured a cup of coffee. There was nothing to say in response to that. He was right. There were probably a thousand details I didn't know about him, a wealth of information that I had chosen to give up in exchange for peace of mind.

He put down his fork. "Come on, Daph, it's not like I'm looking forward to this. But I'm doing what I have to do to get my head straight. So we can have a normal life."

"We did have a normal life," I said.

We bought overpriced organic goat cheese and Jerusalem artichokes and weird-colored olives with the lofty intention of trying new recipes but let them all go bad in the fridge in favor of takeout pizza. We watched terrible movies on Sunday afternoons and actually enjoyed them. We made love almost every night.

We had a normal life—until you flipped out.

After we finished, he went into the bathroom. I followed him, leaned against the door frame while he turned on the shower and peeled off his underwear.

"I just wish we could've stayed home and taken care of this in Atlanta," I said.

"There's no one like Dr. Cerny in Atlanta. He's going to help me, Daph, I really have a feeling. He's going to help me figure out my past—and we're going to be better for it."

He turned to face the stream of water. Ran his fingers through his dark hair. He looked fantastic. Delicious. I wished we could skip the morning's schedule. No, I wished we could get in the Nissan and drive back down the mountain. Get a cabin of our own—one without big, dark, cobwebby furniture and velvet-fringed draperies. We could open a couple of bottles of wine and sit in a hot tub staring at the mountains and wearing each other out all week long.

Solve our problems the old-fashioned way. With sex.

Downstairs we met Dr. Cerny, who, in tweed pants and an expensive-looking black cashmere sweater, looked a little bit like an old duke hanging out at his genteel, slightly tattered countryside castle. When he entered the foyer at the same time we did, I couldn't help but wonder if there were also cameras that tracked our movement through the house. The sensation of being watched never seemed to leave me.

"Daphne Amos," I blurted, my hand shooting out at Dr. Cerny like an arrow. "Nice to meet you."

He clasped my hand, his eyebrows raised. "Nice to meet you too, Ms. Amos. Matthew Cerny."

His eyes twinkled, our secret obviously giving him some mischievous delight. I appreciated his playing along with my charade, but something about it unsettled me. Like the way he'd noticed the band on my wrist last night, picked up on my snack foraging. The odd toast that seemed directed at me.

That old saying ran through my head: *He's got your number.*

"Thank you for having us on such short notice," Heath said.

"I wholeheartedly approve of an emergency relationship intervention. Not to be glib about marriage, of course." Cerny smiled at me. "I'm impressed with people as young as you who take their transition to the institution with such sobriety." He turned to Heath. "Mr. Beck. A pleasure, at last."

"Likewise," Heath said in an even voice. He seemed tense—or coiled for attack, I couldn't tell which.

Cerny rubbed his hands together. "Business first. Dr. Teague has gone down to Dunfree. Family issues, nothing to worry about. So, unfortunately, there's no one who can show you around the property. Or pull up the correct papers for you to sign. Seems I'm helpless without my assistant."

"Well, it's not like we're going anywhere," I said. "And I can show myself around."

And find where Reggie Teague had stashed our car.

"Excellent," Cerny said. "Then Heath and I will have our first session. Meanwhile, I'd encourage you to find a spot outside where you can meditate or journal."

I saw one corner of Heath's mouth twitch.

"Will do," I said.

"Mr. Beck? Ready?" Dr. Cerny gestured toward the hall that led to his office, then looked back at me. "I believe the rain has stopped. You know, Daphne, you ought to go outside and visit the bird garden. Watching the birds, I find, is quite a peaceful pursuit. For most."

His dimples appeared, and I couldn't help it—I flashed to Mr. Al. Then I glanced at Heath, but he'd already turned toward the doctor's office, like he couldn't wait to get started.

Chapter Seven

It hadn't quit raining completely, but I wasn't about to stay inside jotting my thoughts in a journal or go swanning around some bird garden. I needed to get out of this house. Pull off the tentacles of claustrophobia that had started to curl around me and do something proactive.

For starters, I needed to track down a knife. That morning in the shower, I'd suddenly remembered Heath kept a spare set of keys under the car, secured with a zip tie. There was no way the flimsy cuticle scissors in my makeup bag were going to slice through the zip tie, but a kitchen knife should do the trick. Once I got the key, I'd be able to hide in the car and check the iPad to see if Annalise Beard had come up with any answers for me.

What I would do after that, I was less sure of.

Maybe I'd just lay it all out on the table. Tell Heath that he didn't need Dr. Cerny, because I knew what had really happened to him. Maybe it had been an abusive boyfriend of his mom's, some guy who had tormented him physically or, God forbid, sexually. Whatever it was, I'd reassure him that it didn't have to ruin his life, that we could handle anything together, privately, without interference from a therapist.

After we talked, after the truth was out, we'd get the hell off this mountain. Go home, back to the safety of our little house and our orderly lives. Back to the way things used to be.

In the kitchen I nicked a paring knife off the end of a magnetic rack, tucked it up the sleeve of my sweater, and headed back down the front hall to the porch. Outside, the air had taken on a noticeable chill, and everything shone, still slick with rain. The Baskens property was clotted with mountain laurels, oakleaf hydrangeas, and multiple varieties of pine, oak, and maple. The vegetation was thick and lush and heavy with droplets of water. I could hear the faint roar of the waterfall somewhere above me, but hidden from sight on this side of the house, it just sounded like a throaty rumble. I hugged my old, lumpy fisherman sweater around me and hoped the clean-washed air would blow away the thoughts squirreling around my mind.

Just beyond the house, I found where the cars were parked. There were five of them—an old silver Mercedes, a white minivan, a forest-green extended-cab Tacoma, Heath's blue Nissan, and an ancient brown Buick. And at the end of the row sat a John Deere Gator.

I scooched into the bushes and ducked under the front bumper of the Nissan, settling onto a bed of soggy leaves. I planted the knife in the dirt and ran my hands all under the greasy grille, but didn't find the key. I repeated the same thing under the rear of the car. No key there either. Dammit. Had Heath used the spare key recently and not mentioned it?

I palmed the knife and strolled away from the cars toward the backyard. A sad collection of damp chairs and tables was arranged around the mossy stone patio, including an old potting bench that was pushed up against the house. Behind the patio lay a grid of raised beds with the bedraggled remnants of a summer garden. Farther back, set against the line of trees, sat a small, unpainted outbuilding, its lopsided double doors chained closed. No bird garden that I could see.

I ambled to the structure, a barn from the looks of it. The trees ringed it, the tips of their overhanging branches, encased in dense caterpillar webs, reaching like a parent's protective arms. The double doors were fastened with a large, rusty padlock. I fiddled with it a minute, then let it drop with a clank against the door, pressing one eye against the crack and waiting for my vision to adjust to the darkness. The only thing I could see was what looked like a bunch of old furniture draped with dingy sheets. A trio of white moths fluttered in the gloom.

Up at the house a door slammed, and instinctively, I flattened myself against the side of the barn. A woman, maybe in her sixties, stood on the back patio, dressed in hiking clothes—cargo pants and a thermal top and a bandana holding back her hair. Mrs. Sieffert. The woman who'd been watching us as Reggie Teague showed us to our rooms. The woman I'd seen fighting with her husband last night.

I held my breath, watching her. She tucked a water bottle into a small backpack, then slung it over her shoulders and took off at a brisk clip, crossing the yard and then the drive, moving in the direction of the mountain.

After a second or two, I pushed the knife between the cracked barn doors, hoping no one would venture in and find it on the floor. Then I followed her.

The trail was astonishingly steep. A twisted path—merely a rut in a few places—that seemed to climb forever. I stayed far enough back that Mrs. Sieffert wouldn't hear me, which was easy enough to do, because apparently she was in excellent shape and covered an impressive amount of ground with a practiced stride. As for me, after three days of no running, I felt like my lungs had atrophied.

Trees crowded the path, blocking the sky and turning the light around me gray. The leaves were close to peak color—oaks and maples and dogwoods in blazing yellows and reds—with hemlocks and ferns and moss on the fallen trees providing the evergreen accents. The woods smelled faintly of smoke, from campers, most likely. The musty scent made me queasy.

I never could quite believe that people did that voluntarily—drove to the middle of nowhere, pitched a tent, and sat around a fire all night. The people who ran the girls' ranch took the girls up to Amicalola Falls once a year for a while. I hadn't gone, my first year there, and then after that they'd cancelled the trip indefinitely. I hadn't felt like I was missing anything. Even now that I was an adult, the mountains spooked me, with their overhangs and gaps and twisting paths. You never knew what was just around the next corner.

After what seemed like forever, the land leveled out, and I stepped out onto a wide rock ledge. It, in turn, opened onto a stunning vista. The spreading ranges of southern Appalachia. A sea of mountains at my feet. The wind was fierce up top—it whipped my hair into my mouth and stung my eyes—but the sun was strong too, beaming some of that late Georgia heat, now unimpeded by the canopy of trees. I squinted one eye in the light. The woman was standing on the far side of the ledge, hands on her hips, gazing out over the view. She seemed perilously close to the edge.

Alarm filled me, and I had a nearly irresistible urge to run up and grab her by the arm.

I blew out my breath and forced myself to look away from her, out over the scene.

There was no single range that I could identify, no straight line of mountains like on a map. These mountains were different. They moved like ocean waves. An endless undulation of green and gray spreading out in every direction, hiding towns and houses and farms, rivers and creeks and waterfalls, between their slopes.

I turned from the view just as Mrs. Sieffert tipped up her water bottle and caught sight of me. Self-conscious, I raised my hand in greeting.

She lowered the bottle and stared at me. I waited, snapping the band on my wrist nervously. She wasn't exactly waving me over, but didn't look annoyed either. Then, just as I'd made up my mind that I should head back down the mountain, she started toward me. I straightened, tucked my tangled hair behind my ears, but she stopped several yards away and shaded her eyes with one hand.

"I didn't mean to disturb you," I called out. "You seemed like you knew where you were going, so I followed. But I'll go, if you'd like to be alone. I know Dr. Cerny—"

"It doesn't matter what he says," she broke in. "We can do what we want." Then she grinned—a bright flash of white teeth that made her look at least twenty years younger. And she was beautiful. Definitely in her midsixties, with barely lined skin and light, arresting eyes. I wondered, suddenly, what her husband could've done to make her so sad.

"You thirsty?" She held up her bottle. "Take it. I have another."

I approached her, accepted the bottle, and gulped down half of it in one swig. "Thank you. That's one hell of a hike."

"You're not a hiker?"

"No. I'm a runner, actually. I mean, I run around a track for exercise. But I mostly sprint. So that"—I jutted my chin in the direction of the trail—"nearly killed me."

"Yes, up here you find the mountain challenges you in ways you'd never expect. Anyway, you can't set out with no provisions, not under any circumstances. It may not be the Rockies, but things can still go wrong really quickly up here."

I averted my eyes from her penetrating gaze. Things going wrong on mountains wasn't something I liked to think about.

"So you don't think we'll get in trouble for talking?" I asked.

"Not if we don't tell." She smiled again. "Your husband's in his first session?"

"Fiancé. And yes, he is."

"I'm Glenys, by the way," she said.

"Daphne."

"Nice to meet you, Daphne."

I studied her, trying not to think about how I'd spied on her and her husband. How I'd watched them fight and her cry and how I'd defended my eavesdropping to Heath.

"It's Sieffert, right?" I said to shut up my mind.

"Yes."

She looked out over the panorama. "My husband's doing his required reading. So I thought I would come up here. Collect my thoughts. It's very peaceful up here. Wild, but peaceful."

She pulled off her bandana and ran her fingers through her hair, and I sent her a sidelong glance. The woman seemed so calm, so together, like she had a handle on this place. I wondered if her marriage had been a rocky one for years or if she and her husband had just recently encountered a new, insurmountable problem that could only be solved with the help of therapy. Was it an affair? Some knotty financial issue? She looked so placid now, it was hard to believe I'd seen her sobbing last night. Maybe she had that much confidence in Cerny's ability to fix her marriage.

"I hear you're not meeting with him," she said.

I cocked my head. "You heard that?"

"Maybe I shouldn't have mentioned it, but you're a bit of a celebrity, coming up here with your fiancé but refusing the therapy. Very rock-star of you."

"Oh, well. Truthfully, I'm not a big believer in that kind of thing. I mean, not to say I haven't read my share of ridiculous self-help books. You know, *Chicken Soup for the Perpetually Panicked*. But no, I guess I prefer a quick sprint around a track to talking about . . . all that."

Her eyes sparked. "Interesting. So you've never had therapy?"

There was a lump in my throat suddenly, and it was difficult to talk around it. I coughed.

"I actually did meet with someone once, after an incident at the place where I lived." The lump in my throat felt like a boulder now. "Anyway, I think I was supposed to see her, the doctor, I mean, a few more times after that, but for some reason it never happened. The system was overloaded, and things like that seemed to fall between the cracks a lot."

A vague, non-answery answer, if there ever was one. But if Glenys had questions about what the hell I was talking about, she didn't show it. She just nodded like it all made absolute sense to her.

"Have you?" I asked. "Had therapy, I mean? If you don't mind me asking."

She waved a hand dismissively. "Oh yes, I've seen therapists before. And you're smart to be skeptical. A lot of them have no idea what they're doing. Others go beyond incompetence and are actually destructive. It's almost as if they became doctors in order to mess with people's heads." She ruffled her hair again. "The good ones, though"—she sighed— "the good ones are magic. It's like, when you finally let go, release your problems to them, they take some of the pain away, and suddenly you're lighter. Unencumbered and free to live your life."

I considered this.

"Am I convincing you?" She laughed. I laughed too, then our eyes met.

"Is that what you're trying to do, convince me?"

She waved her hand. "Goodness, no. You seem like a smart woman. Like someone who can certainly figure out what's best for herself."

Silence settled between us. Overhead, some kind of bird cried. Little did this woman, Glenys, know how far off the mark she was about me. I was not a smart woman. I was scared, floundering, terrified over the thought of losing Heath. But I liked that she said it, anyway. It reminded me of the way Barbara Silver used to talk to Lenny. That motherly tone—all at once protective and confident in her daughter's infinite capabilities of resourcefulness. I liked the way it felt when it was directed at me.

"So you think Dr. Cerny is one of the good ones?" I said.

"I do. I saw him for the first time years ago. And I've never found anyone to be quite as perceptive as he is."

I absorbed this.

"I lost my son," she went on. "It was a long time ago, but it happened very suddenly. One day he was with me, and the next . . ." Her fingers pressed against her chest. "It was terribly difficult. It still is, if I'm being honest. Which it seems I am." She smiled sadly at me.

I spoke before I had time to think. "I don't mind. I'm glad you are."

She nodded. "No one tells you that you never get over losing someone you love, do they?"

"No," I said.

No, they didn't.

She sobered. "So. I came here to release some of the pain. To see if there was a way forward for me."

"And your husband."

"Yes. That's right." She regarded me. "I'm sure your issues are different. But you must want the same thing for you and your fiancé."

"I do, but it sounds like a fairy tale. Like something that can't even be real." I glanced away, feeling tears press against my eyes.

"It's real." She said the next thing in such a matter-of-fact tone that it didn't even surprise me. "Why are you here, Daphne? It's not just for your fiancé, is it?"

I shook my head. The tears had sprung up, in spite of my best efforts.

"I'm sorry. I didn't mean to make you cry."

I sniffled and dabbed at my eyes. "Ah, well. I'm probably due."

She seemed to want to say something else but, in the end, turned back to the overlook. Grateful to escape her scrutiny, I sniffed mightily and wiped my running nose on my sleeve.

"Hey," she suddenly said. "A hawk." She pointed, and I looked but didn't see anything. "He just dove into the trees. He must've seen something tasty down there."

We stared at the empty sky for what seemed like a very long time. I wanted to speak, to say something to break the silence, but I was afraid of what would come out of my mouth. It had become a physical sensation now, a painful cramping all the way down in the lowest part of my stomach, the way the memories pressed against my insides. I realized my hand had moved up to my neck. That I was digging my nails into it.

After a while, Glenys turned to me. "I understand why you might not want to talk to a doctor," she said quietly. "Especially one like Cerny. But—would you consider talking to someone else?"

I stared at her, not understanding.

"What I mean is, you could talk to me. I'm not a professional, I know, but maybe that would be easier for you. To talk to a regular person first, before you go all the way with a doctor." She smiled. "That came out wrong."

I smiled back.

"I'm a pretty decent listener. You could consider it a practice run."

I shook my head and thought of Heath. "I appreciate the offer. I really do. But it would be breaking the rules."

"Technically, yes, but we already seem to be doing that."

"I don't know."

She smiled. "Oh well. Just a thought."

She moved to the edge of the cliff, then beckoned me over. "Look. He's back." She pointed at the hawk, wings spread, lazily looping above us.

"Oh my God. He's gorgeous."

"See how he's not flapping his wings? He's soaring. Using air currents to hold him up. He can stay up there for hours, wheeling and watching for prey, without even trying."

I closed my eyes, feeling the sun and the dizzying height and the wind on my face. Picturing the wheeling hawk. I yearned to be like that, weightless and free, circling above the earth. Above my problems and my fear. And somehow this woman, this absolute stranger, seemed to understand that. I wasn't fooling her. So what was I fighting against?

I snapped open my eyes. Filled my lungs with the brisk mountain air.

"My mom was a prostitute," I said quickly, before I could change my mind. "When I was eleven, the state of Georgia transferred custody of me to a girls' ranch."

Chapter Eight

Aside from Chantal, no one took much notice when I arrived at the brown brick house that sat at the edge of the property known as Piney Woods Girls' Ranch. Of course, later on I figured out why Chantal was so interested in me—finally something lower than her on the food chain had shown up on the scene.

I was a chubby eleven-year-old—legs bloodied from mosquito bites, bleary from bad sleep, nerves strung tight, nails bitten raw. It was an early September evening, and for the past week, I'd known something bad was on the verge of happening. My mother had been gone seventeen days this go-round, the longest stretch yet, and I'd finally been turned in to DFCS by Mrs. Tully because, she said, her husband was tired of having me around. She told the caseworker that, by God, she'd done her damnedest, but she couldn't find one single relative to take me in.

Mrs. Tully had sent me into her shower, but my knees and elbows were still caked with grime. My long dishwater-blonde hair desperately needed a trim, and the few clothes I'd brought were stained and ragged. Nevertheless, I was there at the brown brick house and, on the whole, glad of it. I was scared but also relieved that I wouldn't have to wait for my mother anymore. I was also more than a little excited about a warm bed, a meal, and maybe a bathtub with bubbles. It did occur to me—in a vague way—that I might have landed myself someplace far worse than my lonely apartment, but nothing in the house seemed amiss, so I tried to ignore the way my stomach constantly went from fluttering to tight.

There were three tormenters in the brown brick house—the Super Tramps, they called themselves, and whenever Mrs. Bobbie scolded them for it (their nickname, not the tormenting, which she seemed oblivious to), they screeched in outrage: "It's just after the rock band! Mr. Al's favorite group!" They weren't wrong about Mr. Al loving Supertramp. He played that album all the time on the huge stereo system he had set up in the living-room built-ins, so much that "The Logical Song" ran maddeningly on a loop through my head anytime things got a little quiet.

Mrs. Bobbie hated that the girls called themselves after the band. I also think she hated that her husband liked that music so much too. She was just that kind of woman. She didn't appreciate anyone enjoying themselves too much outside of church and school. Which was probably why she was forced to either ignore Mr. Al or be constantly, supremely annoyed with him.

He was a shambling man with a mane of shaggy blond hair and friendly, sleepy eyes. A stoner, even though I didn't recognize it at the time. A man who did happen to enjoy himself on a daily basis and without one ounce of guilt, earning himself Mrs. Bobbie's displeasure, fair and square. I didn't pick up on any of those details at the time. I just knew I liked and trusted the man. He was master of the awkward side-hug, gentle ruffler of hair, bringer of fun. The father we all quietly—unwittingly—yearned for.

Even though the Super Tramps were technically right about the origins of their nickname, Mrs. Bobbie knew they were full of shit and just trying to get her goat, so she usually banished them upstairs. It wasn't much of a punishment. They'd sashay up to the room they shared, slam the door, and giggle themselves limp on the three twin beds that they'd arranged in the center of the room. I heard everything through the walls, and every bit of it drew me in. I especially liked the sound of that laughter. It was throaty and nasty and knowing. I got the feeling these girls always somehow had the last say with Mrs. Bobbie.

The Super Tramps had been living in the two-story brown brick house at the end of the dirt road along with Chantal, who was fourteen, for a number of years before I got there. I didn't know exactly how many. I wasn't allowed that level of security clearance. To me, my new roommates imparted other, more pertinent, information, like:

You have boogers in your eyes, and you smell like an asshole.

You better never, ever fucking look at me. You got that?

The Pinkeys are coming—tomorrow, probably—to adopt you.

The Pinkeys, I learned, were a family of hillbilly cannibals with bear traps for teeth who lived in the national forest behind the ranch. I was told they came around every couple of years to select a young girl to take home with them for housekeeping duties and, if things didn't pan out, possible ritual child sacrifice.

While Mrs. Bobbie kept the daily routine of the brown brick house humming—meals served at six a.m. and p.m. on the dot, a rotation of chores for us girls when we got home from school, and mandatory family Bible study each night before bed—the Super Tramps actually ran the place. Omega, the leader, was seventeen—fiercely beautiful, with a Cleopatra haircut and pillowy woman-lips that, when coated with cheap drugstore lipstick in fuchsia, made her look like she'd just blown out of a photo shoot for one of the copies of *Glamour* Mrs. Bobbie hid in her bathroom cabinet. You wouldn't want to be assigned kitchen cleanup with her, though. She talked to the knives while she washed them, like they were actual people.

"You ever stabbed someone?" she would croon to a blade, then cut her eyes at me.

Tré and Shellie were sixteen, juniors at Mount Olive Christian Academy, where the ranch girls were given scholarships to attend. Shellie was pretty but pale, with a headful of peroxided straw and a perpetual spray of acne across her jaw. Tré was a freckled wraith who wore a pair of men's Carhartt coveralls that Mr. Al had handed down to her; muddy, oxblood-red Doc Martens (that I never figured out how she obtained); and a stack of rainbow-colored hair bands as bracelets. She told everyone she was a Wiccan high priestess, except Mrs. Bobbie and Mr. Al, who were Baptists and wouldn't have appreciated it. I was eleven and had no idea what Wiccan was, but I was duly terrified by my new sisters.

Which was what Mrs. Bobbie said they were. Along with Chantal, they were my new big sisters.

That first night at the ranch, the hot night in September that the social worker dropped me at the brown brick house, I was overwhelmed, although at the time I couldn't have said why. Part of it was that I was used to a small apartment, with a tiny cramped living room and bedrooms the size of closets. This house had walls, but to me, it felt boundaryless. It was the biggest house I'd ever been in, and I had the sensation of standing on an open field, unprotected, my flanks exposed to an unseen, lurking enemy.

Where did everyone belong?

As I stood in the tidy, Lemon Pledge–scented living room, my secondhand backpack of meager belongings hanging off my rounded shoulders, I pictured the pantry—its dimensions and how much food must be kept there and what kind. It was weighing on me, making me feel nervous, the thought that there might not be enough food for me to eat in the morning. Had they known I was coming? Where would I find breakfast way out here in the country? Hunger gnawed at my stomach. In the rush to get me to the ranch, the social worker had forgotten I hadn't had supper.

I trembled in the center of the vast unknown as it expanded around me, and my stomach growled. After Mrs. Bobbie told me there were three older girls upstairs (*sisters*, she called them), she introduced Chantal, who was standing by the plaid sofa, digging her finger in a hole in the fabric. Mrs. Bobbie said Chantal was fourteen, even though she was not much bigger than me. She had long, frizzy hair, blonde with a sickly green tint to it, and when Mrs. Bobbie dragged her closer, I saw that she had different-colored eyes—one green and one blue—that reminded me of a dog that used to wander around our apartment. It was a mean, spindly mutt, and I always tried to feed it scraps when it would let me get close enough.

"Chantal," Mrs. Bobbie said. "Daphne's come to stay with us because her mother's not feeling well."

It was true, to a point. On a regular basis, my mother—jonesing for whatever it was that made her feel better—would disappear for days from our apartment complex, leaving me to fend for myself. This had been going on since I was five or six, and the neighbors had always been kind. Every time I knocked on their doors, they let me in. I didn't blame Mr. Tully. After a while, you were bound to get tired of a hungry, smelly kid eating all your cereal and chips and using up your toilet paper.

Chantal seemed inordinately interested in me, watching me with her strange eyes.

"Hi," she said. Her voice was deep and raspy. It made her sound worldly, older than her years.

"Hi," I replied.

"Why do you squint your eyes like that?" she asked, which I thought was a strange thing for her to notice, considering she had the freakiest-looking eyes I'd ever seen on a person.

"Maybe Daphne needs glasses, Chantal," Mrs. Bobbie said in a singsong voice like I was a kindergarten baby. "Your mama ever take you to an eye doctor, Daphne?"

I shook my head no. Just then, a hulking man in an embroidered button-up shirt passed by the room. He stopped, lifted a hand, and beamed at me.

"Greetings, princess." Two dimples slashed his pudgy, whiskery cheeks. I smiled back. I couldn't help it.

"Mr. Al, come say hey to Daphne," Mrs. Bobbie said.

The man bounded up to me and shook my hand with one of those long complicated secret handshakes. I tried to keep up. "Daphne-Doodle-Do, how do you do?"

"Fine." I giggled softly.

"How old are you?" he asked.

"Eleven."

"Well, I'm thirty-two, so I guess I got you beat." He winked at me.

"Bedtime," Mrs. Bobbie announced, before Mr. Al could say anything more.

I was to share a room with Chantal, down the hall from the Super Tramps. It was a tiny room with a bunk bed and one dresser. Chantal told me I got the top drawers and the top bunk. I used the bathroom, changed into a ratty, pilled-up Strawberry Shortcake nightgown that Mrs. Bobbie had given me, and climbed the ladder. I hung my backpack over one of the posts, then felt a jolt underneath me.

I peeked down. Chantal was lying on her back, mermaid hair fanned out on her pillow, her hands folded over her chest, her feet jammed against the bottom of my bunk. She grinned up at me, and I could tell her front tooth was chipped.

"Earthquake," she said.

I hadn't meant to tell Glenys so much. In fact, when I was finished, my stomach was in knots. Storyteller's remorse.

I looked down—over the sheer cliff that dropped out from under my feet—and backed a couple of steps away. It seemed I couldn't stand that close to the edge without being bombarded by images of a small body tumbling over the cliff.

I forced my eyes down to my watch. "Oh, wow. Lunch in half an hour. I'm sorry, talking your ear off like that."

"Nonsense." Glenys folded her arms and lifted her face to the breeze. "I enjoyed it." She cracked one eye. "Did you find it really horrible to tell me those things?"

I laughed. "A little, I guess."

"Feel any lighter?"

"I do." In fact, I was feeling kind of buzzed now, high from the atmosphere of secrecy and the thin mountain air.

"Would you like to walk back down?" I asked. "We can split up halfway, so nobody knows we were fraternizing."

She smiled. "I think I'll stay a little longer, if you don't mind. I'd like to spend a little more time alone."

"Of course."

"I'm so glad to have met you, Daphne," she said.

I smiled. "Me too."

"And I'm always happy to listen, if you find the need to talk."

I didn't reply, but I had the feeling that didn't bother her. She was a strange woman —who didn't seem to mind stretches of silence or expect to be told anything but the unvarnished truth. I allowed myself a brief moment to consider what it would be like to tell her everything. To open the door I'd shut all those years ago and let the rest of the story pour out at last. I felt a stab of something in my throat and realized it was a sob. I backed a few steps farther away and started back down the path.

I wondered if she watched me go. If she noticed I was dashing tears off my face with the sleeve of my sweater as I clomped over the rocks and roots. I hoped not. I'd cried more in the past hour than in the past ten years, but I'd be damned if I let anyone see it.

My face was red and raw by the time I returned to our deserted room. I guzzled a bottle of water from the minifridge in the corner, then I twisted up my hair and splashed my face with cold water. At twelve thirty, I heard a sharp knock and opened the door to find Heath holding our elegantly appointed lunch tray, complete with a bud vase containing a single branch of red maple leaves.

"Oh, wow." I grinned. "The waitstaff is really hot around here."

I set our table near the fireplace. There was a tiny white worm crawling on the pale underside of one of the maple leaves. I eased it onto the edge of my spoon and gingerly dropped it in the crackling fire. I watched it writhe, then sizzle, and I turned away, feeling sick. Heath sat across from me, unfolded his napkin, and started in on the meat-and-black-bean stew. He looked utterly normal—so normal, it was hard to believe he'd just been in a session with the doctor.

"How'd it go?" I asked lightly.

"It was revelatory."

"Yeah?"

"Oh yes. I'm absolutely insane. One hundred percent. There's no saving me." My jaw unhinged and he broke into a grin. "Daphne, take a breath already. We just talked. It was no big deal."

I jabbed my fork into the concoction of rice and beans and tender pork. Lifted it to my mouth and told myself to chew. It was only day one—Heath wouldn't have made any major progress with Dr. Cerny. There was still time to learn something from Heath's ex-girlfriend, Annalise. Maybe not enough to wrap up every last thing with a bow and convince Heath we should go home, but maybe a start.

"You okay?" he asked.

"Mm-hm."

"You seem . . ." He studied me. "Nervous."

"Really?" I shoveled a forkful. "I feel fine. It's probably the house. I'm just not comfortable here yet. And I'm not comfortable with all this free time."

"I'm guessing you didn't go journal in the bird garden." He snorted.

"I hiked to the top of the mountain."

He put down his fork. "You did?"

I nodded.

"How was it?"

"Nice. Beautiful, actually."

"And better than spying on our neighbors."

I laughed, and we ate the rest of our lunch in silence, then Heath washed up and brushed his lips against my temple. "Gotta go."

"But you already had your session," I said. "It's our free block. Remember, the free block you were so excited about?"

"Oh, God. Yes. I'm sorry. I've got to fill out some paperwork. Personality assessments. Aptitude and diagnostic tests and stuff like that. And the releases—I'll pick yours up too, while I'm at it. You going to be okay up here by yourself?"

"Sure. Of course. I may head down to the library. Find a book to read."

He caught my fingers. "Thank you. For doing this. I know what you're sacrificing."

I squeezed his hand. "Well. I'd rather be here for you than assembling shared workspace pods. That much I can promise you."

He grinned. "That's not really much of a compliment."

"Always us." I kissed him.

After he left, I slipped on my shoes and headed downstairs. I circumnavigated the foyer, listening for anyone, opening cabinets and pulling out the drawers of every big sideboard. No one happened along, and the furniture yielded nothing—not a set of keys, not even the smallest scrap of paper. There were no keys in the library either. Reggie must've stashed them in a more secure place: the doctor's sunroom office or maybe even up in his suite. I'd have to wait for a more expedient time to find out, when his office was empty. For now I'd have to find something else to occupy my mind.

I drifted to the carved bookcase. Most of the dust-coated books looked like they hadn't been read in ages. Which stood to reason. I was probably the only person who came to Baskens who actually had time to read. I perused the shelf. All the oldies but goodies. Dickens, Shakespeare, Hawthorne. Every last one of the Brontë sisters' titles: *Jane Eyre, Shirley, Villette, The Professor, Agnes Grey, The Tenant of Wildfell Hall,* and *Wuthering Heights.*

I thought back to Cerny's strange toast last night in the kitchen: *I wish I were a girl again, half-savage and hardy, and free.*

I took *Wuthering Heights* to the sofa and flipped the pages, the story coming back to me in bits and pieces. Mr. Earnshaw, appearing back at his home, Wuthering Heights, presents a surprise to his children, Catherine and Hindley. Heathcliff, a dark-skinned, dark-eyed Gypsy child who speaks gibberish. The interloper immediately sparks in Hindley an intense jealousy, as Hindley is a bully, racist, and overall dickbag. Catherine, on the other hand, is instantly smitten and sticks to Heathcliff like an imprinted duckling.

I read for a while, then let the book drop to the floor and stretched out on the sofa, my legs and lower back aching from the hike. I knew how the story ended, how Heathcliff and Catherine devoted their lives to loving, then destroying, each other. Emily Brontë may have been melodramatic, but she'd hit on something real. It was true—similar souls sought each other out. Damaged gravitated to damaged, the same way Heath and I had recognized ourselves in each other, then locked into our unshakable orbit. It was too bad the story ended so tragically. Too bad Heathcliff and Cathy couldn't have just admitted that they belonged together.

Because surely they did belong together.

Sleep stole over me quickly. I woke sometime later, and the book was gone, returned to the Brontë section of the shelves. Whoever had done that had also left a bottle of water and a plate of small coconut-dusted cookies on a nearby table. I swung my feet down and chugged the water. In a daze, I headed for the front stairs. My legs felt like tree trunks, my head three sizes too big. Even after the nap, I still felt wrung out. Maybe it was the hike—or the fact that I'd told Glenys about the ranch. I checked the clock on the mantel in the front hall. Five after three. *Great.* In our room, the camera would be up and running again.

I climbed the stairs, thinking about Catherine's and Heathcliff's lovely doomed lives. About how good it had felt to tell Glenys about the Super Tramps and Chantal and Mr. Al while standing at the precipice of a mountain. Maybe there was a pattern to it all. Maybe the universe had brought me here because it knew what I needed—to be hardy and free, to finally let go of my burden and soar.

Friday, October 19
Evening

I'm standing in the middle of the road before it occurs to me that I've finally made it out of the woods. The sun is obscured by clouds, but I can feel the knife edge of twilight in the air. I know I still have a long way to go before I get to town.

There are no sounds—no car engines in the distance, no crunch of feet through the leaves. But it feels like there's a hurricane whipping up in my head, so it's possible I'm not hearing so well. I'm also panting like someone who's never done a jumping jack. I failed to factor in the concentration it requires not to trip on a path studded with boulders and roots and hidden holes.

Part of me knows it's not the exertion that's getting to me, it's the fear. Which is ironic. All those times I was charging around the track like a lunatic, I never considered the way fear could fill a person, weigh them down. I never knew fear had actual mass.

Suddenly I realize why the silence is bothering me so much. I thought the police were coming. I've been expecting them the whole time, but there are no sounds of cars or sirens. The police aren't coming. They never were.

I take a minute to get my bearings—make sure I'm headed down, not sideways across the mountain or, God forbid, back up. I adjust the iPad in the back of my jeans and set off at a trot down the gravel road.

I'll find the police myself.

Chapter Nine

Tuesday, October 16
Three Days Before

I decided all that stuff about the universe knowing what I needed was bullshit. The universe could go suck an egg; what I really needed was some Internet and a Domino's pizza.

And an email from Annalise Beard telling me what she knew, if anything, about Heath's past.

Not that it was going to be easy to hear, whatever it was she might have to say, but it was for the best. Getting Heath away from this weirdo doctor, this creepy mountain and ancient house, was in Heath's best interest as well as mine. What I was doing was for us.

But it was Tuesday already. Three days since I'd gotten the Instagram message from her. And I was losing faith that I was going to be able to get into the car to retrieve the iPad. And if I did get to it, there was still the possibility that Annalise knew nothing. So what would I do then?

My brain raced. Like me, Heath was a loner. Not extremely so, just a little on the introverted side, and mostly focused on getting his career off the ground. He had friends, just not many older ones from his years at University of Georgia. That guy at Divine, the one in the bad suit, was one, but they hadn't been roommates. I'd only met a roommate once—Evan Something-or-Other. Graham? Gilbert? If Annalise was a dead end, maybe I could track him down on Facebook or Instagram. Ask him if Heath had ever talked in his sleep.

I paced the length of the room. Baskens was getting to me, fraying my nerves and making me jumpy. When I first arrived, I was so run down from the nightmares, part of me had hoped Baskens would be the break I needed. But I didn't know how to amble and piddle and lounge like a delicate Victorian lady. My body was used to the exhilarating busyness of dealing with clients, the daily analgesic of sprinting around a track until the copper taste filled my mouth and every bone in my body ached. The relentless quiet of this place was driving me insane.

I needed to find our car keys before I ended up strangling somebody.

After breakfast, I followed Heath down the stairs, then down the hallway that led to the kitchen. I heard the doctor usher him into his office and close the French doors behind them. I waited a few seconds, then, backtracking, inched closer to the glass doors to see if I could get a better view.

All that was visible was the anteroom of the office—a small, unfurnished nook that blocked any view of the doctor's office beyond it. On the wall adjacent to the door, a row of metal hooks held multiple sets of keys, including the Nissan's, which I recognized from the red-and-black Georgia Bulldogs fob. I pushed at the door, and it creaked open a couple of inches.

"How are you feeling this morning?" I heard Dr. Cerny say from the other side of the wall.

"Better," Heath answered. "It's not like I hadn't anticipated the—"

His voice dipped in volume, and I couldn't hear the rest of what he said. But it didn't matter. I was here for the keys, not to eavesdrop on my fiancé's therapy. I slipped through the open door and crept toward the hooks.

"Do you think having her here was really a good idea?" I heard the doctor say.

I froze. Who was he talking about? Me?

"It's so funny to me"—Heath again—"the assumptions you people make, you doctors, that you know what's best for the rest of us. You leave . . ." His voice lowered.

My God, he sounded so brusque. It seemed a little premature to have already developed such a combative relationship with the doctor. But maybe that's how Cerny operated—maybe he encouraged bluntness in his patients. I lifted the keys gently, easily, off the hook and slid them into my pocket, then backed toward the door, tugging my sweater down to hide the bulge.

I slipped out the front door and headed around the side of the house. At the row of cars, I stopped beside the Nissan and unlocked the passenger's-side door. Ducking in and shutting the door behind me, I reached under the floor mat. The iPad powered to life, and as the bars filled in, a thrill ran through me.

"Hi, you," I crooned.

Thanks to the gods of 4G, little red dots sprang out on my apps like a rash of measles. Twenty-one new emails, a handful of texts pushed from my iPhone, and a smattering of notifications on my social-media apps. I opened the texts from Lenny first.

This seems really last minute, D. Not to be an asshole, but we've got a lot going on this week. Could H not have given a couple weeks' notice?

Then:

I'm all for counseling, but H knows how headshrinkers make you feel. He should respect that.

Followed by:

I don't get why you're so willing to drop everything for him like this. And, okay, maybe my feelings are just hurt because you never open up to me. Well, fuck it. I am being an asshole, after all. Look, I know it's not about me. I love you, D. I'm here for you. Can you just check in when you get a chance? Let me know you're okay? This is really nerve racking, not being able to talk to you. And just FYI, my mom is worried, so she's calling me nonstop.

And finally:

Okay, ignore all previous texts. I'm a jealous diva. I love you. We'll talk when you come home. BTW, did you hear? They've shut down Divine's. xx L

I smiled, in spite of my nerves. That was my Lenny, running the entire gamut of emotions in a handful of texts. I felt bad, worrying her, worrying Barbara, but I really didn't know what else I could've done. I'd had no other choice but to come with Heath. I would text her back later, and when I got home, I'd take Barbara out to lunch.

Right now, though, I had other things to do. I needed to see what Annalise Beard had for me. Fingers shaking, I opened her email.

Daphne,

A part of me is relieved you got in touch with me. Not that I'm happy Heath is suffering, I'm just glad someone cares enough about him to make sure he gets help. Heath Beck is a troubled person, Daphne, but you know this or you wouldn't have written me. And maybe I should've reached out to you a long time ago. I'm sorry if I did the wrong thing.

Heath and I were dating when you guys met, but I think you must be aware of that by now. Things weren't going well with us. He'd been having nightmares. They were sporadic at first, but became more constant toward the end. He sleepwalked, tore all the blinds off my bedroom windows. Once he even smashed an antique mirror that I'd inherited from my great-grandmother. I don't know what

89

the dreams were about—he would never say—but after a while I didn't care. I just felt afraid, and not only for my furniture.

As far as his past, Heath told me his parents were strange people who lived this alternative, off the grid, hippie lifestyle somewhere in east Georgia. He said they were physically abusive to him, isolated him from the outside world, and he hadn't seen them since he ran away at sixteen.

He refused to see a doctor, although once he did float the idea of us attending a couples' retreat he'd heard about. By then, though, he'd started not coming home, sometimes for days. And then one of my friends said they saw him out with another woman. You, as it turned out. It was just as well. I was done with him, ready to forget the things that had happened between us. And maybe I was wrong—or just not patient enough—but I didn't really feel like our problems were a relationship issue. I believed something was wrong—is wrong—with him.

I hope you can help him work things out, but I don't know. He's a locked door, Daphne. And he doesn't like it if you knock too hard. Maybe he's found someone more understanding in you. Anyway, if you don't mind, I'd rather you didn't bring up my name to him. I'd rather just forget I ever knew him.

Annalise

I stared down at the email, letting her words sink in. That wasn't quite the story Heath had presented. He'd told me he and Annalise had drifted apart and basically ended things before we met. He'd said they simply hadn't been a match, and I'd accepted the explanation. And, yeah, even if Annalise saw it differently, that wasn't so unusual. There were two sides to every breakup story.

But . . .

A couples' retreat? That was more than a little coincidental. Was it Baskens that he'd wanted to bring Annalise to? If so, he knew about the place at least a year ago and had lied to me about hearing about it from the guy in his office. It also meant I wasn't the first woman he'd tried to get up here, or the first one he'd felt seriously enough about to consider therapy with. What was that stupid phrase? Sloppy seconds.

Another thing: he had told me he was raised by a single mother, with a procession of bullying boyfriends, who died when he was sixteen. And he told Annalise he was raised by a mother and father in some isolated country cabin and ran away at sixteen. Two different stories—so clearly he had lied to at least one of us, maybe both. There was a chance he was still keeping the real truth of his childhood to himself.

Something struck the roof of the car, and I jumped. I looked out the window, but there was no one there, at least no one that I could see. And then something hit again, this time on the hood. *What the hell—*

Outside the windshield I saw a small object bounce onto the hood of the car and roll off onto the ground. An acorn. I collapsed against the seat, heart thundering. The goddamn thing sounded like a missile. I drew in a deep breath and blew it out. I cracked the door and sucked in breath after breath of cool air. I just needed a minute to settle down. This was what I'd wanted—to know the truth about Heath, so we could deal with it. And now I knew.

The next move was mine.

So what was that going to be? Should I march up to Heath and announce that after almost a year of trusting him, after almost a year of believing everything he'd told me about his past, I'd suddenly decided to reach out to his ex-girlfriend? *Oh and hey, FYI, a few of your stories don't line up, and also, is your smashing her house up the only reason she didn't feel safe around you?*

There was no way that discussion was going to end well.

I closed my eyes and saw the child-psychologist's office—worn carpet and dingy walls hung with framed diplomas and certificates. I felt the edge of the slick, uncomfortable sofa under my thighs. Smelled the stale smoke lacing the air. A woman with whiskery, cigarette-pleated lips and bloodshot eyes that regarded me frostily over wire-rimmed reading glasses. She asked me questions, her voice rough and laced with phlegm:

Tell me what Mr. Al did to you, Daphne. Tell me, and you can go home.

For some reason, that doctor kept asking all the wrong questions. Heading down a bunny trail, like Mrs. Bobbie used to say. I could have told her what really happened, who was the real evil person at the ranch, but then I would get myself in trouble. The police would take me away—from Omega and the other girls. From my home.

So, instead, I tried to explain how good Mr. Al was. I'd heard about men like that, but he didn't touch us in that bad way, and he never put a hand on me. He was really nice. He hung out at the clubhouse with us, built doghouses, and took us to the library. He laughed and acted silly with us.

I told her just enough to send her down the right trail. And to get Mr. Al hauled from the ranch in handcuffs. The tragedy was, he was nothing more than a guy who liked to smoke weed—a stupid one, yes, since getting high with teenage girls was not an okay thing to do by anyone's standards. But he was harmless. Better than that, he was kind. His concern for me was sincere, and it comforted me to know someone truly cared about me. Until Hap Silver, he was the closest thing I'd ever had to a father.

I opened my eyes, tucked the iPad back under the mat, and got out of the car, leaving it unlocked for later. Shoving the keys in my pocket, I hurried back to the house, arriving just in time to see a man—Luca, probably—slip into the house through the screen door. I glanced at my watch. Lunchtime. There must have been someone eating out here.

I crossed the lawn and found a graveled walk that led down the terraced levels. At the bottom, I could see a grove of gnarled trees with a concrete bench in the center. Heath sat there, two silver-covered plates beside him.

"So this is the bird garden," I said, coming up behind him.

Heath twisted around. "You weren't in the room, so I figured you went for a hike. Luca brought us lunch, just in case I ran into you."

He smiled at me, and I couldn't help it—I pictured Instagram Annalise, her apartment filled with smashed glass. Cowering in fear before her boyfriend. I blinked the image away.

"That was nice," I said. "But aren't we supposed to take our meals in our rooms?"

Heath shrugged and removed a lid. "So we get a demerit. Who cares?"

I took in the bird garden. A stand of mature redbud trees formed a ring around the small, smooth lawn where we sat. The trees' heart-shaped leaves had gone bronze, and each branch was trimmed, like a Christmas tree, with dozens of wooden birdhouses. The houses were hopping, quite literally, with activity. Birds popped in and out, flying off in search of nest-building supplies or worms or whatever they ate, and returning. A giant avian-party apartment complex.

I inspected one of the houses hanging on a low branch. Its walls had once been painted with a detailed purple-and-green-and-gray paisley design. Miniature birds made of tiny dots marched in a circle around the base of the house. It must've been painted long ago. The mountain weather had faded the colors so much they were only visible if you got close.

"Come eat," Heath said.

I joined him on the bench and dipped into a bowl of thick butternut squash soup. "Was it bad? Your session?"

He shook his head. "Not particularly."

I thought of what I'd overheard Dr. Cerny say in the office. *Do you think having her here was really a good idea?* I tucked my legs up under me. It was perfect here in the garden, sun shining in dappled splotches through the trees. The whistles of the birds. You could only see a red smudge of the house from here, high on the hill above us. I tried to let the peace soak into me. Tried not to think about Cerny talking about me. Or what Annalise had written in her email.

"He asked me about my memories," Heath said. "My first day of college. How strange it felt to be sitting in a classroom the size of a theater with all those other students. The papers shuffling and pens scratching. The smells of other people's laundry detergent." He seemed far away, staring past the trees and the swaying birdhouses. "I was just so glad to be there. To be lost in the crowd, one in tens of thousands. It was good to talk about it, which was a surprise. Easier than I thought."

He went back to his food. "I also told him about my mother." He hesitated. "I told him that I wanted, more than anything, to be able to forgive her." He paused.

I knew what he was doing. He was giving me a chance to engage in his therapy. To help him in his search for closure. I forced myself to speak.

"What do you have to forgive her for?"

He got very still. A chill brushed my skin.

"Were there boyfriends?" I asked.

He put down his fork. "No. What I have to forgive my mother for was something different. Something I've never told you."

I gripped the edge of the bench with both hands, my knuckles gone white. What a fool I'd been, thinking I could control any of this, that I could somehow manage the way the truth came out. This freight train was coming, hard and fast, and I was tied to the tracks.

He went on. "My mother was single when she had me—and older, past forty. She'd been hustling a long time . . . She was a dancer before I was born. And probably more than just a dancer, even though I didn't have any proof of it. After she aged out of that career, she got a job at some taco place. Sold weed—and probably harder stuff—to the rich kids in the suburbs." He let out a long breath. "She'd grown up Catholic enough to feel guilty that she wasn't giving me a fair shot at life. So when I was still very young, she gave me away—to a couple she met. Well, not *gave* exactly. I'm fairly certain money changed hands."

So it was basically what Annalise said. He'd told each of us a portion of the truth.

"From the time I was three or four years old, I lived with them." He ran his fingers through his hair. "They were an older couple. And they wanted me—not because they wanted to be parents, but for other reasons. Disturbing reasons."

His words washed over me, and I started to go numb.

"They owned me. Not to physically abuse. There was no sexual abuse, either, nothing like that. It was . . ." He scanned the woods beyond the garden. "Mind games."

"You don't have to talk about it."

He gave me a quizzical look. "I know, Daphne. But they were my parents. The people who raised me most of my life. I want to tell you about them."

I laid down my spoon, my appetite gone. I shook my head, once, then twice, like some crazy windup toy.

"Daphne," he said. "There's nothing to be scared of."

"It's just, I don't want you to feel any pressure."

He laughed in disbelief. "I lied to you, Daphne. I made up an entire story about growing up with my mother. About her having two jobs, us being poor, and all these guys she brought around that roughed me up. Doesn't that bother you? Don't you care?"

"I do. It's just—" I stopped.

This is the one place I'm afraid to go.

The one place I can't go.

"You're afraid I'll push back," he said. "Expect you to tell me about your past. Isn't that right?"

"I just think you should focus on your sessions with Dr. Cerny right now, that's all. That's why we're here. That's the whole reason we came up here."

He pressed his lips into a thin line. "You've told me you lived in a house at a girls' ranch. You said you had surrogate parents there and other girls you lived with and that they got you a scholarship to art school. That's it. That's all I know. You've never told me anything more."

My face felt hot. My whole body felt engulfed in flames. "Because you didn't want me to!" I practically yelped. "Because we agreed the past wasn't worth rehashing!"

He inhaled and let it out slowly. "You're right. We did agree, but I was wrong, Daphne. It was a bad idea for us to pretend certain things didn't happen. That certain events didn't change us. The things that happened to me did change me. They . . . poisoned me, in a way. And I'm afraid if I don't talk about what happened—if I don't get the poison out—it will kill me."

My eyes burned and I felt tears welling. Shit. *Shit.* I couldn't refuse to listen, couldn't watch him suffer like this. I had to fucking pull myself together and be here for the man I loved.

I sniffed. "So tell me. Get it all out."

"Really?"

I nodded.

He looked down at his hands. "I don't know how to describe it exactly. It was lonely and isolated, so lonely that sometimes I thought I was going crazy. No one ever came to the farm to check on me, no police, nobody from child welfare. I wasn't adopted legally, of course, but who cared? Nobody knew, and honestly, how difficult could it be to buy an unwanted toddler off a half-starved crack whore?

"After I ran away, I was so traumatized, I couldn't bring myself to report them. I believed they could somehow find me, take me back to that place." His voice trailed and he shook his head. "I'm glad they're dead now. I'm just sorry I wasn't able to tell you the truth."

"They're dead?" It was the only question I could think to ask.

He faltered. "I mean, I assume they are. They were old when I was a child. I haven't heard from them since I left."

We were quiet for a moment, then I spoke. "What about the mirror?"

"What mirror?" he asked.

I hesitated. "You always talk about a mirror, when you're dreaming. Break the mirror, smash the mirror, stuff like that. I thought it might be something from your time with those people. I thought it might be some clue to unlock . . ." I laughed self-consciously. "I don't know. Now that I'm saying it, it sounds stupid."

He stared at me for a moment, then got up, walking over to one of the gnarled trees on the opposite side of the lawn. I looked up at a birdhouse hanging just to my right, almost within reach. If you looked close enough, you could see it had been carefully painted with a design of leaves and vines, all shades of green and yellow. Someone had labored over this tiny shelter, taken hours probably to make it unique and beautiful. And for what—a couple of birds, who wouldn't know the difference? It was ridiculous. I wanted to pull it down and bash it against the tree trunk. Stomp it until it broke into a million pieces.

I averted my gaze from the birdhouse. Heath was standing in front of me, a resolute look on his face.

"I don't remember any mirror in the house where I lived that scared me," he said. "Or if there was, I guess there's a possibility that I've blocked it out. Jesus. What kind of fucked up would that mean I am?" He laughed harshly.

I kept very still. "I'm sorry, Heath."

"I'm sorry I didn't tell you." He let out a long, trembling breath, scrubbed his face with his hands. "I was scared if you knew how I was raised, that you would see me as damaged. A freak. I thought you might leave me."

I nodded.

He let his eyes shutter. "Dr. Cerny thinks if I can talk about all this, and how it affected me, the nightmares will stop."

"That's good. Really good. I admire your courage."

He looked down at me again, his face broken and sagging. For the first time since I'd known him, I thought I could imagine what he would look like when he was an old man.

"I want you to know me, Daph," he said. "Even if you don't like what you see. Even if you don't want the same in return."

I started to say something, then stopped.

"Just don't leave," he said.

"I won't."

When I stood to kiss his cheek, it felt cold.

Chapter Ten

We sat in the bird garden for another half hour and watched the birds zoom in and out of their faded houses. They hopped out on the perches and dive-bombed each other, playing some mysterious bird version of king of the hill.

Heath told me a few more details about his childhood. The couple who had taken him in lived in a house deep in the country, east of Atlanta, on a large piece of land bordered by a creek and fallow cotton fields. He was never allowed to set foot off the property.

Public school was out of the question, and there was no church attendance nor any social gatherings. The couple he lived with weren't religious, Heath said—or, at least, they hadn't ever talked about God to him. As far as he could figure out, keeping him separated from peers and other adults was more of a privacy issue. They didn't want to get arrested for buying a child.

I didn't mention Annalise Beard or her email. It seemed like she was beside the point now, and bringing her up would probably just create more noise around the situation. Heath didn't need that, not right now. What he needed was to sit with the story he'd just told, let the realization of it sink in. Then maybe, just maybe, he would come to the conclusion that he didn't have to stay up here to fix it. That he didn't need Dr. Cerny, because there was someone else who was here for him. Maybe he'd remember what he'd said to me when we first met, that the only thing he believed in was the right person.

And I was that person.

I figured Heath could use some space, so when he gathered the dishes and went inside to get ready for his next session, I stayed behind and prowled around the property. I ambled farther than I'd ventured yet—into the woods, following a narrow trail that wound down to a stream and then looped back up to the yard. The double doors of the barn were chained and padlocked. I stared at them, not seeing rotted wood and lichen but picturing a hawk bobbing, effortless, in a cold blue sky. Oh, to be a hawk. To be any kind of bird.

My head throbbed, the pain shooting all the way down my neck and deep into my right shoulder. I reached over and dug at the knotted muscle. Forget being a bird; I'd settle for a stiff drink and a good laugh with Lenny. Or, barring that, another chat with Glenys. I wanted to feel that lightness again, that incredible buoyancy I'd felt up on the mountain after I'd told her about Chantal and the girls' ranch. It was supremely ironic. I'd just fought so fiercely against talking about my past with Heath, but with Glenys, the story had rolled right off my tongue.

What was it that made me so afraid of telling Heath? What stopped me from opening up to him? Maybe that, with him—the only man I'd ever loved like this—I had so much more to lose.

I pushed at the chained doors and put my eye to the crack. Nothing had changed from yesterday—sheet-covered furniture was crammed into the far corner. There was a single twin-bed frame, what looked like it might be a dinette set with four chairs pushed underneath. A wing-back chair and some kind of desk, or maybe it was a dresser.

Something on the floor of the barn caught my eye—the knife I'd slid between the doors yesterday. I squatted and slipped my fingers into the opening, feeling my way toward the handle.

"Sleuthing?" came a voice behind me.

I turned to see Dr. Cerny standing a couple of feet away, hands in his pockets, watching me with an enigmatic smile. I stealthily withdrew my hand. Rose and jabbed my thumb back at the barn.

"I was just . . . seeing if I could get inside. Look around a little bit. There's not much to do around here."

"No, I'm afraid there's not. We're not big on extracurriculars, as most people come for the therapy." He cocked his head and held my gaze. *Smart aleck.*

I raised my eyebrows. "Speaking of which, you're probably keeping one of your patients waiting, aren't you?"

"Waiting's not such a bad thing. Illuminates the true character of a person."

I lifted my chin. "Or perhaps it illuminates the character of the person making you wait."

He smiled. "Did you know, they say people won't complain about waiting if they have something to do, even the most meaningless activity? For instance, turning one of those superfluous corners in line at Disney World. Or studying themselves in a mirror."

A mirror?

He furrowed his brow. "Is there anything you'd like to discuss with me, Daphne? Something about Heath's treatment? You seem . . . annoyed."

"No." I shook my head. "It's just, I was wondering if I could maybe get my phone back? Just to check emails."

He smiled. "You know our policy."

"You could make an exception." I matched his smile.

"I could, but there's no cell service out here."

Not true.

"Wi-Fi, then," I said.

"No Wi-Fi either."

I squinted at him. "You don't have Wi-Fi here?"

He shot me a patient grin. "I have Wi-Fi. You don't."

"What about the LTE network?"

"Daphne, Daphne." He shook his head. "Don't you understand I'm trying to help your fiancé? Disconnecting from your devices is the first step in getting in touch with your soul."

"Okay, fine." I sighed. "You win."

"You know, this house was built by a wealthy prospector, who also didn't have Wi-Fi," he said. "Or iPads or telephones or streaming . . . whatever. But I imagine he and his family found ways to entertain themselves. What do you suppose they used to do for fun?"

"I don't know. Taffy pulls and sing-alongs? The occasional episode of cannibalism?"

"Maybe. Maybe." He laughed. "You know, in our sessions, Heath has shared with me how meeting you changed him. How he is determined to do anything to be the man you need." He watched me, his eyes keen. And I had to admit, I didn't hate the rush of warmth I felt.

"He doesn't need to do anything more. He's already succeeding."

"I like you, Daphne. I hope you don't mind me saying so."

I didn't really know how to answer.

"Did Heath tell you the truth about his family? The couple who cared for him after his mother gave him up?"

"He did, some."

"It was very difficult for him, I expect, opening up about his past. Especially given the fact that you've chosen to be more discreet about yours. I imagine you feel some pressure to reciprocate now. Fulfill the social contract. Perhaps tell him about the ranch and what happened to you there."

I swallowed. "Not necessarily."

"Heath already feels quite protective of you. I believe he would be entirely sympathetic if you told him about your surrogate father being sent away to prison."

I shrugged.

"Just a bystander's opinion, of course." He scratched his cheek absently. "Unless, that is, you had something to do with the man's incarceration. In that case, your reticence would make complete sense—if you were in some way responsible."

His tone was light, but alarm still zipped through me.

"I had nothing to do with it," I said curtly. "And if anyone really wants to know what happened, it's just a Google search away. For those of us with access to Wi-Fi."

"Touché." He grinned, all friendly dimples and casually wavy hair. I had to admit it was a little disconcerting. He was so much like Mr. Al, and yet, not at all. This man was careful, and he didn't appear to miss a single detail.

I inhaled deeply. "You know you're not going to keep cornering me when I'm alone and trick me into spilling my guts for you. So you might as well give it up."

He sobered. "You think that's what I'm doing out here? Have you considered that I simply enjoy talking to you?"

"No. But it seems . . . possibly unethical."

"Psychologists are allowed to converse with people who are not their patients. To have friends."

"Okay, so let's converse. Let's talk about you."

"Ah, ha. So clever." I lifted my chin, and he smiled back at me. "What do you want to know?"

"You don't wear a ring. Are you married?"

He ran his fingers through his hair. "Right to the heart of things, eh? All right. The answer is, no, I'm not married and I never have been. I've no children either."

"That's interesting. A relationship expert who's never been married."

"Marriage isn't the only kind of relationship. I have been in love, plenty of times."

"Okay, not going to touch that one."

He laughed.

"What's with the monster faces in the fireplaces?" I asked.

"Ah." He smiled at me. "The fiery fiend. I believe my ancestor Horace Baskens was a bit of an eccentric. Probably be diagnosed paranoid schizophrenic today. Back in the gold-rush days, he made a fortune for himself, but was always afraid of it being stolen by friends, even family. It was why he built his home so far up the mountain—he was terrified of losing his stash. The fiends were the guard dogs of Baskens, watching over every move of the visitors who came to call. Or his family members. He was obsessed, I hear, that his own wife and children were plotting against him."

"Yikes."

"When I was a boy, I was terrified of them. Their watchful eyes kept me from a great deal of mischief, as a matter of fact."

"And provided the inspiration for the cameras?"

"An astute observation," he said with a smile. "I had begun my practice in Atlanta when my mother passed away and left me the house. I supposed the fiery fiends had not done their job, as all the Baskens money had been frittered away by then. But yes, moving back up here among them probably did spark my imagination. I've never thought of it that way."

"You must have seen some interesting things up here."

He chuckled. "That I have."

I forged on, hoping my voice sounded casual. "Do you get many repeat clients? I mean, do some people ever bring one partner, then a different one later?" I swallowed uneasily. I sounded about as subtle as a hammer.

He eyed me. "I take it you're talking about Heath. You're asking me if he's ever brought another woman to Baskens?"

"I'm just curious if he ever called to check out the program . . . for him and someone else? Before me?"

"I'm sorry, Daphne. I'm not free to give out that information. But, if I may . . ."

I raised my eyes to meet his. Asking the question, laying myself out like that to a stranger, had left me feeling exposed. Vulnerable in a way I hadn't experienced in a long time. I felt an unaccountable rush of grief slam though me. The desire to let down my defenses and cry like a little girl.

"You understand, don't you," he said gently, "that sometimes people hide certain facets of who they are, who they were, from the people they love? Not because they're willfully trying to hurt them, but simply because they're deeply, deeply afraid that the one person they care about most may reject them."

Of course I understood that. It was basically the single motivating factor of my entire life: don't let anyone know the truth, because if they find out, they will leave you. Heath was afraid, just like me. We were the same, in more ways than I'd ever imagined.

"I understand," was all I said.

"That's good to hear." He nodded a few times, like he wanted to say more on the subject, but then decided against it. "Very good indeed." And he turned and walked back to the house.

For the third night in a row, Heath slept. No middle-of-the-night yelling, leaping out of bed, or taking random swings at me. I wondered if it was partly because he'd told me about the couple he'd lived with, somehow the confession letting his subconscious mind off the hook.

And if the therapy was working, why would I complain? Even though I didn't like being here, this was what I had wanted.

I put on my glasses. The clock on the mantel showed past midnight. While Heath snored softly, I stared toward the windows. Where exactly was the camera hidden? It unnerved me, that Cerny might be up in that spooky attic room full of hulking machines, waving needles, and blinking lights, sitting at the metal desk, watching us.

I sat up, grabbed a hair band from the nightstand, and swept my hair up. I wasn't going to sleep anytime soon, but I couldn't lie here, worrying about things I had no control over. I decided I should sneak up to the attic, see what Jerry McAdam was up to with his forbidden phone. Maybe after a little spying—thinking about somebody else's problems for a change—my brain would settle down, and I could get some sleep.

I climbed out of bed, went out the door, and tiptoed past the Siefferts' and McAdams' rooms. At the end of the dark hall, I eased back the pocket door. I climbed the narrow stairs to the attic and felt a welcome slam of adrenaline—the fireproof door was cracked open. I crept in, careful to leave it open behind me, just enough that it wouldn't shut all the way. Locking myself in up here wouldn't be wise.

The oddly shaped room looked exactly as I'd left it, except the desk was bare. No pad or pen. The monitors were up and running—grainy and gray and still. The monitor on the left showed the McAdams, tucked in and fast asleep. The middle screen showed Glenys and her husband in their bed as well, back to back, motionless in sleep. On ours, Heath curled next to my empty side of the bed.

Back on the Siefferts' monitor, something flickered. I moved closer. The screen was dark and the image just a shadowy blob, but I could see clearly. It was Glenys, climbing out of bed. Her back was straight and narrow in her nightgown, and her light hair tumbled over her shoulders.

She walked to the window, threw it open, and leaned out—the way Heath had the other day. She sucked in the night air, then canted back, letting her head drop between her thin arms. She looked like she was doing some kind of strange yoga stretch, but I knew she wasn't, because under her nightgown, her shoulders shook rhythmically. She wasn't stretching, she was crying. Sobbing, to be more exact.

Abruptly, she drew herself up, the cool air caressing her face, drying the tears. Her ghostly figure wavered on the screen. Ever so slightly, her upper body began to incline forward, to lean out the window. Instantly, I felt myself go cold. The bedroom was only on the second floor, maybe fifteen feet off the ground, but it was directly above the concrete patio, and if she went headfirst . . .

I whirled, stumbled forward, blindly tripping over a cable and careening into a tall shelf against the wall. I threw up my arms as a torrent of hard black plastic objects rained down over my head. When the deluge was over, I opened my eyes to find myself standing in the center of a mountain of VHS tapes. I waded out, kicking them to the side, slipping on them, crushing them, frantic to extricate myself.

I clattered down the steps and ran down the hall to the last door on the left. Tapping it lightly, I leaned close.

"Glenys," I said in a hoarse whisper. "Glenys!" There was no answer. I knocked louder, then tried the knob, but it was locked. "Glenys, it's Daphne. Come to the door, please."

Nothing. No answer, no sound of movement from the other side of the door. Had she accidentally fallen? Or maybe jumped on purpose? It was hard to tell from the dark monitor what was happening.

I ran down the steps, taking them two at a time, my pulse pounding in my ears. Near the bottom of the stairs, my toe hooked the hem of my pajama pants and I tripped, tumbling to the floor. I scrambled up and charged back through the house, down the hall, and into the kitchen. I threw open the door and ran outside.

On the patio I stared up in the direction of Glenys's window. The glare from the floodlight on the back corner of the house was so bright I had to shade my eyes. But when I did, I saw the window was closed, the curtains drawn. Glenys was gone.

Friday, October 19
Evening

It feels like forever that I've been staggering down the rutted gravel road to Dunfree when suddenly, I hear something. The faint rumble of a car engine. It is behind me.

I stop, all my senses ratcheting up. The car sounds like it's a good half mile back up the mountain, and my brain clicks through the possibilities of who it could be.

A vacationer from one of the cabins on the road, maybe. I've passed seven mailboxes, all with carved wood signs: "Pete's Peak" or "The Bear's Lair" or "Set a Spell."

Or someone else. Someone who means to do me harm.

The rumble grows louder, and I speed up to a fast walk. This stretch of the road is cut into a crevice, the gradient rising steeply on either side. But there's a stand of bronze-leafed beech trees and a handful of huge boulders dotting the slopes that I can hide behind, if I have to. I strain my ears. At first I don't hear the car, and I wonder if it turned off somewhere. But then . . . no. There it is—a low revving.

I break into a jog. Cut right, slide into the shallow ditch, then scramble back out, bear-crawling up the hill. I'm heading for some boulders a couple of yards ahead of me, clawing frantically at the leaves and moss. The engine growls louder just as I dive behind the rock. With the approaching car and the thundering of my heart, time seems to stand still. But when my breath finally levels out I realize I have to pee in the worst way.

It doesn't matter. There's no time. I edge sideways, positioning myself so I can see between the V of the two boulders. The car rolls into view, then slows and idles. It's a truck, a dark, early-model green truck, with a long scratch near the right bumper.

I pull my big coat around me and scrunch down, making myself part of the stone. Was that one of the vehicles from Baskens? I picture the line of cars. A minivan, a Mercedes. A truck, I think. But was it old or new, blue or black or green? I don't know. I can't remember. But it could be from anywhere, and anyone could be driving it, so I need to stay out of sight.

The engine revs again, and the truck continues down the road, the deep rumble diminishing as it gets farther and farther down the mountain from me. When everything is quiet again, I lie back against the rock, wilting in relief, not even caring that I've just soaked my pants.

Chapter Eleven

Wednesday, October 17
Two Days Before

I woke to the creak and slam of a screen door. A man's voice said something in what sounded like Spanish, and I squinted through the early-morning gray and my gluey eyes. I had fallen asleep outside on an old metal patio chaise. Then last night came back to me in a rush.

Glenys on the monitor, leaning out her window. Me running outside to stop her. The closed window.

Now, as my eyes focused, I saw something—black, plastic—wedged between two patio stones just below me. I blinked, rubbed my eyes, and picked it up. The fragment of a cut zip tie.

I saw boots then and looked up, dropping the zip tie. Luca, the phantom cook and butler, was standing in front of me, hands planted on his hips. He was young, early twenties, maybe, with a compact body and short-cropped, light-brown hair. He wore a faded plaid flannel with the shirtsleeves rolled to his biceps. His forearms looked like they might be attached to a bear, but he had a kind face with high cheekbones and a cleft chin that would probably drive a sculptor wild.

I sat up and swung my legs around so fast, I felt dizzy. I made an attempt to rub my eyes, put on my glasses, and smooth my hair all at the same time. It was a move a woman did when the guy who woke her up happened to be attractive, and I was instantly mortified. I tried to cover by acting like I wasn't doing exactly what I was very clearly doing—the result being, I wound up poking my eyes and garbling something incoherent.

In reply, he said something in Spanish that I didn't understand and disappeared back through the screen door. I took a quick inventory. I was in my pajamas but covered by a quilt. Luca's contribution, maybe. Last night, I had waited and waited below Glenys's window, but when nothing happened, I had to conclude that I'd overreacted, read too much into what I'd seen on the monitor. Still, I couldn't bring myself to leave, and even after the chill in the air had turned icy and the dew had started to form, I'd stayed, curling up on the chaise.

I pulled the quilt around me, shivering in the cold dawn. A few minutes later Luca returned with a mug of steaming coffee and a cinnamon roll. I accepted them gratefully and bit into the roll. I could feel him watching, arms folded.

"Daphne," I said, covering my mouth and swallowing. I took a gulp of the coffee. It burned the back of my throat. "Ah, that's hot. But good. Thank you."

"Luca."

"Luca. Nice to meet you." We did a quick shake, then I slurped the coffee again. I couldn't help it. It was perfect. A pinch of sugar, even less cream. Just the way I liked it. Luca said something and nodded up at the house, but I was lost. And not so certain what he was speaking was actually Spanish. It had an odd twist to it. But that look on his face. Was he judging me? Pegging me for some rich, crazy white woman who liked the idea of her every move being recorded for a doctor's viewing enjoyment?

"Everything's okay," I said around the delicious cinnamon roll. "I came out here last night and fell asleep. I was . . ." I paused. "I fell asleep."

He didn't answer. Either he didn't understand, or he didn't care.

"Well." I stood. "I should go back upstairs and get dressed. I've got a whole lot of aimless wandering around to do today." Not to mention I needed to return the Nissan's keys to Cerny's office before he figured out they were missing. "Okay, well, thanks again for the breakfast. See you around."

Luca sent me a tight smile.

Upstairs, I shucked the quilt and crawled into bed beside Heath's warm sleeping form. In spite of the coffee I'd just drunk, I was wiped out from sleeping on the lumpy chaise, and in seconds, I passed out. When I woke later, he was gone, his breakfast dishes still sitting on the table. Skipping the cold eggs, I picked up another cinnamon roll and wondered if Luca had any hot coffee left.

I threw on a pair of jeans and a sweater, yanked my hair into a topknot, and found the keys. Downstairs, as I neared the sunroom, I heard low voices—Dr. Cerny and Heath.

"It's like somebody put a filter over the sun," Heath was saying, "that makes everything look the same, all the time."

I slipped through the door and edged toward the key hooks.

"You're talking about an obsession," Dr. Cerny said.

My hand stopped a couple of inches from the keys.

"Fine. Tell me how to make it stop."

"You have to decide first. Do you want to involve Daphne?"

There was no answer.

"The question is, do you believe she is capable of understanding?"

I backed out of the door and closed it behind me. *Capable of understanding?* Really? I'd agreed to come to this musty old house to support the man I intended to spend the rest of my life with. Of course I could understand whatever it was he was dealing with. I slammed into the kitchen, and Luca, standing at the stove stirring a pot of soup, glanced up.

"Hello," I said, pointing toward the back door. "I was just heading out."

"Espere," he said and grabbed a bottle of water from the fridge. He wiped it down with the dishtowel over his shoulder and handed it to me. Then he snagged a granola bar from a bowl on the counter. *"Para mais tarde,"* he said.

"Sorry, I'm the asshole who only speaks English." I held up the water. "But thanks. I'll be back for lunch."

"Cuidado," he said behind me.

Now that one, I knew.

I stopped and turned back. His clear, intense eyes were boring into mine.

"Why would you tell me to be careful?" I asked.

He went back to his pot without answering, which was frustrating. But the guy didn't speak English, so I tried not to read too much into it. And I guessed it made sense, his warning. He probably knew that people wandered out without realizing how far they'd gone. I had forgotten water last time I'd trekked up the mountain.

"Oh," I said, the thought coming to me at once. "It's Portuguese, isn't it? You're from Brazil."

Over his shoulder, he sent me a smile. I noticed he had really nice, straight teeth.

"Or maybe actually Portugal?" I asked.

He shook his head.

"Okay, then. Brazil. Rio de Janeiro. Big stone Jesus." I spread my arms. "I've heard it's beautiful there."

He sobered. Then moved to the counter and pointed up at the magnetic knife rack. To the empty space on the end.

"Onde está a faca?" He tapped the magnetic strip, and I met his eyes. Sent him a look of confusion. He raised his eyebrows. *"Você pegou."*

I smiled. "Sorry, I don't understand. And I should really go. The birds are waiting for me, I'm sure. But I'll *cuidado*. Promise."

I fled the kitchen, not stopping until I'd slipped around the far side of the house, in the direction of the bird garden, out of sight of the kitchen. I was fairly certain Luca hadn't bought my confused act. He knew I'd taken the knife. I figured I should probably go get it and wait for an opportune time to return it. I didn't need him reporting me to Cerny.

I glanced over at the barn, at the far end of the yard, and nearly jumped out of my skin. The doors were creaking open just then, a figure slipping out from them. It was a woman—thin, dressed in black yoga pants and thermal top, with a yellow baseball cap pulled low. Glenys. What was she doing in the barn?

She didn't see me. She was slumped against the side of the barn now, hands pressed to her face. She inhaled once, then again, like she was trying to collect herself. Then she slowly straightened, wiped her sleeve across her face, and took off toward the stand of trees behind the barn.

I set off after her. Although the terrain was level and the path mostly clear, she was taking this trail slower. I held back to keep a safe distance between us. It was a risk, following her like this. I barely knew the woman, and really didn't have any right to steamroll my way into her private grieving. I just couldn't get the picture of her poised on the ledge of the window out of my head. The way her thin back curved under the weight of her sadness. I promised myself I wouldn't push. If she didn't want to tell me what was bothering her, I'd leave. But I had to know she was all right. She felt like a friend.

I tromped over sodden leaves, the woods smelling vaguely of mildew, of organic rot and decay. A melancholy scent. Bright as it was, the forest was well into autumn—halfway to dying—and it took some effort not to let the vague feeling of sadness settle over me. After about fifteen minutes, I heard the rippling of water ahead, and I slowed. At the bottom of a gentle slope, where the path converged with a broad but shallow creek, Glenys had stopped.

I stopped too, still several yards back, and watched her. She stared past the creek at a row of red-leafed dogwood trees, then closed her eyes and tilted her head back. Whatever she was thinking about, it couldn't be good. It set my nerves thrumming, knowing she was spiraling into her own dark thoughts.

I approached her. "Glenys."

She turned. Broke into a smile. "Oh, Daphne. Hello." She shifted her weight. "I'm sorry about that. I'm afraid I had a moment and got a little emotional." She waved me over and patted my arm when I reached her side.

"No, I'm sorry for intruding. Are you thinking of your son?" I asked.

She surveyed the creek. "And other things."

"I'm sorry."

She waved her hand. "Ah, well. Life is full of so many things that can break a heart, isn't it? I'm glad to see you, though. Very glad, actually."

"You are?" I felt an unexpected rush of warmth in my chest.

"You're a comforting presence, Daphne." She reached out for me, and I let her catch my hand. "I'm sure that's one reason why your fiancé loves you so much. You seem to be a very safe person. Very trustworthy."

"I hope so."

"You're what they call a deep well." She squeezed my hand, then held it up, inspecting it. "What a beautiful ring."

"It was Heath's grandmother's."

"Lovely." She released my hand. "How are you?"

"Oh, fine, I think." I sent her a rueful grin.

"I know how hard it was for you to share those things you did. I hope you don't regret confiding in me."

"I don't. You were right. It was a relief to let it out."

"This place rattles the nerves, doesn't it?" She looked off into the dense woods. "Which is strange. Since it's supposed to be a place of healing. I don't know. Sometimes I wonder if there's anywhere we can go to escape. The pain that's been inflicted upon us or that we've inflicted."

She sat on a large rock on the bank of the creek, and I sat beside her. Wind rustled the canopy of leaves, and the water burbled below over rocks and submerged branches. I thought of Heath back up at the house, sitting in the doctor's sunroom office pouring out more stories. Stories about obsessions that he wasn't sure he could share with me. But could I honestly say I wanted him to? Wouldn't that mean that sooner or later I would have to open myself up to him in return?

The red-leafed dogwoods on the other side of the creek swam into focus. There were three of them, I noticed, planted in a straight line, parallel with the water's edge. How odd.

Glenys nudged me. "They're lovely, aren't they? Pink dogwoods. Spectacular in the spring. Fiery in the autumn."

"Yes."

"Would you like to talk now?" Glenys said. "I have some time."

I toed at the wet leaves. Underneath, a trio of mushrooms had sprung up, pale white, crusted with dirt. I wondered if they were the poisonous kind. I was a city girl, though, unable to tell the difference between an edible mushroom and one that killed you.

"It was a complicated situation," I heard myself saying. "What happened at the ranch. I was a child, and I didn't know what I was doing . . . what I had done, until it was too late."

Chapter Twelve

After a couple of days at the girls' ranch, it became clear that Chantal had decided she was my own personal earthquake.

My third day there, I'd satisfied my itch to explore every inch of our house and yard. We were the last house at the end of a long dirt road, backed up against the woods, and I'd grown curious about the other houses and the rest of the place. Sunday, after church, Mrs. Bobbie said Chantal could show me around the expansive sixty acres.

The girl took me behind the house and through the woods, looping back around to the entrance, where the ranch's mile-long red-clay drive turned off the state road. A hand-carved wooden sign swung on the branch of a gumball tree, and even though I'd seen it before, I smiled.

"Welcome to Piney Woods Girls' Ranch," Chantal announced in a tour-guide voice and then took off, jogging down the drive. I followed her, panting and struggling to keep up in the sticky south-Georgia September heat, until she slowed at the main offices. The buildings were designed to look like an Old West town, ramshackle and shingled and hung with old-timey signs that said "Office" and "Library" and "General Store." A boardwalk connected them, and our feet made satisfying clomping sounds as we walked over it.

The building on the end was where the director, Mr. Cleve, and his staff worked. I'd met him that first night—he was a jovial man with a white beard. There was a sparse library with homemade bookshelves, a game room with a Ping-Pong table and board games in cabinets, and one other building, for group activities and meetings. From the Old West town we walked down a hill past two large vegetable gardens, to an open-air pavilion where Chantal said everybody from each house gathered together on Sunday evening for something called Vespers. Past the pavilion, we started back down the dirt road where all the houses, including ours, sat in two untidy rows. We dawdled for a minute in our front yard, which was mostly dirt and crabgrass.

"If we go in, we'll have to finish our Sunday-school lesson," she said. "Wouldn't you rather go to the lake? And maybe somewhere else, a place I haven't showed you?"

We'd been to church that morning. And Sunday school after that, where a lady had handed out worksheets on a parable that Jesus told about a woman who swept her house. The teacher had kept staring at me while she put paper cutouts of the characters in the story onto a flannel board, as if it was a lesson she thought that I, in particular, could learn from. A few times, her gaze dropped down to my clothes, and I thought I saw her nose wrinkle the slightest bit. I hadn't had a chance to check the cast-off-clothes box in the hall closet, so I was wearing the old, stained yellow pants with the hems ripped out that I'd brought from home.

And now that I thought of it, why hadn't Chantal shown me the lake in the first place, on our tour? It was just like her, keeping something back. Trying to show me who was boss.

I told Chantal I wanted to go to the lake.

It was a pond, actually, a murky man-made thing crusted over with green algae and rimmed by thick, sharp-edged grass. A cloud of gnats swarmed over it, and I made up my mind that I would never dip a toe in its disgusting depths. There was a short, wobbly dock of splintered wood, booby-trapped with nail heads that snagged at our shoes when we walked to the end of it. In the summer, Chantal said, the girls were allowed to swim or fish with poles they kept up at the ranch house. Onshore, a cobwebbed canoe lay flipped upside down. When I asked about it, she looked at it blankly for a second, like she'd never noticed it until now.

"We don't use it. No oars."

I pushed at one end with the toe of my sneaker, but she grabbed my arm. "Don't. There are probably snakes under there."

Something buzzed in my head—not so much a warning bell as just an indication of the presence of new information. The upside-down canoe was important to Chantal, and I could imagine several reasons why that might be so, mainly because I had immediately recognized it as a prime hiding place.

"You want to see a secret place?" Chantal said quickly.

"Okay."

"Swear on your mother's grave that you won't tell anyone."

"How come?"

"Just swear."

"All right. I swear," I said, not bothering to mention my mother wasn't dead. Besides, there probably wasn't really a secret place, so who even cared?

Chantal and I set off, following the curve of the lake until we reached the woods. About a half mile in, we arrived at our destination— a moldy plywood structure that looked like a cross between a tree house and a fort. It was built by some girls who'd lived at the ranch long ago, maybe even in our same brown brick house. They'd filched the wood from somewhere—probably from Mr. Al, who, since I'd arrived, had spent every afternoon in the driveway, surrounded by stacks of lumber and tools. He was building a doghouse for Bitsy, the ranch hound who wandered from house to house, begging scraps and pooping in every-body's front yards. I thought that was sweet of him.

Inside the clubhouse was another world—a distant planet strung with old Christmas garlands and grimy cast-off pillows, and filled with an impressive stash of snacks, magazines, and tattered paperbacks. It reminded me of what the inside of a genie bottle must have looked like, and smelled like it too—that same scent of sweet cologne that clung to Omega and Shellie and Tré. It was the most beautiful place I had ever seen.

"These woods don't belong to the ranch," Chantal said. "They're a national forest. So we can do anything we want here—smoke, drink beer, or read dirty books. Even if we get caught, there's not a damn thing Mrs. Bobbie can do about it."

I nodded, truly and legitimately enthralled.

"You ever read a porno book? They have them here. And Omega and them bring boys out here and have sex sometimes too. But you're just eleven, so I can't say anything else about that." She ticked a lock over her mouth. I was relieved.

That night, after we all sat down to dinner and Mr. Al said the blessing, Mrs. Bobbie pointed to a large orange pill sitting in the upper-right corner of my place mat. I scanned the table. All the other girls had identical pills sitting on their mats as well. Chantal had two—one orange and one small blue.

"Vitamins first," Mrs. Bobbie said.

I swallowed the pill with one big gulp of cherry Kool-Aid, then noticed the other girls only sipped theirs. I wondered why.

Mrs. Bobbie watched me with a gimlet eye. "It's a multi." She said it like *mult-eye*. "Because I can't afford to be driving you gals into town for this, that, and the other. Around here, if you get a fever, we call the preacher 'cause he lays on hands for free."

"He sure does," one of the Super Tramps muttered.

One of the girls giggled, then all of us got to laughing; even Mr. Al cracked a grin and shook his head. Mrs. Bobbie hushed everyone. She declared she had something else to say, and all at once everything got really quiet. My stomach flipped—the way it used to every time I came home to find our apartment door locked even though it was too early for my mom to have gotten home from work for the day. That stomach-flip feeling meant she was inside and up to no good, and I would have to find a place to wait until dark. It meant I'd have to figure out a way to stay out of sight of the older boys who hung around the parking lot.

"There's some food missing," Mrs. Bobbie announced. "From my top shelf."

She didn't elaborate or say what the food was, but I figured it was something good, cookies or candy or something. I'd seen inside the pantry—counted everything from stem to stern one morning before anybody was up. Mrs. Bobbie was on the ample side, and she probably didn't like it when the kids got into her snacks.

"We don't hide food here, Daphne," Mrs. Bobbie went on, and I jerked in surprise. "There's a gracious plenty to go around for growing girls. And anyhow, when you hide food in your room, it brings roaches, so you need to bring it back to me right away."

I glanced around the table. The Super Tramps were all staring at me—Omega with her beautifully pursed fuchsia lips, Shellie with her languid eyes, and Tré behind her curtain of stringy hair. I could feel the weight of their attention, like stones crushing the breath out of me. Their eyes were aflame with some expression I didn't recognize. It might've been admiration. Or bloodthirstiness.

I looked down at my plate. We'd all been given a scoop of macaroni and cheese with chopped-up hot dog mixed in it. The whole concoction was dusted with crushed potato chips. There were no vegetables or fruit accompanying the meal, only the one half a cup of Kool-Aid to drink. It wasn't a shock that the food had been taken, but all the same, I hadn't been the one to do it.

"Mrs. Bobbie has a special diet from her doctor, hon," Mr. Al said. "She gets sick if she don't take in enough calories." His face was kind under the floppy blond wings of hair, but I had a hard time believing what he was saying. I'd never heard of a sickness like that.

"I didn't take it," I said.

Mrs. Bobbie made a sound like *Of course you did.* She'd been doing this long enough to know better, I guessed. She knew how foster kids were.

Chantal piped up. "I'll check our room."

"Now, hold on." Mr. Al put out a hand, but Mrs. Bobbie shook her head at him. Chantal scooted back her chair, ran out of the room, and, in an astonishingly short amount of time, returned with three small boxes of yogurt-covered raisins. She laid them on the table in a neat row and I stared at them, openmouthed.

"She ripped a hole in the mattress and stuffed them up inside," she announced, then turned to see my reaction.

My face heated and my eyes watered. I hadn't done that. I didn't know there was a hole in my mattress. Chantal would, though. She sure would. That bitch!

Mrs. Bobbie regarded me, her lips pursed. "Where's the rest of it, Daphne? There was more."

"No, there's not. I don't know. I didn't take those raisins." My voice shook.

But there was the evidence lined up beside my plate, three tiny red boxes. I looked at Mr. Al, hoping for some sort of help, but he glanced over at Chantal.

"Let's eat up, girls," he said and hunkered over his plate of hot-dog mac and cheese. He didn't look at me again.

Later, after Mr. Al and Mrs. Bobbie had settled in front of the evening news and we were cleaning the kitchen, the Super Tramps crowded around me at the sink. They were so close, their scent enveloped me. It was sweet, some kind of cotton-candy perfume I didn't recognize.

"What did you do with the rest of Mrs. Bobbie's food?" Omega said. "If you tell us, we'll share it with you."

"I don't know." I stole a glance at Chantal, who was flicking crumbs off the table with a dishtowel, spraying them across the floor I'd just swept. "I didn't take it."

They stared at me blankly for a few more awful seconds, then ordered Chantal and me to finish the kitchen for them. Then they all trooped upstairs to their room.

"Homework, ladies!" I heard Mrs. Bobbie shout after them from the TV room, and a door slammed above us in response. Chantal went back to flicking crumbs from the table instead of coming to help me at the sink. I turned back to the suds without a word.

After lights out, I waited patiently for Chantal to finish kicking my bunk. When she finally quit and I heard her breathing deepen, I climbed down the ladder and tiptoed down the hall. I tapped on the Super Tramps' door as loudly as I dared and immediately it swung open. Tré in a T-shirt, her hair in short braids, stood before me. A pink light glowed behind her. I could see the other two girls were awake too, propped on their elbows, heads close where they'd pushed their beds together. That cotton-candy smell enveloped me again. I really liked it.

"What?" Tré said. Her fingers were splayed out on the door, nails slick with wet black polish.

"I think I know where the food is," I said.

Her eyes widened and she flashed a delighted smile down at me. I thought suddenly how pretty she looked with her hair pulled back. Her skin was porcelain, and her legs were long and toned. I wondered why her mom and dad had given her away. And why nobody had adopted her. Suddenly, Omega appeared in the doorway and, shoving Tré aside, propped her hip against the frame. She was wearing a T-shirt too, but she'd cut the sleeves and neck out of hers and it showed the ribs of her sternum. The rise of small breasts.

"Where?" was all she said.

I told her about the overturned canoe. After which, she clicked the door shut in my face.

In the morning, after our breakfast of cornflakes, there was a flurry of gathering backpacks and jackets and shoes. I didn't have any of the above, so I walked out to where the white bus waited to take us to school. Someone plucked at my shirt. I turned. It was Omega.

"Hold out your hand." I did, and she dropped into it two Chips Ahoy cookies. "Don't fucking eat 'em where anyone can see. You have to be alone in the girls' bathroom. Alone, locked in a stall. Okay?"

I nodded, curling my fingers around the crumbly cookies. My stomach growled as I imagined them melting in my mouth. The sharp, sweet tang of the chocolate chips in the crevices of my molars.

"You know where the clubhouse is, right?" Omega said.

I squinted up into the piercing morning sun, up at her gorgeous face. Her lashes were coated with mascara and lined with a thick black sweep. Her mouth glowed fuchsia. She looked like a girl that should be on TV.

"Chantal showed me," I said.

She pursed her pillowy lips. "I should've known she'd sneak. I bet she lied and said that we let her come in, didn't she?"

I didn't answer. I didn't want to give the wrong answer and ruin my chances.

"Because we don't let her in," Omega said. "And we never will."

I smiled.

Omega did too. "You wanna know why? She's a disgusting piece of shit. She's trash. Her parents killed each other, did you know that? Her mother shot her father in the face, and then shot herself in the face, right in front of Chantal."

My throat went dry.

"You know what she did after that? She ordered pizza and watched a movie. I'm not even kidding."

I waited. There was more, I could tell from the gleam in Omega's eyes.

"Has she thrown up yet in your bedroom?" she asked.

I shook my head.

"Well, she will. She has these fits and throws up everywhere. And we don't want her getting sick in our clubhouse. Having one of her fits and upchucking all over the place like that demon-possessed girl in *The Exorcist.*"

I didn't have the slightest idea what she was talking about, but I nodded. Omega studied me with narrow eyes. I wondered how she got her eyeliner to wing perfectly like that on both sides.

"We got something better than cookies in the clubhouse, if you're cool," she said. She had a devilish tone in her voice. "After school, okay, little Daphne-Doodle-Do? You come to the clubhouse and hang out with us." She reached out and tweaked my left nipple and the shock of it, the sting, actually made my eyes water. "Titty twister!" she shouted over her shoulder. I didn't say anything. My newly budded breast burned.

I watched her saunter away, her hips swaying in her tight, low-slung jeans. Her deputies running to flank her as they approached the bus. They were a force to be reckoned with, the Super Tramps. And I was going to be one of them.

When I got to school, I scooted into the girls' bathroom, counted the cookies one more time for good measure, then threw them in the trash. I brushed the crumbs from my palms, as something warm and strong surged through me. It was a new sensation, one that made me feel ten feet tall. I didn't need cookies. And I wasn't going to be a fat fuck anymore. Omega had given me a gift. And it had made me into someone completely different.

It was the new Daphne.

And she could withstand a million earthquakes.

Chapter Thirteen

After Glenys and I parted, I felt raw and skittish—sandblasted from the inside out from talking about the ranch. That was probably why I forgot my plan to retrieve the knife from the barn and return it to Luca's kitchen.

After I'd finished, Glenys asked if I would tell her the end of the story. Before weighing the consequences, I agreed, promising to meet her at two thirty the next afternoon on the brow of the mountain.

She'd taken my hand once again, before we parted. "I know it may sound strange to you, but hearing your story makes me feel like I'm not so alone."

"That doesn't say much for Dr. Cerny's therapy."

"It's different with him." She pressed her lips together. "Hard to explain. I feel like you and I understand each other in a way that a man like Matthew Cerny never could." She studied my face. "I'm thankful for your friendship, Daphne. And I'm glad we met." She hugged me before I knew it was happening. "See you soon."

Talking to Glenys had felt as natural as the turning of the leaves, but now, back at the house, I was wondering why I'd been so quick to agree to meeting her again. What she'd said about therapy made sense—I did feel lighter after talking to her—but I couldn't say that I was ready to completely let go of all of my story. The truth was, I didn't know this woman, and there was no guarantee she could be trusted to keep my secret. If it even still needed to be kept.

On my way down the first-floor hall, I heard Cerny lumbering up the back stairs to his suite. He called down to Luca that he was not to be disturbed, and I paused.

His office was empty. Possibly unlocked.

I waited, listening for the door of his suite to close. When I finally heard the distant click, I hurried toward the office. I tried the door, and it opened. Cerny probably didn't intend to be away for long. Maybe he'd only gone upstairs to use the bathroom—at any rate, I would have to be quick. If there were any files on Heath, this might be my only opportunity to learn something.

The office was bright and spacious, spanning the length of the side of the house and glassed in, just like our room. It was furnished with a desk, a couple of squishy chairs, and, no surprise, one sleek black leather couch. A few Mark Rothko–esque paintings hanging on the brick wall and a couple of giant palm trees. I turned to the fully packed bookcase. Freud, Skinner, Piaget, Ainsworth, Jung—familiar names from the intro-level psych class I'd taken in school. There were other books too, of a darker sort. Marx and Kipling, Hitler and Machiavelli.

Such a tasteful room for spilling your nastiest secrets.

Cerny's elegant marquetry inlaid desk was bare except for a sleek desktop computer, a black landline phone, and a tablet—an iPad, just like mine. Did the doctor keep his files on the iPad instead of on yellow pads? There were no file cabinets in the room. But he had to keep the personality assessments somewhere. All the interviews and the surveillance videos had to be kept somewhere too. When the avalanche of VHS cassettes fell on me up in the attic, I hadn't noticed any tapes labeled *Beck/Amos*, even though, honestly, I hadn't taken the time to really look. But surely he didn't store them that way, not in this day and age.

I edged around the desk and swiped the screen of the tablet. The lock screen lit up. I sat and opened the one narrow desk drawer, revealing a mountain of envelopes and papers, sticky notes, and receipts. I bit my lip and plunged a hand into the pile, feeling around, and drew out a stack of business cards bound with a rubber band. A couple were Cerny's, a few from a caterer, a lawyer, a limousine service. But it was the one at the bottom of the stack that stopped me.

JESSICA KYUNG, INVESTIGATOR
GEORGIA STATE BOARD OF EXAMINERS OF PSYCHOLOGISTS

I mentally calculated how much time I had before Cerny returned, then decided to chance it. I lifted the phone receiver and tapped in the number on the card.

"Jessica Kyung," a woman said in a brusque voice—so quickly, in fact, that I had to gather myself.

"Hi, Jessica," I stammered. "I was just, ah . . . vetting a particular therapist, and I wondered if you could verify his status with the board."

"I'm sorry, we don't discuss individual cases with the public. Who is this again?"

"I'd rather not tell you my name, if that's okay."

"It is." She hesitated. "There is a license-verification database I can direct you to, if you'd like."

"I don't really have access to a computer where I am. And I think you might've met with him, at one point. Maybe given him your card?"

"I'm sorry. I'm really not—"

"It's Matthew Cerny."

There was a long silence, then she spoke again, her voice low. "I don't mean to push, but it would really help if I knew your name."

I cleared my throat. Time was running out, and I needed to wrap this up. "My name is Daphne Amos. I'm staying at Baskens Institute, in Dunfree, with my fiancé, for the week. I just want to know—is there any reason I should question Matthew Cerny's ability to treat him?"

"Look," she said evenly, "if you have any questions or concerns about a particular doctor, any licensed doctor in the state of Georgia, I would encourage you to go to our site. Since you aren't near a computer, I can tell you that Dr. Matthew Cerny is a licensed psychologist, currently in good standing, in the state of Georgia."

"Okay."

"But . . ." She went quiet, and I glanced toward the door. Even if Cerny's bowels were knotted tighter than a Boy Scout's rope, the clock was running down.

"How about I just hang on to your card?" I suggested and she cleared her throat.

"Yes. Why don't you do that."

I hung up and tucked the card in my pocket. On the desk, the iPad screen had gone black, a reflection of my face staring out at me. Everything could be right here, right in front of me. A recording of my fiancé telling someone all the things he didn't want to share with me. That he didn't feel safe telling me. The real reason for his nightmares. His secrets. His obsessions.

And possibly some professional dirt on Cerny.

I swiped the home screen again. Tentatively tapped out a guess: C-E-R-N. The screen vibrated its rejection. I tried again, another miss, and again. Still nothing. I heard a noise then, the sound of the door banging against the wall. I clicked off the iPad and stepped away from the desk, back into the center of the room, just as Dr. Cerny entered. His sleeves were rolled up, his shirt unbuttoned at the collar. He smiled when he saw me.

"Daphne. What an unexpected surprise. Unexpected, but not unwelcome. What brings you here?"

I arranged my face into a careful neutral. "I was looking for Heath."

"I imagine he's gone back up to your room. For lunch. Isn't it about that time?" He was moving toward me. His dad-smell filled the room: sweat, aftershave, wood chips. "You look well. Full of light and vitality and fresh air. The sun, the moon, the stars. What have you been doing with yourself, Daphne, while we damaged souls toil away in here, attempting to reclaim our sanity?"

"Wandering, I guess. Walking through the woods."

"Pulling a Robert Frost, eh?" He went to the desk. Swiped the iPad. Tapped it a few times. "You go up the mountain or down to the creek today?"

"To the creek."

"Good choice. Tell me, has Heath confided in you any more about our sessions?"

"No, not after the thing about his parents."

"Interesting." He leaned back in his chair. "You know, most people think the key to a successful relationship is communication. But it's not. Communication doesn't have some sort of magical ability to solve problems." He laced his fingers and observed me. "Problems don't disappear—most of them, anyway. Heath is who he is and you are who you are. Talking about it won't change a thing."

"Then why did we come here? And, might I mention, write you a giant check?"

He chuckled. "What Heath's doing with me isn't talking, not exactly. It's more like a recalibration." He leaned back. "The trick to constructing an unassailable relationship is to embrace the unsolvable. You ever heard of the wild problem?"

I shook my head.

"It's from the field of algebra. The wild problem is an unsolvable equation or concept involving classification and graphs and something called a quiver, which I'm not even going to begin to pretend I can explain. The point is, there are unsolvable problems that even the most brilliant among us can't resolve. They're in math but also science, phi-losophy, and art. Everywhere. So why, then, is it that we can't accept unsolvable problems in human psychology? You can talk about your disagreements with the person that you love until your throats are raw. But it won't change anything. And it won't ensure a happily-ever-after."

"But you want Heath to share his wild problem with you," I said. "That seems like a contradiction."

"It's part of the process I lead my patients through. Jung called it bringing the shadow to the conscious self, an essential part of achieving wholeness. One can't deal with a problem they can't articulate. But after that, after you see it for what it is, you must decide how you want to handle it. You can talk and talk about it, circling it endlessly, throwing thousands of dollars down the drain. Or . . ."

I leaned forward. "Or what?"

He mirrored my position, inclining his body toward me. His voice was barely louder than a whisper. "You can pull it close, wrap your arms around it, embrace the anathema you've been led to believe by all the experts and book peddlers and TED Talkers that you should erase."

A lock of hair had fallen over his forehead, and the intensity in his eyes sent a wave of prickles over my skin.

"You do this—you embrace the darkness, the treasure of the shadow—until the lines between you and it dissolve and it becomes an ally. Perhaps even an asset."

The room stilled, and I remembered a rainy Sunday afternoon, several months back. Heath and I were home, and we'd been lying on the floor, watching some action movie I couldn't even remember now. It had played in the background, a soundtrack of tire squeals and gun-shots, as we made love.

Afterward, when he had looked at me, I'd felt that I knew, at last, what it was to be understood and loved—not in spite of who I was, but because of it. In that moment, that hard, hidden vein of metal in me that I'd prayed no one would discover had been exposed. It had been a strange sensation, terrifying but exhilarating, being broken open like that. It felt a lot like standing on the edge of the sheerest cliff in the world.

I cleared my throat. "You're saying our darkness is what gives us strength."

He nodded. "It's our beauty."

"Our secret weapon in the world," I said. "So you think I should let Heath tell me everything. And then we can move on."

He laid his hand on his chest. "Ah, Daphne. You really do understand, don't you?"

"I think so." And it was true. I did.

He smiled. "What a surprise you are. What an absolute surprise. You come here my adversary and now look what's happened. You've gone and won my heart."

I didn't know how to respond to this, what to say to this man who looked so much like the only father I'd ever known, but who was really just a stranger.

"Would you reconsider—" Cerny said at the same time that I spoke.

"I was just thinking I should get back to my room."

He hesitated, then gestured toward the door without protest.

I stood. "Thank you. For the talk and everything."

"The pleasure was mine."

I walked slowly up the stairs, thinking. I was torn about approaching Heath, the same way I was conflicted about talking to Glenys. Part of me wanted to know more about Heath's mysterious past. The other part wanted to close my eyes and make it go away. Since we'd had that talk in the bird garden, the atmosphere around the two of us had changed. Things between us felt different, strange and unbalanced in a way I couldn't put my finger on.

And I was scared if I took things further, we might never find our way back.

In our room, I was greeted by the sound of the running shower. The bathroom door was cracked, and steam poured into the chill air of our bedroom. I tucked the business card into my suitcase and moved toward the bathroom door. I could feel my nerves jangling, stretched taut. I cracked my knuckles, turning back away, scanning the windows. Eighteen panes in all. Eight on the top, ten on the bottom. Eight and ten, eight and ten. I snapped the hair band on my wrist, once, hard, then another time, for good measure. I was safe.

Safe enough to go to the bathroom, strip naked, and join my fiancé in the shower. There didn't have to be any talking. Not yet. Like Cerny said, Heath's wild problem, and mine, weren't going anywhere. And if the doctor was right, we could use them to make us stronger.

I undressed and heaped my clothes on the floor. I stepped into the steam-filled bathroom, so quietly Heath didn't notice. At least not until I swung open the glass door. When he saw me, he dashed the water out of his eyes.

"Look at you," he said.

"Same old me."

"Never. You need to get in here. Now."

God, I loved the gruffness in his voice. I could feel myself getting turned on by the mere tone of it. I stepped in, and he corralled me in his arms. He was dripping but I didn't care. He felt warm and perfect.

"Hi," he rumbled.

I raised on tiptoe, kissed him, and he gathered me close. Held the back of my head and pressed the length of his body into me. His mouth was open and warm, his tongue gentle. I tipped back my head and let him bend over me, enjoying the familiar leap of desire in my belly. We fit together like we'd been made that way, his chest and abdomen lining up with mine. He circled one arm around me, and we staggered back against the shower wall.

"Daphne," he said into my mouth.

Suddenly, the jet spray caught me full in the face. "Oh, God," I sputtered, part moan, part laugh. "Not sexy."

"Hold on," he said and twisted the nozzle down. Turning back, he lifted me up, and I wrapped my legs around his waist. He kissed me again, and I felt the rush of his breath down my neck. When he entered me, I tipped my head back, reveling in the feeling of him inside me, and the water cascading over us. We fit together perfectly. We always had.

I groaned with pleasure, grinding against him. And he was enjoying it too, his hand under my thigh, fingers probing higher and higher as he kissed me. And then, without warning, he lurched forward, pushing me back against the tile. My head struck the wall, so hard stars burst across my vision.

I would've gasped but my lungs wouldn't work. I wanted to cry out, to protest, but I couldn't make a sound. I was flash frozen. I blinked a couple of times, trying to wake myself up. Had he slipped?

I opened my mouth to ask, and it happened again—my head slammed back against the tile.

This time I cried out. That hadn't been an accident. And now, the way his face had turned from mine, the way he was holding me, pinning me against the wall, it was like he was lost in some fantasy that had nothing to do with me. The lights of the bathroom blurred and the sound of the water muted. I couldn't catch my breath from the shock and the pain and the steam. My mind spun out, synapses firing chaotically. I couldn't tell him to stop, to let me go, to—

"Stop. You can't—" I finally gasped. "You have to stop."

He did stop. And he stared at me.

I shook my head. "Why did you do that?"

"What do you mean? Do what?" His face looked so blank, it filled me with fury.

"You hit my head. You hurt me, Heath!" My voice, finally, loud and shrill.

His eyes filled with instant regret. "Oh my God, Daph. I didn't mean . . . I just got caught up . . ."

"Caught up." I pushed my wet hair out of my face and let out a harsh bark of laughter. Or a wail, I couldn't tell the difference. "Did you think I liked having my head bashed on the wall? Are you into that sort of—"

He edged toward me. "I'm not. I didn't realize—"

I put my hand on his chest. "I need you to give me a second, all right?"

I stood there, my fingers splayed against him. Water streamed over my ring and dripped down my arm, and he waited, not moving. But I was already doubting myself. Wondering if I was overreacting. Maybe Heath had just gotten ahead of himself. He was a big guy. Strong. He probably didn't realize the impact of his strength.

He pressed his chest against my hand. "Daphne."

My elbow bent, the slightest bit. I couldn't bear to look at his crushed face anymore. I looked down instead—focused on the tile floor through the sheet of water. It had gone lukewarm.

"Do you want me to leave?" he said. "Just tell me and I'll go."

I couldn't answer him. Yes, I wanted him to go. And I wanted him to stay. I wanted to scratch out his eyes, draw blood from his skin. Scream at him until I was hoarse.

I thought about Annalise Beard. Was this the kind of thing she'd been afraid of? She had said she'd prefer to forget she ever knew him . . .

"I love you so much, Daphne," Heath said. "I would never intentionally hurt you, I swear." He held up his hands and it was such a vulnerable gesture, so forlorn, I felt myself waver. All the possibilities flooded through me.

I rested on the most probable one, the one I wanted. He hadn't meant to hurt me. He loved me, I knew it. This had just been a manifestation of his wild problem—the darkness he hadn't yet embraced. I hugged myself, closed my eyes, and let the warm water run over me.

"Daphne—"

"No," I said. "Don't speak. Don't say a word. We're going to start over."

I took a shaky breath, ran one finger down his streaming chest all the way to his taut abdomen, and let it linger. He closed his mouth.

"None of this happened," I said. "You and I just got in the shower, and we started kissing."

I knew it was unreasonable, maybe even foolish, but I just wanted him back, wanted all the hurt and confusion to go away. And why couldn't we just go back and say it had never happened, if we both agreed to it? The truth was, it wouldn't have, not if we hadn't come to Baskens. This strange place was messing with our minds, making us do things we wouldn't normally do. Feel things we normally didn't feel.

Like, right now, how a small, dark part of me pictured myself folding Heath into my arms, pulling him close, just so I could hurt him back.

I let my finger, which had been drifting along his stomach, drop to a lower spot.

"We shouldn't—" he began, but I shook my head.

"You're a lucky man," I said. "You're getting a do-over."

I took him by the waist, rotating him toward the same wall where he'd just had me pinned. I pressed him against it.

"But I'm in charge now."

Friday, October 19
Night

By the time I stumble into the little town of Dunfree, it's dark. I feel like I've been jogging for hours, but it's probably only been forty to fifty minutes at most. I'm freezing, all except my feet, which feel like they're on fire. My throat is raw with thirst.

Dunfree's main street is punctuated by street lamps and newly planted maple trees with a few red leaves still determinedly clinging to the spindly branches. Its crown jewel, if you can call it that, is a one-story stone-and-green-metal city hall, squatting halfway down the street. Anchored on either end of the street are two home-style restaurants called, respectively, Mama June's and Paw-Paw's. On the drive up, Heath and I ate at Paw-Paw's.

I wander up and down the sidewalk, from one end of the street to the other, but the green truck is nowhere in sight. For the moment, I'm in the clear.

The sidewalks are crowded with people, and it dawns on me that I've hit the Friday-night dinner rush. I haven't eaten since this morning, and I am desperately thirsty, but I have no money, no wallet, no nothing. I push open the door to Mama June's (colorful flyers, jangling bell) and wander in, stopping short in the middle of the bustling dining room. There are several boxy old TVs sitting on precarious-looking shelves in each corner of the restaurant, replaying an old Georgia football game. I spot a half-empty glass of water on an unoccupied table, but just as I edge my way over to it, a waitress appears and sweeps it and the rest of the dirty dishes into a plastic tub.

I veer into the bathroom and, at the lone sink, flip on the faucet and duck my mouth under the stream. I gulp and gulp until my stomach begins to cramp and I worry I may vomit. The sound of toilets flushing makes me jerk upright. When three women simultaneously emerge from the stalls, I shut off the faucet, wipe my mouth with my sleeve, and back against the wall.

Chapter Fourteen

Wednesday, October 17
Two Days Before

We ate the lunch that Luca (appearing, then disappearing, before I could catch sight of him) left outside our door. White-bean, bacon, and kale soup, with a slender loaf of crusty bread. Outside, the temperature had dropped dramatically, the cold seeping in through the cracks of the windowpanes. But we were comfortable. Even though it was a small gas affair, the fireplace still packed a wallop. I tried not to notice the way the black fiend's face glowered out at me from the flames.

After we'd finished eating, Heath swirled the ice in his glass. "I don't know how else to say this, Daphne. I'm so sorry."

"You've got to stop apologizing. Seriously. It's done. Over."

"But we can't pretend like it didn't happen," Heath said.

"I'm not pretending. I just don't think we have to talk it to death. As a matter of fact, Dr. Cerny even agrees that talking isn't what keeps a relationship together. He told me that, just today."

"When did you see him?"

"Earlier. Just briefly, before we . . ."

He nodded. "Hm."

"And you can wipe the smug look off your face," I said. "He wasn't *therapizing* me. I'm just saying that, although I want to hear about your childhood and everything you went through, there are some things—some parts of us—that we just have to accept."

"He wasn't in here, with us. He didn't see what I did to you."

"You got carried away, but I'm fine. And it'll never happen again."

I took a deep breath. I was sitting calmly, across the table from him. In one piece, not obsessively counting or displaying any discernable signs of a mental breakdown. But was I really fine? So much had happened since we'd gotten to Baskens, so many things had begun to shift and upend between us, I wasn't sure if I knew what *us* meant anymore.

Heath moved to the mirror over the dresser, stroked the two days' growth of beard. It gave him a rugged look. Wild and untamed. Normally I would go to him and pull him close, rubbing my skin against his, but my body wouldn't move. I touched the tender spot on the back of my head and pressed it gently. Pain radiated over my head, but it helped me focus on where I was. The fiend behind the flames caught my eye, and this time, I glowered back at it.

After Heath left for his final session, I changed into workout clothes, grabbed a bottle of water from the lunch tray, and headed outside. I needed to fill my lungs with sharp, cold air. Shock my fuzzy brain into clarity. A hike up the mountain would be the perfect thing. Maybe I'd run into Glenys again. Maybe I'd just go ahead and finish my story, tell her the things I couldn't bring myself to tell Heath, and I would finally feel my soul loosen just the slightest bit.

On the way up, memories filtered back to me. Of Mount Olive Christian Academy, where they sent us ranch girls and the boys from Maranatha Ranch, near Warner Robins. The school sounded fancy, but it was really just an old remodeled roller-skating rink off an industrial highway, with a couple of rickety trailers out back that served as extra classrooms.

Every morning, after we said the regular pledge of allegiance, they had us say a different one, to the Christian flag, but I could never quite remember the whole thing, so I just moved my lips without making a sound. At lunchtime a ladies' Bible study from Hollyhock Community Church brought us a meal—peanut-butter-and-jelly sandwiches, Fritos, and Capri Suns.

At the end of my first week at Mount Olive, when the old, hand-me-down school bus dropped us off at the top of the long drive, we all walked back to the brown brick house together. In our room, I dumped my backpack in the corner and then went to pee. From inside the bathroom, I could hear Omega and the other girls trooping down the hall. Their laughter rose up like a thundercloud and shook the thin walls.

Sitting on the toilet, a thrill shot through me. I wanted to live inside their funhouse laughter. It was so big and warm and enveloping, so full of hidden knowledge and inside jokes and stories I imagined were just too crazy to be believed. But I would get to hear the stories soon in the clubhouse. I would revel in the cushiony womb of their laughter. As I walked down the hall, Chantal called to me from our bedroom.

"Do you want to play Skip-Bo?"

She was lying on her back on her bed, her feet tapping out some mysterious choreography on the bottom of my bunk. I didn't want to play cards. I didn't want to be anywhere near her.

"You don't know how to play?"

"I didn't say that. I just can't right now. I'm busy."

She sat up, crossed her legs under her. "How are you busy, Pizza Face?"

That was one of her names for me, after last night. She'd lain on her bunk at night after lights out, kicking my mattress, chanting in a singsong voice: *Pizza Face, Hairy Legs, Squinty McGee, Egg Salad.* I let her talk. I made up my mind, sometime during the endless, droning naming ceremony, that I was going to have to do something about her.

"Where are you going?" Chantal demanded again.

"Out," I said and waited. She hadn't spewed all her venom, and I knew if I let her finish, she'd feel like she won. And maybe she wouldn't follow me.

"You're a pile of egg salad. Rotten egg salad and a fat fuck."

I was careful to keep my face expressionless, but it warmed nonetheless. My arms and legs were thicker than hers, rounded and soft, and I had a belly that jiggled when I ran. I also had cheeks that made me look like a baby. I guessed that made me fat. The egg-salad thing made no sense. I had never considered myself anything but ordinary looking. Plain round face, plain blue eyes, and plain blonde hair. At least, nobody else had ever called me names.

She lay back down on the bed, jammed her feet against the mattress above her. She kicked once, twice, three times—so hard that the mattress popped up and tumbled off the frame. It slid to the floor, and she grinned over at me.

A white-hot needle of fury pierced my heart, and I could feel tears threatening to rise up. I ran out of the room before Chantal could see them. By the time I was at the edge of the backyard and heading across the gravel road, though, she reappeared. I ignored her as she trotted beside me, all the way through the fallow vegetable garden, past the pavilion, down to the lake, then along the shore and into the woods.

Her long frizzed green hair gently flopped behind her as she jogged, and her breathing had a whine to it, like an old dog. I tried to ignore her, and thought about running faster, but I didn't want it to turn into a race. If anything was likely to turn Chantal into a rage monster, it was competition.

"You can't go to the clubhouse when the Super Tramps are there," she said as we began to navigate the brushy woods.

I didn't answer, just kept picking my way over fallen logs and thornbushes.

"They won't let you in. You have to be in the club, and you can't be until you pass the test."

I glanced at her. She jutted her chin, and her eyes glittered dangerously.

"Why do you take two vitamins?" I said.

For once, she looked taken aback. "Because none of your business."

"Do you have a disease?"

"No."

"Is it contagious?"

"No." She was getting agitated. I had done that, and it felt good. I wanted more.

"So why do you take them?"

"I just need extra vitamins, that's all. When I lived with my mom, she starved me for a week, once, and I got malnutrition. So Mrs. Bobbie gives me an extra vitamin. One you have to get from the pharmacist."

"Okay, fine. I was just asking."

She was quiet the rest of the way, and when we got to the club-house, the little hut was empty. I thought Chantal might barge in any-way, but she hung back, quiet all of a sudden. Her eyes had gone wide, her bottom lip caught in her teeth. I knocked on the door, but no one answered. She gave it one more shot.

"They aren't going to let you in."

And then they were upon us, a whirlwind of laughter and acrid smoke and sweet perfume and Bubblicious gum, breaking through the trees. The queen and her two handmaidens. Omega saw me first, then saw Chantal, and stopped. Tré and Shellie pulled up short behind her.

Omega pointed at Chantal. "You. What did I tell you?"

"She wanted to see inside the clubhouse," Chantal spat, but she was already edging her way around Tré and Shellie, giving them a wide berth. "She'll tell on you. She'll tell Mrs. Bobbie. She's a fat fuck."

"You're a fat fuck," Tré said quietly. Ominously.

Omega looked at me. "Are you going to tell Mrs. Bobbie?"

I shook my head.

"Even if we let you in but not her?" Omega said, sliding her eyes to Chantal. Her perfect lips had curved into a small smile, and I felt afraid and elated, all at once.

"She'll tell. Fat fuck," Chantal said, and Omega lunged at her. In a flash, Chantal sprang to life and took off running, up the hill, weaving around the thin saplings, slipping on the rotted leaves.

Shellie giggled. "Oh my God. Look at that little jackrabbit go."

They all started laughing then, and for a moment, I felt just the tiniest bit sorry for Chantal. But then they swept me into the genie's bottle, into the warm embrace of their laughter, and they clicked on a string of rose-colored lights (battery powered, I asked) and turned on a CD player that had only one working speaker.

They showed me everything they had hidden there (two dirty books, each with a man's oily torso on the cover; sour-cream-and-onion chips and Snickers bars from Mrs. Bobbie's stash; and a crushed package of L&M cigarettes), and told me we had to wait there for a special surprise. Then there was a rap on the moldy, split plywood door.

The surprise turned out to be Mr. Al, although I didn't quite understand what made his appearance so astonishing. He was basically our dad, after all. Surely, he knew about the clubhouse and had been down here. When the girls heard him at the door, they immediately leapt up and filed out. Tré, the last one in line, turned to me.

"Don't come outside," she said, her black eyes flashing in her white face. "I mean it."

I nodded vigorously so she knew I could be trusted. "Okay."

The door slammed shut, but I could hear their giggles and Mr. Al's low voice. And then all the sounds dropped away and I was left in the silence. I opened the book to one soft dog-eared page.

Everlane felt the heat and weight of Dex's body pressing down on her, pressing her into wet sand. She felt the crush of his chest and pelvic bones and muscled thighs against her body, the rash of his rough beard against her face, and her mouth opened involuntarily. He took the opportunity to cover her mouth with his, and she wondered if she would be able to breathe or if she would be smothered. When his tongue entered her mouth, every cell of her body melted liquid, and she realized she didn't care. "Let him crush me," she thought. "Let him obliterate all I am so I will become one with him . . .

"Hey, little one," Omega said and I looked up, startled. "You're still here?"

It felt like it had been ages since they left, but it couldn't have been longer than half an hour. Omega was standing in the open doorway, backlit by a halo of sunlight. She sauntered in, followed by Tré and Shellie. They brought with them a current of sweet-smelling smoke, and all three dropped cross-legged on the pillows scattered on the floor. They smiled and played with their hair and shirtsleeves—half-lidded, slo-mo princesses. I looked around expectantly, not really understanding but knowing something significant had changed about everyone but me.

"Ah, reading about Dex and Everlane?" Omega said.

"Did you get to the part where he does oral on her?" Tré asked. Omega swatted her. Mr. Al stuck his head in the door, took a gander around the dim room.

"All right, ladies," he said, and then zeroed in on me. His face went slack for a second or two, then he blinked and broke into a sunny smile. "Well, my goodness. Hey there, Daphne Doodle Dandy," he said. His voice was a warm, deep, twisting river, and it wound its way to me.

"Hey there," I said.

"I didn't know you were here," he said.

The Super Tramps all burst into laughter, which made no sense, since he hadn't said anything funny.

"Hush up, ladies. I'm talking to Daphne here. Look here, Miss Doodle Dandy. I'm going to go up to the house and get to work on

Bitsy's doghouse. Maybe you could help me with the painting a little later on. How would you like that?"

I nodded wordlessly.

"All right, then. Good." He flicked a glance down at the book in my hands. "And look here. If you want to go to the library sometime, I'll take you."

I set the book aside, a flush of shame creeping along my neck. I wanted him to approve of me. I wouldn't read any more about Everlane and Dex. I wouldn't read anything but books Mr. Al helped me pick out at the library.

He grinned at me and I grinned back. It was hard to explain, but, like Everlane, I felt the weight of him. Not his body, and not in any kind of a sexual way. It was instead the gentle, steady sound of his voice, his kindness, and the reassurance that he really and truly cared about me.

All of those things had weight to them. They could really mean something, something big and important, I thought, and I couldn't help but wonder what it would be like if Mr. Al was my real father.

Chapter Fifteen

I pushed myself up the mountain, not pausing for rest or even a swig of water. On the level stretches of the path, I jogged, scrambling and leaping, mountain-goat-style, over the boulder outcroppings when it steepened.

A mountain hike wasn't quite the same as a balls-out sprint around the track, but it would do in a pinch. And truthfully, my lungs felt like they were about to burst. Also, at some point, that elusive inner switch had flipped, kicking over the endlessly spinning hamster wheel and allowing my mind to settle into a quieter frequency. By the time I broke out onto the curved limestone cap that looked out over the mountain range below, my heart was thundering, my body bathed in sweat. But I felt better.

Glenys wasn't there. After I got over my disappointment, I reasoned that she was probably having a session back at the house or had other assignments to complete for the doctor. When I'd headed out, I hadn't thought of the schedule, only my claustrophobia and need to move—to get away from that creeping, oppressive house. I couldn't get my mind around how the other patients—clients—were okay to hang out in their rooms, submitting to the watchful eyes of the doctor's cameras. I wished

I'd run into one of them, even snooty Donna McAdam. I'd welcome seeing another human face about now.

I planted my hands on my knees, waiting for my breath to slow. At the edge of the brow, wind gusted, and to my left, a bank of dark clouds heaped up and roiled, dumping rain on the distant mountains. The clouds were moving this way; even now I could feel the spit of raindrops. I would have to run if I wanted to make it back without getting soaked.

My sweat chilled by the wind, I started back down the path. By the time I was descending the final slope toward the house, I was shivering. And dreaming about a cup of scalding hot chocolate, with a splash of Baileys, preferably. Maybe I could pop in on Luca in the kitchen and make a special request. I was so caught up in my plan, I didn't see the bird until I'd almost stepped on it.

It was a cuckoo—a female, I thought, a long, slim brown body with a white underside and a bright-yellow beak. Mr. Al had once pointed one out to me, sitting on the hitching post of the ranch office. He whispered that sometimes they laid their eggs in other nests. "Like us girls," I had replied. "We live in other nests too."

This bird lay in the grass, unmoving. I nudged it gently with my foot, but the body was limp. I squatted down and rolled the tiny body over gingerly. There were no puncture marks, no gashes from a cat's claw or teeth, none that I could see, but I was no veterinarian. I wondered if something had happened to it down in the bird garden and it had flown up to the lawn to die.

I scooped it up and carried it to the patio, to the long, rickety potting bench against the house. I sifted around the plastic pots and nearly empty bags of soil until I found a trowel. Then I scanned the yard, looking for a good grave site. My gaze settled on the barn. It seemed an appropriate resting place, sheltered from the wind and rain.

On the far side of the barn, hidden from the view of the house, I laid the cuckoo down and went to work. In no time, I had a perfect little rectangle about six or seven inches deep. I hoped it was deep enough. I couldn't stand the thought of a cat—or whoever the killer was—sniffing out the body and digging it up for more macabre fun.

I ripped a couple of strips of moss off the dirt, fashioning a makeshift burial shroud around the bird, then laid the pitiful package in the hole. With its head twisted to one side, it looked like it was sleeping. That was what people said about the dead, wasn't it? That they looked so peaceful. It was what they had said about Chantal, when they filed past her casket.

"I'm sorry, little one," I said, and immediately a grunting sob rose and tears sprang to my eyes. I clapped a hand over my mouth. Then both hands, even though they were crusted in dirt and dead-bird germs. What was my problem? It was just a bird, just one of a million birds who died every day. I was being dramatic.

I tamped down some loose dirt and tried to scatter some bits of grass and straw over it. Blotting the tears with my sleeve, I walked back to the house.

I paused in the middle of the yard and took a minute to suck in a lungful of cool, rain-tinged air. To brush my hands against my running tights, then gently press the swollen skin around my eyes. This place—it was making me crazy, playing on my frayed nerves, messing with my head. I didn't know how much longer I could take being trapped on the mountain. I considered asking Luca if he had any whiskey.

Then I remembered the iPad and nearly leapt with elation.

"Hell to the yes." I'd run a bath out of sight of the stupid camera and watch the dozen episodes of *The Americans* I'd downloaded a couple of weeks ago. Nothing like Russian spies wreaking havoc to get your mind off real-life ones. I pivoted and headed for the gravel drive and the Nissan.

I checked to make sure the coast was clear, then slipped between the cars. I pulled at the Nissan's door handle, but it was locked. Stepping back, I stared, perplexed. I'd left it unlocked yesterday, I knew I had. I scanned the backyard. Empty. But maybe Dr. Cerny had seen me out here. Maybe he'd waited for me to head up the mountain and come back to lock the car.

Or somebody else had done it. You didn't need the actual key, you could also just manually punch down the old-school lock. But why would somebody do that—other than to mess with me?

I jogged back to the house. In the empty kitchen, I helped myself to a whiskey soda. I knocked half of it back, then poured another slug. Snagging a half-finished bottle of Chardonnay from the fridge, I made my escape into the hallway. On my way past the doctor's office, I peered through the French doors. The sunroom was dark and quiet. I tucked the bottle of wine under my arm and tried the door. Locked.

The front of the house was quiet as well—the salon, library, and dining room all doused in darkness from the approaching clouds. I climbed the stairs and let myself into our suite.

There was no sign of Heath having returned to the room after lunch. Our bed was made and the room looked like it had been freshly vacuumed. I set the bottle of wine aside and headed to the bathroom, whiskey in hand. I was already warmer, pleasantly loose limbed.

I soaked until the whiskey was gone and the bathwater was cold. I dressed, then grabbed the Chardonnay and headed out into the hall, surprised to find our dinner tray outside our door. I hadn't realized it had gotten so late. Both the McAdams' and Siefferts' doors were shut, but their trays had already been collected. I tapped on the Siefferts' door.

"Glenys? It's Daphne. I was just wondering . . ." I cradled the wine. "Would you like to come hang out in my room? I've got a nice Chardonnay, if you like Chardonnay. I wasn't sure."

No answer.

I tried the knob. Locked.

Where was she? It was like the house had swallowed them whole, left me to knock around the empty rooms. I crept past the McAdams' closed door to the end of the hall, where I pushed open the pocket door and eased into Dr. Cerny's nook. His door was open, the room beyond it dark but seeming to offer an invitation.

I didn't know what I expected to find, but it looked to me like a pretty normal apartment. There was a bed (queen size, with a gray duvet), a dresser, a small desk and chair, all gleaming Victorian antiques. Also, by the window, there was a wardrobe. A beautifully carved piece, inlaid with glossy burled walnut, with cherubs flitting across the top portion. I set the bottle of wine down, swung open the door, and plunged my hands into the dark depths. Silk, cashmere, wool. I pulled out one shirt, a soft cream woman's blouse with black pearl buttons.

I moved to inspect the desk and sleek computer. I jiggled the mouse, and the screen lit up.

Counting compulsion—true OCD? Or connected to childhood food hoarding/fixation?

Possibly deprived of regular, healthful nutrition until age 11.

Childhood obesity? Excessive exercise, orthorexia?

Comorbid psychiatric issues?

I felt my face redden. So Dr. Cerny was taking notes on me—or, rather, my secret habits, which weren't such a secret after all, apparently. I shouldn't be surprised. He was a psychologist and undoubtedly connected the dots that first night when he caught me in the pantry. And of course Heath had told him I'd been a state kid. But none of that made it feel any less invasive, any less of a violation.

Feeling sick, I minimized the document, and a series of images filled the screen. The window that was already open behind the other document.

I stopped breathing.

Jesus.

It was shocking to see our room this way, viewed from nine differ-ent angles by nine different cameras. But that was definitely what I was looking at—our room. Cerny had a whole different surveillance setup for our room. Something way more modern and vastly more extensive. Just for us.

My God . . .

Reggie had been very specific about how there was just one camera, one camera that we were to pretend didn't exist. I minimized the win-dow, revealing the desktop screen and a row of four files labeled with numbers and letters. I enlarged the program again and pulled down the main menu. Nine cams and no indication of more. So nothing in the McAdams' and Siefferts' rooms, unless I was missing something.

I was standing there trying to absorb it all when I heard a sound. The distant wail of a trumpet, coming from somewhere down the hall. I froze, straining to hear it again. A moment passed and the sound disap-peared, but I waited, holding my breath, and it returned. The trumpet. And singing. A man singing.

I headed toward the sound. Out on the shadowy landing, I shut Cerny's door gently behind me, then turned and yelped in shock.

Luca was standing a couple of feet away, beside the attic stairs. There was a doorway behind him, one I hadn't noticed before. An under-the-stairs, Harry Potter kind of door.

"Luca," I said. "You scared me."

We stared at each other, the smoky, sultry voice of Sinatra filling the space between us, then both started to speak—

"I got turned around," I said.

"Vim para sua bandeja," he said.

Sinatra hit a high note, and, in tandem, we looked down the hall on the other side of the pocket door. Luca put a finger to his lips. He motioned for me to follow, and we crept through the doorway and into the hall, stopping at the McAdams' door.

In the dark, our eyes met, and I leaned against the door to listen. The next song started. It took a minute for the notes to register—the clarinet and piano and cymbals—before the memory crystallized in my brain. That song "Why Can't You Behave?" The one that had been playing that night in the restaurant, when Heath had joked about Sinatra being a deal breaker. And here we were in this weird red house, stuck halfway up a mountain, and the exact same song was playing in the McAdams' room.

Suddenly, over the music, I heard voices. Two of them, floating up the staircase, a man and a woman. Cerny and Glenys, maybe? I couldn't be sure, but it definitely sounded like they were fighting. I tiptoed to the banister, careful to keep out of sight.

". . . doesn't matter," the man was saying. Dr. Cerny, it sounded like. "And this is neither the time nor the place."

I could only hear fragments of the woman's response. ". . . manipulating you," she said. "Why can't you see that? The Hawthorne Effect changes everything . . ."

Luca put a hand on my arm, and I jumped. He was beside me, his hand warm through the sleeve of my pullover. He gave me a little push toward my room. I moved in that direction, but when I looked back, he was already closing the pocket door behind him. I stopped, straining to hear the rest of the conversation.

"Go, lie down," Cerny was saying. "We'll talk when you feel better."

I couldn't hear all of Glenys's reply, only the last few words. ". . . you've taken away from me . . ." But there was nothing more, and after a few minutes, I hurried back to my room. It was only after I'd slammed the door and changed into my pajamas that I remembered the bottle of Chardonnay. I'd left it in Cerny's room.

By late September, I'd heard all about the fall camping trip. Along with the director of the boys' ranch forty miles away, Mr. Cleve, the girls' ranch director, organized it every year and used it as a carrot for good behavior. Every girl wanted to go—every girl did her chores, kept up her grades, and refused to sneak out of Sunday school in order to be allowed to go. We in the brown brick house were no exception.

Every house from the ranch except the baby house went. We all packed tents and sleeping bags the church had donated and drove up in white vans to a public campground in north Georgia. Amicalola Falls. A wildly beautiful place, Mr. Cleve announced at Vespers, with a set of creaky stairs that scaled the rocky face of the waterfall.

Even Omega admitted it was the prettiest place she'd ever seen.

The festivities would kick off at one of the park's picnic pavilions. The director, Cleve, would lead prayer, then everybody from the boys' and girls' ranches would eat lunch. After that there would be a time of what Mrs. Bobbie called "fellowship," which consisted of a bunch of super-lame (according to Omega) team-building games while the older boys and girls did the important work of scoping each other out and figuring out who was going to meet up later that night. The ranches would split up then. Mr. Al and Mr. Barry would take the girls hiking up the mountain one way, and the boys' leaders would head in the opposite direction.

Separate campsites would keep us in "the pure zone," Mrs. Bobbie said, although, from what Omega and the other Super Tramps told me, a couple of girls had once been intercepted on their way out of camp after curfew. Also, one boy had gotten lost on his way to meet up with a girl. Deep in the woods, he'd run smack into a black-bear cub and its mama and gotten so scared he'd started screaming at the top of his lungs. The next morning, before anyone woke up, that boy's housefather marched him down the mountain and drove him all the way back to the ranch.

"Those ranch boys may sneak out, but it's not because they're getting any of this." Omega leaned forward and shimmied, and her boobs practically fell out of her shirt.

"Hey!" Mrs. Bobbie snapped, banging her fork on the table. Mr. Al said nothing.

"Most of them guys are as gay as my Aunt Fannie. They don't need to sneak out, long as they get a cute tentmate." She had a sly expression on her face. Mrs. Bobbie looked like she was about to burst into righteous flames.

Two weeks before the camping trip, Chantal and I were in the tiny, mildewy laundry room off the garage, doing the weekly load for the house. Chantal held up a pair of rainbow-striped cotton panties and danced them in my face.

"Hi! I'm Omega and I shake my smelly ass in front of all the boys because I think they all want to have sexy-wexy with me!"

I kept shoveling clothes from the basket into the washer. She reached around me again, extracting another pair of underpants. These were plain white cotton—mine. She inspected them coolly, then grinned at me.

"Just what I thought. Skid marks." She pinched her nose. "What's the matter, Daffy Duck, you can't hold in your poop at school?" She started a jig around the room, waving the threadbare cotton, and my face burned. "Hey, look at me," she crowed. "I'm Daffy Duck, and I shit my pants. I'm just a fat fuck baby who poops her little-girl panties."

I couldn't bring myself to look close enough to see if she was telling the truth, but it didn't matter. The thought of Chantal telling everyone at school was mortifying enough. I swiped at the underwear and tossed it in the washer with the rest of the clothes. Chantal dumped in an overflowing scoop of soap powder.

"Hey," I said. "That's way too much. You're gonna get us in trouble."

Her other arm lashed out so fast I didn't see it coming, but the backhand sent me reeling into the set of wire shelves where Mrs. Bobbie kept her cleaning supplies. A wire protruding from one shelf dug into my skin, and a thin stream of blood spiraled down my arm and dripped onto my favorite olive-green capris.

"Whoops," Chantal said, then widened her buggy multicolored eyes at me. She yanked open the dryer door, grabbed a dry shirt, and started dabbing it on my arm.

"Hey, stop!" I said and backed away. "That's my shirt." And it was, my favorite pink sleeveless baby-doll top that I'd found in the castoff closet. But the damage was already done. She threw the shirt into the washer with the rest of the clothes and banged the lid shut. I stood there, the scratch on my arm throbbing.

"Blood comes out, you doofus." She twisted the dial and pulled it out, and I heard water gush into the machine. "Quit being such a baby."

Back in our room, I tried not to cry. I only had three good shirts, and one of them was too short and showed my stomach if I had to reach up for something. Now my favorite top had a bloodstain on it. Great, just great. Not that any of the ranch girls had fabulous wardrobes to begin with, but I dreaded the necessary trip to the clothes closet in the main office. Those clothes smelled funny and looked like they'd come from a thrift shop in the 1970s. To keep myself from crying, I cursed Chantal in my head, using every evil word I could think of.

Pizza Face, Fat Fuck, Egg Salad.

Jackrabbit.

Devil Eyes.

Nobody.

When I returned to the laundry room, she had folded the clean clothes neatly, stacked them, and told me she would take care of the remaining load. I stood there, unsure of what to say, waiting for I didn't know what—another insult, a good reason for me to fly at her and slap her. But she only smiled and handed over my stack of warm clothes, which made me positive, beyond a shadow of a doubt, things weren't over between us.

Chapter Sixteen

I woke sometime later in the night, overheated and drooling. My neck was twisted in such a way that I knew, instinctively, that I was going to feel it for days. We might be catching up on our sleep in this creepy old house—enjoying the respite from Heath's nightmares—but I didn't feel any more rested.

I just felt uneasy. About the nine extra cameras that were watching us at all times. And the creepy Sinatra music playing in the McAdams' room.

Heath was sitting in one of the chairs by the fireplace. He wasn't doing anything in particular, just staring into the middle distance. A feeling of disquiet—a premonition, maybe, of something to come—stole over me. I wanted to reach out to him, to comfort him. But I couldn't make myself do it. I sat up, clutching the bedcovers to my chest.

Heath shifted in the chair. "I'm sorry I woke you." His voice was so gentle, so soft, that the fear in my heart was almost quelled.

"It's okay. I don't mind."

"What did you do this afternoon?"

I kept my voice light. "You're looking at it. Nothing much. You?"

He just shook his head.

"Heath. What's going on?"

He was running his finger along the arm of the chair. Watching the movement, fascinated by the journey of his own hand. Or maybe he just didn't want to talk to me. I didn't know whether to feel relief or concern. It seemed like everything that happened here divided me.

His finger stopped on the curve of the chair arm, and his back bent. It looked like he'd suddenly been struck with a pain in his stomach. He stayed there a moment, hunched and still, and then I heard a sound. It took me a minute to figure out what was happening, but when I did, I almost couldn't believe it. He was crying.

I didn't know what to do. Should I go to him? Try and comfort him in some way or just hang back and let him alone? I clenched the covers in my fists and did nothing.

He was really weeping now. Convulsing heaves punctuated by pathetic wails. I resisted the tears that rose to my own eyes.

"Heath," I said. "What's wrong?"

He didn't look at me, didn't even seem to notice I'd spoken. But at the sound of my voice, his sobs lessened some. Eventually, they wound down to sniffs and then there was complete quiet. He finally faced me. Leaned forward, lacing his fingers together.

"I'm not who you think I am," he said.

The panic slammed into me with a force that took my breath. And then my next thought, *Not in front of the cameras.*

But I couldn't think about that. If this was really happening, if Heath was finally going to talk to me, Cerny's secret backup cameras were beside the point. I threw off the blanket and crawled off the bed. Knelt at the chair and grabbed his hands. He gripped mine back so tightly that a fresh wave of panic sluiced through me.

"I'm not good for you," Heath said. "You deserve—"

"No." I shook his hands. "I love you. I love you more than you could ever know, and whatever you had to do to survive, I understand.

And I forgive you, without even having to know what it was. That's how much I love you."

He pressed his lips into a tight line. I could tell he wasn't convinced. "I won't judge you, I swear. I had to do things to survive too."

"You don't understand—"

"Please, stop. Just listen to me." I pressed his hands to my chest. I was sure he could feel my heart racing.

And then, I suddenly knew. I was going to do it.

I am going to tell him everything.

"I did a terrible thing," I said. "It was a long time ago, but it changed everything. And to survive, to stay sane and function in the world, I had to keep it a secret."

I didn't know what I expected him to do. Leap out of the chair? Faint with shock? Suddenly regard me with disgust? Whatever dramatic reaction I'd imagined, he didn't do any of them. He just studied my face like it held a secret he wished he could be privy to.

"You're an angel," he said.

"I'm not." I shook off his hand. "I'm . . ."

. . . half-savage and hardy, and free . . .

"You are an angel," he repeated dully. "You're trying to make me feel better. And I love you for it."

"You don't know what I've done." I tried not to think of Cerny's high-tech spy cameras consuming my pain, crushing it to ones and zeros and storing it until the doctor decided to watch it.

"What? You stole a pack of gum at the dollar store? You cheated on a chemistry exam? You had unprotected teenage sex behind the bleachers with a boy everybody told you to stay away from?" His expression grew distant. "This is different. If I told you this, you'd leave. I know you would."

"You're not Jeffrey Dahmer, are you?"

He shot me a rueful smile.

"See? We're good."

The wind buffeted the glass panes, the loose joints and eaves of the house. I could feel the pressure inside me, building. We'd both kept our secrets, kept the doors shut and locked tight. And now, I had the worst feeling that those doors were about to burst wide open. That our secrets—beasts with claws and fangs and foul breath that had grown in the dark and transformed into something hideous—were on the verge of escaping.

He spoke again, his voice deliberate. "I don't know where we go from here, Daphne. I don't know how to go forward anymore. I've done things I'm ashamed of. I am a fraud. A *perpetrator*."

His face was still, a mask of calm, his eyes glittering in the semi-darkness. He didn't look ashamed. He looked unflinching.

"I used to think I could be in a marriage where we kept secrets," he said. "I don't anymore. I know we're both scared as hell to do this, but one of us has to bite the bullet. One of us has to lead the way."

There was a moment of quiet, then I spoke in a low voice. "I'll do it."

"Really?" He looked surprised. "That's what you want?"

Yes. It was what I wanted. Finally, after all this time of covering up and running from the truth, I wanted to show Heath who I really was. I saw then, in the darkness, the way his lip curled up and his head tilted to one side, and I knew it was what he wanted too. This moment would draw us even closer, our dark confessions. This moment would bind us forever.

He was ready to hear my story. And I was ready to tell it.

"I killed someone," I began, my voice trembling. "I hid the evidence, and no one ever knew."

Chapter Seventeen

I found out the meaning behind Chantal's smile a couple of days later, when Mrs. Bobbie called Omega and me back to her bedroom.

Earlier that afternoon, the ranch girls had spilled out of the bus and streamed down the long red-clay drive, ready to get down to the business of the weekend. We'd slung off our backpacks in our bedrooms and scattered to our own activities for a few hours. Fridays were chore-free. For Omega, that meant trooping off with the other Super Tramps, toward the lake and the clubhouse.

For me, it meant figuring out wherever Chantal happened to be and making sure I was as far away from that place as humanly possible. Sometimes that was the clubhouse, but the last couple of times I'd gone down there, Mr. Al had shown up, and Omega had told me to scram. I was happy enough to comply. I'd made a chart for myself of all the books I'd finished since Mr. Al had first taken me to the enormous library in Macon after we'd gone to pick up my new glasses. *Harry Potter and the Sorcerer's Stone* was my seventeenth. And anyway, I'd spied on them before, and all they ever did was sit around and smoke lumpy-looking cigarettes.

Our small Christian school's puny football team was playing a nearby public school that night, and Mrs. Bonnie had promised that Mr. Al would load all us girls in his ancient minivan and take us to the game. Not only that, she said we could swing by the pizza parlor with the old-fashioned pinball machines beforehand. But around four o'clock, when I saw Omega and Mr. Al approaching me where I sat cross-legged on the dock with *Harry Potter*, my gut flip-flopped nervously.

Omega's head hung low and her eyes kept to the ground. I didn't think I'd ever seen her like that—she usually had such a defiant tilt to her chin. Alarm rippled through me, even though they were still several yards away. All my foster-kid alarms were going off, in fact, readying me for fight or flight. I closed the book, laid it to one side, and I scrambled up. Began methodically popping my knuckles, one by one.

"Hey, Daphne-Doodle-Do," Mr. Al said when they reached the dock. "I need you to come on up with me to the house. Mrs. Bobbie wants to talk to y'all for a minute."

I glanced at Omega, but didn't move. Omega was staring at the ground, her shoulders hunched into her hoodie like she wanted to disappear.

"What about?"

"Come on now," Mr. Al said. "It'll be over before you know it."

Which must've meant he didn't know what this was all about either. But that wasn't a surprise. It hadn't taken me but a week at the ranch to figure out that Mrs. Bobbie was the ringmaster and Mr. Al was the clown that cleaned up the elephant poop. Now that I thought about it, he was looking every bit as miserable as Omega.

My palms pricked with adrenaline. I wondered if the trouble was about what Mr. Al and the Super Tramps did outside the clubhouse. I didn't know any specifics, but maybe Mrs. Bobbie had suspicions and she wanted me as a witness. I didn't want to tell on anybody, but I also didn't want to make Mrs. Bobbie my enemy.

My mother was long gone. Never coming back for me—that's what the social worker and lawyer had told me as they'd driven me to the ranch in the lawyer's shiny red car, which smelled like Christmas trees and hot plastic. The courts had signed parental rights over to the ranch until I turned eighteen, and because they were designated as only a "children's institution," they didn't have the legal authority to place me for adoption. I'd stay here until then, and afterward get to go to college, maybe, if I made good grades and one of the state schools awarded me a scholarship. Omega said there were tons of scholarships out there, that she was probably going to go to FIT up in New York, then get a job in fashion design.

If I betrayed the Super Tramps, they'd never let me back in the clubhouse, and I'd be left to handle Chantal on my own. On the other hand, if Mrs. Bobbie wasn't happy with my answers, she might send me to a different house—maybe the blue-shingled one at the other end of the road where Mr. Barry, an ex-marine, woke the girls up at four thirty every morning before school and made them do exercises, then cook their own breakfast. Or I could be sent back to my caseworker. Even though she hadn't returned to check on me since she dropped me off, that didn't mean she wouldn't take me to another group home. I'd heard about those homes where the people took in foster kids for the money.

That fat fuck. Chantal must've done this. She must've tattled to Mrs. Bobbie about the clubhouse or what went on in the woods or something. She was the cause of this—she was the cause of all my problems, the root of all evil. That fat, ugly, mean fuck. I wanted to shove the heel of my hand right into her stupid upturned nose, a move that I'd heard could kill a person.

I could kill her. The words made my scalp prickle deliciously and the adrenaline surge from my hands all the way through me. The simple thought of Chantal being dead settled my nervous stomach. I wrapped my arms around my torso, tucked my book under my arm, and followed Mr. Al and Omega up to the house. I wasn't scared any longer. A new power nestled safely inside me, a hard little nut no one could crack.

Fat fuck, I repeated silently to myself the whole way up to the house. Not the whiny way Chantal said it to me, but the way Tré and Shellie had flung it casually over their shoulders at me the first couple of days I was at the ranch. Just an afterthought, a bad girl's inside joke. And then it hit me—the name-callers had only been Tré and Shellie. Omega had never said anything mean to me, not one thing, not once. She'd intimidated the hell out of me, but she'd only ever spoken to me in a kind way.

Warmth filled me, an unreasonable optimism. We'd stand together against Mrs. Bobbie, whatever happened. Omega was my friend. My sister.

Mr. Al ushered us into the bedroom, where Mrs. Bobbie sat at her sewing table, a huge swath of gauzy mauve fabric cascading around her chair and over her lap. She was in charge of making all the pillows and curtains for all the houses at the ranch. She kept her back to us, the whir of the machine filling the air. I wondered for a brief, wild moment if there was a new girl already on her way to replace me, and these were the new curtains for her room. Chantal and I had white plastic blinds. Maybe Mrs. Bobbie thought the new girl should have curtains.

"Thank you," Mrs. Bobbie sniffed at Mr. Al. "You can go, hon. And don't let them girls hang around outside the door. We need privacy." She flicked her hand at him, then went back to arranging the fabric under the needle, folding and pushing and smoothing the material. Her thick French-manicured nails tapped on the machine. Mr. Al nodded at me and Omega. When the door clicked shut behind him, I attempted to catch Omega's eye. She wouldn't look at me.

Mrs. Bobbie turned to us, her blue eyes wide. They looked like doll's eyes, flat, expressionless. Empty. "Ladies," she declared. "Do you know why you've been invited back here, to my private rooms?"

She said it like her bedroom and bath comprised a whole wing of Versailles.

We shook our heads dumbly, and the woman heaved an enormous, pained sigh.

"Because what we have to discuss is very"—she glared at me, then Omega—"very private." Then, reaching under the avalanche of neatly arranged fabric, she drew out a pair of rainbow-striped girls' underwear. She held them aloft between two fingers, her face puckered in distaste. "What is this?"

"They're underpants," I piped up, eager to set things right, sooner rather than later. Mr. Al and Mrs. Bobbie's bedroom smelled funny. And I couldn't help looking at the bed and wondering what went on in it. I knew about sex, but I couldn't imagine sweet, puppyish Al doing things like that to shellacked Mrs. Bobbie with her perfect hair-sprayed hair and enormous boobs. "They're Omega's underpa . . ."

My voice trailed off. Omega's face was a stone, and Mrs. Bobbie was smirking. I glanced from one to the other, struggling for a foothold.

"Give them back," Omega growled. Her ominous tone made me shrink inside.

"Not until you explain what they were doing in her"—at this point she waved the panties in my direction—"backpack. They were found in Daphne's backpack with this message written on them." Bobbie looked at the panties and read theatrically: "9-27 midnight." She looked at Omega. "That's the night of the camping trip, isn't it? September twenty-seventh. Daphne, did you promise to deliver these underpants to someone? To a boy?"

Omega pivoted and leveled her destroying laser-beam stare at me. Like she'd flipped a switch, I began to shake. "I don't know how they got in my backpack. I've never seen them." I thought back to the last time I'd had laundry duty with Chantal. Her smile as she'd sent me on my way.

"Yes, you do," snapped Mrs. Bobbie. "You know and you're gonna tell me right now or I swear, I will snatch you up and march you down the drive and cut you loose." She shook the panties some more and they danced like a puppet. Omega pressed her lips together—her beautiful, perfect bright-pink lips—and kept her narrowed eyes on me. They paralyzed me. I guessed she wanted to know how I'd ended up with a pair of her panties as much as Mrs. Bobbie did.

"You want me to cut you loose, little girl?" Mrs. Bobbie bellowed. "Is that what you want?"

I shook my head. I could feel warmth beginning to creep into my neck, the tears rising. I thought I might throw up as well. And now I had to pee really bad.

"Jesus wants you to tell the truth, Daphne. Don't you know that?"

I didn't, not on any kind of literal level, but I nodded my head anyway.

"Jesus don't want me to turn you out on the road, because there's all sorts of things—people—out there who don't necessarily care about a little girl's purity. They do awful things to little girls out there. Shoot them. Stab them. Choke them with ropes. Tie them up with duct tape and throw them in the back of the trunks of their cars and drive them to the woods—"

Omega cleared her throat, and Mrs. Bobbie shut her mouth abruptly.

"I didn't . . ." I began. But I couldn't finish. I honestly could not conjure up a lie that would satisfy Mrs. Bobbie and get both of us off the hook.

"Chantal told me," Mrs. Bobbie spit out, growing impatient with her interrogation.

At that, even Omega looked dumbfounded.

"Told you what?" I asked.

"Don't play games with me, missy!" Mrs. Bobbie screamed. Then she collected herself, dabbed at the liner smudge beneath her blue shadow-ringed eyes. "I know you're protecting her." She flapped the panties in Omega's direction. "Daphne was supposed to deliver your panties to a *boy*. As a *message*"—now the underwear snapped in my direction—"and I *caught* you."

Omega was silent. I was silent. Mrs. Bobbie looked overwrought.

"I'm only glad your sin was exposed before you had the chance to follow it through." She drew in a tremulous breath. Stood. "Omega. I have had my fill of your whoring behavior. Your whoring and sneaking and laughing. Your *attitudes*."

The room suddenly felt so warm, so filled with hate, I couldn't breathe.

Mrs. Bobbie jabbed her finger in Omega's direction. "You listen to me and you listen well, missy. You will not agree to meet a boy. You will not so much as *look* at a boy until you leave this house. You are a child, not an adult. Sex is for the sanctity of marriage. For two married adults such as Mr. Al and myself. It belongs in the marriage bed, not out in the woods, in the *dirt*. Am I clear?"

She was inches from Omega now, and I saw clearly Mrs. Bobbie was wrong. Omega was an adult and this was an argument not between a woman and child, but between two peers of equal standing, each with their own particular weapons of warfare. I also recognized I had no idea what this battle was being fought over. I just knew I didn't have a part to play in it. I didn't belong here, and I wanted out.

"I'm sorry, Mrs. Bobbie," I said. She didn't look at me.

Omega grabbed the panties. Her face was burning but her eyes were grim. She turned, as if about to leave.

"No camping trip," Mrs. Bobbie shrilled at her back. "Neither of you. You'll both stay behind. Here with me, to do chores."

Omega hesitated for a fraction of a second, then wrenched open the door and stormed out. I waited a moment longer, wringing my hands, wondering if I was dismissed, or if I should stomp out like Omega. Mrs. Bobbie didn't even bother to look at me. She sank on the bed, her fingers picking imaginary lint from her pilled black trousers. Smoothed and cupped her hair. Smoothed and cupped, smoothed and cupped.

"There you go," she croaked. But I didn't think she even realized I was still standing there. "See how you like that, Mr. Sneaking Off to the Woods."

I crept out as quietly as I could and went and climbed into my top bunk. I fell asleep and slept through the pizza and the football game. But it turned out it didn't matter, because Omega and I had been forbidden from going to that too.

Chapter Eighteen

"Go away," Omega said.

I was lurking in the doorway of her room, gazing at her the way Bitsy looked at us through the dining-room window when we sat down to supper. I'd been circling her all weekend, far enough away not to aggravate her, close enough to gauge her mood. So far, she'd acted like I was invisible. Now it was Sunday night—fifteen minutes until lights out—and I was desperate. Somehow I sensed that if I did not repair whatever it was that had broken between us before Monday morning, she and the rest of the Super Tramps would be lost to me forever.

"I know who did it—" I started.

She twisted around, her face a thundercloud. "I said get out!"

I darted away before she got really mad and chucked a book or something more substantial at me. Back in my room, I knelt on the floor, pulled out my backpack, and went through my binders and books, smoothing and sorting every homework paper and book report and math worksheet. I checked and double-checked to make sure I'd completed every assignment for the upcoming week.

Sometimes I thought I was just like Mrs. Bobbie, with the organizing. Smooth and cup. Smooth and cup.

Every now and then, I would stop and chew one of my already-ragged nails until a tiny bead of blood would bubble out. Like the papers, my thoughts shuffled themselves in order of importance in my head, then flew apart and reshuffled. But on the inside, I could feel something winding tighter and tighter, like a coil. Mrs. Bobbie might be annoying, but she wasn't dumb. She had to know Omega would never send her underwear to one of the boys at school. There were plenty of reasons:

All of the boys at Mount Olive Christian were greasy haired and acted weird when they got around the Super Tramps, whooping and giggling and clobbering each other like a bunch of chimpanzees.

None of us girls had more than three or four pairs of underwear to begin with, and even those we had to wash in the sink just to have enough to make it through the school week.

If Omega was going to give a boy her panties, I'd seen enough TV to know she would never, ever give him a faded-out pair like that. She'd give him filmy, delicate, lacy panties—the kind none of us had ever owned and, if we did, we sure wouldn't throw away on some greasy-haired chimpanzee.

Even if Mrs. Bobbie was dumb enough to think Omega had done that, Omega *knew* I hadn't done anything. So why wouldn't she speak to me? Why was she angry? Didn't she understand we were both being falsely accused?

She had to know Chantal had set the whole thing up. Omega knew everything that went on in this house. She ran the place. Orchestrated every event that went on inside these walls, every change in temperature, every passing storm, every ray of sun.

I knew somehow, even though I was young, that it had to do with the fact that Mr. Al liked to hang out at the clubhouse with us. That must have made Mrs. Bobbie really jealous. Which made sense but also seemed odd to me, because Mrs. Bobbie was an adult who could do anything she wanted. We girls got stretched-out hand-me-downs and mac and cheese out of the box, and she got weekly manicures, bubble baths, and Pepperidge Farm cookies. Plus, she and Mr. Al had been married for a long time, over ten years, I thought. Seemed like she wouldn't mind him spending an hour or two with the kids he was house dad to. That was his job.

I shoved my binder in my book bag, rocked back on my heels, and pushed my new glasses up my nose. I had to do something—something big and real to prove to Omega that I'd never betray her. To make her know that her friendship was more important to me than anything else in the world. But I would wait until the time was right, like I'd done with Chantal and the stolen food. I would wait until an opportunity presented itself, then I would make my move.

I went to sleep easily that night—Chantal's regular jolts didn't bother me. Her whispers—*Fat Fuck, Four Eyes, Egg Salad*—barely registered as I nestled deep into the warm covers. The girl was beneath me in a literal sense and a figurative one too, I thought with satisfaction. And she would be sorry for ruining my friendships with Omega and Shellie and Tré. She would be very, very sorry.

Two weeks later, we had a brilliant blue-sky October Saturday morning. Orange leaves drifted and the smell of far-off smoke in the cool air lent an air of expectancy. For most of the girls, the anticipation had everything to do with the camping trip.

For me, it meant destroying Chantal.

Mrs. Bobbie had assigned Omega and me a list of chores as long as our arms. Omega had torn the list, thrust half of it at me, and gone to work spraying Lysol on the grout in Mrs. Bobbie's pink bathroom without even a glance my way.

She was still mad. But she'd also stopped talking to Tré and Shellie, which made me feel somewhat better. I was more determined than ever to bring our leader back to life. To see the spark in her eyes again. To hear the house filled with her mocking laughter. Things had grown so gloomy.

I'd found an excuse to walk to the main office—picking up a box of fabric that had been sent to Mrs. Bobbie from some church in Atlanta—and was dawdling near the small parking lot. I was wearing a new sweater—pale-blue angora with a white stripe across the chest. Well, it wasn't new. It was one Omega had outgrown and thrown into the box in the hallway closet. I'd seen her do it one afternoon, and the minute she'd disappeared back inside her room, I'd tiptoed down the hall and fished it out. Now, I ran my fingers lightly over a downy sleeve. The day was too warm for it, but I didn't care. I felt like the new Daphne wearing it.

I watched the girls who were going on the camping trip swarm around the three white vans parked in the lot. They dropped their duffels and sleeping bags and pillows in a pile that grew rapidly. They clumped in groups, one or two separating and joining another group, chattering excitedly. They didn't seem to notice me, and I didn't join them or wave or anything. I wasn't mad or even really disappointed anymore about missing the trip. I was thinking.

This wouldn't be my big moment. I hadn't come up with that one yet—the final, glorious act of revenge that would bring Chantal to her knees and show her she'd better never mess with me again. But the camping trip . . . it did provide an opportunity.

I went inside the office and told Miss Lacey, the lady who answered the phones and sorted the mail, that I was there to pick up Mrs. Bobbie's package. She went into the back to get it, and I glanced around the office. It was done up in a Western theme, with horseshoes hung on the wall and cactus plants in pots. The curtains were made of red bandanas stitched together. By Mrs. Bobbie, probably.

A large omelet flecked with bits of orange cheese and pink ham sat on a paper plate, a few bites taken out of it by Miss Lacey. I heard a thump from the back room and quickly lunged forward, scooping up a handful of egg and cheese and ham and dropping it into the pocket of my jeans.

Miss Lacey reentered the room, box first, huffing. "Can you carry this all the way home, Daphne?" she asked. "It's a booger."

"Yes, ma'am."

I took the box and pushed against the front door with my rear end. The sun nearly blinded me. It really was too hot for this sweater. I set the box down on the porch and leaned against the hitching post. The mountain of camping gear had grown substantially, and now there were two houseparents milling around the vans too. Mr. Barry, the marine, and his wife, Mrs. Vessa.

I approached one group of squealing girls. They sobered when they saw me.

"Sorry you can't go," one of them said. Her name was Tiffany J. There were two other Tiffanys in her house, Tiffany L. and Tiffany B. The other girls all clucked sympathetically and said how unfair it was. How Omega and the other Super Tramps were mean and ruined everything for everybody. I nodded and glanced toward the pile of gear. Mr. Barry, Mrs. Vessa, and the rest of the adults were gathered at the rear of the vans, discussing something animatedly.

I moved to the pile. Chantal's frayed backpack was toward the bottom. It had been red once, but was now bleached out to an uneven pink. On the back, with a black marker, Chantal had written *NSYNC in big block letters. Probably the same marker she'd used to write on Omega's underwear, that jackrabbit. That Devil Eyes. That big bunch of Nothing with a capital N.

I scooped the omelet from my pocket, crouched, unzipped the pack. Inside, I felt clothing—a sweatshirt, a pair of jeans, and some underwear. A brush and a tube of toothpaste. I smeared the egg over it all, really smashing it in good. Then, at the bottom of the backpack, my fingers closed around a plastic bottle—the kind you got in a pharmacy. *Ha!* Chantal's vitamins. I pulled it out and stuffed it in my pocket.

I looked furtively over one shoulder, then stood. The girls had migrated to the office porch and were pushing the porch swing and singing some song from the radio. Chantal had joined them and, as usual, was shouting over them, bossing them around. She hadn't even noticed me yet or she'd be over here, running her stupid mouth. I squatted again, pulled Chantal's sweatshirt out of her pack, then zipped it up and shoved the pack under the bottom of the pile.

I thought of Chantal shivering in her sleeping bag up at the falls, wondering if she'd dropped her sweatshirt on the way up the mountain. I grinned, then bit my lip. She'd wonder what happened to her vitamins too. I didn't know how bad she'd feel without them—maybe she'd just get weak, feel sick or dizzy and have to sit out some of the activities. I hoped she'd feel miserable the whole weekend. That would teach her. And sometime later, after she'd been back for a while, I'd leave the medicine bottle on her bunk, for her to find. Then she'd know who was boss. She'd be sorry she messed with me.

I stood and fluffed out the sweater over the bottle in my pocket. The sweatshirt I tossed under the closest van, then shuffled over to the porch and retrieved Mrs. Bobbie's box, feeling the gaze of the girls. As I walked away, I heard someone call out.

"Have a nice weekend, Daphne Doodle-Do."

I turned. It was Chantal.

When I got back to the house, I dropped off the box outside Mrs. Bobbie's bedroom door and ran to my room, where I put the pills on Chantal's bed.

I hadn't bothered to read the label on the bottle or to even consider that Chantal had not told me the truth about the pills or why she had to take them. Even if I had seen the word on the label—*Depakote*—it still wouldn't have meant a thing to me.

I wouldn't have known that it was not a vitamin at all, nor that it wasn't prescribed for girls with malnutrition, but for people who suffered from epileptic seizures.

Chapter Nineteen

After I finished talking, Heath spoke. "What happened to her? To Chantal?"

We'd migrated to the bed and were lying on our sides—bodies aligned, heads propped on our arms, faces inches apart. Heath smoothed a lock of hair from my face. His breath smelled of mint and wine. His eyes were fastened on me. They hadn't left my face the whole time I'd been talking.

"She got sick. Up on the mountain, on the camping trip, the first night. She had wandered away, they think maybe looking for Tré and Shellie. She had a seizure and fell off a cliff. There was a search party. They found her the next day. Her body."

He just stared at me.

"Say it," I said. "Say what you're thinking. It was my fault."

"You thought they were vitamins, Daphne. You didn't realize what you were doing."

"No. I knew. Somewhere . . . somewhere inside, I knew. And I wanted something terrible to happen to her."

He was quiet. Still studying me with that look that cut through my very soul. But I couldn't stand it. I didn't want him looking at me that way—full of pity or judgment or whatever it was he was feeling. I turned so I couldn't see his face.

"What happened then?"

I rolled onto my back and laced my hands over my chest. "The police questioned everyone who was there on the trip. The kids from Piney Woods and Maranatha. All the houseparents. Then they showed up at the house. They just talked to Mrs. Bobbie, though, I think just to find out if she knew where the pills were. No reason to talk to me and Omega, since we hadn't been on the trip. It was an accident, they said. Chantal forgot her pills and she had a seizure, simple as that. It was terrible. But it was just an accident."

"What did you do with the pills?" he asked.

I hesitated. To say the words aloud . . . what would that feel like? For the truth to finally come out of my mouth? Would it change things? Would I feel at peace with the fact that I was a monster who had hated a young girl? Who had wanted her dead? Wished her dead and made her die?

"Daphne?"

I had to force the words out of my mouth. "Mrs. Bobbie had given Chantal her pills to pack in her bag before the trip. I just pushed them up under the dresser, so it looked like they rolled there and she had forgotten them."

He was quiet.

"They took all us girls in the brown house to see a child psychologist in Macon. They brought us in, one by one, to talk to her. She asked questions about Chantal and our life at home. At the ranch and the house. She asked about Mr. Al. About . . ."

"What?"

I cleared my throat. "Apparently, the night of the camping trip, the night Chantal wandered off, he and a couple of the older girls had left their tents to go smoke weed in the woods. Chantal found them. They made her leave, and on her way back to the campsite, she lost her way." I touched my forehead. A sharp pain had begun to stab me right behind my left eye.

"That's terrible."

I inhaled. "She pushed, the psychologist. She kept asking me questions. What kind of father was Mr. Al, what did he do with us at the ranch? Did he spend time alone with us? Did he find ways to get us away from Mrs. Bobbie?" I shook my head. "I was a kid, and surprisingly still pretty innocent. I didn't understand what they were getting at. And to tell the truth, I don't think they had anything on him other than the whole weed-smoking business. But . . ."

"They fired him."

I nodded. "He went to prison."

"Good God. Seriously?"

"The judge was up for reelection and needed someone to prove she was tough on drug crime."

He waited.

"Mr. Al was an idiot for doing what he did, yes, but he loved us girls. And he was always kind to me. But everything good he did got lost in the chaos of Chantal's accident. He was the convenient scapegoat, the one who prevented the ranch from having to deal with any major repercussions. I don't know specifically how it all went down, but I do know that's what happened. Believe it or not, in that whole world of child-welfare services, there's a lot of money at stake. Plenty of winking and nodding and looking the other way. At least, there was back then."

"Did you ever look him up? Try to find out what happened?"

I shook my head. "Even if I could find him, I don't think I could face him. Not after what I did. It was my fault he went away."

"It was his fucking fault he smoked weed with a bunch of minors," Heath said flatly.

"Mrs. Bobbie left the ranch," I went on. "And we were all redistributed—Omega, Shellie, Tré, and me. My new house was fine. Nice parents, sweet girls, and I was safe. Reasonably happy, I guess. And no one ever found out that Chantal's death was my fault."

He touched my face. Then he kissed me, tenderly. And as he did, I began to cry. I didn't want to, but I couldn't stop myself. I'd finally ventured down that dark hall, pushed open the door, and told someone. The relief was enormous.

"Daphne," he said. "Look at me."

I did.

He held my face. "You were a child. A little girl. You couldn't have known she was taking medication for epilepsy. And you were probably confused by the questioning about Mr. Al. Did you even understand what marijuana was?"

"I knew it was more than cigarettes that they were smoking outside the clubhouse, and I had the feeling that if Mrs. Bobbie had found out what was happening, she would have killed them. But it felt wonderful too—like a happy secret they all shared together. And I wanted to be a part of it. I wanted to belong."

I shifted on the bed. Our legs were entwined now.

"The child psychologist said if I knew anything at all about how Chantal had died and didn't tell, I was an accessory to the crime. I didn't know what she meant exactly, just that it sounded like Mr. Al had committed a crime, and it was possible that they could put me in jail too. I was scared. But I should've done the right thing. I should've told the truth."

"They would've put you in jail. Or some hellhole of a detention. You did the smart thing."

I sighed. "Maybe. Maybe not, I can't know for sure. I never actually talked to a lawyer, but my understanding is, if they ruled the death a homicide, the DA could have prosecuted me as an adult. Some of these guys are known for taking a really preemptive approach with juvenile offenders. Maybe the worst they could've come up with was criminal negligence, but still, prison was a possibility. The fact that everybody knew I hated her. That certainly would've been used against me."

"Okay, Daphne, so let's say you wished Chantal was dead. Somewhere in your eleven-year-old brain, you understood the law of the jungle was in play—that it was either you or Chantal. So, yes, you struck first, but that doesn't make you a criminal, it makes you a survivor."

I shook my head. "I don't know. It definitely makes me a liar."

"Not anymore. You just told me everything."

I swallowed, feeling something delicately reaching a balance between us. Then he smiled.

"Daphne." He lifted his eyes to meet mine. "I want to be involved in this. I want to be with you. Everywhere you are. That's why I am alive. The only reason."

"You really mean that, don't you?" I whispered.

He nodded. "And we will be safe together, no matter what we meant to do or not do. No matter what we've done. We will be always us."

I bit my lip.

"Say it."

"Always us."

He pressed his lean body against mine, and I felt his lips on mine, his tongue in my mouth. I closed my eyes. The room was warm and dark, and I let myself relax against him. I imagined the protective armor I'd always worn falling off me, joints breaking, pieces of metal clanking to the ground. I felt the distance between us evaporating, its dense black form shrinking until there was nothing left. I watched it go—sensed it going, rather—without a shred of remorse. It was easy to let Heath come close now. An easy, beautiful, shining thing to lie next to him and be fully known.

. . . *what we've done* . . .

That's what he had said.

Sleep started to nibble away at the edges of my consciousness. The bed felt like a boat that was rocking gently over waves. I'd forgotten to take off my earrings and ring, so I pulled them off, dropping them on the nightstand. I was drifting, drifting, drifting—back to the apartment where I lived with my mother. To the small pink room, my white-painted bed with the spindled posts and daisy-chain comforter. The purple lampshade. The little TV on the chest of drawers.

I was six or seven. Or, I don't know, maybe I was older. Mrs. Tully, our down-the-hall neighbor, had used her extra key to let me in. She'd persuaded the super to let her cut a spare after the first half a dozen times my mother stayed out all night and Mrs. Tully had seen me boarding the school bus the next morning in the clothes I'd been wearing the previous day. Mrs. Tully unlocked the door and told me to go put on my pajamas and brush my teeth. She would gather some of my dirty clothes she could throw in her washing machine.

I heard her from the bathroom, talking in a low, urgent voice. When I came out, toothbrush sticking out of my mouth, I saw my mama hunched over the recliner. She'd dropped her purse on it, pulled off the scrunchie that had held back her yellow-blonde hair, and dragged her fingers tiredly over her scalp. She was wearing a denim miniskirt and a ruffled eyelet halter top that showed a strip of doughy skin between the two. She leaned over to shuck off her sandals—the high-heeled brown strappy ones I used to like to clomp around in. I wondered what had made her have such loose skin. It was like some of her insides had been pulled out, and left her body like a week-old balloon.

"Where have you been?" I wanted to ask, but I didn't. After Mrs. Tully left, Mama finally noticed me standing in the hallway, the toothbrush still in my mouth.

"You want to come along next time?" she said. "I bet I could get a stack of pesos for your hot little ass." She laughed, a loud, honking noise, and I melted back into the bathroom.

As I spat into the sink, I thought it over. Since she was high, it would be easy to push her off our second-floor apartment balcony, up and over the railing, and down to the cracked, weedy parking lot below. Maybe she would hit a car. Or crack her head on the concrete. I wondered what she would look like, dead, all that pale, flabby skin below the balcony.

And then I wondered how bad a child must be to think things like that about her own mama. Children were supposed to love their mothers, even I knew that. Good children.

Maybe I wasn't good. Maybe I was a monster . . .

In our room at Baskens, sometime later in the night, I woke to use the bathroom. Back in bed, I was restless. Had my mother really said such a horrific thing to me, or had I, through the haze of years and bitterness, painted her more of a villain than she really was? Our minds were tricky things, manipulators of time and space, coloring events with our personal palette of rage, fear, or desire.

I wasn't going to be able to get back to sleep, I thought, not now. And I couldn't bear to lie here, being recorded by the extra cameras Cerny had hidden in our room. I decided to go outside, let the night air wash over me. Maybe I'd sit on the metal chaise on the patio, try to get a glimpse of the stars, and fall asleep there. Let Luca cover me with a quilt when he found me in the morning. I fumbled for my glasses, wrapped myself in the fuzzy throw from the foot of the bed, and crept down the stairs.

The moon was high and bright, and frost had crystallized on the velvet grass of the backyard. But between the two, just above the ground, a layer of fog hovered, wispy and spectral. At the far end of the yard, it shrouded the barn. Down the terraced levels to my left, it gathered thickly over the bird garden. How strange, that the sky above me should be so clear but down here, all was obscured.

It was cold and I was barefoot, but I felt myself pulled to the bird garden. Something worrying at the edges of my mind, an insistence. I picked my way past the vegetable beds and down to the redbud trees, each step filling me with greater dread, until the weight of it was as tangible as the mist I was passing through.

Just as the birdhouses materialized through the haze, I felt a lump of something under my bare foot—soft and solid at the same time. I jumped, then looked down to see a dead bird on the grass. My hand flew to my mouth, but then, after another moment, I had to adjust my glasses. I couldn't believe what I was seeing.

The grass beneath the birdhouses was strewn with dead birds. Dozens of them.

I was standing in a graveyard.

Friday, October 19
Night

In the bathroom of Mama June's restaurant, I press against the floral-papered wall. But the three women don't even look my way. Chattering nonstop, they head to the single sink and crowd around it. One woman, with long, carefully curled red ringlets and a knee-length crocheted vest, jabbers as she washes up.

"I told her, I said, 'Dee, if you don't do something, he's just going to stay up all night looking at porn, chatting with those inter-sluts.'"

"Inter-sluts," cackles another, yanking paper towels out of the dispenser.

"Lord, Natasha," the third one says. "That man is not chatting with women. He's a pastor."

They rotate places. Natasha flips back her curls and points a French-manicured finger at her friend who's now at the sink. "That man hasn't stuck it in her in over six months. Mark it, he's either sticking it somewhere else or talking about it. You know as well as I do, you gotta watch them pastors."

When they're finally finished, I follow them back into the restaurant. Natasha and her friends settle at a table in front of the long, plastic-shielded buffet where three men—their husbands, I guess—are working on plates of pie, locked in on the boxy TV.

I sit at a small table a couple of yards away. There's a check printout and a five-dollar bill near a plate with a couple of soggy fries in a pool of ketchup and an uneaten biscuit. I pull the iPad out and start to open it, then stop.

Across the room, Natasha has her arm draped around a man I recognize. Round, shiny face, swoop of mud-brown hair. Dr. Reggie Teague. The face is the same, but he looks different from when I last saw him. He's not dressed in a suit and bow tie or wearing the preppy glasses.

He's wearing a firefighter's uniform. All three of the men are.

I am shaking now. Reggie Teague, or whoever this man is, is a firefighter. Not a therapist who was called back to Dunfree on a family emergency. Not Matthew Cerny's jovial associate.

I'm shaking so hard, I'm not even sure I can move. I close my eyes and try to slow my breath. If I have a panic attack in this diner, Reggie Teague will see me. I'm not sure where his loyalties lie—how deeply involved in this thing he is or how far he might go to protect his own interests—but I can't risk getting caught. If he stops me from getting to the police station, I'm done. This much I know.

I resist the biscuit, despite my gnawing hunger, but I slip the five-dollar bill out from under the plate. The familiar act of self-preservation gives me a boost of adrenaline, which turns out to be the necessary motivation to get my legs working. I stand up as inconspicuously as I can and make for the door.

The bell jangles, and back in the restaurant I hear Reggie and his two firefighter buddies cheer lustily in response to something wonderful that just happened on the TV.

Chapter Twenty

Thursday, October 18
The Day Before

Heath's breakfast dishes were already cleared from our room. My plate, still covered, waited on the table.

I yawned. The clock said it was past ten—which was hard to fathom. I hadn't slept this late in years. I nestled farther under the covers, warm and contented, until a wave of nameless anxiety washed over me. I bolted up, remembering last night.

The fog. All those dead birds.

When my brain had finally registered what I was looking at, I'd bitten back my screams and run back to the house. I'd woken Heath and told him what I'd seen. He explained that it was probably a coyote or some other predator that had gotten after them, that I should try and get some sleep, and he'd tell Cerny about it in the morning. I was so distraught I'd almost told him about the Sinatra song I'd heard in the hallway. But I stopped myself. Something told me it wasn't a good idea.

Maybe it was the fact that Luca and I had been together when we'd heard the song—sneaking around the house like some kind of detective duo—and Heath might misread the situation. Or maybe I worried he was beginning to doubt my stability. Last night, as I'd ranted about the dead birds, the expression on his face had seemed so patient. So completely unconcerned, like dead birds in the yard were an entirely normal situation, and he was merely allowing my neuroses to spin themselves out.

He'd held me until I'd finally fallen asleep, which hadn't been until around three in the morning, reassuring me that everything was fine. His voice had remained calm. The voice of reason in the midst of my hysteria.

I returned to bed and drifted back to sleep almost instantly. When I awoke again, light in the room had shifted, and the room shimmered in the cold. I burrowed deeper under the blankets and looked up at the ceiling, at the unseen camera that was, no doubt, recording me. I felt the tension creeping back into my neck and shoulders. I needed to run. I needed to sweat, to feel my heart swelling and pounding like it was going to explode. To feel my jaw ache with the lack of oxygen, taste the trace of blood in my mouth.

I rolled over and looked at the clock. One forty. I cursed aloud. Glenys and I were supposed to meet at two thirty at the top of the mountain, that's what we'd agreed at the creek yesterday. She'd be glad to hear I'd finally talked to Heath and told him everything about Chantal. And she'd probably want to hear the story too. I owed her that much. If it wasn't for her, I didn't think I would've ever been brave enough to come clean with Heath. If I threw on clothes now and sprinted up the mountain, I'd only be a few minutes late.

I pulled on running tights and a zip-top, then inspected the meal under the cover. The eggs had gone cold, but the bacon was still good and the fruit too. I pulled apart a biscuit and stuffed a flaky half in my mouth. At the nightstand, I stopped. My earrings and ring were gone, probably swept to the floor in the chaos of last night. I peeked under the table, but the floor was bare. I'd just have to search for them later.

I popped a beanie and gloves on and stepped into the empty hall. It was freezing. The temperature must've dropped fifteen degrees since yesterday.

I glided down the front staircase and across the foyer, ducking into each of the front rooms for a quick check. No one was in the library, dining room, or salon, but as I retreated to the rear of the house, I could hear voices in the doctor's office. I stopped and let them roll over me. In a strange way, the sound of humans talking was the most warming, comforting sound in the world. Life went on, didn't it? On and on and on.

In the kitchen, Luca was bustling around, chopping, mixing, sliding pans into ovens. He turned when I came in, and at the sight of him, my stomach executed a flip-flop. He reciprocated my smile—the spontaneous, easy grin filled his eyes with light and the space around us with electricity. He handed me an apple from a bowl on the counter.

"Thanks," I said. "I guess you saw I slept through lunch."

He shook his head. His face had turned somber and he was watching me intently, like he expected me to say something.

"I know, I know, *no hablas*, although I can't help wondering if it's just a put-on."

His gaze didn't waver, his eyes that shade of hazel that looked green in one light, gray in another. It was strange. It was as if he was trying to send me a message, but I was too boneheaded to decipher it.

"Or you really can't speak English," I forged on. "And I'm just being an utter asshole. In which case, my sincerest apologies, and thank you again for the apple. I'll try not to miss dinner."

He nodded once, then moved to the sink and started to clear the dishes. I beat a hasty exit.

The backyard matched my mood—serene and golden in the afternoon sun. From my vantage point, it looked like the birdhouses down in the garden were deserted and the lawn clear. The air around me was sharp with a smell of smoke, though, and I wondered if there was a fire on the mountain.

Or one started in the woods behind the house, maybe, to dispose of the birds' bodies.

Feeling unsettled, I turned and headed for the mountain trail. The cold air burned my lungs, but I welcomed the pain. The faster I went, the more alive I felt. I was bursting with the endorphins and the anticipation of seeing Glenys. If I hurried, I wouldn't be late.

I wiped my fogged lenses and checked my watch. Two thirty on the dot. I walked to the edge of the limestone slab where the cliff dropped away and breathed in the clean, cold air. No trace of Glenys up here, nor of any smoke. Maybe the smell had come from a campfire or someone's chimney.

I stretched, did a couple of yoga poses, which would've cracked Lenny up if she could've witnessed it—me, the dedicated runner who couldn't even be bothered with more than a cursory stretch before I started off. I checked my watch again. Twelve minutes had passed and still no Glenys. She could've forgotten, but it seemed unlikely. It wasn't as if there was a schedule of activities to get swept up in.

After another twenty minutes or so, I headed back down the mountain, trying not to worry. I ticked through the possible reasons she hadn't shown up. Maybe I'd inadvertently offended her. Maybe she'd had a particularly rough therapy session, and it had wiped her out. I remembered how distraught she'd looked outside the barn yesterday. I wondered what she'd seen in there that had set her off. Or maybe she hadn't seen anything. Maybe it had just been a private spot where she could grieve, away from the camera in her room.

But suddenly it occurred to me—she'd obviously unlocked the chain on the barn doors. There'd been a huge padlock on it, for God's sake.

I caught a sapling, stopping myself midstride.

How did she manage to open it?

The question was a valid one, even if I didn't want to ask it. Even if it made me uncomfortable. As much as I wanted to deny it, none of what I'd experienced this week was normal. Not the locked Nissan, the Sinatra song, the arguing voices, the dead birds. The list of strange, unexplained things was getting longer by the minute. And now this: the barn-door chain, roped and padlocked for me, but not for Glenys.

I'd read enough self-help books to know what I was doing was called catastrophizing. But what if this was an actual, real-life catastrophe? Sometimes they did happen. Sometimes the signs were all there, right before something went terribly wrong. And the people who didn't heed the warnings—who didn't evacuate or board up their windows or brace themselves for the storm—were usually the ones who got swept away.

"This is not normal," I said aloud. And broke into a run.

At the bottom of the trail, I charged toward the barn. On the doors, the chain hung limp. Unlocked. I ducked inside, waited for my eyes to adjust to the shadows. There were a couple of grimy, cobwebby windows up high in a loft area that let in what light was left of the day. It made the space look extra spooky—the set of a play, before the actors walked onstage and brought it to life. I wrapped my arms around my torso and surveyed the space.

The collection of sheet-draped furniture I'd seen, the day I'd first peeked through the cracked doors, filled the far-left corner of the barn. I approached it and gingerly lifted the corner of one sheet. A small bed, twin size. I pulled at the sheet and let it settle to the dirt floor. The bed was a simple light-wood four-poster with a chipped headboard. A set of old-fashioned springs rested on the slats.

I drew the sheet back over the bed, then moved to the next piece of furniture. A school desk, one of those old-fashioned all-in-ones, with a green metal seat and wood desktop that lifted up. It had a narrow groove at the top, for a pencil. I ran my fingers over the surface. It was scratched up pretty good. Maybe it had been Cerny's. He had mentioned growing up here. How the fiery fiends had frightened him. How much mischief they'd kept him from.

The light through the high windows was fading fast. It was getting late. I dragged the desk over to the nearest one, angling it so the beam of light hit it at just the right angle. The surface of the wood was scarred over its entire surface. Someone had been busy . . . and not with their lessons. I squinted. I picked out the letter *H*. Then an *A* and a *V*. An *E* and *N*.

Haven?

I felt my way along the surface, identifying each subsequent letter. "*O, P, I, T, Y, S, O* . . ." I shook my head. Went back to where I started. Felt the scratches there. "*I*," I said and furrowed my brow. "*IHAVENOPITYSO* . . . What in God's name?" I shook my head again, hard, clearing the cobwebs. "*I have no pity,*" I murmured. Ran my fingers over the letters again. "*I have no pity so* . . ."

I imagined Matthew Cerny, a small boy with floppy blond hair, carving this phrase into his desk during his lessons. What a strange thing for a child to carve. How desolate.

"Daphne?" I heard behind me, and I whirled. Even in the gloom, I recognized the voice. Heath. And then I saw the knife, lying on the floor of the shed, just beside his feet.

Chapter Twenty-One

"Daphne, I'm sorry to take you away from your activities."

Dr. Cerny took my hand between his. The overhead lights of his office were dimmed to a soft amber, turning the glass-paned walls opaque in the dark. We couldn't see out, but anyone looking in could see us. Like actors on a spotlit stage.

Heath wandered across the room to peruse the bookshelves. In the barn, he'd simply asked if I'd be willing to go back to the office to speak with Dr. Cerny. On our way out, I trailed behind and gave the knife a gentle kick into the shadows.

Now Heath ran his fingers down the spines of Cerny's books, leaning in periodically to get a closer look at a few of the volumes.

The doctor tapped his iPad. "I wanted to speak to you, Daphne. Get your input on some subjects Heath and I are accessing. Would you be comfortable with that?"

"I think so," I said. "I'd like to help if I can."

Heath turned and sent me a look—a signal I didn't quite understand. Looking at him usually made my heart feel tender, swollen with love to the point of being painful, but ever since I told him about

Chantal, I sensed something was different between us. An unnaturalness that hadn't been there before. Something cold and stilted.

The doctor leaned back, folded his hands across his sweater. "The nightmares Heath was having before you came to Baskens—he says he is unable to remember them. You said he referenced a mirror."

I felt the low rumble of panic in my gut. The nerves all over my body sang to life. I dropped my hands behind my back and snapped the band on my wrist.

"Are you all right?" Cerny asked. "Can I get you something?"

I swallowed. "No."

"You don't look well."

"I'll be fine."

"You're having a panic attack," he said calmly.

I shook my head. "I don't think so." And yet I could feel myself dying to count the books on the shelves or the blacked-out panes of glass around me. Anything to ease the discomfort. I snapped the band again and again, not caring anymore if they noticed.

"Sit. I'm going to get you some water and a paper bag to breathe into. Do you take medication for anxiety? Or do you just employ the . . . other coping mechanism?" Cerny was up now, bustling in a circuit around the room, but it made me too dizzy to watch him, so I sat, dropped my elbows to my knees, and closed my eyes.

"Daphne?" Heath's voice seemed thin with concern.

"I don't do meds," I said, to no one in particular.

Dr. Cerny returned with a glass of juice and a paper bag.

Maybe I was having some kind of attack. At the very least, Baskens was unraveling me. I felt untethered here, without an Internet connection, without any of my familiar tasks and boundaries and outlets. Paranoid because of the cameras. Dull and hazy. With Heath's nightmares no longer waking me, I was sleeping substantially more than usual, but instead of rested I felt groggy. My dynamic with Heath had shifted ever so subtly too, after the thing in the shower. Or maybe it was that I'd told him about Chantal. It was hard to tell.

It was like my mind had become an unruly child, running wild through the dark, dusty corridors of the mansion, up and down the wind-whipped mountain, body-free and heedless. And somehow, in the process of investigating the dark nooks, watching the glowing monitors and seeing the secret lives of the other patients here, I had fallen into the strange offbeat rhythm of the place. I had become unclenched and vulnerable.

A child again.

And like an obedient child, I finished off the juice the doctor gave me.

Heath spoke. "I'll take you back upstairs, Daphne." He glanced at the doctor, and some form of communication that I couldn't decipher passed between the two of them. "We'll finish this later," he said firmly, then touched my arm.

I lifted myself out of the chair. I felt as heavy as an elephant, which had to be from the panic. Or was it . . . I stopped and turned to Cerny. Heath plucked at my elbow, but I pushed away his hand.

"Dr. Cerny . . ." I said.

The doctor, just settling into his chair behind the desk, raised his eyebrows.

"I was supposed to meet Glenys Sieffert this afternoon, at the top of the mountain."

He froze.

"We were just going to do some yoga. On the mountain."

Cerny's eyes flicked over at Heath. "We have a policy."

It was only the millionth time I'd heard someone at Baskens say that, and frankly I was over it. "I know," I said. "And I'm sorry I broke your rule, but I couldn't not say something. I mean, it's more than her not showing up. I haven't seen her in a while."

He pushed aside a stack of papers, retrieved his iPad, and unlocked it. He tapped at the screen a few times. I watched, bleary eyed and zoned out, until something occurred to me. Something wonderful—I'd just watched him tap in his passcode.

I closed my eyes. Pictured the screen. Saw the pattern his fingers had traced.

5353

Easy. No way it was his age. Cerny had to be in his mid to late sixties, at least. Maybe it was someone's birthdate—May 3, 1953. That seemed more likely. Possibly his. Possibly the woman's whose silk blouses were hanging in the wardrobe upstairs.

"I've talked with her recently," the doctor said, interrupting my thoughts. He pushed the iPad away, but the screen still glowed. A page of notes. Glenys's last session, possibly. "Everyone here at Baskens is accounted for. No need for concern."

The image of Glenys leaning out her bedroom window flashed in my head. "I'd just like to know where she is. For my own peace of mind."

"Well, that's solicitous of you." The doctor picked up a pen, inspected it, then put it back down. "But she's probably in her room, reading or perhaps napping. Maybe talking with her husband."

"I thought I heard the two of you arguing. Earlier."

"Daphne . . ." Heath said.

Cerny fixed me with an inscrutable look. "She's my patient, Daphne, not yours."

"I'd like to know if she's okay," I said. "That's all."

Cerny's gaze stayed on me. "We have a policy, and we were very clear regarding it. I understand, though, growing up the way you did, you probably associate the idea of policy with the legal system . . ."

I flinched. *Nice shot, Doc.*

"But I can assure you," he went on, "it's in everyone's best interest." He sat back, lacing his fingers. "Daphne, I need you to understand. My patients are all here for counseling, primarily because they're encountering obstacles in their lives they cannot manage on their own. In other words, everyone here is *struggling*."

He enunciated the word precisely. Like that had anything to do with what I asked. Like I didn't know what the hell the word meant.

I put a hand on the chair and pivoted myself toward the door. I felt the rush of the room readjusting itself around me, just a split second later than it should have.

"Did you put something in the juice?" I asked.

Cerny pursed his lips. "Do you feel all right?"

"Yes," I mumbled. "Just a little . . ." My mind drifted, then swung back to Glenys. "I was just concerned she might've left, that's all. Have you had time to watch any of the tapes? The surveillance tapes of her and her husband, from the time in their room? Maybe something happened when she was up there?"

Heath sighed. He was losing patience with me, I could tell.

"Daphne, I can assure you, everyone here is safe," Cerny said. "You are safe."

He was missing the point. It wasn't my safety I was concerned with. It was his lie about the additional cameras in our room. The Sinatra music. The goddamn dead birds strewn across the grass.

I was concerned about a woman who might be missing, but he wasn't listening. No one was. I pressed my fingertips to my temples. Confronting him in my impaired state was useless. I'd wait until I had my wits about me. When I felt myself again, I'd figure out what the hell was going on.

I propelled myself toward the door, spotting the row of car keys hanging on the hooks. I'd done some minor shoplifting in my day, at the Flash Foods, after school. All the girls at the ranch did it. I was pretty good, too. Just a quick reach and a sprint to the door . . .

I could make a run for it. Pick any car and drive down this mountain. They couldn't stop me, not if I was smart about it. I could drive down to Dunfree, even, hunt down Luca or Dr. Teague. Bring the police into it, if I had to. A sense of well-being washed over me—or maybe it was power. I was only here because I chose to be. I could leave anytime. I was in charge of my life, not this grinning, Mr.-Al-looking bullhorn of lies.

I turned to face Cerny. "You said you wanted to know what else Heath said? During the nightmares?"

He stilled. "Ah, yes. But we can discuss it later, when you're feeling better."

I eyed the doctor, then Heath. I had their full attention now. I lifted my eyebrow just a fraction, hoping Heath would get my message—*Two can play this game, Doc*—then closed my eyes, as if conjuring up the memory. The reality was, I didn't have to. I remembered every time Heath had cried out in his sleep. Every scream and roar and whimper that had woken me.

Break the mirror . . .

Cerny stared at me, and a delicious frisson of superiority went through me. Whatever game he was playing with Heath and me—and with Glenys—he wasn't going to win. I sure as hell wasn't going to give him any more information until I figured out what he was up to.

He may have looked like Mr. Al, but he wasn't my fucking father.

I cleared my throat. "One time—and I remember it very clearly—one time he said . . ."

I could've sworn Cerny's pupils dilated in anticipation.

"He said, 'I have no pity.'" I looped my hand through Heath's arm, gripping his bicep. I could feel him staring down at me.

"I did?" Heath asked.

"Hm." I glanced back at Cerny. His face had gone slack.

"Does that mean anything to you, Dr. Cerny?" I asked.

"I don't know. I can't really say." His eyes were hard and narrowed and laser focused on me. I wondered if he knew I had broken into his barn and seen the old desk. I wasn't sure. I couldn't imagine he'd be anything but annoyed at my little game. But he didn't look annoyed. He looked furious.

I was so relaxed now; there was no question he had dosed me with something, but only a distant part of me was afraid. Mostly, now, I was feeling about ten feet tall.

"I'm sure," I said breezily, "that, as his psychologist, you'll enjoy solving the mystery. Good night."

I walked to the door and was about to reach for the keys, when I felt Heath beside me, his breath in my ear. I froze as his hand clamped around my wrist. I had the keys in my sights, right there, within a literal arm's reach.

"No." His voice was only a whisper, but he was shaking. Before I could protest, he pulled me away from the keys and out the door.

Chapter Twenty-Two

"Why did you say that to Dr. Cerny?" Heath asked.

It was almost dinnertime, and if I was serious about finding Glenys, I probably should've been keeping an eye out for Luca. But the episode in Cerny's office had thrown me off. I was more than a little high and way past done with this place. All I wanted to do was go home.

Dully, I scanned the room:

In the frame of the oil painting above the fireplace.
In that floor lamp in the corner of the sitting area.
Somewhere along the mirror above the dresser.
In the fan above the bed.

Behind me, Heath cleared his throat. "Did I really say that 'I have no pity' thing?" He was speaking carefully, like he was picking his way over broken glass.

Should I tell him about the other cameras in our room? Would it convince him that we had to leave? I didn't know anything anymore. This place was turning me upside down.

"No, you didn't say that." I scrubbed at my eyes. "It was just something I saw on some old furniture in the barn, a phrase scratched on a desk."

He leapt up. "Daphne! God!"

I straightened in surprise. "What?"

"You can't do that!" he yelled. "You're messing with my treatment. Don't you understand?"

"I'm sorry. I didn't—"

"You don't like Cerny, it's obvious. But that doesn't give you the right to lie to him about me."

"I'm sorry, okay? It's just . . . I feel really weird. Not myself. I'm pretty sure he put something in that juice he gave me."

He made an exasperated sound. "Oh, come on. You wanted to fuck with him, and you saw your chance. Don't pass the blame."

"I'm not!" I shouted. Then, aware again of the cameras, I lowered my voice. "Okay, you don't have to believe me. But you have to admit nothing here makes sense. Why aren't we allowed to talk to anyone? Why does Dr. Cerny act so goddamn weird all the time . . ." *Why does he have a state investigator's card in his desk and a closetful of women's clothing? Why is the yard full of dead birds?*

And the cook seems to be trying to send me a message every time I run into him . . .

Heath shook his head. "You can't just make stuff up. This is a serious process."

"So get him to prescribe you some sleeping pills and let's go home. There's nothing that says you have to offer him your soul."

"I know how you feel about therapists. I know this is hard for you . . ."

"This is not hard for me," I said evenly. "I'm not afraid of Dr. Cerny. I know what the Internet says, that he's a qualified doctor and everybody thinks he's a miracle worker. It's just . . ." I trailed off. "I'm not comfortable talking to him about your nightmares. You can talk to him, but I can't. I don't trust him."

"You're saying you don't trust me."

"No. Yes. Yes, I do."

"You're pissed that you told me about your past. You regret it."

"Stop it, Heath. Don't turn this around on me."

"You're so full of bullshit," he spat. "You only told me about the ranch, about Omega and Chantal, because you were scared to hear more about my past. To really go there with me, all the way to the darkest part. And now you're acting weird and distant and cold. You can't stand it, the reality of actually being close to me."

My face flushed. "No."

But he'd hit on something. Being here at Baskens had changed us, set us on what felt like an irreversible course. I couldn't pretend like our pasts didn't exist, but I didn't want to go forward and deal with all of it, either. I was stuck, here in this twisted house.

He fixed me with a hard look. "So you just happened to see that phrase, *I have no pity*, carved on a piece of furniture?"

"It was on this old school desk I found in the barn. I don't understand why it bothers you so much. Am I missing something here?"

A knock sounded on the door, and I jumped like someone had set off a bomb. I went for the door, but Heath caught my arm.

"Hold on." He kept a tight grip on me. "It's just dinner. He can wait." He folded me into a hug. "You scared me, Daph. I didn't understand what you told Cerny or why you hadn't ever said anything about it before. It made me feel . . . it made me worry I might never get to the bottom of whatever is going on with me."

I pressed my face against his shoulder, guilt flooding me. "It was shitty of me. I'm sorry."

"I just need to feel you for a second."

He tightened his arms around me, but all I could think was that I was missing my chance to see Glenys answer Luca's knock on her door. If she answered it at all. When Heath finally let go, I opened the door. Our dinner tray was the only one in the hall.

"God*dammit*," I said under my breath.

"What?" Heath said behind me. I picked up the tray and scooted around him.

"Nothing. It's nothing."

In the room, I lifted the cover on my plate to find fragrant shrimp and quinoa and slender asparagus. Heath moved to fill my glass with wine, but I put my hand over it to stop him. I couldn't afford to mix alcohol with whatever I'd ingested, especially if I intended to keep looking for Glenys tonight. Heath poured himself a healthy serving, then forked violently into a slice of coconut cake. I watched him with raised eyebrows.

"Dessert for dinner?"

"Long day," he grumbled through a mouthful.

I went at my shrimp, feeling belligerent. "So you really think Glenys is okay?"

"I don't see any reason to think otherwise."

"If I could just call her or text her or something . . ." I shut my mouth abruptly. A kernel of an idea had just broken open in my mind. A way to get word to somebody that didn't necessitate Wi-Fi or cell networks. I tucked the idea away for the time being. I'd need to wait until I was alone. "I just hope she's okay, that's all."

"Do you have any reason to think she wouldn't be?"

"No. Not specifically. She's been having a hard time about some things in her life."

"Like what?"

"She lost her son."

"Lost him?"

"He died."

Heath absorbed this. Dropped his napkin. He hadn't eaten any more than a few bites of the cake. "How did it happen?" His voice was calm but he was watching me intently.

"I don't know. I didn't ask."

"Weren't you curious?"

I shifted uncomfortably. "Not necessarily."

He met my gaze. "Everybody's curious about death—how it happens, what it feels like."

"I guess."

"Doesn't a small part of you wish you could've been there at the bottom of the cliff at the moment Chantal died? At the exact moment her spirit left her body?"

"Are you serious?" I stared at him.

"I'm just being honest, Daphne. It doesn't make you a bad person to admit you have a touch of darkness inside you. We're all just hanging out together, here in the morally ambiguous quagmire. You don't need to be afraid of the darkness in yourself. Or in me. We're in this together, right?"

"Right," I said. Because that was what I always said. But this time I didn't feel it. In fact, I felt more alone than ever right now. Our favorite phrase, *always us*—what did it actually mean? Would we really always be us? Always the same? Always together?

We finished our meal in silence. I left the tray outside our door. The hallway was deserted. No people, no trays, even, but the pocket door leading to Dr. Cerny's suite was half-opened. I leaned out, peering into the darkness beyond. I couldn't see a thing. It would only take a few seconds to run up the small stairs to the attic and check on Glenys on the monitors.

"Come to bed." In the open doorway, Heath's hand settled on my shoulder. The other one snaked under my sweatshirt and around my bare waist. I tensed. When I turned, his face was tilted toward me, so close that I could smell the wine on his breath.

"What about if something happened to her on the mountain?" I said. "What if she's lost? Or hurt?"

"Cerny's a doctor. He's not gunning for a lawsuit, I promise you that."

I thought of Jessica Kyung's card. Her clipped voice on the phone. *I would encourage you to go to our site.*

"I'm sure your friend is fine." His fingers traced the outline of my ribs. "Come to bed. We don't have to do anything. I'll give you a back rub."

I let him lead me back into the room. He lifted my sweatshirt over my head, then I stretched out on the comforter. He lay down beside me, molding his body to mine. He planted one kiss on my temple, but nothing more, then started kneading my knotted shoulders. I closed my eyes.

I could feel my tension lifting, feel myself drifting. When I looked through the windows, the light outside had gone dusky purple, and Heath's hand had slowed to a tickle that traveled the curve of my neck. I was so blissed out by the pill, the food, and his expert touch, I knew I wasn't going to get up. I closed my eyes again, telling my body to wake up at ten.

My internal clock must've been in good working order, because I woke at 9:58. I scrubbed away the grit in my eyes, letting them get adjusted to the dark. Only two minutes until the cameras went down. Perfect. I slipped out from under Heath's arm and snagged a small pad and pen from my purse.

Faint light from downstairs illuminated the hallway. Hopefully, Mr. Cellphone was still up, texting merrily away while his clueless wife slept. I moved closer to the stairs, flipped open the pad of paper, and jotted the message I'd formulated hours earlier.

> *Mr. McAdam,*
>
> *I think one of the other patients, Glenys Sieffert, may have gone missing. I realize this may sound strange, but last night, I believe she was on the verge of hurting herself—maybe even jumping out her bedroom window. Now I can't find her anywhere. I think she may be in*

trouble. I know you have a phone, I've seen it on the monitors (I apologize for the invasion of your privacy). Will you please call 911—ask the police to please come up here and make sure she's okay? I swear I won't mention who made the call.

Thank you,

Daphne Amos

I ripped the note out of the pad, carefully folded it, and headed to the McAdams' door. I slid the note under the door, then tiptoed to Glenys's door. I paused, straining my ears, but there was nothing—no sounds, no light—so I returned to our room. Back in bed, I burrowed against Heath but couldn't settle my scattershot pulse.

I kept seeing Glenys, the way she looked the other night on the monitor. Poised on her window ledge, her nightgown rippling in the breeze, her face an etching of grief and despair.

Heath was right, as it turned out. I did wonder if Chantal's face looked the same the moment before she had died.

Chapter Twenty-Three

Mr. Cleve let me skip school for Chantal's funeral, even though it was only supposed to be for the eighth graders and up.

"It'll give you closure. Since you girls shared a room and all," Mr. Cleve explained when he came to see how I was settling in at the new house. The word *closure* seemed like it didn't fit in his mouth. It looked like somebody else had told him to say it. Probably the psychologist.

I didn't have a proper dress to wear to the service, so Mrs. Waylene, my new housemother, said I could go back to the brown brick house and look in the castoff closet there. I found a dark-green sweaterdress one of the Super Tramps had ditched and some maroon tights from Chantal's drawer, and I changed in our old room. Her black clogs, still arranged under the bed, were too big for me, but I slid my feet in them anyway.

When I got back, Mrs. Waylene made a clucking sound.

"Should I not wear the clogs?" I asked.

"No, honey. You look just great," she said and went to call the rest of the girls.

The group of us drove to Hollyhock Community Church in silence. They'd set up the white casket on some kind of stand that had been covered with a white cloth. Vases of plastic flowers and pots of greenery ringed the casket. I was pretty sure they'd gathered them from the houses at the ranch. I recognized a big potted palm Mrs. Bobbie kept in our old dining room.

Mrs. Bobbie and the other house moms were bustling back in the fellowship hall, setting out deviled eggs and ham rolls and sugar cookies for after the service. Somebody said Chantal's aunt and uncle were there, and there were a few grown-ups sitting in the pews who I didn't recognize, but I couldn't say for sure. As far as I knew, Omega's story was the gospel truth: Chantal's parents were dead, and she had been alone in the world. Part of me did hope her whole family was gone, so there would be no one to see me there, walking around in her clogs.

The top half of the white casket was propped open, and the preacher quietly announced to all the kids that we were to view the body. Everybody was extra quiet and reverent and got in line without the usual rowdiness. Then we all filed down the aisle. The choir director was playing the piano, something really sad and pretty, and there was only a low murmur of the kids' voices under that. When it was my turn to walk past the casket, I looked down at Chantal.

She lay nestled in swaths of white satin, her eyes closed, hands folded over her chest. She had on a lot of foundation and even pencil on her eyebrows, which I'd never seen on her when she was alive. Her greenish hair had been curled and fanned out around her. She didn't look alive, not at all. She looked more like a Chantal mannequin. A Chantal doll.

The white satin made me think of Mrs. Bobbie and all the fabric she kept in bolts stacked around her room. I pictured her cutting a length of white satin and gently arranging it around Chantal, making sure she was safely tucked in for the long sleep ahead. The girl looked warm in there. Safe. Like she'd actually fallen straight from the top of the mountain down into the pillowy satin casket, her hair fanning out like an angel's.

She'd had a seizure—an epileptic seizure because she'd forgotten her medicine—and then she'd stumbled and fallen from a high rock ledge. It was nighttime and she'd wandered away from the campsite. Later, after I'd seen the psychologist, the police would blame Mr. Al, but Shellie told me it hadn't been his fault. After everyone had gone back to their tents for bed, she and Tré had snuck out with him. They'd hiked up the gorge to smoke some weed, and that's when Chantal had woken up and come looking for them.

When she showed up, Mr. Al told Chantal to go back to her tent and go to bed. But she never made it. A parks search party had found her the next afternoon in a crevasse near the base of the falls. She was dead, but hadn't been that way for long. That was the worst part. She'd lived a good long while after she hit the bottom.

It took twenty-seven crew members from the Fire and Rescue to get her up. The doctors who examined her said she'd had a grand-mal seizure, then probably lost her footing. She'd tumbled over eighty feet to the bottom of the falls. Broken her neck and her back. Smashed the back of her skull to smithereens.

Since I'd heard the news, I hadn't been able to eat. My stomach had been in knots every day, and each night, as I drifted to sleep, I pictured Chantal lying at the bottom of the cliff, mangled and dying. I knew something no one else knew, that she'd had the seizure because she hadn't taken her meds. And she hadn't taken them because I'd stolen them.

But at Mrs. Waylene's house, in my new twin bed, there wasn't anyone kicking my mattress, so I slept surprisingly well. Eventually, the stomachaches stopped too, and I got my appetite back. I liked Mrs. Waylene and her husband, Mr. Bob, and the other girls in the new house.

All of it worried me, though. What kind of person could sleep so soundly, could be happy and even laugh, knowing what they had done? A monster, I guessed, which was what I had become.

Inside the church, the pianist hunkered over the keys, playing with an extra measure of gusto. The tune was so melancholy and beautiful, tears pooled in my eyes. I realized I was gripping the edge of the casket.

"It's from *Anastasia*," a girl next to me whispered. I'd never seen her before. It was possible she went to our school and she and Chantal had been friends, although I couldn't remember seeing Chantal hanging out with anyone.

"It was her favorite movie. She knew all the words," the girl said.

All the words in the whole movie or just the songs? I wanted to ask but didn't. I'd had no idea Chantal liked *Anastasia*. We never watched movies. Mrs. Bobbie thought they were a bad influence on us.

"Did you live with her?" the girl asked.

I nodded.

"Did she ever talk about Cynthia? That's me. Her cousin. My mama was trying to get her to come live with us, before she . . ." She nodded at the casket.

I didn't know what to say. My ears were ringing now, so loud I couldn't hear the *Anastasia* song.

"Hey, stop," the girl said then.

I looked down. My hand had stretched out into the white sea of satin and taken ahold of one of Chantal's green-tinted curls. Alarmed, I snatched my hand back, then broke out of the line and ran, across the church, weaving my way through the throng of kids and adults, until I found a door. I pushed against it and burst out into the sunshine.

I stood in a parking lot full of pickups and beat-up Cadillacs, dusted red from dirt roads. I blinked in the bright sun, trying to decide which direction to run. The church was a long way from the ranch and not all that close to town either, so my choices were limited. If I didn't want to go back inside there, I would have to hide.

I spun, looking around for a spot to duck under until the coast was clear. That's when I saw them: Omega and Mr. Al, on the far end of the parking lot, standing in the shade of a mimosa tree that had lost all its fern-shaped leaves, so that only the brown seed pods remained, clinging to its spindly branches.

Under the tree, Omega's head was tilted up to Mr. Al's. She wore a black off-the-shoulder dress. Where she'd gotten it, I couldn't imagine; I'd never seen such an exotic thing in the closet. Mr. Al was dressed in a dark suit and tie, and his floppy hair was, for once, slicked back. He kept starting to reach out to touch her, then putting his hand back in his pocket. I thought of Mrs. Bobbie, busy in the church kitchen. She would be pissed if she could see the two of them, standing so close. Even I could feel the strange tension in the air.

The wind blew, and the mimosa pods rattled like bones over their heads. Omega was talking loudly—the consonants rat-a-tatting like gunshots across the parking lot. I couldn't hear what she was saying, but I could tell she was upset. She shook her head violently, and then she started beating against Mr. Al's chest with her fists. I couldn't move. I was mesmerized. I'd forgotten all about touching dead Chantal's hair and the sad, lovely piano music and her friendly cousin.

And then they shifted toward each other. And for a second, they looked like kindling sticks laid for a fire, their bodies making an upside-down V. It occurred to me that Omega no longer seemed like one of the Super Tramps—a high-school girl talking to her foster father—but like an adult, just like Mr. Al. Like Everlane pleading with Dex.

Especially when Mr. Al caught her by the wrists, and she wilted against him. Then when she lifted her face, I saw her reach up and press her lips against his. He jerked back, reeled back almost, releasing her from his grip. She let out an anguished sob, stumbled through the cars toward the highway, and started running in the direction of town.

After a moment or two, Mr. Al turned and lumbered toward the church. When he caught sight of me, his face broke into a sad smile.

"Hey there, Daphne-Doodle-Do. Why aren't you inside?"

I lassoed him with my arms and let him hold me. His spicy aftershave-and-coffee smell comforted me. I wanted to stand there with him forever, my face pressed into the stiff material of his suit jacket. I didn't feel one bit cold. Just electrified and scared by what I'd witnessed.

"You know, Daphne, what just happened—" he started.

"Is Omega your girlfriend?" My voice was muffled in his jacket.

He let out a *harrumph* sound, but I couldn't tell if he was laughing or it was something else. I stayed very still, hoping he wouldn't let go. He circled his hand between my shoulder blades. "No, darling. I love her, just like I love you. But not that way."

"Why did she kiss you?"

He was quiet for a moment. "She's confused. And she's sad," he said.

The idea of Omega being sad felt like the world being folded up with me inside of it. I couldn't bear it.

"We should go get her in your car," I said. "She'll miss the funeral." *And the food afterward, in the fellowship hall,* I was thinking too.

Mr. Al let out a heavy sigh. "Mrs. Bobbie has the keys."

It was the last thing I wanted to do, tear out of his embrace, but somebody had to go after Omega. Somebody had to cheer her up. So I did. I wove my way through the cars in the parking lot and, when I got to the road, kicked off the clogs and started running as fast as I could in the direction I'd seen Omega go.

Chapter Twenty-Four

Friday, October 19
Morning

I was peering through the crack in our door, hoping to catch sight of Jerry McAdam, when I heard Heath roll over in bed.

"You showered already?" He squinted at me though sleep-swollen eyes.

"I woke up early," I said, glancing at the clock. It was six forty-five now, but I'd been wide awake since around five, snapping the band on my wrist. My head throbbed dully.

Obviously, McAdam hadn't called 911 last night; it was possible he hadn't even seen my note. The hallway was deserted and silent, and no sign of Luca. Breakfast wouldn't be ready yet. There was no certainty that even if McAdam got the note this morning, he'd do anything. He could think it was a joke and throw it away. He could tell Dr. Cerny and get us thrown out.

Not that I'd mind going home. In fact, that would be hunky-dory with me.

Heath groaned behind me. "Daphne, leave it. She's a grown woman. She can stay in her room if she wants to. Cerny's therapy is really intense. She may not want to talk to you. You should respect that. Give her space."

"And if something happened to her, if she's lost somewhere up on the mountain—"

"Or at the bottom of a cliff . . ." he said.

I glared at him, then turned my back.

"She's not Chantal," he said gently.

"I know." A rustling sound and a couple of thumps rose from the foot of the far stairs. Luca, bringing up the breakfast trays. I closed the door a fraction of an inch more and positioned my eye at the crack.

"Good God," Heath sighed. But I didn't care. I was going to stay at the door until I saw something. Anything—McAdam or Glenys or anyone—and then I would make my move. From the bathroom, I heard the squeak of the faucet and the shower start to run. *Fine, Heath. Take a leisurely shower even though a woman's gone missing. Wouldn't want your day inconvenienced in any way.*

At last I spied Luca rounding the corner, bearing a single tray. Poor guy. He had to make three separate trips, three times a day, up those endless stairs. I was surprised the doc had the place wired up like the CIA, but he couldn't manage to rig up some kind of dumbwaiter for poor Luca.

He stopped when he saw me, then pivoted, depositing the tray in front of the McAdams' door, giving it a light rap. He nodded at me, then headed back down the hall to the back stairs. I thought of all the cameras, whirring away from the safety of their hiding places. I was just going to have to risk Dr. Cerny diagnosing me as a voyeur or paranoid or some other type of mentally ill person. I wasn't leaving my post.

But the McAdams' door never opened, and the tray sat untouched outside the room. When Luca returned with the next tray, he seemed to hesitate at the top of the stairs. I lifted my hand in greeting, and he deposited the tray in front of the Siefferts' door. Before heading down again, he glanced back at me. I withdrew, leaving the door cracked wide enough to spot Glenys or her husband, if either one happened to retrieve their tray. Which they didn't.

Presently Luca was back at the top of the stairs with our food. I hurriedly pushed the door closed and scuttled backward farther into the room, which was a ridiculous move, seeing as I'd obviously been watching him throughout the whole process. Still, when he rapped, I lunged forward, swung the door open, and smiled like I was astonished to find him there. He froze, bent halfway to the floor.

"Hi," I said.

He straightened and gave me a look, but it wasn't a friendly one like we'd shared in the kitchen. He seemed annoyed, maybe even angry. I stared back at him, either waiting to understand the hidden meaning behind his eyes, or daring him to speak—which he eventually did.

"Café da manhã."

"Come in." I beckoned him into the room, but he didn't move. I stepped back, gestured to the table. He entered tentatively, like he thought Heath—or an angry bear—might come crashing in at any minute. "You can put it on the table," I offered, and he did, as quickly as I'd ever seen any hotel room-service waiter do.

He started to back away, but then stopped. Slid his eyes toward the closed bathroom door.

I took a deep breath. Plunged right into the deep end. "He's in the shower. And the cameras don't record sound, I don't think." I held my breath. "I know you want to tell me something."

His eyes flashed for a brief second, then he moved to the open door.

He spoke in heavily accented English, then melted back into the dark hallway.

"Look behind the mirror," was all he said.

The police receptionist—if that's what they call her—is sitting at a small desk right inside the front door. The waiting area is lined with plastic chairs, and one of those huge, chainsaw-carved wood bears stands guard in the corner. When I tell her I need to speak to an officer because of something that's happened up at Baskens, she gestures at the chairs.

"I'll have an officer out to talk to you soon as I can. Can I get you something to drink?"

"Yes, please," I say. I'm starting to feel light headed. Nauseated from the water I gulped down earlier. In my fog, I notice yet another TV, this one a flat-screen affixed to the wall beside the reception desk. No football game playing on this one, it's the local Atlanta news.

"Co-cola? Sprite? Diet?"

I try to concentrate on what the woman is saying. "A Coke, please. Thanks."

When she returns from the back—and presumably telling one of the officers I have a crime to report—she hands me a cold can. I pop the top and tip it up.

She slips behind her desk again.

"Oh. One more thing." I hold up the iPad. It's fogged and slick from being tucked against my sweaty back. "You wouldn't happen to have a pair of earbuds, would you?" She can't disguise a quick furrow of her brow, but she produces a pair of black earbuds from one of the desk drawers and hands them over.

"Thanks."

She nods, but she doesn't make eye contact. I wonder how long it's going to be. There can't be that much going on in Dunfree, Georgia, on a Friday night.

I return to my seat, plug in the earbuds, and tap in the numbers *5353*. In the Notes section, I find the patient folders and click on Heath's. When his voice fills my ears, goose bumps cover my body.

Chapter Twenty-Five

Friday, October 19
Morning

By the time Heath emerged from the shower, I was already well into breakfast. He joined me, digging energetically into the stack of pancakes. A lock of wet hair fell over his eye as he ate.

But all I could think of were Luca's hazel eyes fastened onto mine, his voice in my ears.

Look behind the mirror.

Behind the mirror above the dresser in our room? Or some other mirror? I didn't know. It was all he'd said.

My pulse was racing so fast now it felt like I was about to kick into a panic attack. I played with my food, pretending to eat, pushing the pancakes and bacon around. I'd broken into a sweat despite the frigid room.

I leapt up. "I'll be right back."

"Where you going?" Heath said, working his way through the pancakes.

"I left the book I was reading downstairs."

"There you go, read a book. Much healthier than worrying about everybody else around here."

"Back in a sec," I chirped and scooted out of the room.

In the hallway both trays were still untouched. I still had a chance to make contact with Jerry McAdam. I tapped on the Siefferts' door, but there was no answer. I moved on to the McAdams' and knocked quietly.

"Mr. McAdam, it's Daphne Amos." There was no answer. I bounced on the balls of my feet. "Jerry, I really need to talk to you. I know you have a phone. So I need you to call the police for me. For Glenys Sieffert, okay? That's her name. Glenys Sieffert. She and her husband are staying right next door to you. Just call 911, please."

At the end of the hall, the pocket door was open. Beyond it, I could see that Dr. Cerny's bedroom door was shut. He was either still inside or he was already downstairs in his office getting ready for the day. In either case, I had a chance to get up to the attic without him hearing me. I gauged the time. Soon Heath would be done eating, and Luca would be back up to collect everyone's trays. I had to go now.

I made it up the stairs in seconds. The monitors were on, but the Sieffert screen showed nothing. No people. No activity. The room was empty.

The McAdams were eating breakfast.

But how was that possible? I'd just seen both trays still sitting by the respective doors.

I leaned closer. Their faces were hidden, but I could see the meal clearly enough. Soft-boiled eggs in old-fashioned cups and what looked like grapefruit halves. Which was strange, because back in our room, Heath was shoveling down pancakes and bacon.

"What the hell . . ." I said softly.

So Luca cooked different breakfasts for different guests? That was an extraordinary amount of work for one person, and above and beyond providing dietary substitutions. Something about this felt off. Way off.

I backed out of the room, headed down the stairs, but stopped dead at the pocket door.

Both breakfast trays still sat outside the McAdams' and Siefferts' doors. They looked exactly like they had when Luca had dropped them off, like they hadn't been touched at all. I hesitated. I knew what I'd just seen—the McAdams eating their made-to-order eggs and grapefruit. Was it possible that in the time it had taken me to climb down the stairs, they'd put the tray back out?

I crept toward the McAdams' door and the tray, knelt, and lifted one of the metal lids. The plate underneath was empty. Not just cleared of food but absolutely clean, like it had just come out of the cupboard. I lifted the cover off the other plate, and it was the same. A perfectly pristine plate. No food. Nothing.

I unscrewed the lid of the coffee carafe and turned it upside down. Nothing came out. It was completely, utterly empty. I dropped it, ran over to the Siefferts' tray, and lifted those covers too. The plates were clean.

I flung the covers across the hall. Kicked at the tray, and utensils and glasses and carafe shot in all directions, clattering across the runner and bouncing off the opposite wall. My brain wasn't computing the images. They didn't make any sense. Not in the world where I was living and breathing—the dark hallway in a crimson house hidden away on a mountain. Where my fiancé ate syrupy pancakes down the hall like everything was perfectly normal and right.

But it wasn't. Not by a long shot.

There was something terribly wrong here. Utterly and irrevocably wrong. I couldn't zero in on what it was exactly, but I did know a few things: I knew Matthew Cerny had led me and Heath to believe we were on a retreat, a weeklong retreat with two other couples . . .

. . . who were nowhere to be found.

. . . who were being delivered trays of empty dishes for their meals.

But the other couples had been here at one point, hadn't they? I'd met the McAdams, Jerry and Donna, just a few days ago. I'd seen them with my own eyes. Had they left? Gone down to Dunfree, like Reggie Teague, for some reason? But why would they? And why had Glenys and her husband left too?

Was it possible that Heath and I were actually alone here?

I tore down the hallway, charged back up the cramped staircase to the hexagonal attic. Sure enough, on the monitors, the McAdam and Sieffert rooms were buzzing with activity. Mrs. McAdam was making the bed while, across the room, her husband tied his shoes. Mr. Sieffert was pulling on pants, tucking in his shirt, staring at his reflection in the mirror on the closet door. Glenys was nowhere in sight.

I moved closer to the Sieffert monitor. Waited until the bathroom door opened, and a woman emerged, then sat on the bed, her back toward the camera.

It looked like Glenys, but honestly, I couldn't see her face, only her back and profile. It could have been anyone. Any woman who was tall and slender with lightish hair. The next monitor over, Jerry McAdam—or somebody that looked a lot like him—watched his wife disappear into the bathroom and shut the door. He waited a second, then pulled out his old-school flip phone.

I spun to face the wall behind me. Studied the massive blocks of metal, their complicated faces of knobs and dials and gauges humming and clicking away. It sounded the same as every other time I'd been up here, but I'd just assumed it was part of the doctor's J. Edgar Hoover setup. And I'd never bothered to really examine it.

Even though it was broad daylight outside, the attic was still dark. I ran my hands over the machinery, and all the way at the end, I found a section of boxy-looking green metal units, stacked four high. They were almost hidden, wedged between the bigger machinery and the wall. Each of them had one vertical slot.

Four in all.

I studied them, waiting for my brain to catch up with what my gut was already telling me. I knew what this was, I did. It was just that I was used to seeing one of these gadgets as a slim black box, sitting on top of a TV, with one horizontal slot and a few buttons underneath. But this was the same thing. It was the exact same goddamn thing.

A VCR.

A whole VHS system connected to the monitors up on the shelf.

I stuck my hand in one of the slots, and my fingers hit plastic. I could feel the mechanism whirring under my touch. I pushed on it, thinking it might release and eject, but it didn't. I stepped back. Started randomly pressing every button, turning dials and knobs indiscriminately. I hit a black square button and, like magic, one of the tapes popped out from the last slot on the row.

"Shit."

I pulled it out of the slot and looked at the label. *Sieffert, Randall & Glenys—2006.*

I practically smashed the other buttons, and another tape popped out. I yanked it out and looked at the label. *McAdam, Jerry & Donna—2007.* I dropped it, then shoved the Sieffert tape back into the deck. The tape chunked into the player and began to whir.

When I turned back to the monitors, the woman—the Glenys Sieffert doppelganger—was on camera. She was dressed in a sweater and trousers, her hair still dripping from the shower. She stood in the middle of the room, in a block of sunlight from the window, fluffing her hair. I watched her, mesmerized.

I couldn't believe that I'd missed it. It was so obvious. I'd expected to see the Glenys I knew—I'd wanted to, and so I had. But this woman wasn't Glenys. She was tall and thin, yes, but her face was all wrong. Her eyes too close together, her nose long and slightly hooked in profile, instead of Glenys's straight, elegant one.

I felt my breath go shallow, my whole body tingle in alarm. The woman I'd been talking to all week had told me her name was Glenys.

Cerny had made sure he had a tape of her look-alike playing at all times on the monitors. All of this was part of a carefully thought-out plan. A plan designed to fool me and Heath.

But why?

What possible reason could Cerny have for hiding the identity of the woman I'd befriended?

I heard a door slam somewhere downstairs. I backed out of the attic and flew down both flights of back stairs just as Luca was entering the kitchen from outside. We each stopped dead at the sight of the other.

I waved at him, wildly, probably looking like a crazy woman. "You need to go. Get out of here."

He shook his head. I could tell he was worried about me, that he wanted to stay and help, which was sweet. But this was not a time for chivalry. No good could come from either of us hanging around here for one minute longer.

"I'm fine. I'm safe." I looked over my shoulder. "But Dr. Cerny is crazy—he's a fucking lunatic—and you don't need to be in this house with him." If I could've physically pushed him out the door I would have, but he retreated of his own accord, right out the door he'd come in.

I ran back up the stairs and down the hall to Glenys's room. *Correction. Not Glenys, not her room.* I squared up to the door, drew in a deep breath, then kicked it as hard as I could. The door rattled in its frame but held fast. Which stood to reason. The thing had been built to last for generations. Twice as thick as modern doors and solid as stone, made from impenetrable, age-hardened oak.

I kicked again, feeling something bitter and strong rise up in me, the fear that had been seeping through my insides since the first moment I'd set foot in this house. It had been leaking from the poisoned well of my past, pooling in all the cracks, drowning me from the inside out. But now, each time my boot struck the door, I felt the fear transform to fury, giving me strength. I closed my eyes and thought of them all.

Mrs. Bobbie. Kick. *Mr. Al.* Kick.
Omega. Kick. *The psychologist.* Kick.
Chantal. Kick, kick, kick.

A crack appeared right down the center of the door, and the door banged open so hard, it slammed back and hit me smack on the nose. Eyes watering, I pushed it open again and entered the room.

Or, rather, the suite. The apartment—because that's what it was—was made up of three identical rooms, just like I'd been seeing on the monitors, only I hadn't noticed they were actually connected by doors. The doors were opened now, and as I turned a full three-sixty, the realization dawned that the suite ran the length of the entire hall. The room I was standing in was papered in faded brown roses just like I'd seen on the tape, the wood-plank floor worn bare. Cobwebs waved from the ceiling corners and edges of the windowsills. A film of dust covered everything. There was no furniture anywhere in sight. Not a bed, not a table, not one chair. Not even a stray rug or scrap of a curtain. It was completely bare.

No one had been here in a very long time.

I walked all the way through the apartment to the room at the end. It seemed to have been retrofitted for another use. One half was a kitchenette, the other half a makeshift classroom. A large chalkboard with bits of chalk and an eraser in the tray covered the window. I imagined a desk, a child's desk like the one in the barn, situated in front of it, the board covered in history dates or math equations or diagrammed sentences. I envisioned the sharp point of a pencil as it dug into the soft wood of the desk's surface. *I have no pity.*

Against the far wall, in between the two sections, sat a cherry buffet over which hung an enormous, rectangular gilt-framed mirror. The thing was a monstrosity, an overly ornate piece that seemed out of place in this bare, dusty room. I walked to it, drawn to my own reflection. My hair was sticking out all over, wild and frizzing in the humidity, my face flushed. I looked like someone I didn't recognize. Someone angry and strong and determined. I touched my face, feeling the pressure of my fingertips against my skin.

I backed out of the room, returning to the middle one. This room had the same faded, scarred wood floors, but was papered in grimy gold grass cloth. Along the bathroom door, cut into the vertical wood molding, was a series of pencil marks. A growth chart, a lot like the one Mr. Al made on the garage door of the brown brick house.

So, a growth chart.

A chalkboard.

And a child's desk.

All of which added up to one undeniable conclusion. Before being used as rooms for Cerny's patients, they had been someone's home. A child's home.

That's when I heard the music. Frank Sinatra. I looked over my shoulder, back into the bedroom with the faded brown-rose walls. Heath was there, standing in the center of the room, frozen. There was a look of horror dawning across his face. I walked toward him, slowly, as Frank's velvet purr filled the room.

"Did you turn that music on?" I asked him.

It took a minute for his eyes to focus on me. He didn't say a word. I walked past him. The iPod was lying on the windowsill, a long, snaking white cable connecting it to a small stereo receiver on the floor below. The iPod was an older generation, one of those oversize models with the big, chunky wheel. I spun the wheel and the screen lit up.

The song title scrolled across the screen: "Why Can't You Behave?" I hit "Reverse" and saw the playlist. *Matthew & Cecelia*. All Frank Sinatra songs, scores of them. I felt dizzy.

"Heath?" I turned back to him. He still hadn't moved. "No one's been staying in these rooms," I said. "We're alone in this house."

He shook his head. "That doesn't make any sense."

"I know. But look at this place. He lied to us. Made us think we were here with two other couples. But it was a game. He's playing us." I looked at him. "Why did you turn on the music?"

"I don't know." His voice was calm, eerily so.

I felt like someone had grabbed my heart and was squeezing it so hard it might stop beating.

"Do you remember it—this song?" I asked him.

He shook his head. "Should I?"

"You said you hated it. You said Frank Sinatra was a deal breaker. Don't you remember?"

He just stared blankly at me.

"Are you okay?" I asked.

"We should go back to the room," he said.

I took his hand. "We're not just going back to our room, Heath. We have to get out of Baskens."

He looked at me, expressionless. "Yeah."

Somehow I maneuvered him back into our room, grabbed my bag, and started stuffing clothes into it. In the process, I fished out Jessica Kyung's card and slid it into my jeans pocket. I'd be giving her a call about Dr. Matthew Cerny as soon as I could find a phone. The authorities were sure as shit going to hear about this insanity. In the bathroom, Heath seemed to have snapped out of whatever fog he was in and was gathering our toiletries and dumping them all into his bag.

"We should confront him," he kept saying as he went back and forth between the rooms. "Get our money back."

"Forget the money," I snapped. "The guy's a whack job. A lunatic. And we don't need to engage with him. He could be dangerous. He could hurt us. He could hurt Luca. We have to leave."

"I just think we should take a minute and think. Make a plan."

"He tricked us, Heath. He set this whole farce up to make us think we were up here on this mountain, in this creepy house, with other people. But we're not. We're alone! And, incidentally, not only that, he's got more cameras hidden around here, which we didn't agree to. They could be running around the clock, and we'd never know—because he never told us. He's gone to a whole hell of a lot of trouble to watch us night and day, and it's not just because he wants to help us. Trust me. The man has got a screw loose. He's got about a thousand fucking screws loose." Grabbing a poker from the fireplace, I leapt up onto the bed.

"What are you doing?" Heath said.

"I'm showing him exactly what I think of his game." I yelled out into the room. "You watching, Doctor? Remember how I said I didn't do therapy?" I smiled. "Well, I changed my mind. I'm finally ready to express myself."

I swung up at the lazily spinning fan, missed, then swung once more.

The poker hit the fan with a loud metallic clang. I swung again and again, beating the thing until it began to sway crazily. One final whack, and the blades caught the poker and flung it like a missile across the room. Heath and I both ducked. I snatched it up and headed for a painting. I whacked at it, as hard as I could, and the painting separated from the frame. In the crack between, I spotted a tiny lens and yanked it out.

But I wasn't done. I circled the room, smashing lamps and pictures and the mirror above the dresser. Things shattered and ripped, fell off the walls, and crashed to the floor. Cameras sprung out of the wall, crazy, high-tech jacks-in-the-box.

I let the poker clang to the floor, panting.

Heath lifted his head from his hands. His face was ashen. "What the hell did I drag you into?"

I grabbed his wrist. "It doesn't matter. What we need to do now is get the car keys. And get the hell out of here. The keys are hanging on hooks in his office. And get the cell phones too, if you can. I saw Luca—"

"Luca?"

"The cook, the waiter guy. I told him to run. He's probably gone already. I'll get the car and bring it around front."

"Cerny will be in his office."

"Okay, then. Forget the cell phones. We don't need them."

He followed me down the front stairs. We dropped our bags in the front hall, and I followed him to the sunroom. He gently eased the door open and slipped in. Snagging the keys, he tossed them to me. I darted back through the hall to the front door. Outside, I ran for the car. The Nissan was still there, thank God. I looked across the yard. Without the chain, the barn doors gaped open. I ran over.

The knife was wedged between the concrete floor and the rotted wood-board wall, right where I'd kicked it when Heath hadn't been watching. I grabbed it and ran back to the car, slid behind the wheel, and dropped the knife into the pocket of the door. But what the hell did I think I was going to do with a kitchen knife? Stab Cerny? Or Glenys? If things got dire, would I even have the guts to do such a thing? I guessed I was about to find out.

I turned the ignition, and the engine sputtered. *Dammit, not now.* I gave it one more go and, thank God, it turned over. Shaky with relief, I shifted into reverse. The next sound I heard, the crunch of metal on metal, made me stomp on the brake. *Shit.* I'd sideswiped the car next to me, the green Tacoma truck. I bit my lip, then kept going, scraping all the way down the vehicle until I was past it. We were getting out of here, and there was no turning back. Shifting into drive, I swerved around the side of the house just as Heath was striding across the porch with the bags. He climbed in the car.

"I couldn't find them," he said. It took a minute to understand what he was saying. Our phones. He wasn't able to find our phones. But it didn't matter. The only thing that mattered was getting away from this place. I punched the gas, and we spun away from the house.

Chapter Twenty-Six

Heath's Nissan fishtailed over the gravel road, hitting every rock and rut as I maneuvered around the hairpin curves like a madwoman.

"Jesus, Daphne," Heath said. He was pressed back against his seat, clutching the handle over his door in a death grip. I didn't slow down. We could do that when we got to Dunfree. We would talk then, make plans, argue, whatever. As for now, I was getting us off this miserable mountain.

"Did he see you?" I asked.

"No. He wasn't in the office. Watch it!"

I took the corner fast and felt the tires skid under us. "I hope he's taken a dive off the mountain—that sleazy charlatan. That lying, garbage, snake-oil-selling sonofa—"

Out of nowhere, a figure appeared—a man in dark trousers and a tweed coat—and stepped into the road, right in front of the car.

I stomped on the brakes, hard, and the car jerked to the right, jolting us. We dropped, one time, then again, my stomach flopping like I was on a roller coaster. My head snapped sideways, bone connecting with tempered glass, and as my arms flew out to brace myself, I heard a loud, metallic *chunk*. I slammed back into my seat, and everything went deathly silent.

No. Not completely silent. I could hear the sound of my breathing, and after a few seconds, other sounds too. Heath breathing. The birds and the wind in the tops of the trees. I took stock of my situation. My wrist hurt, and my head, and I was wedged down between the seat and the dash, so far down all I could see was the door of the Nissan. I didn't have my seatbelt on. I hadn't taken the time to fasten it.

I looked out the cracked windshield. The Nissan was rammed against a tree, a small pine. I twisted around. We weren't that far off the road. But where was the man? Had I hit him? And then I heard a groan. Oh my God, Heath.

I lifted myself back onto the seat and saw him slumped against his door, his back to me. I tugged gingerly at his arm.

"Heath? Are you okay? Talk to me."

His head rolled to face me. Blood dripped from his nose, and a nasty red lump rose just above his eye. He groaned again.

I touched his face. "Heath?"

He shook me off. Pressed himself back against the seat. He dabbed his sleeve to his nose. Blinked a few times. "I'm fine."

"That was Cerny. Jesus, he just jumped out in the middle of the road. Did I hit him?"

"I don't think so." He was massaging his temples now.

I climbed out to inspect the front of the car. It had cracked the pine clear through its trunk. I could smell the sharp aromas of sap and green wood. If I'd hit Cerny, there certainly didn't appear to be any sign of it—or him—on the bumper. And we really weren't that far off the road. It was just that it was so steep here. We were lucky we hadn't flipped on our way down.

I heard the passenger door creak, and Heath emerged from the other side. He straightened, then went down hard. I ran to him.

Although he'd already managed to right himself again, his face looked pale. I reached for him, but he shooed me back.

"I twisted my knee. Maybe tore something. God*dammit*." He stood, balancing precariously on one leg, grimacing.

"We have to get you to a doctor," I said. "I'll try to get the car started again. Do you want to sit down or something?"

"This car isn't going anywhere."

"I'll try." I slid behind the wheel and cranked it, but all that resulted was a forlorn clicking sound. A thin stream of smoke rose from a crack between the crumpled hood and body of the car.

"She's gone," came a voice behind us. For a second, I thought it was Heath, talking about the car. Then Cerny step-slid down the slope into sight, using the trees to balance. The knot of his brown silk tie was pulled loose, and his shirttails flapped. I struggled out from behind the wheel, leaping toward him.

"You idiot! You almost got us—" I began.

Heath put out a protective hand. "Don't."

"I can't understand it." Cerny was on the other side of the car now, regarding both of us with a look of sincere confusion. "I just can't understand it," he repeated, then leaned against the car and let out a wail, a low sound that made the hairs on my arm stand on end. After a few seconds he looked up. His face was puffy and red. "You know, you said she was missing, and I didn't believe you. But I thought, *I'll drive down the road a bit, see if I can't catch a glimpse* . . . We have to call the police. She's gone, and I need your help."

The clouds had hidden the sun, and the wind was biting now. Heath pressed his jacket sleeve to his bleeding nose, then leaned against the car. He looked dazed, like he was on the verge of fainting.

I spoke up. "We can't help you, Dr. Cerny. I have to get Heath to town. He hurt his knee as we were swerving to avoid hitting you."

Cerny addressed Heath. "It's Cecelia." He looked at me then. "Glenys, as you know her. I need your help."

I shook my head. "What do you mean she's gone? Like missing, or—"

"Daphne." Heath sent me a look heavy with meaning. I shut my mouth.

"Show us where she is, Doctor," he said. "And we'll do what we can. But then we have to go."

"Heath, your knee," I said.

"It's fine."

Cerny started into the trees, sliding on the dry leaves blanketing the slope, grasping at branches for balance. I followed him, my arms folded tightly over my chest, and Heath fell into line, limping behind me. My nerves were vibrating, singing along with the wind and panic inside me.

Less than a dozen yards into the woods, Cerny stopped. I did too, then covered my mouth. The body lay on the ground, partly covered by brush and leaves. I could see, even from where I stood, who it was. But only from what she wore, the same thing she'd been dressed in the other day at the creek—black yoga pants and top. The yellow baseball cap on the ground a couple of feet away. The breeze lifted strands of her hair. Her face was a waxy greenish blue, an unrecognizable, bloated mass.

I took one more step forward, caught a whiff of decay, then stopped, suppressing the automatic response of sick that rose in my throat.

"She was hanging up there," Cerny said beside me, and automatically, I looked up at the oak tree. I wished I hadn't. There was a length of rusted chain hanging from the lowest branch. It looked a lot like the chain that had been wound around the barn doors. "She must've hanged herself."

I lurched back and vomited into the leaves. When I was done, I sat down, gasping and wiping tears and snot and vomit. When I stood again, I felt Heath's hand on my shoulder, leaning on me for support.

"Are you okay?" he asked me in a low voice.

I nodded. "It's her. It's Glenys."

He pressed his lips into a thin line, then pulled me back toward the car, a couple of yards away from Cerny and Glenys's still form. I grasped his jacket, two fistfuls, and held on to him as tightly as I could.

"Do you think he killed her?" he asked me.

"I don't know. But we have to get down to Dunfree. Report it to the police there."

"The car is wrecked. My knee feels like a truck ran over it. We can't walk down to Dunfree."

My eyes cut to Cerny. "We could take his car. Or one of the others."

Heath shook his head. "And let him get away? No fucking way. Let's just get him back to the house and see that he's . . . I don't know, secured, I guess. He seems pretty distraught. Maybe if we just talk to him, he'll stay put. I'll get a bag of ice on my knee. We'll call the police and then, when they show up, get the hell out of here."

The temperature was falling, and I felt a few drops of rain hit me. It had gotten colder, just in the time we'd been out here. I felt myself begin to shiver uncontrollably.

"The whole thing is just wrong," I said.

Heath glanced over at the doctor. "Agreed. The guy's a kook—and, I don't know, maybe he even had something to do with this whole . . . Glenys situation—but either way, we need to let the police handle it."

He was right. I knew he was, but the last thing I wanted to do was go back to that house.

"Don't worry." Heath touched my face. "I may have a bum knee, but he's old. If he tries anything . . . if he tries to hurt you, I'll beat the ever-loving shit out of him."

Heath gestured at Cerny to get his attention. "It's going to take the police a good half hour to get up here," he yelled. "We'll go back to the house and wait there with you. It's getting cold. And dark."

"We can't leave her. There are animals . . ." Cerny's voice trailed off. *Oh my God.*

Heath snapped at the doctor. "Cover her with your jacket, if you want."

Cerny shucked off his tweed jacket and Heath hobbled through the leaves and draped it over the upper half of Glenys's body. A makeshift shroud. Would that really keep the animals off her? I didn't know how these things worked—these very basic, human events of life and death and nature. Other than Chantal in her nest of white satin, I'd never seen a dead person.

"Go get your car. Wait for us up at the road," Heath said to Cerny, who nodded like an obedient child and lumbered away. I pulled open the door of the Nissan, scooped the knife out of the door pocket, and held it up.

"Okay," Heath said dubiously.

"Just in case." I slid the blade between my wool sock and boot, then pulled my jeans over the handle. I offered him an arm. "One of us should have a weapon."

Cerny drove us back up to the house, disappeared into his office for several minutes, then rejoined us in the front hall. "Dunfree police are on the way." He raked a hand through his wet hair.

I glanced at Heath. "Maybe we should call too."

Cerny handed his phone to Heath, who limped into the library to make the call.

"I'm sorry for running out in the road," Cerny said. "For behaving so . . . erratically. I was distraught. Not thinking straight." He shook his head. "I didn't expect to find her in that state."

The image of Glenys flashed into my brain. Her body covered by Cerny's tweed jacket, anointed by the freezing rain, slowly stiffening, cold under the low white clouds, the dampness soaking to her skin. The temperature would probably plunge tonight—the first drop of the fall—but it would be okay, the police would get to her before then. They would zip her up in one of those black bags, and she would be protected from the cold and wet.

I wanted to ask him who she really was and why she'd lied to me, but that would have to wait for when the police arrived. For now, I just wanted to make sure Heath was comfortable and keep this maniac as calm as possible.

The doctor sighed and scrubbed at his eyes. "I could use a drink. Join me?"

"Yeah, no," I said with a twist of my lips. "No drink for me."

Cerny scuttled back to his office, and I went into the library. Heath was leaning against the mantel, just hanging up the phone.

"Are they coming?" I asked.

He nodded.

"Do you think Luca got out? Maybe he's called the police too."

He shook his head. "I wouldn't count on any help from him. Ten to one, he's illegal."

"What if Cerny killed him too?"

"Daphne, come on. We don't know for sure that he killed Glenys— or whatever her name is. He said she hanged herself with the chain."

"He also said this was a couples' retreat, introduced us to a fake couple called the McAdams and told us they were staying in an empty room upstairs." I was on a roll. "Glenys was in her sixties, and that branch was at least seven or eight feet off the ground. Tell me how a woman that age, or any age, for that matter, could"—I swallowed—"loop a heavy metal chain around her neck, throw it up over a tree, and attach it all by herself? Not to mention I didn't see a clip or a lock or anything that would've held it fast. The whole thing defies the laws of physics."

Heath shook his head wearily. "I don't know, Daphne. Maybe we overlooked whatever Glenys used on the chain. I mean, it could've fallen in the leaves, right? And look, obviously, the guy's a nut. But I don't think he's dangerous. If he did kill her, wouldn't he be long gone by now?"

"You're assuming he's in his right mind."

"Anyway, when the police get here, we'll tell them everything. Let them handle it. I'm going to sit down."

"I'll get you some ice."

"No." He put his hand on my arm. "We stay together until the police come."

He eased himself down on the dusty, threadbare sofa and leaned his head against the back. His dark hair and jacket were still damp, but he made no move to dry off. He seemed too focused on the pain. Cerny—or Luca—had lit the gas fire and it was crackling in the grate, animating the fiend behind it.

I moved closer to the fire, rolled my stiff shoulders, and closed my eyes. I pictured Jerry and Donna McAdam the way I'd seen them when we first arrived at Baskens, standing by the bay window, wineglasses in hand. It was hard to believe they were nothing but actors in a play, random people who Cerny had convinced or paid to come up here and lie to us.

Jesus. It was all so preposterous.

Shortly, Dr. Cerny returned with our phones and a tray with two crystal tumblers of brown liquor. He'd already partaken back in his office—I could smell it in a cloud around him, bourbon or scotch, I couldn't tell the difference.

"Did you drug it again?" I asked Cerny. Across the room, I could feel Heath stiffening, wanting to intervene, but I didn't care. I was through holding my tongue.

Cerny met my gaze. "I'm sorry about before. I thought it was for your own good."

"Have a seat, Dr. Cerny," Heath said. "I think it's time we all had a talk."

"I'm not—" Cerny said at the same time, but at the look on Heath's face, he shut his mouth. I suddenly felt inexplicably gripped with fear.

"I don't want to talk," I said.

"I know you don't, my dear," Heath said. And, for some reason, I wanted to say something nasty in return. Heath had never called me that—*my dear*. I hated the way it sounded coming from his mouth. But I was just on edge.

"The police will be here soon," I said.

"Yes, they will," Heath said. "But we have a while before that time comes. Can you listen?"

I nodded wordlessly.

"You must already realize this by now," he went on. "That I brought you here under false pretenses. It was my idea, the story about participating in a couples' retreat."

Suddenly, I felt excruciatingly hot, my entire body bathed in a fine layer of sweat. My heart slammed in my chest, and I couldn't catch my breath.

"Not that I expected the doctor to take the ruse to such elaborate extremes," he continued. "But then again, he's always been a bit on the theatrical side."

Something very bad was about to happen in this room. I understood that now. And there was no way I could stop it.

"We're going to talk," Heath said. "The three of us, right now."

My head had begun to feel buzzy, and I couldn't shut out the images of Glenys's dead, bloated face. A rusty chain slung over a branch. An empty three-room apartment. A lawn strewn with dead birds. I breathed deeply, willing my body to settle.

Heath sighed. "I needed you here with me, Daphne. I was scared if you knew what was really going on, you would refuse to come. So, the doctor arranged the week. He arranged the McAdams and Dr. Teague. The economy up here has been squeezed for years. With the promise of cash, it wasn't that hard to convince a few locals to help us out."

He shifted, easily. Too easily. His knee didn't look like it was bothering him any longer, as a matter of fact.

"I wanted us, the four of us—you, me, Cerny, and Cecelia—to come together so the truth could finally come out. I've never told you the truth about myself, but I would like to tell you now, if you want. Would you like to hear the truth, Daphne?"

"Of course," I said. I was trembling, and he saw it and smiled.

Strange, what a relief it was to finally say those words, even though I had spent our entire relationship avoiding both his truth and mine. Yes, I did want to know the truth—even though I was certain that, when Heath was finished telling me, the world would look like an entirely different place.

Friday, October 19
Night

"I'm supposed to just start talking?"

"That's the way it's always worked, Heath. Or have you forgotten?"

"I haven't forgotten anything. And it feels strange for you to call me that."

"Would you prefer Sam?"

"Either way."

"All right, then. Sam. Why don't you start at the point when you left us? What was it like for you during those years on your own?"

"Different, I guess. For a lot of reasons. Mainly all the unsupervised time. The freedom. I was on my own. Homeless, essentially. Drifting around Georgia, Florida for a while. Louisiana. Working odd jobs, painting crews, ditch digging. Sleeping in alleys, on sidewalks. In cars I could break into."

"Must have been a heady feeling. Finally being free to do what you wanted."

"I don't know if heady's *the word I'd use. I was free, yeah. But I didn't have any idea what I wanted to do with that freedom. Of course, I wanted to drink and smoke weed. Meet girls, and . . ."*

"And what?"

(silence)

"What did you want to do with those girls?"

"You tell me, Doctor."

"How could I possibly know that?"

"All the times we talked? All the things I told you? The birds."

"That was a long time ago, Sam. You were a boy then."

"Boys grow into men."

"What do you mean by that?"

"I mean the fantasies never went away. They never . . . lessened in their intensity. I couldn't stop thinking about them. Playing them out in my mind every day. Dreaming about them every night."

"So when did the thoughts become actions, Heath? Tell me about that."

Chapter Twenty-Seven

Friday, October 19
Afternoon

"What we did," Dr. Cerny said. "What happened to Heath . . . it was all because of my ego. My need to be recognized—"

The doctor stopped, as if he couldn't continue. I wondered if it was a real reaction to everything that was happening, or something put on just for effect. *Bastard,* I thought. He wasn't remorseful. He had brought this all on himself—and I wasn't so sure he hadn't killed Glenys as well. It certainly was plausible.

Cerny had resumed talking. "From my days as a student, I'd always been fascinated by one area of psychiatry—an understudied, misunderstood, popularly maligned personality disorder. Doctors said there was no cure for it. No treatment and no hope of improvement. But there was no research to back up those claims. No hard, incontrovertible data."

He folded his hands.

"In an absence of data, we experiment. And for experiments we need test subjects. But certainly no parents were willing to offer up their children. No fit parents, anyway."

Heath was sitting very still.

The doctor continued. "There were studies, few and far between, MRIs that revealed anatomical differences in the subgenual cortex and the paralimbic system. Underfunctioning of the amygdala and so on. But they've never been adequately tested on children suspected of having the disorder."

The doctor's words flowed around me like a riptide. I gripped the nearby edge of the bookshelves, as if that could keep me from being swept away.

"I knew, if I found the right subject, if I was allowed to create the perfectly modulated test environment, I could conduct the research we needed to truly understand the disorder. It would involve intricate, meticulous planning. Careful monitoring and the utmost discretion, allowing a level of experimental observation and behavior modification that I'd never undertaken. I realized"—his eyes flashed—"that a study of groundbreaking significance was within reach. One that could revolutionize a formerly dark area of psychiatry."

I glanced at Heath.

"I moved to Atlanta after receiving my degree and opened a practice there with a woman I'd met in school, Cecelia. We ran it for many years—but she knew where my interest truly lay, and eventually, together, we began the search for our first subject."

Silence settled over the room. I looked at Heath and cleared my throat. "You still haven't said what disorder you're talking about." He and Heath each shifted in their seats.

Dr. Cerny spoke. "A nonspecified disorder not officially listed in the DSM—commonly known as psychopathic disorder."

Something changed in the room, something in the air—as if the barometric pressure had dipped dramatically and everything had to reset. After a second or two, I laughed, but it sounded hollow. Strange. "Heath's not a psychopath," I said.

No one contradicted me. No one said a word.

"I know him," I went on. "He's a good man. Kind. Considerate. And he cares about me."

Cerny stood. "Psychopaths aren't what you see in the movies, Daphne. They're not sadistic killers or violent criminals. They are simply devoid of some of the human emotions we consider basic and, dare I say, essential. Emotions like empathy, shame. Remorse and fear."

I glanced at Heath. He was looking down at his clasped hands.

"Without these emotions, they are untethered by normal connections to humanity. This enables them to pursue their own ends without being restrained by inconvenient feelings. The threat of punishment means nothing to these people. The only thing that motivates them is reward. And they'll do anything to gain it."

"That isn't Heath," I said. "That isn't him at all."

Once again, silence.

Then, in the calmest, most level way imaginable, Heath replied, "It is me."

I fixed him with a defiant stare. "No, it's not," I said. "It's not. Fuck you. Fuck both of you."

Heath stood and moved to me, and I slapped him, hard, once across the face. His head snapped away, then swiveled back like I hadn't even struck him. When he looked at me, he seemed so sad. There was a bright-red spot where I'd hit him.

"Stop doing this," I whispered. "Please."

He spoke calmly. Quietly. "Daphne, I've learned over a long time how to operate on an intellectual level. I know I should have empathy, so I display a facsimile of it. I don't feel it, but I make you think I do. I'd like to say I do it because of some altruistic seed deep within me, but that's not true." He shook his head. "I do it because of the reward I get."

"No . . ."

"You."

I slapped him again, then a third time, with all my strength. He took each one stoically, absorbing the force of my blows, then gently reached for my trembling hand.

"For example . . ." I followed his gaze down to our entwined fingers. "Right now I'm holding your hand not because some inner impulse deep within me is compelling me. I'm doing it because I know this is what a supportive boyfriend, a loving fiancé, is expected to do in a moment like this."

I shook my head.

"I know it's what you want," he said. "And I want to give you what you want. Because then I get what I want. Which is you, by my side. If I do what I should according to the laws of society, I get us, together. Always us."

My eyes swam with tears, and I pulled my hand out of his grasp. Dr. Cerny crossed the room to stand at one of the front windows. The rain was coming down hard now outside.

Heath spoke again. "I was born Sam O'Hearn. When I was four years old, the doctor took me from my mother. We'd been living in downtown Atlanta. A crack house, for all intents and purposes. My mother was an addict, a prostitute, and I don't know what else. And I was a difficult child. I screamed for hours, all night sometimes. I used to bang doors, over and over, sometimes until their hinges broke. It was a wonder she could care for me, a wonder I didn't end up in the system, but for a couple of years she was able to manage it."

His eyes registered pain. Or they seemed to. But maybe this was just another trick of his—intellectualizing normal human emotions and passing them off as authentic.

He sighed and went on. "She came across an ad in the Personals section of the Atlanta paper. The people, a doctor and his assistant, wanted test subjects and would pay for the privilege. That was the magic word, apparently. She let them come to our apartment, where they questioned me. And her."

I shook my head. "I don't understand."

"Dr. Cerny and his assistant, Cecelia Beck, were looking for children who displayed early indicators of antisocial behavior. Frequent, uncontrollable tantrums. An imperviousness to punishment. They arranged for an MRI and got their confirmation, that I had less gray matter in the prefrontal cortex. Abnormality in my white matter. How'm I doing, Doc?"

Cerny puffed out a breath at the window. "Just fine."

"The assumption was that I would continue down the path my brain had set for me. I would grow up to become your run-of-the-mill psychopath. You know—the guy a couple of doors down who you'd prefer not to hang out with. You don't know why exactly . . . just that something isn't quite right about him. He's charming, but he doesn't connect on a deep level. Maybe he's a jerk to his kids, maybe he cheats on his wife and at golf every Saturday at the club. Mostly, though, he's the guy who just does whatever the hell he can to get whatever it is that he wants. Probably more of us walking around than you would ever think."

Heath flicked a look at Cerny, who still hadn't turned around. "Dr. Cerny and Cecelia believed I deserved a chance, that I could learn to override my genetics, learn to operate in a different way. They might not have been able to cure me—save me from who I was on a DNA level—but they were convinced I could be conditioned to rise above it. They believed they could prevent me from going off the rails later in life—from getting into trouble, at a criminal level or otherwise."

"And they did," I said. "Look at you. We're getting married. You have a good job, friends."

The doctor finally spoke. "No one really knows what exactly flips that switch that transforms a basic psychopath from someone who merely cheats on his taxes to someone who commits more serious crimes. We believed, with careful conditioning, we could discover the mechanism in order to dismantle it. So we asked Heath's mother to let him come live with us."

My head swiveled back to face Heath. "She signed away her parental rights?"

"She needed the money," Heath said simply. "And they gave her a lot of it. They brought me here, up the mountain, to live with them in this house. I stayed upstairs, never leaving the grounds, under their constant surveillance. Cecelia became my mother." He hesitated. "The doctor, my father. I believed Cecelia and the doctor were married, that they were my actual parents, and we were a real family. The doctor and Cecelia weren't abusive, physically or in any other overt way. They simply withheld certain natural human interactions that might corrupt the research."

"But I thought they wanted to help you."

"We were helping him," Cerny said. "By gathering information. Collecting data that would be used in all future research on psychopathy. We had to be very careful, very deliberate in our methods."

Heath let out a long exhale.

"What does that mean?" I asked Cerny. "What did you do to him?"

"No one was allowed to touch me," Heath said. "No hugs, no kisses, no gesture that could be considered affectionate in any way. My conditioning was to be strictly reward based. B. F. Skinner, all the way. Anything outside the parameters could skew the results."

I interrupted. "And you were going to publish a paper—"

"A book," Cerny said. "A groundbreaking work that would change the course of psychology forever."

I couldn't stifle my laughter. "And you actually thought the scientific community was going to accept a book like that with no objections? That they would look the other way and let you get away with what was clearly a breach of ethics and guidelines and God knows what else?"

"Scientists understand that the greatest minds must bend the rules to achieve their ends." He pushed up his sleeves. "I was a well-regarded psychologist with my past practice. And I continued to see a few patients down in Dunfree, in order to maintain my license. I knew, though, when the mental-health community saw what Cecelia and I had accomplished, when they read about our findings with Sam, I would be named among the greats like Freud, Piaget, Pavlov."

"But you didn't write the book. You ended up leading couples' retreats. What happened?"

His eyes clouded and he glanced at Heath. "A scientist can't draw a conclusion without analyzing all the data."

"And your data ran away before you could do that." I turned to my fiancé. "So that's why we came? So he could finish his book? Somehow I don't believe that. There's more, isn't there? There has to be more. What about the nightmares?"

Cerny chuckled softly. "Oh, Daphne. What a perfect match you are for our boy. Tell her, Sam. Tell her the real reason you brought her to Baskens."

Heath regarded him coolly. "She needs to see the tapes first."

"Tapes?" I said.

"I don't think that's—" Cerny said.

"I want her to see," he said. "I want her to understand everything." He turned to me. "You're right, Daphne. That's part of the reason why I came back to Baskens, because the doctor wanted to find out how his experiment turned out. But also because of the nightmares. That's why we set it up the way we did—as a couples' retreat. I had to get you up here with me, and there didn't seem to be any other way."

"So what else do you need to tell me, Heath?" I asked. "What is the truth?"

"It's on the tapes," he replied simply.

Cerny cut in. "The tapes Cecelia and I made of him when he was a boy. Our research. When he lived here with us at Baskens. He brought you here because he wanted you to understand what he is. Why he is."

My gut twisted. I could still taste a trace of the vomit in my mouth from earlier. Cerny reached for his iPad from a nearby table. Held it out to me. I didn't move.

"I don't want to watch them," I said. My voice was shaking, and I realized I was afraid. Afraid in a way I'd never been before.

"Heath wants you to know who he is," the doctor said. "He needs it."

I took the iPad, swiped the screen, and the keypad came up. I met Cerny's gaze.

"Cecelia's birthday," I said. "5-3-53."

"Clever." His eyebrows lifted. "Like I said, a perfect match."

I tapped in the code with trembling fingers. I found a file labeled "Sam O'Hearn" and opened it, and the screen filled with folders. Each was labeled an age, beginning with four all the way to sixteen.

I clicked on a folder at the top of the screen labeled *Age 4*. Another window opened then, this one stacked with video files. I selected one on the top row, and a video player filled the screen. A wide shot of one of the rooms in the apartment—the one on the end with the kitchenette, chalkboard, and gilt-framed mirror. Only, in the video, the room was fully furnished with a gleaming table and chairs, lamps, and scattered vases of hydrangea. A rich Persian rug covering the scratched wood, and the walls hung with paintings. The room looked elegant and lived in. It looked like a home.

A small boy ran around the perimeter of the room under the watchful eye of a woman, seated in one of the chairs at the table. She was dressed in a light blouse and slim dark skirt, her hair gathered neatly into a twist. She held a yellow dump truck. The boy, motoring around the room like a battery-powered toy, was a blur of stocky legs and floppy black hair.

"Sam," the woman said. "Would you like to play with the truck in the sand?"

He continued to run.

"Sam, if you'll sit down with me—quietly, for a few minutes—I'll give you the truck and let you take it outside."

The boy let out a shriek as he dodged the table and chairs.

"Sam—"

The shriek rose to a steady scream. I paused the tape and closed the file. I was shaking, and my scalp prickled in creeping horror. What was this?

"Open another one," Heath said.

I did, one labeled *Age 5*.

The camera showed the sitting room—the space between the dining room and bedroom. Music played in the background, and Dr. Cerny and Cecelia danced in the center. The little boy—Sam—sat on the sofa and watched, stone faced. He looked bored. I closed it and moved on to the next file.

The boy, slightly taller and thinner now, sat in the sitting room beside the coffee table. He and Dr. Cerny were playing cards. Cerny's hair was a rich golden brown, with only a hint of silver, his face unlined and handsome. He dealt the cards slowly and methodically, across the table, his eye all the while on the boy. There was no music in the background, no drone of a TV, only the scrape of the cards and Cerny's low instructions.

The camera was positioned perfectly to capture the boy. The messy shock of black hair crowning a delicate, sallow face. A pair of wide, thickly lashed brown eyes, slender nose over full lips. A fine spray of freckles across his cheeks.

Heath. *My* Heath.

It was the strangest thing, seeing him this way. As a child. Especially since I'd never seen so much as a snapshot of him as a baby. But here he was, more than just a badly lit school photo in a scrapbook. He was a living, breathing human being—the same person I knew and loved. The man who sat before me now.

But this wasn't just a record of a birthday party, a picnic, a random spontaneous moment of his childhood. This was a carefully planned-out experiment. The card game was beside the point. The doctor and Cecelia had positioned Heath in front of the camera for optimum study. So every gesture he made could be catalogued. Every expression as it flickered across his face. Every tone of voice.

The psychopath's every move was of the utmost interest.

On the iPad there was a wail and a scraping sound as Boy Heath's chair flew out from under him. He doubled over, his body going rigid, fingers fanning wide beside his head. He screamed at the floor, the veins in his temple popping, the cords lining his neck standing out. The sound was chilling.

Heath upended the table, the cards spinning across the room. Dr. Cerny stepped neatly out of the way, then moved slowly in the direction of the kitchen. He stood in the doorway for a beat, erect, expressionless, then backed into the kitchen and pulled the pocket door closed behind him. In his absence, the destruction amped up. A lamp flew. A vase. A book. A spread of newspapers covered with sticky pieces of painted wood. The chair Heath had been sitting on shot across the floor.

Heath flung himself against a wall, then ran to the door that led to the bedroom on the far side of the room. He opened and slammed it repeatedly, with all of his strength, the door bouncing back, doorknob punching a hole in the opposite wall.

Eventually, he wound down and began to stagger around the room, finally collapsing on the bare wood floor. After several seconds, the kitchen door slid open and Cerny emerged. He calmly walked across the room—stepping over the boy's inert body—and switched off the lamps and lowered the blinds.

He left, shutting the hallway door quietly behind him. I didn't know where he went—upstairs to the surveillance room to confer with Cecelia or downstairs to his office—but no one else entered the apartment. No one helped the boy lying on the floor into pajamas or guided him to brush his teeth and into bed. No one tucked him in, smoothed his hair back, or kissed his forehead. He was left to fend for himself.

I felt a wave of sorrow rise and begin to overtake the earlier shock and horror I'd felt. I lowered my head and wept into the crook of my arm. No one said a word; then, after a minute or two, I felt Heath's hand on my back.

He doesn't mean it, I thought. *It's not real.*

Nevertheless, his hand was there, radiating warmth into my skin. Even if he was doing it because in his cold, analytical brain, he knew that he was supposed to comfort me when I cried, I didn't wish it away. It *was* comforting. It was what I wanted, and maybe I didn't care why.

Could I honestly say I'd be able to go on with a normal life after discovering who Heath really was? Was it possible to live a full, satisfying life with a man who didn't feel emotions the way I did? I truly didn't know the answers to those questions. What I did know was that I wasn't ready to say no to the firm, warm, reassuring pressure of Heath's hand on my back.

Heath wasn't a diagnosis. He was a flesh-and-blood person. The man I loved.

I turned to him. He was staring at me with those same dark eyes, that same stillness. He was the same man I'd come to know. The same man I'd fallen in love with when I first saw him standing in the glare of the lights. For now, that was enough.

I caught his hand. "I want to go back upstairs," I said. "I want to see your home."

Chapter Twenty-Eight

It was surreal—standing where Heath had played and eaten and slept as a child.

Twelve years. All spent in these three small rooms.

He'd been isolated from other people, but he hadn't been held prisoner, not technically. He'd been allowed to roam the grounds, hike into the forest and up the mountain to the overlook. He'd been educated in a broad range of subjects and encouraged to expand his knowledge with books. It wasn't the confinement that was the problem—plenty of kids were raised in apartments tinier than this one in cities all over the world. It was that he'd been considered a specimen. An object to be observed rather than loved.

If he'd started out an anomaly, a peculiarity of human DNA, at the end he became a freak. Or, at least, that must've been how he felt. Just standing in the dingy apartment at Baskens, even I felt like an alien.

Heath had shown me his old bedroom—the one I had thought was the Siefferts', that was papered in the brown roses. And then through the grass-cloth-papered sitting room. We were in the far room now, and I glanced at Cerny, standing by the chalkboard. I thought of Glenys—Cecelia—out in the rain, stiffening in the wet leaves.

"Where are the police?" I hissed at Heath, acutely aware of the knife in my boot.

"Don't freak out. They're on their way. In the meantime, just listen to what he has to say."

I caught my reflection in the huge mirror over the sideboard. I looked so different now than earlier. Pale and lifeless.

I turned to Cerny. "Tell me about Cecelia."

"She was my assistant, for many years. We had a brief dalliance, but there was a disagreement—"

Heath snorted. "She was in love with you. And you treated her like shit."

"It was a mutual decision to part ways. She moved out west. Found a position at another institute, doing research on attachment disorders. And I opened the Baskens Institute."

"She disappeared, like that, from both of your lives? Then showed up in time for this heartwarming family reunion?"

"I let her know Heath was coming home," he said. "To try to untangle the past so he could move forward with his future. She came back because she wanted closure, just like I did. Just like Heath. Cecelia was always troubled by what we did. She never got over it." He nodded at Heath. "She never got over losing him."

I folded my arms. "Is that why you had to kill her? Because she loved Heath more than you?"

He smiled. "I'll admit, when she returned to Baskens, I found that I . . . I still had a certain fondness for her. We had a reunion, of sorts. Those were her clothes, of course, that you found in my room."

Heath looked sharply at me.

"But I assure you, Cecelia's death was a result of her own actions. She was a troubled woman. Watch the tapes, Daphne. You'll see."

I looked down at the iPad. Opened the next file.

Heath's boyhood unfolded before me. I watched him scream and run. Bang doors, throw lamps, books, and plates. He slammed his head against walls and floors. Toppled chairs, upended tables, urinated in every corner of every room.

There were calm moments too—when he ate or read or did school-work. He built birdhouses. On a canvas drop cloth spread on the living-room floor, hammering, sanding, and painting quietly. In these interludes, he appeared focused and relatively content. It looked like he worked on the birdhouses for countless hours.

Cerny cleared his throat. "The birdhouses were one of the primary rewards we used when Heath brushed his teeth or ate his lunch or bathed himself without oppositional behavior. Unfortunately, at some point along the way, he unearthed my old pellet gun and began to use the birds for target practice, shooting them right out of the houses. Needless to say, we had to find another reward."

Heath had moved closer to the mirror and was staring into it. I wanted to ask him if he'd found that pellet gun again. If—sometime when I was up on the mountain or in the house and couldn't hear the sound of the shots—he'd taken it to the birds I'd found yesterday. I wondered if he'd gathered them up later, in the weak morning light, dew drenched and cold, and flung them somewhere in the woods. If he'd burned them.

I turned away from him and opened the next file.

Music was the other reward Cerny and Cecelia offered Heath. Cecelia had an old-fashioned boom box, and, in the later years, an iPod attached to a speaker. She usually played music at Heath's solitary mealtimes, in the dining room, but sometimes she did it at night in his bedroom. As he would settle himself in bed (alone, no kiss, no tuck-in), the room would fill with the strains of Count Basie, Tony Bennett, Ella Fitzgerald. And Frank Sinatra, of course. Lots and lots of the Chairman of the Board.

"I take it you don't appreciate fish for dinner," Dr. Cerny's voice suddenly rang out from the iPad, tinny but clear.

The time stamp at the bottom of the screen showed 9:36 p.m., and the brown floral walls were doused in shadow. They were gathered in the bedroom—Cerny, Cecelia, and what looked to be a young-teen Heath. Heath was sitting in bed, his knees drawn up under the covers. Cerny stood, arms folded, in one corner of the room, Cecelia in another.

Heath didn't answer Cerny, and Cecelia shifted her weight. There was a strange feeling in the room. Something electric and dangerous even I could feel, just viewing the tape. I glanced at Heath, remembering how strange he'd acted when Reggie Teague had told us our first meal at Baskens would be fish.

On the tape, Heath spoke. "I warned you," he said, his adolescent voice cracking. Goose bumps broke out on my arms.

"You don't warn me," Cerny said. "I'm the adult. I set the rules. You choose to either follow them or break them. Following rules brings rewards. Breaking them results in a zero sum."

"I told you," Heath said. "And I told Mom."

"Cecelia."

"Mom." Heath's voice was edged with an ominous tone.

"Oh, for God's sake," Cecelia interjected. "Give him the music, Matthew. He's tired, and he's making an effort."

"I'm making an effort," Heath parroted.

Cerny folded his arms. "I disagree. You're not making an effort. You're mocking me."

"Matthew—" Cecelia said.

Cerny held up his hand. "Let him advocate for himself. This is good practice. The world is full of people, Sam, and you are going to have to absorb this lesson—if not in your heart, in your head. How to negotiate with them. How to give them what they want sometimes. How to let them win. Others deserve to get what they want just as much as you do. You said you believed that. Do you?"

Heath said nothing.

"I didn't ask if you felt happy about it or if you liked it. It's called a cognitive moral conscience. You don't have to feel things to know they are true. Do you agree, Sam, on principle, that others deserve to win occasionally?"

Heath didn't answer. Cecelia, agitated, fussed with the buttons on her blouse.

"From time to time, out there in the real world, you may be given food you don't particularly enjoy—fish, perhaps. Maybe even, *dear God*, liver. But because you value the person who prepared it for you, because you need something from that person who took the time to buy and prepare the fish or liver or what-have-you, you eat it. And while you are eating it, you pretend to experience *enjoyment*. You pretend to *relish* it. You feign *gratitude*. And after you have eaten it, you thank the person."

Heath dropped back on the pillows with a loud huff.

"You do not throw the plate against the wall and grind the fish into an expensive hand-knotted wool rug with your foot."

"Am I allowed to say, at any time, politely—honestly—that I don't fucking like fish?"

"You can say anything you like, Sam. We've gone over this again and again. But if you want more . . . if you wish to override your particular brain wiring and genetic markers . . . appear like other neurotypicals around you—"

"Sheep," Heath muttered.

Cerny drew a slow breath. "If you desire lasting connections with neurotypicals . . ."

The two stared at each other—man versus nearly-man.

"You will not throw your dinner," Cerny finished. After a beat he nodded curtly at Cecelia. "No music tonight," he said and left.

There was a long period of silence, then Cecelia switched off the lamp on top of the dresser. She walked to the bed and sat on the edge of the mattress.

"Go away," Heath said, his voice muffled by the pillow.

She put out her pale, slender hand, letting it hover over Heath's motionless form like she was casting some sort of spell. After a few seconds, she lowered it slowly, rested it on his back. It was possible I was imagining it, but I could swear I saw Heath's body go rigid under her touch. She sat that way for a couple more moments, staring down at her hand on Heath's back as if it was something disconnected from the rest of her body.

After a while she spoke. "Heath? My darling Heathcliff. It's your Catherine. And if you'll just thank me for the fish, I'll give you a back rub."

He lifted his head from the pillow, but it wasn't tearstained. It was flat. Hard.

"Do you want to give me a back rub?" he said. His voice was a mocking singsong, and she didn't answer. "Tell me, Catherine, does it make you feel like we're connected?"

She lifted a shoulder. "It does. A little bit."

"And you like that?"

"I do, Heath. I enjoy feeling connected to you."

"Must be nice. The doctor doesn't think I can ever experience an authentic, noncognitive connection with another human being." One side of his mouth curled. "Do you?"

"I . . ." She faltered.

"Be honest."

"I hope so, for your sake. So you can know how it feels. It's wonderful to feel love for another person. For your child." She touched his arm. Her voice was barely more than a whisper. "Heathcliff. Just thank me for the fish. Won't you? Won't you do that for me? So you can have a back rub?"

A long pause. And then his subdued voice—

"I enjoyed the fish. It was delicious. Thank you, Catherine."

I couldn't tell if he'd capitulated or if he was mocking her. If he'd won or lost the battle.

She looked up at the camera—the one recording everything I was seeing—and then slipped off the bed. Grabbing a blanket from a chair, she walked toward the camera and covered the lens. Everything went dark.

But after a few seconds, the picture reappeared—bobbling, filled with sounds of fumbling and from a different angle. The angle was shot from the far room, the camera aimed through the sitting room into the open door of the bedroom. The camera zoomed in and focused on Heath's bed.

I stared in shock. "It's a two-way mirror," I blurted.

In the dining room, Heath rapped on the mirror hanging over the buffet with one knuckle. "There's an observation room on the other side of the wall. Where the doctor could monitor me in a more direct way. I didn't know about it, not until much later." He cut his eyes at Cerny. "But Cecelia did, even though sometimes she liked to pretend she didn't. So she could push the good doctor's buttons. Isn't that right, Cerny? She did always enjoy playing us against each other."

Disgust twisted through me. The sound was still being recorded. Cecelia hadn't shut that off. And even from this distance and angle, it was clear from Cerny's camera that she'd started to rub Heath's back. Exactly what a mother might do to lull her son to sleep. And singing to him the way a mother would croon a lullaby—only it was a goddamn Sinatra song.

"Human contact wasn't part of the treatment," Heath said as I watched. "The operant conditioning meant neither of them could touch me in an affectionate, familial way, because showing warmth or affection could skew the results of the case study."

"That's abuse," I said.

"B. F. Skinner would disagree," Cerny said.

"Well, Skinner put rats in boxes to neutralize their environment," Heath said drily. "So . . ."

The doctor held out his hands, a conciliatory gesture. "Look, Daphne, I understand how cold and unfeeling our experiment must appear to you. But it was rooted in solid science. The research Cecelia and I were doing was based on Skinner's time-honored, research-based theories. He called it behavior shaping through operant conditioning. It involves a very particular schedule of positive and negative reinforcement and necessitated a truly, wholly isolated subject."

"But he was a child," I protested.

Cerny forged on. "Heath's home life was unpredictable, chaotic. His birth mother was loving at times, neglectful and overly harsh at others. The truth is, if he'd remained in the home, Heath would've probably ended up as an adult with a slew of mental-health issues and a treatment-resistant personality disorder. Probably in prison. Cecelia and I gave him a second chance at life. We removed him from that environment and brought him to Baskens, a place where all his basic needs were provided and variables were controlled."

The preposterousness of what I was hearing was just starting to sink in. My mouth felt dry, my lungs constricted. I kept picturing the knife in my boot. I imagined what would happen if I pulled it out. Brandished it in Cerny's face. I saw myself aiming for his neck. Slashing. Blood everywhere.

Cerny's voice jarred me out of my fevered daydream. "It was profound work, what we were endeavoring to do. If we were successful with Heath, imagine the impact. Children with antisocial precursors, like oppositional defiant disorder or conduct disorder, could be flagged for early intervention and offered treatment. Families could be restored, marriages rescued, lives saved. The world would never again have another Mengele or Jack the Ripper or Jeffrey Dahmer. Psychopaths could learn to assimilate, to contribute to society, just like Heath has done."

I glanced at Heath. His body was tense, back curled.

"But what about the nightmares?" I asked. "If your experiment was so successful, why was he waking up every night, screaming and ripping bedsheets and breaking windows?"

Cerny furrowed his brows. "I don't know. The nightmares could have something to do with what Cecelia did. The way she interfered with the study. She broke protocol. It was very damaging to our work."

It was ridiculous, the assertion that Cecelia attempting to show Heath a shred of kindness could cause nightmares. Cerny was delusional, at the least. But we needed to keep him talking, and I was curious.

"Why didn't you fire her?" I asked him.

Heath and Cerny exchanged a brief glance.

"I considered it. There were mitigating factors."

"Would you like to see it?" Heath said suddenly. "The observation room on the other side of the mirror?"

He had turned his back to us and was staring at his reflection in the gilt-framed mirror. He was so beautiful, this man. This survivor of an unimaginable childhood. How was it that he could even stand here, in this space, and not break down completely? I felt a pain grip my heart, so that I could barely breathe.

"I would," I said.

Heath led me back out into the hall, through the pocket doors. Under the attic stairs, he reached up to the top corner of the small door and slid a bolt lock open. He jostled the door in a practiced way, yanking the knob up and out, and the door swung open.

"The doctor kept files in here. A camera. He kept it bolted so I couldn't get in. Later, when I was older and I figured out it was here, he padlocked it, because he knew I'd destroy it if I had the chance." He put a hand on my arm. "I'm glad you're seeing it, Daphne. I'm glad you're finally seeing everything."

I entered the small room and stood very still, letting my eyes adjust to the dark. Inside wasn't much—just a dusty, dark cubicle with a sharply pitched ceiling above one metal desk and a metal chair, identical to the one in the attic surveillance room. The far wall was dominated by a large, smoky pane of glass—the reverse side of the mirror. I could see, in the dim half light, Dr. Cerny standing in the room on the opposite side, hands in his pockets, a thoughtful look on his face. He was staring directly at me. Staring but not seeing.

I was suddenly acutely aware of Heath's body next to me. I could feel heat emanating from him, a human heart pumping blood, and cells responding. This man was more than just a set of learned behaviors, fossilized by years of conditioning. Surely inside him there was a glimmer of empathy. Of love. It couldn't have all been an act. We weren't an act.

"This is where he preferred to watch me," he said. "The cameras were always running, one to a room, but I think he preferred this old-school setup. He told me once, later, when I was older, that he could tell what I was feeling by the way I moved around the room, the way I breathed and blinked my eyes. He said he could sit all day and night, watching my brain at work."

"Jesus." I shook my head. "So you've been back in contact with him? For how long?"

He took my hand. "Do you want to know the truth, Daphne? Really? All of it?"

I was paralyzed, unable to make any kind of reasonable decision about which path to take. It was like my brain had suddenly dumped all its storehouse of information and in doing so, lost the ability to decide. Was there anything I could do to escape this nightmare and still be with Heath? I didn't know. I had absolutely no halfway-reasonable frame of reference for any of this.

"If you do," he continued, "then watch the rest of that video."

I still didn't move.

"But only if you want to."

Which, all of a sudden, because of the glint of his eyes in the dark and the broken sound of his voice, I found I wanted to. I tapped the screen, and the video sprang to life.

From the perspective of Cerny's camera behind the two-way mirror, I could tell Cecelia was still rubbing Heath's back and singing Sinatra in her soft, clear voice. Instantly, all my hackles went back up, but I told myself not to flinch or look away. It was important to Heath—to us— that I watch it all. At last, when Cecelia finished the song and turned off the light beside Heath's bed, she bent over him.

"She kissed you good night," I said, surprised.

"She'd been doing it for a while, in secret. She sometimes hugged me when he wasn't looking. Ruffled my hair. Nothing out of line in the eyes of normal people, but at Baskens, a mortal sin."

He jutted his chin at the iPad. On-screen, Cecelia was closing the door between the bedroom and sitting room, then she walked toward the dining room. Slowly, purposefully, defiantly, her gaze fixed on the two-way mirror and the camera Cerny had aimed at her.

"She was messing with him," I said.

And then, after a couple of seconds, she veered out one of the side doors that led to the main hallway. Inside the observation room, Cerny turned the camera, and the room where we were standing now materialized on-screen.

It was still and silent for a beat, then the door banged open. Cecelia stood in backlight, ferocious and ready for battle. Off camera, Cerny began a slow-clap.

"Bravo, darling," he said. "Nine years of work, nine years of grueling, tedious, groundbreaking work, compromised. All because of your pathetic maternal yearnings."

He stood, crossing into the frame. Cecelia squared her shoulders.

"He's a child, Matthew. A human, who will, one day, hopefully, be able to survive in a world of other humans. He needs to understand how to move among them. To relate to them on more than an intellectual level."

"We agreed on the terms of the treatment."

"To thrive, a child needs warmth."

"No," Cerny snapped. "You need warmth. And it disappoints me to see how easily you will sacrifice your scientific ethics in order to get it."

He moved closer to her, and I could hear her swallow audibly in response. Her body tensed as he spoke again.

"I was very clear with you that I needed an assistant who possessed the discipline and endurance to grapple with the complexities of a difficult project. You told me you would be that person."

"And I am," Cecelia said. "But you can't keep treating me this way. I've done everything you wanted. Given up my life. Given you everything I had . . ."

He was so close to her, their bodies were touching. I could see she was trembling as he laid his palm on her face, then moved it to cup her chin.

"You still go down to the creek, don't you?" he asked. "To stare at those goddamn trees. To wallow in the past, to mourn the things you can't ever have."

"They're a memorial, Matthew." Her voice was breaking now. "For the children. Our children."

"Not our children, Cecelia. Cells, that's all. Cells that never developed."

She let out a whimper. "It's hard for me. Be patient, please. I can be what you need."

"You can't," he roared, grabbing her face and squeezing it. "You've already compromised everything. We are scientists, Cecelia. We deal in facts. In quantifiable data, not in yearnings of the soul. We don't play house. We don't pretend to be Heathcliff and Cathy. We do important work that will change the course of psychiatry forever. That could change the understanding of mental health universally. And you so cavalierly throw it away? If you're so pathetic, so desperate for the touch of a—"

"Please—"

"—another human being, then go down to town and find yourself one of those mouth breathers sitting at the bar, drinking beer and dreaming they're the ones running the football down the field."

He still had her face clenched in his hands, and now he'd shoved her up against the wall. I saw a tear slip down her cheek, then her hands rise up to press against his chest. Only she wasn't trying to push him away—instead she seemed to be caressing him.

"He's your son, isn't he?" she said. "Yours and that woman's—"

"Oh my God! Cecelia, no! Listen to yourself! I've told you a million times, I found that woman through an ad in the newspaper. The boy is not my son. He is ours. *Ours*. And, if you remember, we made a pact to help him . . . regardless of how difficult it got. We promised to help this boy, and disregard our weaknesses and desires and endless longing to receive love in return—"

She swung at him, awkwardly, catching him on the side of the face with her open palm, but he caught her hand. Then, pushing her against the door, he pressed forward and kissed her. She let him. In fact, she opened herself to him, softening, throwing her arms around him as he ground her against the door. The camera captured it all, the whole torrid moment, but as I watched, something occurred to me. Something I hadn't thought to ask Heath this whole time.

"I don't understand," I said. "Why didn't you ever tell anyone what they did to you? Why didn't you call the police?"

There was no answer.

He was gone. Just as I realized it, I saw the door shut and heard the unmistakable sound of a bolt sliding into the lock.

Chapter Twenty-Nine

I put the iPad on the floor and pounded on the door with both fists as hard as I could.

"Heath! Let me out!"

The lock held fast. I kicked at the door anyway, fury and fear spreading in me like a drop of black ink in water.

"What are you doing?" I screamed. "Heath!"

There was no answer.

The iPad played behind me, and I looked at it in distaste. Dr. Cerny and Cecelia were going at it now—one side of her blouse had fallen off her shoulder and his hand was up her skirt. Good God. What a pair of sickos. Rutting like a couple of animals while a child suffered alone in those dusty, desolate rooms. And capturing the whole train wreck on film. It was beyond disgusting.

On the other side of the mirror, I saw Heath reenter the dining room. I pushed the iPad aside and moved closer to the mirror. Heath had joined the doctor, and the two men stood in silence in the middle of the empty room, both of their faces pale and haggard.

I watched, heart beating against my chest like a trapped bird, waiting for something to happen, for them to tear into each other or for the heavens to fall, but all that happened was they started talking like a couple of guys who'd just run into each other at the bar. I couldn't hear what they were saying—if there was some sort of audio connection from the apartment to the observation room, it had been disabled. I kicked at the door one more time. Nothing.

Clearly, Heath wanted to confront the doctor alone. And he deserved that much.

I sat, rebooted the iPad, and opened a file labeled *Age 15*. The dazzling young man pacing the sitting room on-screen made me suck in my breath. From all indications, he'd reached his full height, over six feet, and even though his face was still rounded with baby fat, his shoulders had broadened and his jaw sharpened. His hair was a shock of shiny black, a buzz cut that had grown out. It was my Heath, raw and coiled, oozing with fresh testosterone and ready to launch at the slightest provocation.

I felt the familiar curl in my stomach. That delicious tightening I felt every time I laid eyes on him.

Cecelia sat on the sofa; her feet were tucked up under her, and a lock of blonde hair fell across her face. She was knitting—a big, nubby, ivory thing fanned out over her legs. An afghan, maybe. Or a circus tent, who knew. I wondered if she and the doctor were still playing their twisted game of push-and-pull, ripping each other's clothes off in the observation room and using Heath as their pawn.

Cecelia sent Heath a reproving look, then dropped her knitting. "Sit, my dear. Read or work on the birdhouse. Something."

"Fuck the birdhouses."

"Heathcliff."

"Don't call me that."

She cleared her throat carefully. "Sam. There's schoolwork to be done. Reading."

"I finished."

"All of it?"

He tromped to the window, and she resumed her work.

"What happened at the end?" she asked lightly.

"Everyone interesting died," he snapped. "And the ones who didn't, got married."

She laughed, but then shook her head and sighed. He dropped down beside her and let his head fall on her shoulder. She shrugged it off immediately, but the needles in her hands stopped moving. There was a moment when neither of them moved. Then Heath scooted down to the far end of the sofa, stretched out, and gingerly laid his head on her lap.

"Heathcliff," she whispered. And then laid her hand on his hair and began to stroke it.

As she worked her fingers through his hair, his eyelids fluttered closed, and I could see hers lower too, as she watched him. Then, without warning, her hand stilled.

"We shouldn't," she said. Her voice sounded tired.

"You said he went into town."

"I know, I know, but he'll look at the tape later. And he'll be angry."

"I like it when he gets angry. It's funny."

"It's not funny. I hate the way he treats you."

"I don't mind it. It's worth it."

She was silent.

His voice rose. "I just want you to touch my hair, okay? Just touch my goddamn hair. Is that too much to ask?"

"I can't," she whispered.

"You can," he said. "He doesn't fucking own you. Or does he? Does that lunatic get to tell you how to spend every minute of every day, like he does me?"

She spoke calmly. "I'm not your mother, Sam. I don't do the things a mother would do. And besides, it feels like it's . . ." She faltered.

"Feels like it's what?"

Her hand went to her chest.

"What?"

"Like maybe . . . it's inappropriate."

He stared at her, openmouthed. "What are you talking about?"

She shook her head, but kept playing with the buttons on her blouse. He straightened and shook his head.

"Oh, God. My God." He laughed, but it was a sharp, harsh sound. "You think I want to . . ." He laughed again, this time a deep eruption from the depths of his belly. "Oh my God. No. You nitwit. You sad, desperate, lonely, dried-up old woman." He moved closer to her, leaned into her face, and her eyes widened. "You want to know what I want? You want to know what I dream about?"

She didn't move. It looked like she'd stopped breathing.

His voice was a whisper. "I dream of velvet skin. Of long, silky hair. A perfect face and full, soft lips. Green eyes, blue eyes, brown—I don't care. I picture them closed when I touch firm tits, flat stomach. A tight, wet—"

She slapped him, hard, across the cheek.

He recoiled, then charged into the adjacent room, the classroom/kitchen combo. Underneath the mirror, there was a long cherry buffet where he stopped. Gripping it with both hands, he reared back his head and banged it against the edge of the wood.

I gasped.

He lifted his head and did it again. Then a third, fourth, fifth excruciating time. When he lifted his head, blood was pouring down his face from the gash on his forehead, dripping, separating, forking in the shape of a tree's branches down his face and neck. He blinked as the blood coated his eye. I clapped my hand over my mouth when he smiled. His teeth were entirely red, a demon's fangs behind his lips.

In the next room, Cecelia screamed. She ran to him, just as his knees buckled. She caught him, and he reached up to touch the split skin on his head.

"No, don't touch it." She pushed his hand away. "Oh, my dear, what have you done?"

His teeth glistened, one wild, white eye fastened on her.

"I have no pity," he mumbled. "That's what Heathcliff says in the book, isn't it? I have no pity, because I'm not normal, but you are. I've hurt myself, and you feel pity. So now you want to touch me."

She gathered him into her arms. "Yes, yes, my darling. My dearest dear."

He pressed his face against her shoulder, smearing blood across the sleeve of her blouse. She touched his hair, raking her fingers through it over and over, then pressed a kiss on his head. She rested her cheek against him.

He reached up and took her hand. Worked the ring from her fourth finger, over her knuckle and off. She watched him slide it onto his pinky and study it intently.

I looked down at my left hand, still bare. The ring I'd misplaced—supposedly Heath's grandmother's ring—it had actually been Cecelia's.

On the tape Heath spoke. "This is what people who love each other do. They give each other rings." He looked back up at her. "Don't let him tell you I can't love. Don't let him tell you that."

She sobbed and rocked him for a little while longer. When they finally stood, they were locked into each other's orbit. Like there was nothing and no one else in the universe but them. A chill ran up my back, all the way to the top of my head.

Cecelia sniffed and smoothed her hair. Cupped his face with her hands. "I've left the keys to the Nissan under your pillow, Sam. Take it. Take it now."

For a minute it was as if she hadn't said a word. Or he didn't understand.

"Go," she said faintly. Then Heath tore away, bolting out of the camera's frame. I heard a scuffling sound, a slamming door, and a keening wail from Cecelia as she sank to the floor.

A loud thud in the observation room shook me from the iPad. The wall separating me from the dining room shuddered, and I found myself staring into the bulging eyes of a grotesquely contorted face. It was a deep purple, the smashed skin, and the veins along the temples pulsed. Even the veins in the eyes were visible, like tiny red starbursts against the glass. Cerny's eyelid twitched against the mirror—an attempt to blink.

The iPad bobbled in my hands and clattered to the floor. I backpedaled, propelling the chair back against the far wall. Cerny, still pressed against the mirror, was beating his fists on it, clawing at the glass for purchase. I fisted both hands and pressed them to my mouth. Now I could see behind Cerny. Heath was holding him fast by the neck with the doctor's own brown silk tie. He worked the tie, twisting it, cinching it tighter and tighter.

I screamed.

Cerny clawed at his neck, but it was useless. The tie had cut into his skin and blood was seeping into it. Changing the brown silk to black.

I leapt up from the chair and yanked at the door, but it still wouldn't budge.

I turned back to the mirror, just in time to see Heath pull Cerny back by the tie, then slam his head into the mirror again. It cracked—on their side, not mine—and the doctor's cheek split open. Heath jerked the doctor around by the tie and smashed the other side of his head against the mirror. Again and again, he bashed Cerny's head against the glass until I heard a sickening crunch—either the layers of thick glass or the man's skull—and Heath finally released him. Cerny hit the sideboard, then slid to the floor with a thud.

Heath backed up a few steps, panting and looking down. I couldn't see the doctor, but I knew he was dead. There was no way he wasn't after that beating. Heath lifted his blood-speckled face, and although I knew it was impossible, it seemed like his eyes were looking directly into mine. And then he calmly walked into the next room.

I took a couple of steps back. I hit the wall—no, it was the door—and, like a needle finding the groove on a vinyl record, my mind switched into flight mode. Maybe the mirror was weakened enough that I could break it out with the chair. Or maybe the table would do the trick. If that didn't work, there might be an air vent—

The door slammed open and I screamed. Heath was still breathing hard, and blood was spattered across his shirt. I moved away, the repelling pole of a magnet. My breathing had shallowed, matching his. My heart was beating so hard it hurt.

"No," I said. "Stay away from me."

Heath held out a hand. "Please."

I heard a low groaning sound—half crying, half protest—and realized it was me. "You killed the birds. You killed the doctor. And Glenys."

"Please, Daphne," he said. "Please don't be afraid of me. I can't take it if you're afraid of me."

I couldn't say anything—there were no words to reassure him—and I couldn't stop myself from making the strange wailing sound. I was shattered. Broken into a million pieces.

"I had to do it," he said. "Don't you understand? To be free."

I clasped my hands together to keep them from shaking and pressed them to my face. It was wet with tears. I didn't even know I'd been crying.

"He kept me prisoner here, for twelve years. He abused me emotionally, mentally, even physically. It was torture. Real, honest-to-God torture. I can't—" His voice broke, and he swiped at his eyes with one bloodstained sleeve. "I didn't kill Cecelia. He did. He lured her back here. He let us see each other again because he knew how to twist the knife—and then he killed her." I noticed he was crying too. Tears had tracked through the blood.

Do psychopaths cry?

"So it was all about Baskens, then—the nightmares? That was why you came here? Because you wanted to kill Cerny?"

"The nightmares were about more than just this place. They were about other things—thoughts I couldn't stop, thoughts I couldn't make sense of."

"What does that mean?" I said.

"You know," he said. "You know."

"No, I don't!" I shouted.

"I loved Cecelia," he said. His voice was calm now. Level. "She was the only mother I ever really knew. I could never hurt her, just like I would never hurt you. She and Cerny had some kind of sick obsession with each other. In addition to the obsession they had with me."

He moved to the chair and sat, his arms resting on his knees. For one crazy second, I imagined I had inadvertently been swept up in an elaborate stage play. Now it was over, time for the curtain call and the bows. Time for us to get in our car and drive home and get back to real life.

"I may be a psychopath," he said tiredly. "But it takes one to know one. Cerny was antisocial too. He was a warped man who manipulated us so he could inflict his abusive fantasies on us. Science may say I have a disorder—they may call me antisocial or oppositional—but that doesn't make me any less deserving of love. I didn't deserve to live in this torture chamber."

"No. You didn't," I said.

"He told me, when I turned eighteen, he would publish his brilliant paper. He would be the first to achieve the impossible—identifying, treating, and curing a psychopath. He would be showered with awards. And I would too." He shook his head. Laughed. "But you can't grow empathy in someone, like a kidney in a petri dish. If he was any kind of doctor, he would've known that. Matthew Cerny never wanted me to get well. He wanted to entertain himself."

My throat constricted. "So—"

He lifted his eyes to meet mine. "You know what you want to say. Say it."

"You weren't cured." The words fell out of my mouth like broken glass all around me. And now I couldn't step without slicing myself open.

"I told myself I was. I wanted to be. I ran away. Even though I did everything to forget. This place—*his existence*—was a thorn in my side that I could never dig out. That just festered and infected everything. The nightmares. The fantasies. I couldn't take it anymore. I had to face it."

I felt a weight in my chest, hot and crushing. It was becoming increasingly difficult to breathe. "You could've reported him to the authorities."

"But they would've blamed Cecelia too. Maybe put her away forever. I couldn't do that to her. She was as much a victim as me."

Heath stood and limped toward me. I let him get close enough that the air between us fairly hummed with electricity. More than just my hands were trembling now. He took a lock of my hair and wound it around his fingers. Brought it to his nose and inhaled. His eyes shuttered closed, and his face lowered to mine. His skin was rough. Slicked with blood.

"Please say you understand why I had to do what I did," he whispered into my ear. "Please say you won't leave me."

I pictured Cerny's blood smearing from Heath's skin onto mine. He took hold of my arms, his touch sending a series of shocks zinging through me.

"Everything you told me about Chantal and Mr. Al and Omega—it meant so much to me."

He was holding me so tightly now, I couldn't move.

"When you told me, I knew that finally there was someone who understood what I'd been through. What I had to do. We're the same, Daphne, and it helps me so much to know you're with me now. That we're together."

He wrapped his arms around me, and I closed my eyes. Inhaled his scent—woody, animal scent and copper tang of blood. A brief moment passed, images flashing in my head: Heath whispering in my ear at the photo shoot. His lips on mine. Us at home, in bed, sunlight slanting in from the blinds. The light catching on my ring, the diamond band that he'd taken from Cecelia's finger, casting rainbows on the wall.

In the frozen moment, my senses telescoped to a mere pinpoint, my brain slowing.

This is your fate, it said, *where your life has been leading all along.*

You are both damaged. Both beyond repair. But together, you make something whole.

And then, Heath's arm encircled my back, and he lowered his face and kissed me. Like with every kiss before, I felt the softness of his lips, tasted him, breathed him in. Then, just like it always happened in fairy tales, when the handsome prince's kiss breaks the spell, my heart woke up.

Friday, October 19
Night

"It wasn't that she was beautiful—or plain or ugly. As a matter of fact, I don't remember what she looked like. That wasn't the point."

"What was the point, Heath?"

"Connection, I suppose."

"But that isn't possible for you, Heath. Isn't that what this is all about?"

"I've found a way, I think. I just don't believe it's sustainable. I need you to help me adapt it."

"So you're telling me that you are, indeed, able to connect with another person?"

"If it's the right person, yes. If I think there's something more beneath the hair and the makeup and the clothes. But I can only truly know if I'm able to get to that place—"

"What place?"

"The place beyond the hurt. When the hurt finally opens the door—I only know then whether a true connection is possible—"

Something on the TV across the room catches my eye. A local news alert. *MISSING*, in a red banner, crawls across the bottom of the screen. *HOLLY ELAINE IDLEWINE*, it reads. Along with a picture.

It's the picture that stops my heart.

She is dressed for a night of club hopping in a tight black dress. She has long honey-colored, flat-ironed hair, beige lipstick on her pursed lips, and a fringe of blue around her eyes.

Blue eyelash extensions.

At that exact moment, there's a flash just outside the door of the police station. A green Toyota Tacoma truck driving past with Luca at the wheel.

Chapter Thirty

Friday, October 19
Afternoon

I stopped in the doorway of the dining room. Cerny lay on the floor, one arm flung behind him, legs splayed. A lake of blood pooled under him, already congealing into the cracks of the floorboards and around the slivers of glass from the broken mirror. The side of his head was a caved-in mess of blood and white bone. I even thought I could see his brain.

But I didn't have time to get sick or panic. I had to figure out how to get away from the man who had his hand resting protectively at my waist like he owned me. I could feel him monitoring my reaction. And the truth was, I knew I should be reacting—just standing here had to look suspicious, so I buried my face in my hands. My eyes were dry, though, and my mind raced.

What was I going to do? Stab Heath with a kitchen knife and make a run for it? The idea of it was ridiculous. He was taller than me, stronger and faster as well. I'd never overpower him. Never outrun him.

Stay calm. The answer will come.

Heath cleared his throat. "It's terrible, I know."

I nodded. He reached out for me, and I let him catch my hand.

"We have to go back," I finally said. "To the woods where Cecelia is. We should be there when the police arrive."

He didn't answer, and then I knew.

"You didn't call, did you? The police aren't coming?"

"No."

I thought fast. "Well, they will, eventually. Two people are dead. Luca's going to come back and find them. Or maybe Reggie Teague."

"We need to make a plan," he said. "Figure out how we're going to explain what happened here and why we left."

"We could throw them off the mountain," I said.

He blinked at me. "What?"

"No one would find them for months, if ever."

I had the sensation that time was speeding up. Like I'd jumped off a cliff, into a rushing river that was sucking me down, pulling me toward a destination I couldn't see, but that was inevitable.

"That's what we'll do," Heath said, and that cemented it.

In Dr. Cerny's room, we found a down coverlet to wrap him in and I snagged one of the doctor's big canvas barn coats. Heath hefted Cerny over his shoulder and carried him down the back stairs. I darted back into the observation room long enough to scoop up the iPad and tuck it in the waistband of my pants, then hurried down the stairs too.

I caught up to Heath in the kitchen. "Maybe I should stay behind? Keep an eye out?"

"I don't know if I can make it all the way up the mountain alone with him," Heath said. "I might need your help."

Desperation threatened to smother me, but I nodded my assent. I'd have to figure something else out. Something once we reached the top of the mountain. We headed out of the house toward the trail.

I ran after Omega until my stockinged feet burned and the green sweaterdress was heavy with sweat. Thick gray clouds had rolled in and banked, and a cold wind whipped across the soybean fields along the road. I was a fast runner, faster than I knew, because even without shoes, I'd caught up to her.

She had slowed at one of the town's newer municipal parks nestled among the fast-food places, office complexes, and car dealerships, then cut down the hill toward the blue tennis courts. There was no one playing, of course—it was freezing and overcast, and I could feel raindrops pelting me.

On the rise above the courts, I saw her sitting on a white bench against the chain-link fence. She slumped, hands jammed in her jacket, her legs stretched out in front of her. I'd been down here a couple of times, on school picnics. Seen the tanned ladies who played there— ladies from nearby neighborhoods who wore flippy skirts and visors and always had the picnic tables covered with food and wine during their matches. They didn't seem to have kids. Probably they were in school or with nannies. I thought suddenly how out of place Omega looked. She would probably never be the kind of person who played tennis here.

I sat at the top of the hill and watched her for a while, until a rust-edged, dented-up silver car pulled in behind me. It sat idling, and after a minute or two, Omega stood and made her way across the tennis court in its direction—and mine.

I stood, my nerves jangling. When she neared me, she stopped. I bit my chapped lip, feeling tears swimming to my eyes.

"Hey, Doodle-Do." She smiled down at me, but her eyes looked flat and tired.

"Hey, Omega."

She looked past me. At the car, I guessed. I wondered who was sitting in it. How had they known to meet her here? Had she called them? I hadn't seen her stop at a pay phone. But Omega's ways were sophisticated and mysterious. I couldn't begin to know them. Or maybe, in the warrens of memory, I'd forgotten how things had really happened.

"I know what you did," she said to me.

I turned cold.

"I saw you put the pills under the dresser."

I started to stammer out an excuse. "I didn't—"

"Shush," she cut me off. "Whatever you do, don't you ever fucking tell them, okay? It won't bring Chantal back, and it won't bring me back either. It doesn't matter, what you did, Daphne. It doesn't have anything to do with anything, not now."

I didn't understand everything she was saying, except the most important part. The part about keeping quiet.

"Where are you going?" I asked.

She cast a dark glance at the idling car. "Do you understand me?"

I nodded.

"Tell me. Say it."

"Don't tell them," I said.

"Not for any reason."

"Not for any reason," I echoed.

"Good girl." She bent down and gently, tenderly pressed her perfect, pillowy lips against mine, and I felt a thrill roll through me, all the way down to the tips of my toes.

"Don't go," I said.

She just looked at me, her face congealed in sadness.

"Don't go," I wailed and started to cry.

Then she left me and went to the silver car and climbed in. There was a man driving. He looked almost as old as Mr. Al, but he didn't look near as friendly. His hair was shaved down to nothing, and he had a bushy red mustache. The man with the red mustache drove Omega away in the silver car, and I ran after them.

I kept up for a while because the car was old and the man drove slowly. But then, after a few blocks, the silver car accelerated, blew through a couple of yellow lights, then turned down a street that led toward town. It was raining steadily now, and my feet made slapping sounds on the cold pavement. They hurt too. My left toe was poking through a hole in Chantal's maroon tights, and I watched it, counting my strides, letting my breath synch up. I felt like I could do this forever.

Run and run and run and run.

I ran into town, past the pawnshops and tattoo parlors and donut shops. Past the old houses that had been made into offices. Past the courthouse on the square and all the stately old buildings where people used to do their shopping. Now there were mostly junk shops and stores that sold medical supplies or wigs.

I ran until I found myself in the leafy, flat neighborhoods with one-story wood houses and dogs that wandered in the street. I ran past a fire station and the library, then there were more fields and farmhouses and a bridge. I stopped and threw the tights over the bridge and watched them swirl away in a brown creek. And then I ran some more.

I ran all the way through Macon and made it almost to Rutland before fainting in the parking lot of a Hardee's. The manager found me slumped against his dumpster and called the police. Around ten or eleven, Mrs. Waylene came to pick me up. The manager had given me a double bacon cheeseburger and a Coke, and I slept the whole way home, exhausted, my secret hidden deep inside me.

The wind buffeted the mountain, and I shivered in Cerny's too-big work coat. Heath sloughed Cerny off his shoulder like a sack of concrete, and when the body hit the rock, I winced. The sound was muffled but heavy—flesh and bone and blood. Heath groaned and flexed his arms behind his back, his spine cracking. I glanced at the rolled-up blanket with Cerny's body inside. Sometime on the journey up, a spot of blood had bloomed on the side of it.

"Daphne."

I turned away from the body, gathered my hair back against the blustering wind, and looked out over the edge. I felt like I'd been dropped into some gothic horror novel. How could I have gotten here? About to dispose of a body? To cover up a murder?

"Can I ask you something?" he said.

I met his eyes.

"Do you still . . ." He faltered, then tried again. "Will you . . ."

"Yes," I said quickly. Maybe too quickly. "I will, Heath."

He knit his brows. "Even after knowing what I am? After seeing what I've done?"

I mustered a smile, even though the sight of him made me physically ill. Even though I wanted to scream and run and forget I'd ever met him. "I love you, Heath. That hasn't changed."

He heaved a sigh. "I can't tell you how much it means to me to hear you say that." He eyed me. "I can't believe how lucky I am. That you understand why all of this had to happen."

A lump rose in my throat. I jutted my chin toward the drop-off. "So, you should do it."

He rolled the blanketed body to the edge of the rock slab, then straightened and kicked it off. I heard tree branches snap and the echo of them reverberate through the valley, and I turned away. I was feeling light headed. Nauseated.

Heath hitched up his pants and wiped his brow. I knew he'd come back with Cecelia and roll her off the cliff like he'd done with Cerny. And then what? We'd head back down to his car and drive off into the sunset. Bonnie and Clyde, the millennial version. Only, how long would I have to wait to make my move? To run like hell and hope to God he didn't catch me?

He took my face in his hands. Smiled down at me. "He was a hell of a guy, you know, and I got a kick out of coming back here and watching him do his thing. The fake couples, the video playbacks in the attic. It was what they did best, he and Cecelia—turned real life into a show." His expression softened. "It's worked out better than I could even have hoped. I love you, Daphne, and I would do it all again. I would go to the ends of the earth to hold on to you."

His hands were so cold and hard against my cheeks, and I'd begun to shiver uncontrollably. I needed to get away from this place. From this man. Just being in his presence was eating away at my sanity. I realized, suddenly, that I was looking past Heath to the stone cliff, out over the tops of the trees. I realized also that the precipice was only a few short steps away from where I stood.

It would be so easy, I thought, just a matter of forward motion, of closing my eyes and letting gravity take me.

"My dear," he said.

His face swam into focus again. It was the second time he'd called me that, and the word sounded saccharine coming out of his mouth.

"You should hurry," I said. "Go back down and get Cecelia. I'll wait here."

He gave me a long look, his eyes two black unchanging pits, then left. When the sound of his crashing footsteps on the trail below had faded away, I sank to the ground, my back against a pine.

Maybe, if I could just be patient, an opportunity would present itself.

Maybe I didn't have to end my own life to save it.

I just needed to think. To plan.

I don't know how long I sat there, but eventually I felt the air change, the temperature drop, and raindrops start to fall again. I pulled out the iPad. All the video files popped up—the archived footage from Heath's childhood, but there were other files as well. Files simply labeled *Heath*. I touched one of them.

This one was just an audio file, dated only a few days ago. I hit "Play," and Cerny's voice rang out.

"Go on."

"I didn't plan it. I hadn't been thinking or fantasizing about it, in any way. Not lately."

"Because of Daphne?"

"I think so. But then it came back, like before. A fully formed idea— more detailed than the others, not just thoughts. More like plans."

"Describe what you did, Heath."

"I didn't go home after work. I went out. To a bar. I had a drink, met a woman, and we left together . . ."

I tried to swallow, but my throat felt raw. I felt like time was rushing past me, a huge rocketing freight train, and I couldn't stop it. I couldn't stop listening to the tape. I couldn't stop Heath from returning with Cecelia and throwing her off the cliff either. I couldn't stop any of it. Sweat beaded under my arms and breasts.

"Where did the two of you go?"

"We got in my car and drove around for a while. We talked. I told her about my life—how I grew up. About you and Cecelia. About the time I hurt myself, and Cecelia held me in her arms."

"How did she respond?"

"She felt sorry for me. She wanted me to have sex with her."

"Did you?"

My heart slammed in my chest.

"No. I drove her east of town, outside the perimeter, and down this gravel road. I explained to her that the only way I could connect with another human was to hurt myself or them. And then I told her that I was not going to hurt myself."

"Was she frightened?"

"She tried to run."

"You stopped her."

"Yes. I stopped her. I strangled her. It felt . . . it was good."

"How so?"

"I felt close to her. We talked . . . I talked to her."

"About what?"

"Everything."

"For how long?"

"I don't know. A couple of hours."

(laughter)

"What's so funny, Heath?"

"I don't know. That I thought you actually could do something to stop me from being me."

"I can help, if you'll give me a chance. This doesn't have to be a life sentence. But I can only do it if you'll stay here at Baskens. I need you here, where I can administer intensive therapy. We need time and privacy—"

"No. We agreed: one week to wrap up your study, and to help me stop the nightmares, and then you owe me. You help me tell Daphne. But there's more. You need to do something about Cecelia."

"Why?"

"She's been talking to Daphne. Telling her things she doesn't need to know."

Leaves rustled and twigs snapped just below the trailhead.

Heath, back with Cecelia.

I leapt up and gripped the iPad, my heart skittering wildly. He would pitch her off the edge of the mountain, and we would troop back down to our car and drive away from this hellhole. We'd head down the switchback roads, back through Dunfree, slowly, coolly, like he hadn't just murdered someone—maybe two people—and I'd helped him dispose of their bodies.

I couldn't do this anymore. This was the end of the line. The end of everything.

I walked to the edge of the cliff and closed my eyes, Heath's crashing footsteps echoing in my ears. He was almost to the top. And he would expect to find me here, waiting.

Friday, October 19
Night

When I see the green truck drive past, relief and elation wash over me. Luca is okay. And if I can get to him, I will be too. I burst through the door of the station.

But it is a mistake.

The minute I hit the sidewalk, I'm blindsided, football-tackled and pushed to the dark side of the building. I yelp once—a swallowed cry—then find myself looking up into Heath's eyes. They glitter, catching the light from the street lamps lining the sidewalk behind us. Or maybe it's the reflection from the sparkly cutout jack-o'-lanterns and ghosts tied to the lamps.

Heath snatches the iPad I'm clutching and tucks it into the back of his jeans.

"Is that why you're running from me? Because of what you heard on that?" He's in my face now, and I can see that even though he's wiped most of Cerny's blood off, a trace of it has settled into the creases around his eyes. The bloody crow's-feet give him a demonic look.

"Please, Daphne," he says. "Can't you see that running's not a possibility for you now? Too much has happened. What you've done, what I've done . . . we've gone too far. We can't go back."

I can't answer. My throat feels used up, rusted out.

"We have to face this together. Can't you see that I'm the one person in this world who understands you? I read you like a book from the first moment I met you. I read you, and I gave you everything you ever wanted. A hero, a rescuer, the strong, silent type, right out of a romance novel, who wouldn't ask too many questions, who wouldn't get too close. I played it perfectly and you believed me. And now we're a team. I know you. And now, finally, you know me."

I don't answer, and I can tell it frustrates him.

"I was going to tell you about who I was, but I wanted to do it on my own terms. That's why I took the extra key from the Nissan. I couldn't take the chance of you running away. But then Cecelia wouldn't let up, constantly trying to meet with you, acting like the two of you were friends. I told her to stop—that it was my story to tell—but she wouldn't listen. She was jealous of you, how much I loved you. She was going to tell you everything just to spite me."

He lets go of me and rakes his fingers through his hair. The crazy thing, the thing that doesn't make an ounce of sense, that the most astute therapist in the world couldn't untangle, is that even after all I know, I still have the impulse to comfort him.

"I'm smarter than this," he says. "I swear, I just miscalculated." His eyes are wide pools of innocence. I wonder how he makes them look that way, how he fakes it so well. "You have to believe—I only killed the other ones, the other girls, because I wanted to prove to Cerny that he had hurt me. I thought it would make him feel guilty when I told him how he'd driven me to do it. But the man has no remorse. He didn't care, not about the girls, not about the fact that telling you about my past had to be handled very delicately."

The girls.

Girls, plural . . .

"You're lying, Heath." My voice is shaky. "You told him you wanted him to help you adapt what you did. Make it SUSTAINABLE."

He claps a hand over my mouth, but I claw it away.

"You didn't kill anyone to prove a point to Dr. Cerny. You did it because you enjoy it."

His eyes widen. "Okay, yes. Yes. See how bad he messed me up? Do you see? But it doesn't matter, does it? The bottom line is, Cerny couldn't cure me. I am who I am. We are who we are."

"What do you mean, 'We are who we are'?"

"What you did," he says, like I'm unbelievably dense. "What you had to do to survive. It was just like me."

"What I did? You mean . . . hiding Chantal's medicine?"

He's cocked his head and is regarding me with an amused expression.

"No, Daphne. I mean what you did to Holly Idlewine."

"What I . . ."

"At the bar last week," he continues. "You flipped her off, then gave the bartender your credit card. You told him to charge all Holly Idlewine's drinks to you."

He's right. I did do that.

"That doesn't prove anything," I say weakly, but I know it doesn't matter. He has been planning this day, this moment, for a long time. He is way ahead of me. I am outmatched in every way.

"You paid for all her drinks because you wanted her so completely smashed that when she stumbled out of Divine, you could easily drag her to your car. Put her in the trunk and drive her to some dark, isolated location."

My lips part.

"A nothing piece of property so far out in the country, nobody would ever think to look there. That's where you tied her up. Tortured her and killed her."

I can no longer feel my fingers and toes. The electrical impulses in my skull have dulled to a low buzzing. It feels like my body is shutting down.

"They haven't found her yet, and they won't until I want them to. What they do know is a woman named Daphne Amos, a woman who was once questioned in the suspicious death of a fourteen-year-old girl in a state park in north Georgia, paid for Holly Idlewine's drinks the same night she disappeared."

He pulls me by the wrist into a hug, and around his shoulder I see Cerny's silver Mercedes parked just a couple of feet away. It's idling. Then Heath speaks again, low and soft.

"When they find this on the ground near her body, the case will be closed."

I jerk back. He's holding up my engagement ring. Cecelia's ring. I feel like I'm having a heart attack. My hand dips toward my boot, fingers between the leather and wool, and I draw up the knife.

"No, no, no . . ." is all I can say. I am shaking and crying, swinging the knife in wild arcs.

He catches my wrist easily, wrenches the knife out of my grasp, and tosses it into the bushes beside the police station. I can't stop crying—nose running and mixing with the tears—as he hustles me to the car.

"Don't worry, Daphne," he says once we're locked in. His voice is soothing and he pulls the seatbelt across me. "If they find her with the ring, I'll tell them that you were with me all night that night. That you couldn't have kidnapped Holly or taken her to the woods and tied her up. That you couldn't have done all those horrible things to her." His face splits into a grin, but one so full of evil I cannot move. "You see? We can't go back."

$\sim$

Heath stops for gas on 515, at a place just south of Ellijay. It's one of those shiny new mega-stations with endless rows of gleaming pumps and a combo convenience store and Ye Olde Donut Shoppe. And it's hopping, even this late at night. Inside, I walk past a bank of cappuccino machines sandwiched between the sizzling hot-dog rollers and slushie station. I'm starving, but Heath's got my purse with him in the car, and he hasn't given me any money.

The ladies' room is down a short corridor, a spacious, exceptionally clean single. He's let me go alone—there's no reason for him to follow me in there. If I run, he'll just plant the ring and then tell the police I killed Holly Idlewine.

After I use the bathroom and wash up, I stare into the mirror. I remove my smudged glasses and splash water on my face, then wash my glasses. My face looks so normal—pink and healthy. I touch my cheeks. My skin is warm. I am still alive. Still breathing. Still able to think and to reason and to act.

I am still myself.

When I emerge from the bathroom, a yellowed old woman with a thick head of glossy chestnut hair and a purple terry tracksuit is waiting. A brown fake-crocodile purse is slung over her stick arm.

"Whew," the woman says in her Marlboro-roughened voice. "Thank you, sugar. You'd think they'd have more than one potty in a place this big."

I smile and she locks herself in. I stand there, letting the information filter through my consciousness: that was a wig she was wearing, and her skin had a yellow tinge to it. She's ill—cancer, most likely. And then, I can't help it, I picture myself waiting until she unlocks the door, then pushing my way into the bathroom with her before she realizes what's happening. In my mind, I snatch the wig, the tracksuit, and her purse. Disguise myself and walk out right under Heath's nose like something out of a bad spy movie.

But no. I close my eyes and turn away from the door. I'm going to have to find another way. Assaulting ill old ladies isn't an option. I haven't sunk that far yet.

I head toward the doors of the convenience store, and I'm just about to push through when something stops me. Outside, parked a couple of pumps down from Cerny's Mercedes, a green pickup truck. The driver's-side door is ajar. It has a long white unbroken scratch down the side of it. I inhale sharply.

A young man, medium, compact build, wearing a gray hoodie, jeans, and a black knit cap, stands on the other side of the truck at the pump, hand on the nozzle. His cap is pushed far back enough to see the brush of close-cropped light-brown hair. He is scanning the pumps.

I start to move forward again, but something yanks me back by my coat collar.

"Hold up," a voice behind me says. It's Heath. I can smell him—the stink of Cerny's blood on his clothes or skin—but surely I'm imagining that. "He must've followed us here. Did you see him at Baskens? Did you tell him what we did?" Heath twists the collar tight and pulls me back against a rack of Grandma's cookies and beef jerky.

"No," I say.

He nudges me. "He sees the car. Look."

He's right. Luca's edged past the pump and is staring at Cerny's Mercedes.

"He knows," Heath says.

"'Scuse me, sugar."

It's the elderly woman in the purple tracksuit. As she passes, she smiles at us both—a warm, grandmotherly smile. Then, in an instant, she's out the door, and I realize I have a plan. Or, at least, the beginning of a plan. I face Heath, inch closer to him.

"We can put it all on him. Cerny, Glenys, all of it."

"What?"

"He knows I'm in danger, and he's trying to be a hero. We can use that."

There's a beat, then Heath lets out a soft sound of disbelief.

I meet his gaze. "We lead him somewhere, maybe to the woods where you left Holly. Make it look like he was threatening me. Then kill him."

My heart is racing. I'm not sure if anything I'm saying is making sense, but I can see his gears grinding.

"If we don't do it now," I add, "we're going to have to do it later. You said it yourself. He knows."

Heath clears his throat. Runs a finger down my cheek all the way to my lips.

"We should go back to the car," I say. "Get him to follow us."

His eyes are locked on mine, their intensity dizzying. "Let's do it," he says.

We push out the door. I don't look in Luca's direction, but every nerve in my body tells me we have his attention. I'm right, because as soon as we step off the curb and head in the direction of the Mercedes, something whizzes past me, hitting Heath square in the center of his back. He whips around.

"The fuck—"

I look down. A set of car keys at our feet. A gift.

A gift meant for me.

It only takes me half a second to scoop up the keys, pivot, and run like hell for Luca's green Tacoma. At the same time, I can see Luca take off, jogging away from the gas station toward the highway. It takes Heath a second or two longer to figure out what's happened—and to figure out who to chase, me or Luca—but by the time he reaches the truck, I'm locked safely inside, jamming the key in the ignition. Heath yanks at the handle and blazes at me.

We lock eyes, and I don't think I've ever seen so much hatred condensed in one human's face. But he can't make too much of a racket because there are people everywhere. I put my foot on the brake and grip the key. My body is practically vibrating.

I look up the highway and see Luca, about a dozen or so yards up the northbound side, pounding the gravel on the shoulder, all stops out. He's heading in the direction of Dunfree. *Run, run, run,* I think. *Straight to the police.*

Heath follows my gaze, then turns back to me. He runs his finger across his throat. I feel sick, but I crank the truck anyway.

The next thing I know, he's darting through the pumps, sprinting in Luca's direction. Heart punching in my chest, I maneuver around the other cars and roll out onto the highway. Ahead, Luca veers from the shoulder onto the highway too, directly into the oncoming traffic. Heath follows him, and I gasp. A couple of cars screech and skid to avoid hitting them, as Luca tears up the center of the highway, adjacent to the median. Heath is only a couple of yards behind him now, narrowing the distance.

I'm closing the distance too, between them and me, white-knuckling the wheel, weaving around traffic. Maybe cars are honking. If they are, I don't register them. I've become my heartbeat. My pulsing blood and gulping breath. Every function of my body transformed into a laser aimed at stopping Heath.

I will hit him with the truck. Crush him under the wheels. I won't stop until there are smashing lungs, spurting blood, crunching bones.

We're the same . . .

I shake his voice out of my head. It's not true, it never was. And yet here I am, foot on the accelerator, calculating the shrinking distance between the nose of the truck and his body. I'm about to do this monstrous thing. But it has to be done, I know it. And I am the only one who can do it.

Not because I'm a monster, but because I am not.

I pull up behind Heath—there's only a few feet between us, a few yards between him and Luca—and hold steady. This is it. I have to do this now or I'm going to lose my nerve. I inhale, squeeze the wheel, and gun it, the truck leaping forward. But at the same time, Luca swerves up onto the median and onto the other side of the highway, and Heath does the same.

The next instant, I'm thunking up onto the median too, slowing between the clipped crepe myrtles, then grinding to a stop. Cars whiz past me and I catch my breath, scanning the southbound lanes. Where did Heath go? And where's Luca? A few seconds pass, and I spot them at last, Luca scrambling up the embankment toward the woods. Heath sprinting across the road in pursuit.

And then what happens, happens so quickly, I almost can't believe it.

A maroon SUV appears out of the dark, slams into Heath, flips him up and over the hood. I watch him slide onto the top of the SUV, then tumble to the asphalt, and a pale-yellow Cadillac runs over him. Front and back wheels. When the Cadillac is past, I can see Heath's body, a shapeless, motionless lump on the highway. He looks like a stray dog, I think. *Roadkill.*

Do I scream? I don't even know; I don't hear a thing, not even the sound of my own voice. I only see Heath, motionless on the pavement.

The SUV and Cadillac screech to a stop, and both drivers jump out. I don't move because I can't. A wave of nausea, so intense I'm paralyzed, is slicing through me. I grit my teeth so hard I can feel my temples pulse, and I pray for the sensation to pass. It doesn't. I lean over and vomit onto the passenger's-side floor mat.

When I look up again, I see Luca's made it all the way up to the top of the embankment. He stands for a minute, surveying the situation below. Back on the road, one of the motorists, the guy from the SUV, is already on his phone. The Cadillac guy is pacing up and down in front of him and yelling. Nobody has approached Heath, not yet. I wonder if it's because it's obvious that he's dead. In an instant, I see Luca turn and disappear into the woods.

I grip the steering wheel and try to remember how to breathe. The police will be here soon. They'll figure out that the Mercedes abandoned at the pump is Dr. Cerny's. They'll find the iPad inside—the files and Heath's confession. They may not know how I fit into the equation, but before long, they'll be looking for me, even if I wasn't the one who hit him.

Now more cars are slowing and stopping, their headlights illuminating the road. Another guy's out and on his phone. An older woman who stopped has got her arm around the Cadillac guy, leading him toward the median. There's no sign of Luca. I shift into reverse, my hand trembling, then ease onto the gas.

I roll off the median and go farther up the road where I can hang a U-turn. I drive slowly past Heath and the clot of stopped cars. Nobody even glances my way.

I ease up to sixty miles an hour. Still nothing happens. No police lights, nothing. I drive and drive and drive, slow and steady down the highway, keeping the truck at an even sixty. All the while, a constant, low humming vibrates through my brain.

I don't know how long it takes—maybe thirty, forty-five minutes— before I realize it's actually me, humming a tune. Sinatra, if you can believe it. Goddamn Sinatra.

And then I'm sobbing. Loud, inhuman wails and tears pour out of me, and I don't try and stop them. I am due. Past due. I drive and cry. Drive and cry. For the little girl in an apartment alone. On top of a bunk bed at night, hungry. Sitting in a psychologist's smoky office, terrified, telling a partial truth that will slither and encircle and squeeze the life out of her for years to come. I cry for the woman who, even for a split second, actually believed she could stay with a murderer. That she could love him.

But I am alive. I'm alive and driving away from him. I was not willing to dig up a grave and climb in with the monster inside.

I switch on the radio, and the tears stop. Strangely, I don't feel the urge to count anything or snap a band on my wrist. I'm wrung out, my body quivering like a dog in a thunderstorm, but just driving seems like enough for me right now. I have no idea where I should go. South, for now, I guess. Back roads all the way, until I hit I-20.

Then I'll go west. I don't have a phone, no money or identification. But west has a good sound to it. I remember having heard somewhere that getting a forged driver's license, passport, birth certificate is possible—even though I don't have the slightest clue how to go about it. I think I still have Jessica Kyung's business card somewhere on me. She might be willing to help me. I hope so. She's the only option I have right now.

A cursory inventory of the truck reveals Luca's stocked it with food, bottles of water, and a wad of bills that looks like it could last me several weeks. And something else. The truck's license plate is tucked in the sun visor. Luca must've taken it off before he caught up with Heath and me at the gas station. The next time I have to stop, I'll screw it back on. I'll keep to the side roads. Someone could have witnessed the green truck that was bearing down on Heath Beck right before he was hit. It's impossible to know.

The only thing I am sure of is that I want to live. So I will run.

It's the one thing I know how to do.

Eight Months Later

Twilight in the Canadian summer is a lovely time. Enchanting, some might call it. People who use words like that. People who believe in magic.

The sun kisses the southwestern side of Bowen Island good night, then disappears into Tunstall Bay, and in an instant, you can see the container-ship lights wink against the purple dark. It's quite a thing. As often as I can, I watch the whole show from the rickety Adirondack chair on the hilltop deck of the house I look after. I'm usually sipping a glass of whatever I've chosen from the local wine shop down near the harbor. I'm not picky—red, white, rosé—as long as it smooths over the rough edges. My current brand of magic.

A jaunty horn section drifts from outdoor speakers, making its way through the pines and over to my deck. My next-door neighbors, who I haven't met and don't intend to, playing their favorite Pandora jazz mix. First Mel Tormé, then Sam Cooke, and Dean Martin, which is fine. Inevitably, however, Sinatra always comes on. Tonight when it happens, my entire body tenses, but that's the extent of it. I'm past the counting and hair-band snapping. I know another song will always come after.

Today's sunset—blue melting into pink, then warming to orangey red—is as spectacular as always. Even so, I'm surprised to find tears dripping down my cheeks. I blot them with the sleeve of my flannel shirt, but don't move from my chair. I don't want to go inside—don't want to take a pill or put on my running shoes and head out for a jog. I mostly walk now, anyway. It feels kinder to my body.

It's been eight months since I escaped Heath. Not the first time I've sat on this deck and cried. Just the first time I've done it because I know everything is going to be okay. So I can sit here and ride out the tears, I guess. Sometimes it's good to just feel things.

Behind me, on the drive, there's the sound of crunching gravel. It sends jolts of electric fear into my arms and legs. Under the chair, my fingers close around my ever-present canister of bear spray. A reflex.

"Ms. Green?" a man calls from around the side of the house. Somewhere near the foot of the steps.

The voice is oddly familiar.

He must've cut through the thicket of blackberry bushes alongside the driveway and come around to the back deck. It doesn't mean he's a threat. He may have already tried the front door. I keep the alarm on and everything bolted up even when I'm here.

"Sydney Green? Are you here?"

Leaping up from my chair and knocking over my glass of wine, I run across the deck to the giant spruce that grows up through the middle of it. I slip behind the tree. Press my back against the trunk and carefully ease off the safety on the bear spray. The man is standing on the far side of the deck. I can practically feel the vibration of his breathing across the planks of wood. I wish for a gun. A good old-fashioned American revolver, but this is Canada, and I'm not that resourceful.

"I saw the last name on the mailbox," the man says. "And the lady down at the market in the cove said she knew a Sydney Green who's caretaker of this cabin."

I can't place the accent—I think I've heard it somewhere, but my heart is hammering so hard, I can't be sure. Footsteps thud, and that out-of-body panic sensation takes hold. He's getting closer. I will myself to stay put. To wait until he's within spraying range. When I judge it's time, I jump out, executing a neat one-eighty and depressing the trigger in short bursts like the YouTube video instructed. The man leaps backward, yelling and windmilling his arms, eventually stumbling down the deck steps.

I throw the can at him, run inside the house, and lock the door, just before I hear him yell out.

"Daphne!"

At my kitchen table, Luca takes the damp washcloth I offer and mops his red, swollen face for the umpteenth time. From a safe distance, I study him. Navy sweater and black jeans. Worn black combat boots, laced halfway up. Wavy brown hair that he keeps raking off his forehead, even though it just falls back in his eyes every time. It's grown out since I've last seen him.

My hair's different too. Pixie length and dark brown. I keep fiddling with it, oddly self-conscious. Also, I keep apologizing. But that's only fair. I'm a crack shot with bear spray, and even though the level of capsaicin in it is substantially lower than in the human variety of pepper spray, it still hurts. Good thing I didn't have a gun.

"It's okay." Luca manages to make eye contact with me through one not-so-puffy eye. "You did the right thing."

"Oh. So you do speak English."

He does the *so-so* thing. "Learning. Slowly."

"No, it's good. You're doing great."

Weirdly, inappropriately, all I can think about is that he's built exactly like a bear—a human-size, disconcertingly sexy bear—and I'm worried I'm going to say it out loud. It's been too long since I've been alone in a room with a man. I'm fairly certain my filter's out of whack. Thankfully, he fills the silence.

"You stay here all the time?"

"So far, yeah. The owners only use it for two weeks at the end of every summer. I'll figure out something to do when they want it."

He nods. "I should explain. About Baskens."

But I'm not sure I'm ready for that. I think I'd prefer to ease around the subject for a little longer, if we could, so I say, "How did you find me?" Quickly, lightly, to divert his attention.

"Jessica," he replies. "Jessica Kyung."

Surprise ripples through me. Why would Jessica give me away now? Back when I first drove out of Georgia, she was the only one I called when I was finally able to get my hands on a phone. It turned out to be the right choice. After listening to the whole sordid story, Jessica had told me a story of her own. How, around a year ago, she'd caught wind of rumors about goings-on at Baskens in the mid to late nineties, before Cerny started the retreats. She'd embarked on a bit of unofficial, off-the-record investigating, though was never able to turn up anything solid. But she always sensed bad mojo around Matthew Cerny and that place.

After I contacted her, Jessica went full-on fairy godmother on my behalf—telling me to head west and wait for her call. I don't know how she did what she did, contacting God knows what shady characters and pulling God knows what strings, but the woman made disappearing a reality. I basically owe her my life.

She was the one who informed me the police had found three bodies buried back behind my house on Ansley Street—Holly Idlewine plus two other women. And she said Heath was clinging to life, just barely, at Grady Hospital. The police were looking for me, if only to ensure I wasn't buried somewhere too. I felt terrible about that—and it pained me that Lenny and her parents were probably wild with worry. But Jessica told me to sit tight, that, for the time being, it was best for me to stay gone, and she would meet privately with the Silvers and fill them in.

I'm not sure why she helped me, but I was glad she did. Now I'm somewhat alarmed to know she gave away my information.

"She contacted me," he says. "Asked me to come see you."

He does that hair-raking thing again and sends me a tentative smile. It's a warm smile, and it occurs to me—again—that he's remarkably good looking. Which shouldn't matter, even though I seem to be thinking about it a whole hell of a lot. Maybe it's just a defense mechanism.

"It's over," he says. "Heath Beck is dead, and they close the investigation. Everyone knows he killed Cerny, Cecelia Beck, Holly Idlewine, and two other women. Maybe one of them his birth mother."

The world tilts a little. I put a hand out flat on the table.

"A woman named Annalise Beard say you contact her for help, before? She told police you were asking questions, maybe afraid of Heath like she was."

I nod.

"Everyone knows you had nothing to do with the murders," he says. "You're clear. Jessica says it's safe to come back. To come home."

So there it is. The horse is out of the barn. The boulder's rolling down the hill. The dam . . . the door . . . All the metaphors morph into one singular, unified shout.

He is dead.

I will get to go back home to Decatur, feel the southern summer's sticky humidity and the thrum of energy around the square. I'll see Lenny and her parents again, eat Barbara's strawberry-and-rhubarb mousse. Feel Hap's wince-inducing backslap when he hugs me. I'll pick up a white-chocolate latte at my favorite coffee shop on the way to work, listen to Kevin and Lenny singing along with Britney Spears on the office Pandora.

I will live again.

"You okay?" Luca asks. He digs in his pocket and lays a ring on the table. I stare at it.

"The police give me this. They say it belongs to you."

I stare stupidly at the ring I once thought was so beautiful. Cecelia's ring. I don't touch it.

"The news say there could be others," he tells me. "They think after Heath ran away from Baskens when he was sixteen, he was homeless for two, maybe three years—in Florida, Alabama, Louisiana. In New Orleans a church take him in, collect money so he can go to community college. He transfer to Georgia second year but the church . . ." He explodes his hands.

"They disbanded?"

He nods. "Maybe because he mess around with the pastor's wife and some of the other ladies? I don't know. No one say. At Georgia, he make good grades, get student loan, make friends with rich kids. He meet their parents. He get a good job. A lot of good jobs. Then he meet you."

I nod. Heath never told me any of this. Of course, I'd basically assured him he didn't have to, because I didn't want to reciprocate. I had let him off the hook to protect myself.

"Now they look around Florida and Louisiana for missing persons," Luca adds. "For others."

Others.

"The other woman, Annalise, says now she don't know why he didn't kill her. You wonder why he never hurt you?" he asks. It's a mountain of a question, but his voice is gentle. A voice to curl up in.

I do know why. Heath was looking for a partner, in life and in his crimes, and he chose me over Annalise because I was clearly an easier target. I was the perfect mark. The woman he fantasized who would stand by him—adore and cheer him on—even after knowing his horrifying secret. Because she had secrets of her own.

But there was more to his motivations. In the past months, I've had plenty of time to study people with antisocial personality disorder. They are a strange breed. Contemptuous of others' rights, they operate outside the moral and civil law, and they do not change. At first, like Heath did with me, they idealize their targets, flattering and praising to win their trust. To control their targets, they must keep them close, hence Heath's manipulating me into going with him to Baskens. From the moment we met, he'd made up his mind that I belonged to him, and nothing could sway him.

It gets even more chilling than that. Antisocial personality disorder combined with malignant narcissism and Machiavellianism forms what experts call "the dark triad"—a lethal combination of nature and nurture that creates a perfect storm in the human brain, compelling sufferers to destroy everything around them. And they do it with glee. I've come to understand that, based on the chemistry in his brain and his abusive childhood, Heath had every reason to hurt me.

Only he didn't—because that would've been hurting himself.

He believed that, at our core, we were the same. When he looked at me—the abandoned girl who had lashed out once in violence—he saw himself. In the glare of his narcissism, I was nothing but a reflection of him. With me, he wouldn't have to live his life alone. He would have someone to sympathize with his urges, to admire his handiwork, maybe even, at some point along the way, take part in it. I've only begun to understand it myself, but the strange truth is, in his twisted way, Heath Beck loved me.

Luca speaks. "You want me to go?"

I realize I've been somewhere else entirely, and I touch his hand. "No, please. I'd like it if you stayed."

"Okay." His eyes are so kind, so steady. "I come to say it's safe for you now. But also to say I'm sorry for what they did to you back in Georgia. I didn't help you."

"But you did. You helped me get away."

He shakes his head. "I should know something was bad at that place. My sister, she works for the doctor for many years at his retreats. She quit to go back to school, but when he calls her about a new job—just one week, really good pay—she say I should do it. She tell me I only cook for four people, and maybe he'll help me with my citizenship, like he helps her. When I get there, Cerny say I have to deliver empty trays—breakfast, lunch, and dinner. I know it don't sound right, but I'm scared to say no."

I nod.

"I think if I tell police, they come after me. Or call Immigration—and I can't go back to Brazil, it's not a good place for me there, not anymore. My sister is new citizen, but who knows what the authorities do if Cerny say something? And then I find that locked room behind the mirror. I know something is wrong, but I don't know what it is." He rubs his forehead. His face looks pained.

I put my hand on his arm. "I opened a bottle of wine earlier. Would you like a drink?"

"Sure. Yes."

We take the bottle and two glasses outside. Luca tells me to sit in the Adirondack chair and insists on cleaning up my earlier spill. When he's done, he pulls up a chair, and I fill his glass. We talk. Well, he talks—he tells me about emigrating from Brazil two years ago, moving in with his sister and her husband into their tiny apartment in Dunfree. He'd been in med school in São Paulo but had gotten involved with a woman who turned out to have a husband with some seriously shady connections. After being bodily threatened by these guys—organized-crime types, he learned—he left the country.

He goes on to say that he told the police everything about his involvement with Cerny and Baskens, and recently, he's started culinary school in Atlanta.

"And my last name is Isidoro," he concludes.

I smile at this personal detail, glad that he wanted me to know.

"I want to say something earlier, but . . ." he says.

"What?"

He looks embarrassed. "Forget it."

"Tell me."

"I was going to say"—he does this kind of adorable shrug thing—"your hair . . . it looks good."

I'm touched in an unexpected way. It's not that spectacular, as far as compliments go, but it's the way he's said it. Like he was thinking it all along and only now just got up the courage.

"Yours looks good, too."

The worst comeback in the history of haircut banter, but it's all I've got. And now the words are hanging out there, and we're just sitting in a semi-uncomfortable silence, staring at each other's heads. After a moment or two, I realize gravity's kicked in, and we've gone from staring at hair, down to eyes, then mouths. I have a moment of panic. This is the point where Daphne Amos would've felt a tingle. Where she would've gotten swept away by hormones and idiotic notions about soul mates.

But there's no tingle or sweeping away or any of that nonsense, because I'm no longer Daphne Amos. I am Sydney Green, and she doesn't traffic in that currency. There is something else, though, something I am feeling. It's like the negative of a film print. The barest hint that I may, at some point, in some wild, possible future, feel something for another person again. It unsettles me, and I don't know exactly what to do with it, but it is still there, all the same. Glimmering in and out of sight in the space between Luca and me.

I decide, before we can move forward, two things must happen. First, that diamond ring on my kitchen table must be pitched over the side of the deck and into the valley below, never to be seen again. And second . . .

"Can I tell you something?" I ask. "About my past?"

He looks a little surprised, but unguarded. "Sure. Okay."

I take a deep breath. "I lived for a while at a home for children in south Georgia," I begin. "In my house, there was a girl. Her name was Chantal."

ACKNOWLEDGMENTS

This book is an unabashed love letter to Emily Brontë. I have often thought since we shared a first name, we must share some kind of psychic simpatico. That may or may not be true, but I still thank you, my dear, passionate Emily, for your beautiful, dark, heartrending story that helped create the gothic genre. How you continue to confound readers with the lines you blurred between love and obsession is a marvel to me.

Unending thanks go to my superstar agent, Amy Cloughley, and the rest of the team at Kimberley Cameron & Associates. Also thanks to Mary Alice Kier and Anna Cottle for their unwavering support of my books. Thanks also to my editors Alicia Clancy, Danielle Marshall, and Kelli Martin of Lake Union—a group effort this time, but, as always, such an affirming experience. I always know I am in the best of hands with you all.

Shannon O'Neill—I cannot thank you enough for understanding what I was trying to achieve with this one. Your support and incredible perception, smarts, and willingness to get on the phone and discuss cuckoo birds as a motif were a godsend. Rex Bonomelli, your cover was right up badass alley, and I thank you. To Kate Orsini, thank you for being the voice of Althea and Meg. You inspire me.

Special thanks to M. J. Pullen for your insight into the world of therapy and psychology, and to Charles Bailey and Brad Stephens for their advice concerning legal matters. And to my other beta readers/ critique partners Kimberly Brock and Chris Negron. I count on y'all in a way that is probably not healthy. Thank you to Erratica: M. J., Becky Albertalli, Chris, and George Weinstein. And to the ladies of the Tinderbox Writers Retreat, who talked floor mats and ponytail holders. Also a huge thanks to the folks at Happy Writers Hour: J. D. Jordan, Ellie Jordan, Jane Haessler. A special thanks to Katy Shelton for her unwavering understanding and support, and to Henry and Kathleen Drake for always being my Birmingham home away from home.

Finally, to Everett, Noah, and Alex, thanks for your love and support and not minding when I don't cook dinner. Rick, you're perfect. Always us (but not in a creepy way).

ABOUT THE AUTHOR

Photo © 2015 Christina DeVictor

Emily Carpenter, a former actor, producer, screenwriter, and behind-the-scenes soap opera assistant, was born in Birmingham, Alabama, and graduated from Auburn University with a degree in speech communication. After a stint in New York City, she moved to Atlanta, Georgia, where she lives with her family. She is the bestselling author of *Burying the Honeysuckle Girls* and *The Weight of Lies*. You can find Emily at www.emilycarpenterauthor.com and on Facebook, Twitter, and Instagram.